PAST MASTER

Mary turned her head and perceived the new-comers. Her dark eyes locked with those of her father. After a moment or two, she moved, coming straight towards him, even though her route inevitably lay close to the sparring, panting swordsmen. With quiet assurance she raised her hand a little to them, spoke a word or two, and without pausing came on.

He had not ceased to gaze at her. So they stood, so uncannily alike. There might have been no one else in all that noisy, chaotic room.

Patrick it was who acted. He did not move, but slowly his hands rose, open, towards her, arms wide. 'Mary!' he said, throatily, huskily.

She ran, hurling herself into those arms, to clutch against him convulsively, to bury her dark head against his white padded shoulder. 'Patrick! Oh, Patrick!' she sobbed.

Past Master

Third in The Master of Gray Trilogy

Nigel Tranter

CORONET BOOKS
Hodder and Stoughton

First published in Great Britain in 1965 by Hodder and Stoughton Ltd.

Coronet edition 1973

Second impression 1990

Printed and bound in Great Britain for Hodder and Stoughton paperbacks, a division of Hodder and Stoughton Ltd., Mill Road, Dunton Green, Sevenoaks, Kent TN13 2YA (Editorial Office: 47 Bedford Square, London WC1B 3DP) by Cox & Wyman Ltd., Reading.

ISBN 0 340 17837 X

PRINCIPAL CHARACTERS

In Order of Appearance

(Fictional characters printed in *italics*)

Robert Logan of Restalrig: Adventurer; cousin of the Master of Gray.

Mary Gray : illegitimate daughter, publicly unacknowledged, of the Master of Gray.

Ludovick, 2nd Duke of Lennox; second cousin of King James and near heir to the throne. Lord High Admiral of Scotland.

Patrick, Master of Gray: son and heir of 5th Lord Gray former Master of the Wardrobe, Sheriff of Forfar and acting Chancellor of Scotland. Condemned for treason, banished 1587, returned two years later, again fled country 1591.

King James the Sixth of Scots: son of Mary Queen of Scots and Henry Lord Darnley. Contender for the throne of England to succeed Elizabeth.

John Erskine, Earl of Mar: Keeper of Stirling Castle; boyhood companion of the King.

Lord Robert Stewart, Earl of Orkney: one of King James the Fifth's many bastard sons. Former Bishop of Orkney, uncle of the King and father of Lady Marie, Mistress of Gray.

Queen Anne: formerly Princess of Denmark, wife to King James Sixth.

John Maitland, Lord Thirlestane: Chancellor of Scotland.

Master Patrick Galloway: a prominent minister of the Kirk.

Master Andrew Melville: Moderator of the General Assembly, Rector of St. Andrews University; Kirk leader.

William Douglas, 6th Earl of Morton: a powerful nobleman.

Francis Hepburn Stewart: Earl of Bothwell: son of one more of James the Fifth's bastards, and nephew of Mary Queen of Scots' third husband, Bothwell.

Henry Frederick, Prince of Scotland: infant son of James and Anne. Died young.

George Keith, 5th Earl Marischal: Hereditary Marshal of Scotland.

Archibald Campbell, 7th Earl of Argyll: Chief of Clan Campbell, Justiciar of the West.

Master James Melville: nephew to Andrew Melville; a prominent divine.

The Lady Marie Stewart: wife of the Master of Gray.

David Gray : illegitimate eldest son of the 5th Lord Gray, half-brother of the Master; land steward and schoolmaster.

Sir Lachlan Mor Maclean: Highland chief and famous fighter.

Donald MacDonald, 10th Captain of Clanranald: important Highland chief.

Sir Christopher St. Lawrence: one of Queen Elizabeth's sailors.

Donald Gorm MacDonald of Sleat: leader of the Clan Donald Confederacy, claimant to the Lordship of the Isles.

Sir George Home: a favourite of King James, later Earl of Dunbar.

Sir George Nicolson: English envoy at the Court of Scotland.

The Lady Jean Campbell, Mistress of Eglinton: later Duchess of Lennox.

Patrick, 5th Lord Gray: the Master's father.

James Elphinstone: one of the Octavians; 4th son of 3rd Lord Elphinstone; later Secretary of State, and Lord Balmerino.

The Lady Henrietta Stewart, Countess of Huntly: sister of Duke of Lennox; wife of the Earl of Huntly.

John Ruthven, 3rd Earl of Gowrie: a young nobleman, Rector of University of Padua, son of former Lord Treasurer.

Alexander Ruthven, Master of Gowrie: brother of above.

Sir Thomas Erskine: a courtier, kinsman of Earl of Mar; later Lord Erskine of Dirleton.

John Ramsay; a favourite page; later Sir John.

Dr Hugh Herries: the King's physician. Created Sir Hugh Herries of Cousland.

Patrick Leslie, Lord Lindores: a courtier.

Andrew Henderson: chamberlain to the Earl of Gowrie.

Sir Thomas Hamilton: (Tam o' the Cowgate) Lord Advocate, later Earl of Haddington.

Sir Robert Carey: English courtier, son of Lord Hunsdon, a cousin of Queen Elizabeth.

Sir Charles Percy: brother of the Earl of Northumberland.

Chapter One

The servant, intending to show the hulking, travel-stained visitor into the lesser hall of Methven Castle, was shouldered roughly aside, and throwing the door wide, the newcomer stamped within, tossing his sodden cloak to the other and shaking the raindrops from his half-armoured person like a dog. Robert Logan of Restalrig was not the man to stand on ceremony, even with dukes.

A few strides inside, and he halted on the deer-skin strewed floor, to stare past the young woman who seemed to be that pleasant and comfortable room's sole occupant, peering into the corners already shadowed by the early February dusk of a wet day, as though he would root out, with his keen glance, anyone lurking therein.

Calmly the girl considered him, as she stood, a slight but shapely figure, beside the wide open fireplace where the birch logs sizzled and spluttered beneath the great stone-carved coat-of-arms.

'Well, sir,' she greeted him evenly. 'So it is *you*! Not a messenger from the King's Grace.'

The newcomer dismissed that with a flick of the wrist. 'A device, no more,' he jerked. 'To gain entry without names. I do not want my name shouted the length and breadth of Strathearn, lassie. H'mm,' he coughed. 'Mary? Mistress? Or my lady? How do I call you, these days?'

'Mary Gray will serve very well, sir,' she answered him coolly. 'But Mistress if you prefer it – since mistress is a true description of my situation. What may I do for you?'

'He's no' here? Where is he, lassie? Lennox. The Duke. Where is he?'

'My lord Duke is from home, sir.'

'Fiend take him, then! I've ridden far and fast to see him. And secretly. Where is he, Mary?'

She did not answer at once, considering him closely, thought-

7

fully, with her lovely dark eyes. She was very lovely altogether, that young woman, with an elfin fine-wrought beauty of feature, a slender but full-breasted figure, and a natural grace of carriage and inborn serenity of bearing which was as disturbing as it was fascinating to men.

'What is your business with the Duke?' she asked, at length.

Logan grinned. 'I said that I came secretly, did I no'? My business is private, lassie. Even from Lennox's courtesan!'

She nodded, accepting that. 'You are alone? You seldom ride alone. I think, sir? Usually with a band of cut-throat moss-troopers.' That was said no less calmly, factually, than the rest.

The man laughed, nowise offended. The Laird of Restalrig indeed was not a man who offended easily – nor could afford to be in sixteenth-century Scotland.

'No need for my brave lads this journey, Mary. When will Lennox be home? I know that he was here two days back. And that he has not been to Court in Edinburgh since Yule.' That was sharp.

'You are well informed, sir. My lord Duke is but at St. John's town of Perth. He will return tonight. At any hour. He could have been here by this.'

'Ha! Then I shall await him. Here. In comfort. With your permission, of course, Mistress!' He chuckled, unbuckling his steel half-armour. 'You will not deny me some small hospitality, Cousin? To stay a hungry and thirsty man who has ridden ninety miles and more this day. You will pardon my mentioning it – but you show no haste to sustain me!'

'I have never known your appearance herald aught but ill tidings,' she answered. But she moved to pull a bell cord hanging amongst the rich arras, to summon a servant.

He laughed again. Logan was a great laugher, an unfailingly cheerful rogue. He sat down on a settle, unbidden, to pull off his great heavy thigh-length riding-boots.

'You do me injustice, Coz,' he declared. 'Often my news is good indeed – for the right folk! As I swear it is on this occasion, lass.'

'I doubt it,' she said. 'You are apt to be too close linked to ... my father!'

He looked up, and his fleering grey-blue eyes met her dark

glowing ones. The grin died on his florid fleshy features.

'I'ph'mmm,' he said.

The servant reappeared, and was told to bring victuals, cold meats and wine.

The young woman paced over to the rain-blurred window that looked out over the fair prospect of green Strathearn, water-meadows and wide pasture-lands lifting and lifting through rolling foothills to the great heather bastions of the Highland Line, all grey and indistinct today under the thin curtains of the rain.

'You say that you have ridden ninety miles,' she said, without looking back. 'Edinburgh is little more than fifty, from here. So you have not come from Restalrig. Your castle of Fast would be near to ninety, I think. In the Borderland. Near to Berwick.'

'You are quick,' he acknowledged.

'If *you* come, in haste, and secretly, from that airt, then I cannot but fear the reason for your mission, sir. Vicky . . . the Duke, is not apt to be concerned with doings from those parts. Berwick and the Border only spell trouble. *He* is not one of those who accept secret doles and gold from Queen Elizabeth!'

'He is fortunate, no doubt, in not requiring to do so,' the other said lightly.

'No man, I think, requires to be a traitor to his country,' the girl gave back. 'Even the Master of Gray!' She turned round to face him. 'It *is* he that you came from, is it not? From my father? It is on his behalf?'

Restalrig drew a large hand over his mouth and chin. 'On whose behalf I come, Cousin, is my affair.'

'If the matter concerns my father and my . . . concerns the Duke of Lennox, then it concerns me also, sir. Though God knows I want none of it! It *is* Patrick, is it not? My father?'

'You are hard on him, lassie. Must you hate him so?'

'I do not hate him. Would that I could! My sorrow is that I love him still. But his works I hate, yes.'

'His works are for the good o' this realm, most times, girl. Statecraft. Patrick Gray can save Scotland. As he has done before. And, Deil kens, Scotland needs saving, in this pass!'

Her sigh had something almost of a shudder behind it. 'Has it come to this again?' she cried. 'So soon!' It was not often that Mary Gray allowed the tranquil assurance of her demeanour

9

to be disturbed thus. 'Patrick's works are evil. You know it. If he seems to save the realm on occasion, it is only for his own ends. And at the cost of untold misery, treachery, deceit. I say better far for the realm not to be saved – not by the Master of Gray!'

He padded across the floor to her in his hose. 'What so ails you at him, Mary? Has he ever done you hurt? God – I'd say it ill becomes any woman to speak so of her sire! However he conceived her! He loves you well, I swear.'

'I have told you – I love him also. To my grief, my shame. But I shall never trust him again. I have learned my lesson, learned it sorely but surely. A year ago and more I sent him away. Drove him away. Forced him to leave Scotland . . .'

'*You* did? Patrick Gray?'

'I did.' She nodded, with a quiet certainty, an authority almost, that sat but strangely on a young woman of only nineteen years. 'I forced him into exile. Never heed how. When his wickednesses became too great to be borne – even by me, who had condoned so many, God forgive me. When he turned against Vicky. When he would have betrayed the Duke. Who was almost as a son to him. You understand? Understand why I must know what now is toward? I *must* know.'

The other scratched his head. 'I canna tell you, lassie . . .'

'I thought, in my foolishness, that we should have peace from him. From Patrick. From his plots and schemings and treasons. That, banished the realm, he would no more endanger Scotland. Nor Vicky. Nor others. A year ago. Eighteen months. So little a time of peace! And now . . . ! Where is he, sir? Where is my father?'

Logan shrugged. 'That isna for me to say.' He turned away – and in doing so his eye took in the significance of a piece of furniture in the shadows to the right of the window. He stepped over to peer down.

'Ha!' he exclaimed. 'What have we here? Guidsakes, girl – what's this?'

It was a wooden cradle into which he looked. Within it lay a tiny infant that stared up at him with wide dark eyes, silent.

Mary Gray came at once, to kneel down by the cradle and smile into it gently, warmly. 'That is Johnnie,' she said, nodding simply but proudly. 'Johnnie, my heart! My little pigeon! My troutie! Three months old. Is he not an angel from heaven?'

At the change in her, so sudden, so complete, the great hulking man looked almost embarrassed, ill at ease. He grinned, and then guffawed. 'Shrive me!' he cried. 'Some, I'd swear, would call him otherwise!'

She did not look up, nor even alter her tone of voice. 'The bastard son of a bastard mother?' she said calmly. 'That is true. But what of it? He is no less an angel. And he is mine.'

'And my lord Duke's!'

'Why, yes. Of course.'

'Oooh, aye! Johnnie Gray, eh. My new cousin!'

'Not so,' she said. 'John Stewart. His father would have it so. Bastard he may be, in the eyes of men. But he is John Stewart of Methven also. Already. This castle and all its demesne is settled upon him. John Stewart of Methven, sir – not Johnnie Gray. And the King's cousin as well as yours!'

'My God!' Logan stared at her. 'Is this truth? You are none so blate, lassie! You do things in style, I'll say that for you!'

'There is nothing of my doing in it. All was his father's doing. On the day after I gave birth, he brought the papers to show me. All signed and witnessed and sealed.'

'So-o-o!' Logan looked round him at all the quietly comfortable splendour of that hall. 'All this is yours! Mary Gray's. All this – Methven Castle, one of the finest houses in the land. All yours – Davy Gray the land-steward's brat!'

She shook her dark head. 'Not mine. His. John Stewart of Methven's.'

Robert Logan of Restalrig was right about his cousinship. Both cousinships were true, as cousins go in Scotland, a country where clanship was always important. The Lady Agnes Gray, daughter of the fourth Lord Gray, sister of the present Lord and aunt of the Master, his heir, had married Logan's father. So he was a full cousin of Patrick, Master of Gray, and half-cousin of the latter's illegitimate daughter Mary. As for Ludovick Stewart, second Duke of Lennox, he was in second-cousinship to King James the Sixth. His father Esmé, the first Duke, was full cousin to Henry Stewart, Lord Darnley, who married Mary Queen of Scots and became James's father. For lack of closer relatives he was accepted as next heir to the throne of the so-far childless monarch.

Servants brought in food and drink for the visitor, who fell to without delay or ceremony. Mary picked the baby out of the cradle and moved about the great room with him in her arms, crooning softly. They made a pleasing picture, the beautiful girl, her exquisite finely-chiselled patrician features flushed with the bloom of tenderness and mother-love, and the solemn great-eyed infant. But Restalrig had no eyes for other than the viands set before him. More than once the young woman paused and looked at him, lips parted to speak, and then moved on again.

The faint sound of clattering hooves and shouting from the courtyard at the other side of the house, turned both their heads. In a few moments the door opened again to admit another man, preceded by two lanky steaming wolf-hounds, soaked and muddy. Long-strided he came across to enfold Mary and the baby in a boyish impetuous embrace without so much as a glance at the visitor – who indeed rose to his feet only belatedly, and still chewing.

The newcomer was a young man, younger-seeming even than his twenty years, of medium height, stocky but markedly up-right of bearing, with an open freckled countenance, blunt-featured and pleasantly plain. He could make no claims whatsoever to either good looks or aristocratic distinction – in marked contrast to that of the girl he so eagerly saluted. Carelessly dressed in comfortably old clothing which had never been more than moderately fine – much less fine even than Restalrig's, who was no dandy – Ludovick Stewart seemed an unlikely character indeed to fill the role of next heir to the throne, second Duke of Lennox, Lord High Chamberlain of Scotland, Commendator-Prior of St. Andrews, Seigneur D'Aubigny of France and former Viceroy of the Realm.

'We have a guest, Vicky,' Mary said warningly, wiping a smear of mud from the baby's face. 'The Laird of Restalrig – who you will remember, I think. Related to . . . to my family. But here, I understand, for reasons less frank!'

Quickly the young man looked at Logan, and back to the girl. 'Indeed!' he said. 'M'mmm.'

'My lord Duke,' Logan said, nodding briefly. 'Your servant.'

'And yours, sir.' Lennox's manner was civil but stiff. wary, and little more courtly than Restalrig's. 'I have not seen you for some years, I think.'

'True, my lord.' The other grinned. 'I but little frequent His Grace's Court, I fear.'

'That I understand. Myself, I care little for it. But . . . this is a matter of taste. Whereas with you, sir, I believe, it is more than that. The last meeting of the Privy Council which I attended put you to the horn, did it not? For conspiring with the King's enemies? And declared you rebel also, for robbery, rape and assault, if I remember aright!'

Restalrig's grin was succeeded by a scowl, and his fleshy jowl thrust forward noticeably. 'You have a fair memory, my lord Duke. But also, no doubt, some knowledge of the justice of His Grace's Council! I seem to mind your own self being in trouble with them, two years back, over the Bothwell business! But never heed. It is no matter.'

'It matters, sir, that a pronounced rebel should be received in my house.'

'Tcha! I came secretly. None knows that Logan of Restalrig is at Methven. I have word for your private ear.'

'If it is treasonable word, sir, I had better not hear it.'

'Treason is a word for clerks and frightened fools! In affairs of the realm, only to lose is treasonable!'

'He comes on Patrick's behalf, Vicky, I fear,' Mary put in, urgently. 'He will not tell me what it is. But I am sure that it is Patrick again. And if it is, then it is better, I am sure, that you should not hear it. Should not listen to him.'

Frowning, the young man looked from one to the other. 'Is this true, Restalrig?' he demanded. 'That you come on behalf of the Master of Gray?'

'My instructions are that what I have to say is said in your ear alone, my lord.'

'Vicky – either do not hear him or let me hear him also! If it is my father's words he brings to you, then it is *my* concern. You know it.'

'This is no women's business, my lord Duke . . .'

Lennox interrupted him. 'If I hear you, it is in the Lady

13

Mary's presence – or not at all, sir. She . . . she is my other self, in all matters.'

The other snorted. 'God save us!' But Logan was no fool, and perceiving the expression on the young Duke's face, he shrugged. 'Och, well – so be it! If Mistress Gray can hold her tongue . . .'

'You will refer to her, sir, as the Lady Mary.'

"Ho! I will, will I? Mary Gray, the . . . ! A-well, a-well – if that's the way o' it! Aye, then – the lady is right, my lord. I bear you word from Patrick Gray. Privy word. Important word. Word that could hang men . . . and save Scotland.'

'Where is he? The Master? We heard that he was in London. Then Rome . . .'

'He is in my house at Fast Castle, my lord.'

Mary and the Duke exchanged glances.

'Back in Scotland!' the girl exclaimed. 'So soon! So near!' She clutched the baby tighter to her, as at a threat. 'Endangering his own life. And others'!'

Restalrig barked a laugh. 'Patrick's no' the man to shy at a small whiffle o' danger! No' that he's in danger so long as he bides in Fast. It'll take more than the Chancellor Maitland and the Council to winkle him out o' my house! Or King Jamie, either. I'm at the horn, am I no', and biding there secure? They'll no' touch the master o' Fast Castle. Folk ha' tried it before this – and learned differently!'

'You are not in Fast Castle now!' Lennox reminded.

'I' faith – that is true,' the other nodded. 'But Patrick is my friend, see you. As well as my cousin. A man must take a risk for his own blood, his friend. Or no?' He looked from one to the other.

'What does he want with me?' Ludovick asked heavily.

'He wants you, my lord Duke, safe in Fast Castle before the morning's light.'

'God in Heaven! Are you mad, man?'

'Save us all . . . !'

'With fresh horses, I can have you there before cock-crow. Ninety miles. Hard riding – but you are no shrinking lily, my lord. And I have already ridden that ninety here. None will see you, by night. Ride back tomorrow night. None will know that

14

you have been to Fast.'

'Why should I do any such thing, sir?'

'Patrick would speak with you. Urgently. And since he may not come here ...'

'But, dear God – I cannot do this! Is *he* crazed, or you? I am Chamberlain of this realm, one of the King's ministers. Of his Council. I cannot wait secretly upon one banished the realm as an enemy of the King! It is treason for the Master of Gray to be back in Scotland, at all. For me to ride to him at Fast would be treason likewise. He knows that.'

'Nevertheless, my lord, that is what he's sent me to bid you do. He said – "Tell the Duke that the Protestant cause, the throne itself, may hang on this. And the English succession".'

Mary Gray emitted something near to a groan. 'This again! The same fell game!'

'This is no game, lassie! You ken the state o' the realm. Near enough to outright war, wi' our slobbering King pulled a' ways! A blow is to be struck that will topple Jamie into the Catholics' arms first of all. And then off his throne. And that will mean real war. Civil war. Aye, and invasion too.'

'I understood that you were of the Catholic persuasion yourself, sir?' Lennox charged him.

The other shrugged. 'You may say, like Patrick, that I dinna take religion ower seriously. Not to discommode me. That I'm fine and content to worship God in my ain way, and let other folk do the like. A plague on them both, I say . . . wi' due respects to your Dukeship that's of the Kirk party!'

'M'mmm ...'

'There is nothing new in all this,' Mary put in, wearily. 'It is all as it was – ever the same. My father has been playing the Protestants against the Catholics and the Catholics against the Protestants for years. There is nothing new here, that should send the Duke hurrying to Patrick's beckon ...'

'Aye, but there is. That's where you're wrong, Mary – there is. Patrick said to say that it was life and death. For the King. Aye, and for yourself, my lord Duke. Because you're near the throne. He says both your deaths have been decided upon.'

'Vicky!' The girl stepped close, to clutch the Duke's wrist with her free hand. 'Sweet Jesu – no!'

'Heed nothing, Mary,' Lennox told her, encircling mother and child with a damp arm. 'Nobody is going to kill me. It is but one of Patrick's alarums. My death would serve no cause, benefit none. I take no part in any of their affairs, neither Catholic nor Protestant. Besides, no one would dare . . .'

'Not even the Earl o' Bothwell?'

'Bothwell! But . . . Bothwell is of the Kirk party. A Protestant.'

'Patrick says that Bothwell is about to change sides. To turn Catholic. And Bothwell, like yoursel', my lord Duke, is the King's cousin – though on the wrong side o' the blanket. A right bold and fierce man!'

'By the Powers – Bothwell!' There was no doubt about the Duke's perturbation now. Yet he shook his head. 'I do not believe it!' he declared. 'Bothwell has always been a Protestant . . . if he has any true religion at all. Devil-worship and witchcraft, perhaps. But to turn Catholic – no!'

'If religion matters little to him, and this changing could give him the sure rule of Scotland, think you he'd scruple? Patrick says that he is changing – and have you ever kenned Patrick Gray wrong in his information?'

Mary Gray had, but not often – and she was in no state to contest Restalrig's claim. 'Why should he, Bothwell . . .' She swallowed. 'Why should he seek Vicky's hurt? Or the King's?'

The other shrugged. 'It's no' me you've to ask that, lassie – it's Patrick. I'm but his messenger in this, see you. To bring the Duke to him.'

'It is but a device. This threat to Vicky. To entice him to Fast Castle. To seek to entangle him once again in Patrick's evil affairs. Do not go, Vicky. Even if it is true about Bothwell, if you stay quietly here at Methven, far from Court, you can be of no danger to him. Why should he seek your death?'

'But James, Mary – the King? Is my duty not to the King? If *he* is threatened? Am I not sworn, as a member of the Council, to defend him, my liege lord, with my life? If Patrick *has* discovered some desperate plot against the King, am I not in duty bound at least to hear of it, for James's sake?'

'He canna come near to the King himsel',' Restalrig pointed out. 'He is banished the realm. Outlawed. He needs an ear close to Jamie's. That the King will heed. If his warning is to be in time. And there's no' much time, he says . . .'

Lennox took a few paces away from the girl, and back, staring at the floor. 'I believe that I must go, Mary,' he said, at length.

She emitted a long quivering sigh, but inclined her lovely head.

'I shall hear him - no more. Do not fear that he shall cozen me, carry me off my feet, Mary. I know Patrick for what he is . . .'

'Would that I could come with you, Vicky! Two heads are even better than one, in dealing with my father! But . . . Johnnie, here. Nursing the child, I cannot leave him.'

'Nor would I let you ride ninety miles through a winter's night, lass . . .'

'I *could*, Vicky. You know that I could.'

'May be. But you will not. This is not for you.' He turned to Restalrig. 'When do we start, sir? I have fresh horses.'

'The sooner the better. Give me an hour, my lord. It will be full dark by then . . .'

'You will be careful, Vicky? Oh, you must be very careful! Watch Patrick. Do not let him deceive you, charm you, hood-wink you . . .'

Chapter Two

For fully an hour none of the three men had spoken – save to curse their weary drooping mounts when the all-but-foundered brutes slipped and stumbled on the rough and broken ground, benighted and water-logged. Coldingham Moor was no place to be in the dark, at any time – but especially not at four o'clock of a winter's morning, with a half-gale blowing sleet straight off the North Sea in their faces, and after having ridden across five counties.

Though he had no fondness for Logan, Ludovick Stewart's opinion of the man's toughness and vigour could hardly have failed to have risen during those past grim hours. Although of middle years and notorious for gross living, he had led the way, and at a cracking pace, right from Methven in Strathearn, across South Perthshire, Strilingshire, the three Lothians and into Berwickshire, on a foul night, and having already ridden the entire journey in the opposite direction. Not once, despite the thick blackness of the night, had he gone astray to any major extent.

The last lap of that long journey was, as it happened, the most trying of all. Coldinghamshire, that ancient jurisdiction of the once princely Priory of Coldingham, thrusts out from the rest of Berwickshire eastwards like a great clenched fist, where the Lammermuir Hills challenge the sea. At the very tip of the resultant cliff-girt, iron-bound coast, amongst the greatest cliffs in the land, Fast Castle perches in as dizzy and savage a situation as can well be imagined, an eagle's eyrie of a place – and a particularly solitary and malevolent eagle at that. No other house or haunt of man crouched within miles of it on the bare, lofty, storm-battered promontory.

Even high on the moor here, amongst the whins and the out-cropping rocks, Ludovick could hear the roar of the waves, a couple of miles away and four hundred feet below. Heads down, sodden cloaks tight about them, soaked, mud-spattered, stiff with cold and fatigue, they rode on into the howling black emptiness laced with driven sleet. The Duke imagined that hell might be of this order.

He was jerked out of what was little better than a daze by his servant's beast cannoning into his own, all but unseating both of them. He had been aware that his horse had been slipping and slithering more consistently, indicating that they had been moving downhill. Taking a grip on himself, and shouting at the groom, Ludovick brought his black under control.

Only a short distance further, Logan halted. Indeed it appeared that he had to halt, poised on the very brink of nothingness.

'Care, now,' he announced, having to shout above the sustained thunder of the seas which seemed to be breaking directly below them – but notably far below; as though all before had been the merest daunder. 'Dismount and lead.'

Himself doing so, he picked his way along a narrow twisting ledge of a path, steep hillside on one hand, empty drop on the other. It was a place for goats rather than men and horses.

They came to a naked buttress of the cliff, a thrusting rock bluff round which it seemed there was no passage. Down the side of this their path turned steeply, and then abruptly halted. They faced the abyss.

Logan pointed in front of him, eastwards, seawards – but in the almost horizontally-driving sleet Lennox could see nothing. Then the other drew a small horn out from his saddle-bag, and blew a succession of long and short blasts on it. Waiting a few moments, he repeated this, and at the second summons a faint hail answered him from somewhere out in the darkness. This was followed presently by a creaking, clanking noise, and the rattle of chains.

'A drawbridge!' Ludovick exclaimed. 'I' faith – it is *here*?' He was peering into the murk. Vaguely, monstrously, something loomed up there, he believed, blacker than the surrounding blackness.

With a rattle and thud the end of a drawbridge sank into position almost at their very feet. This seemed to be little wider than the path itself; never had Lennox seen so narrow an access.

'Hold to the chain,' Logan shouted. 'The wind. Bad here.'

That was no over-statement. As they followed their guide out on to the slender gangway, which echoed hollowiy beneath their feet, the wind seemed to go crazy. It had been blowing gustily hitherto, but consistently from the east; now it seemed to come at them from all sides – and especially from below – tearing at them, buffeting, shrieking and sobbing. It was presumably some trick of the cliff-formation and of this detached projecting pinnacle on which the castle must stand. Certain it was that without the single, swinging guard-chain to hold on to, the men would have been in grave danger of being swept right off that narrow cat-walk. Even the horses staggered and side-stepped, having to be dragged across in their nervous reluctance. Although Ludovick did not make a point of looking downwards, he was aware of a paleness far below, which could be only the white of the breaking seas which roared in their ears and seemed to shake that dizzy timber gallery. The salt of driven spray was now mixed with the sleet and rain which beat against their faces.

At last they lurched into the blessed shelter of an arched and fortified gatehouse, with solid level rock beneath their feet, and a relief from the battering of the wind. Rough voices sounded, hands took their horses' bridles from them, and flickering lamps were brought. The bare dark stone walls of Fast Castle may not normally have spoken of kindly welcome, but that night they were as a haven of peace and security for the reeling travellers.

Lennox, shown to a draughty small chamber in the main keep, where the arras swayed and rustled against the walling and a candle wavered and guttered, throwing off his wet clothing and donning a bed-robe, bemusedly considered that he had seldom sampled a fairer room. When Logan himself brought in food and wine, his guest partook of only token portions before collapsing on a hard bed and sleeping like the dead.

It was nearly noon before Ludovick awakened, but even so he did not realise the time of day, so dark was it still in his little chamber, with its gloomy hangings and its tiny window only half-glazed, the lower portion being closed by wooden shuttering. The storm still raged apparently, and little of light penetrated the small area of glass, not only because of the heavy overcast sky but because the air was thick with spindrift.

When the young man had prevailed upon himself to rise, and went to the window to peer out, he could see nothing through the streaming glass. Opening the little shutters, he stooped and thrust out his head – and all but choked in consequence; it was not so much the violence of the wind that took his breath away – it was the prospect. He hung directly over a boiling cauldron of tortured seas, riven and torn into foaming, spouting fury by jagged reefs and skerries, just about one hundred and fifty feet below – hung being a true description, for the masonry of this tower rose sheerly flush with the soaring naked rock of the precipice, which itself bulged out in a great overhang, sickening to look down upon. Ludovick's window faced south, and by turning his head he could see, through the haze of spray and rain, the vast main cliff-face that stretched away in a mighty and forbidding barrier three hundred feet high separated from his present stance by a yawning gulf. In other words, this castle was situated half-way down that cliff-face, built to crown an isolated and top-heavy pillar of rock that was itself a detached buttress of the thrusting headland, on as cruel and fearsome stretch of rock-ribbed coast as Scotland could display. How anyone could have achieved the task of building a castle here in the first place, apart from why anyone should wish to do so, was a matter for uneasy wonder. How many unhappy wretches had dropped to their death on the foaming fangs beneath, in the creating of it, was not to be considered. Lennox well remembered King James himself – who, of course, had only viewed the place from the sea – saying once that the man who built it must have been a knave at heart.

Noting, however, that despite the grim aspect and evil reputation of this robber's stronghold, not only had he survived a particularly heavy sleep therein but that while he had been thus helpless his clothing had been taken, dried and brought back to him, along with adequate wherewithal to break his fast, Ludovick dressed, ate, and went in search of company. Descending two storeys by a narrow winding stone stairway in the thickness of a wall-corner, wherein chill winds blew at him from unglazed arrow-slits and gun-loops, he came to the Hall of the castle on the first main floor. It was a small poor place compared with the great hall of Methven, bare and stark as to furnishings but better lit than might have been expected by four windows provided with stone seats, and with a great roaring fire of sparking driftwood blazing in the huge fireplace which took up most of one wall. Here he encountered the Lady Restalrig, Marion Ker, Logan's frightened-eye young second wife, whose nervous greeting to her ducal visitor and swift self-effacement thereafter, seemed perhaps suitable behaviour on the part of the chatelaine of Fast Castle.

Ludovick, gazing into the fire, was wondering at the reactions of any young woman brought to live in such a place, when a voice spoke behind him from the doorway.

'My dear Vicky – here is a delight, a joy! On my soul, it is good to see you! It was a kindly act indeed to ride so far to see me, through so ill a night. I hope I see you well and fully rested?'

The young man swung round. He had looked for this, been prepared, anticipated the impact of the Master of Grey, knowing so well the quality of the man. Yet even so he was somehow taken by surprise, confused, immediately put at a disadvantage. This was so frequently the effect of Patrick Gray on other men – although on women it was apt to be otherwise. The Duke found himself mumbling incoherencies, not at all in the fashion that he had decided upon.

It was partly the complete contrast of the man with his surroundings, the so obvious unsuitability of everything about Fast Castle as a background for the Master of Gray. Exquisite without being in the least effeminate, laughing-eyed, friendly as he was entirely assured, vital and yet relaxed, the handsomest man in all Europe stood in that harsh, sombre, savage place, and was somehow almost as much a shock to the beholder as had been that plunging, throat-catching prospect from the bedroom window. Even his cordial, courteous and so normal words, spoken in light but pleasantly modulated tones, seemed as much at odds with the true situation as to be off-putting.

Smiling, hands out, the newcomer stepped forward to embrace Lennox to kiss him on both cheeks, French-fashion – for Ludovick had been brought up in France, and it was the Master who had brought him as a boy of ten from that country to Scotland, on his father's death. The younger man coughed, stiffened within the other's arms, and found no words adequate to the occasion.

'Eighteen months it has been, Vicky? Twenty? Too long, at any rate. Too long to be separated from my friends. How often I have thought of you, sought news of you, wished you well. In strange and foreign places. But, heigho – that is now over. A happiness, I vow, a good omen indeed, that the first man that I should meet on my own native soil again, apart from my host and cousin Restalrig, should be my good friend Vicky Stewart, Lord Duke of Lennox!' Patrick Gray had stepped back a pace, though still holding the other by the shoulders the better to smile upon his friend in warm affection.

That was such an astonishing misconstruction of the situation as to set the younger man blinking – and to make his protest sound even more abruptly ungracious than he had intended. 'Dammit, Patrick – I am here only because Restalrig dragged me, under threat of God knows what dire disasters! As well you know.'

'Ha, lad – ever the same forthright, honest Vicky! It does me good to hear your plain, frank candour again. After all of these months with dissemblers and sophists in half the Courts of Europe. Now I know that I am home again, in truth!'

Helplessly, Ludovick stared at him. He knew that he was being unreasonably, unprofitably boorish – and knew too that part of this boorish hostility stemmed from the very fact that this man was so devilishly and winsomely like his own Mary. He had tended to forget just how alike they were, and marvelled anew that so beautiful a man could be so essentially masculine, virile, while his daughter, so similar in looks, bearing and calm assurance, should be all womanly woman. Patrick Gray, clad now, as ever, in the height of fashion but less spectacularly than sometimes, as befitted a courtier on his travels, had reached the age of thirty-four, although he looked even younger – certainly too youthful-seeming to have a grandson like little John Stewart of Methven. Yet the Duke saw the resemblance even to his child, with a sinking heart. The man was of medium height, of a lithe and slender grace of figure and carriage, his features finely-moulded and clean cut, enhanced by brilliant dark flashing eyes beneath a noble brow. His black wavy hair was worn long, but carefully trimmed, and the smiling lips were somewhat countered by a wicked curved scimitar of moustache and a tiny pointed beard.

'You are home, Patrick, only in that you have somehow managed to set foot on this outlandish doorstep of Scotland,' the younger man said harshly. 'You are still banished the realm under pain of death. Nothing is changed. And you must know that, in insisting that I come here to meet you, *my* head is endangered likewise!'

'Tut, Vicky – you are too modest, as always. No one is going to have the Duke of Lennox's head, for any such small matter – least of all our sovereign and well-beloved monarch, your cousin! He loves you too well, my friend, as well he might. And secretly, you know, I do believe that he in some small measure loves me also! Poor Jamie is ever a little confused in his loving, is he not?'

'What . . . what do you mean by that?'

'Merely that our liege lord is apt to be pulled in different ways than more, h'm, ordinary mortals! A matter which his enemies seldom forget – so that it falls to his friends not to forget either.'

'And you count yourself that? A friend of the King?'

'Why yes, Vicky – to be sure. Albeit a humble one. Is that remiss of me?'

'After . . . after all that you have done?'

'After all that I have done,' the Master nodded, easily. 'So much done, or at least attempted, for the weal of James Stewart and his realm. So much endeavoured, over the years, to guide and draw the frail ship of state on a sure course through the perilous seas of statecraft – with alas, so many failures. But, heigho – my small successes also, Vicky. *You* will not deny me them? When His Grace was away in Denmark winning himself his bride, we ruled Scotland passing well together, you and I, Vicky. Did we not? You acting Viceroy. I acting Chancellor.'

'I did what you told me, Patrick – that was all. No more than a tool in your hands. And who gained thereby? You, and you only.'

'Not so, Vicky. You gained much also, in experience, in public esteem, in stature. And the realm gained, in peace and prosperity, did it not? So James gained, since he and his realm are one – as he will assure you most vigorously! But enough of this, my friend – such pry talk of days past is no way to celebrate this happy occasion. Especially since I now come to prove my friendship for King Jamie in much more urgent fashion. But first, lad – tell me of Mary. Here is what I long to hear. How does she fare? I learned that you had taken her into your own keeping. No doubt a convenient arrangement – although bringing its own problems! And the child . . . ?'

'Mary is well. And content,' Lennox interrupted shortly. 'She sent . . . greetings. She is as she wishes to be. And the child. A boy. Like to herself in looks. We are very happy.'

'How fortunate. How excellent. Felicitous. All the satisfactions of marriage – without the handicaps! At least, for yourself, my lord Duke!'

'No!' the younger man cried. 'It is not that. Not that at all, Patrick. You mistake – as do all. I would have married Mary. I prayed, pleaded, that she would marry me. But she would not. She would have it this way – this way only. Her mind was set on it. Still it is – for I would marry her tomorrow, if she would do so. But she will not. She says that because I am Duke, and close to the throne, it is not possible. That she could not be Duchess. That the King and the Council would end it, annul the marriage, declare it void – because of her . . . her birth. We are both under age. They would separate us, she says – where they will not separate us, as we are.'

'I see. She is probably right. Yes – I think there may be a deal of truth in that.'

'It is a damnable position!' Lennox declared. 'I care nothing for the succession, or for this matter of dukes and position at Court. I hate the Court and all to do with it – save only James himself. I want nothing of all this. Only Mary for my wife, and to live my own life at Methven . . .'

'No doubt, Vicky. But, alas, we are not all the masters of our own fate. Born of the royal house of Stewart, you are not as other men, whether you wish it or not. It has its handicaps, yes – but its great benefits likewise. These you must hold, use and pursue to best advantage.'

'But that is not my desire. Why, because I am my father's son, must I live a life I do not want to live? Why must I concern myself with affairs of state when they mean naught to me . . . ?'

'I' faith – and there you have it, man! Affairs of state may mean naught to you – but *you* mean a deal in the affairs of state! That indeed is one reason why I am here. That you may be spared from certain of their more violent attentions!'

'Aye – what folly is this . . . ?'

'Folly indeed, Vicky – but dangerous folly.' The Master seated himself on a bench at the side of the fire, and gestured to the other to do likewise. 'There is notable violence afoot– and you, I fear, are intended to be part of it. You and the King, both.'

'Restalrig said something of this. That is why *I* am here. He swore that the King was endangered. So I came. In duty. To James. As no doubt you intended.'

'As I hoped, yes.' Gravely the other nodded. 'For if the King is to be saved, and you with him, I need your help.'

'A plot? A conspiracy?'

'You could name it so, indeed. Though it is more than that. A strategy, rather – part of a great strategy. To turn Scotland Catholic again, to isolate England, and to bring Bothwell to power and rule.'

'That mad-cap! You believe it serious?'

'When Bothwell makes common cause with Huntly, all Scotland must need think it serious!'

'Huntly! But . . . they have always been enemies.

'Ambition can make strange bedfellows.'

Lennox did not require the other to elaborate on the menace, if these tidings were true. The Earl of Huntly was his own brother-in-law, even though there was little love lost between them, and Ludovick well knew both the arrogant savagery of the man, and his military strength. Chief of the great northern clan of Gordon and hereditary Lieutenant of the North, he was probably the most powerful nobleman in Scotland, and a militant Catholic. He boasted that he could field five thousand men in a week, and, with his allies, double that in a month – and he had proved this true on many an occasion. Only two other men in all the kingdom could produce fighting-men on this scale. One was the Earl of Angus, head of the house of Douglas – and his religious allegiance was to say the least doubtful, though he had leanings towards Catholicism; but he was a hesitant man

26

of no strength of character. The third was Francis Hepburn Stewart, Earl of Bothwell, who controlled, after a fashion, a vast number of wild Border moss-troopers as well as his mother's free-booting Lothian clan of Hepburn; moreover, he was married to Angus's sister. An alliance between these three could have fifteen thousand men in arms within days, without even calling upon friends and supporters for aid.

The young man moistened his lips. 'If this is true . . .'

'It is true, Vicky. I have seen a letter from Bothwell to Huntly. All is in train.'

'They would rise in arms? These two? Against the Protestants? Against the King?'

'Aye. And more than that. They will discredit the King first, and so weaken the Protestant cause. And that is not the worst of it. James, unhappily, has played into their hands. You recollect the bad business of the Spanish Blanks?'

The Duke's eyebrows rose. He had hardly expected the Master of Gray to mention that wretched and treacherous affair, since he was believed to have had a controlling hand in it. 'Who could forget it? But that spoiled the Catholic cause, not the King's.'

'Wait, you. Those were blank letters, sheets of paper already signed by Huntly, Erroll and other Catholic leaders. Angus too. With their seals attached. Sent to the King of Spain, for him to fill in his own terms for the invasion of Scotland in the Catholic interest – a stupid folly if ever there was one. Their courier, George Ker, was captured, and the blanks with him. Put to the torture, he revealed all. Or, at any rate, much! That was a year and more ago. All Scotland knows this. But what Scotland does not know is that more than the blank letters were found on George Ker. There was also a letter from James himself to Philip of Spain. Asking on what terms Philip would send men to Scotland to help put the Kirk in its place!'

'God be good! no! That I do not believe!' Ludovick cried.

'It is fact, nevertheless. George Ker himself told me. He who was carrying the letter. I saw him in Paris. James was most foolish. But he is much browbeaten and bullied by the Kirk, as you know. He has to play one side against the other, to keep his throne. He should not have committed himself in writing –

that was a major blunder. But then, His Grace has been but ill-advised, of late.' The Master smiled slightly. 'Since I left Scotland and his side.' That was gently said.

Lennox answered nothing, as his mind sought to cope with the duplicity, the bad faith, which all this implied, amongst those in the highest positions in the land.

Gray went on. 'It was the Kirk authorities who captured Ker and his letters. They have not revealed that they hold this letter from James to King Philip. Not to the world. But they have, I assure you, to James himself! Melville and his other reverend friends hold this letter over our hapless young monarch's head like a poised sword! In order that he may do as they say. And it has served them well, of late – as you must agree. The King has truckled to them in all things. Hence the Catholics' fury. The Kirk goes from strength to strength, in the affairs of state. All goes down before the ministers and their friends. They threaten James with the letter read from every Protestant pulpit in the land! And worse – excommunication! If he does not play their game.'

'Excommunication! By the Kirk! The King?'

'Aye. And that dread word has poor Jamie trembling at his already wobbly knees!'

'I knew naught of this . . .'

'My dear Vicky – I think that you have been further exiled from Holyroodhouse at your Methven in Strathearn, than I have been in London, Paris and Rome!'

'And gladly so! I hate and abominate all this evil scheming and deceit and trickery, that goes by the name of statecraft! Give me Methven . . .'

'Ah-ha, lad – but it is not Methven that you are to be given! But something less pleasant. The Duke of Lennox, unfortunately, must pay heed to all this, whether he would or no. Bothwell and Huntly have planned shrewdly – indeed so shrewdly that I needs must think that there is some shrewder wit behind all this than the furious, half-crazed Francis Stewart of Bothwell, or that turkey-cock, George Gordon of Huntly! Through Ker, the courier – who of course is in their pay – they know the contents of the King's letter to Philip of Spain. They intend to have it shouted abroad from one end of Scotland to the other.

The Kirk will have to deny it – or lose its hold over James. Either way, the King's credit will suffer greatly. So the Protestant cause will be divided – King's men against Kirk's men. And Bothwell and Huntly, with Angus and the other Catholics, will strike.'

'With their thousands of men? War?'

'That too. But first, rather more subtly, I fear. James, discredited and isolated, will be struck down. Assassinated. Whether by dirk, poison, or strangling like his father Darnley, I have not yet discovered.'

'Precious soul of God!' Ludovick was on his feet, staring. 'Assassinated! Murdered! You . . . you are not serious, Patrick? Not that! Not the King! They would never dare . . .'

'You think not, Vicky? James would have had Bothwell burned for witchcraft had *he* dared. Huntly slew James's cousin, the Earl of Moray, with his own hand.'

'But not the King!'

'Why not? His father, King Henry Darnley, your uncle, murdered at Kirk o' Field. His mother, Mary the Queen, harried, imprisoned, executed. James Third murdered at Sauchieburn. James First murdered at Perth. What is so sacred about our shauchling Jamie?'

'But how would the King's death aid them? Bothwell and Huntly? Neither of *them* can aspire to the throne. Bothwell is a Stewart, yes – but his line is illegitimate.'

'Aye. And here we come to it, my friend. Here is the beauty of it all. Our youthful Queen Anne at last, after so many alarms and make-believe, is with child. As all know. She is due to be delivered very shortly. In a month. Less. Hence my haste to come here, to have you brought here – for the time is short indeed. All the plans are laid. Within days of its birth, the child will be seized, captured. Held by the Catholics. And proclaimed King. Or Queen, if it is a girl. For James will be dead – having been murdered the same night. And Bothwell will rule in his name, as Regent. And in the King's name, the Catholic armies will march.'

Ludovick shook his head, wordless.

'Moreover you, my dear Vicky, unfortunately have to die also. None greatly hate you, I think – but you stand in the road of these men. You would still be next heir to the throne – and since a new-born babe is but uncertain of survival, you could be dangerous. A figure round which opposition might rally. You are a Protestant, well spoken of by the Kirk. They might set you up as alternative Regent. Or perhaps even as King. So you too must die. At the same time as James. And Bothwell, son of one of James the Fifth's many bastards, will rule this holy Catholic realm secure. Indeed, I have heard that he intends to divorce his wife, and marry the widowed Queen Anne. A thoughtful gesture! Especially as, that same eventful night, and possibly successively thereafter, she is to be bedded. H'mm forcibly. In order that she may conceive another child. Er, promptly. By Bothwell – but reputedly by James. A nice precaution, in case the first child dies. To ascend the throne. A useful second string to Bothwell's bow. You will perceive that nimble wits are here at work, Vicky?'

Lennox's appalled youthful face was a study. 'This . . . this is the work of devils!' he whispered. 'Fiends of hell, rather than men. It must not be! It must not be! What would you have me to do?'

'Bring me to the King, Vicky. Without Chancellor Maitland's knowledge. Maitland is my enemy, and will thwart me before all else, if he can. If he knew that I was in Scotland, he would have me imprisoned forthwith. And then done away with, before word could reach the King's ear. I am still banished, on pain of death. So all must be done secretly. And swiftly. For there is little time.'

'How can I do this, Patrick? James lives in fear, dreading attempts on his person. Since Bothwell's last venture. He is guarded at all times. With the Chancellor ever close. You know that . . .'

'I know that he trusts you. That you have his ear at all times. Also that my brother James is still a Gentleman of his Bedchamber. And that the Earl of Orkney, my wife's father and the King's uncle, will aid you.'

'If I tell James. What you have told me. Then he will be warned. Can take the steps necessary. Without . . . without you having to be brought to him . . .'

'Would he believe you? And if he did, how would he behave? I vow he would weep and take fright. Go straight to Maitland and babble all in his ear. And that sour and desiccate lawyer would counsel inaction, saying that it was all a plot of *mine?* I know them both. Nothing would be done that could halt these resolute and powerful men. Moreover, I have told you but the broad strategy. The vital details are still to be told.'

The Master nodded in most friendly fashion. 'And by me alone. No, no, Vicky – I fear, in all modesty, that you need Patrick Gray. Unless you flee the country, without me, you and James both, I have no doubt, will be dead men within the month.'

Helplessly the young man looked at the handsome, sympathetic and wholly assured face of the man who lounged there across the wide hearth. 'Mary said . . .' he began, and stopped.

'Ah, yes – what did Mary say?' That was quick.

'She said that I must be careful. Not to let you deceive me, hoodwink me, charm me.'

'M'mm. She did? Ever she had a pretty humour, that one! But, Vicky – even Mary, I swear, would not wish her child an orphan!'

The Duke turned to pace the floor. 'What is to be done, then?'

'Have my good-father, Orkney, hold one of his deplorable entertainments. In his Abbot's quarters at Holyrood. To celebrate some family event. A birthday, a betrothal, anything! He has sufficient offspring, God knows, lawful and otherwise, to arrange such at any time! The King to be invited. Coaxed by some means – pretty boys, a witch to question, a request to recite some of his terrible poetry! Anything. Maitland will never show his thin nose in such a company. An ascetic, he loathes Orkney and all his hearty brood. As do the Kirk divines. So I shall win into the King's presence unknown to my enemies. For the rest – never fear.'

'But I do fear, Patrick. Once before, you'll mind, I aided you to the King's presence, from banishment. And lived to regret it.'

'Lived to doubt me and misjudge me rather, Vicky – to my sorrow and your loss,' the other corrected, gently. 'Allowed your mind to be poisoned and your trust in me cruelly slain. This time, even if you doubt me, you will continue to *live*! The poison and the slaying being . . . otherwise.'

Ludovick sighed. 'Very well. But, I warn you Patrick – do not fail me in this. Or, 'fore God, I promise you that you will fail no others hereafter!'

'On my soul. Vicky – such suspicions are unlike you! Banish them from your mind. Myself it is that takes the risks. Has this not struck you? I need not do this. I need not come to the rescue of James and yourself. As it is, I am putting myself in your hands entirely. I trust you with my life, see you. Come, lad – here's my hand on it! Now – tell me about my grandson. A pox – what a thought! That Patrick Gray should be a grand-father ... !'

Chapter Three

The ancient Abbey of Holyrood, nestling beneath the soaring bulk of Arthur's Seat, had witnessed many a stirring scene in its day, with so much of Scotland's turbulent history apt to take place in its vicinity, even within its walls. Of late years the character of these scenes had tended to change – for the times themselves had changed, the Reformation had come to Scotland, and abbeys and the like were not what they had been. Indeed the magnificent Abbey church, formerly as great as any cathedral, was now largely demolished and reduced to form a royal chapel and a parish kirk. But the monastic buildings still remained, to the east of the handsome new palace of Holyroodhouse which King James the Fourth had erected at the beginning of the century. These, centring round the old Abbot's House, were now the residence of the man who, after the Reformation, had been granted the secular control of these valuable church lands, as Commendator-Abbot - Robert Stewart, one of the numerous illegitimate sons of King James the Fifth, a brood for which the newly-seized ecclesiastical properties had come as a godsend indeed. Robert Stewart had done notably well out of it all, becoming in due course, as well as Abbot of Holyrood, Bishop of Orkney and later Earl thereof. Now an elderly man but by no means palling of his vigorous appetite, he lived here, surrounded by a vast number of his children, legitimate and otherwise, grandchildren, mistresses current and pensioned-off, and general hangers-on. No one, least of all Earl Robert himself, ever knew the total population of the Abbey precincts at any given time – or greatly cared. Undoubtedly, in numbers, it was the largest private establishment in Edinburgh, certainly the most raffish, and probably almost the most seedy also – for Orkney's revenues were never up to the strain their lord put upon them. Nevertheless, it was a most cheerful and lively household, a haven of refuge, if not peace, for all and sundry, where tolerance and liberality and licence were the rule, and

33

few questions were asked so long as visitors were of a hearty disposition and uncensorious.

Not infrequently, of course, it became something of an embarrassment to the palace to the west which, however it turned its back on it, could never quite disassociate itself from the uninhibited, decayed and rambling establishment next door. Not that the King himself suffered much in the way of embarrassment – for James, whatever his shortcomings and peculiarities, was far from prudish or conventional; the offence was felt by his spiritual advisers of the ruling Kirk party and their more devoted adherents, and especially by the sternly Calvinist Chancellor Maitland, first minister of the realm and recently created Lord Thirlstane. Strait-laced as he might be, however, he was hardly in a position as yet to do more than frown caustically upon his sovereign's reprobate uncle.

Robert Earl of Orkney's eldest legitimate daughter, the Lady Marie Stewart, was wife to the Master of Gray.

Tonight, that of the 13th of February 1594, the Abbot's House with its appendages was truly bestirring itself, so that its ancient and ill-maintained fabric seemed to be all but bursting at the seams. Every window was alight, every door open, every chimney smoking. The very walls seemed to throb and quiver with noise and hilarity, music, shouting, laughter and female squeals emanating from every corner and precinct. Numbers of the citizenry of Edinburgh, with a well-developed instinct for free entertainment, thronged the nearest public stance in the Abbey Strand, looking, listening, questing the air, hopeful for spectacle and scandal.

The Duke of Lennox waited, in a fret, near the main door on the inner or courtyard side, just across from the tall frowning bulk of the palace which, notably less well-lit tonight, appeared to stare haughtily in the other direction from its randy, rackety neighbour. Ludovick was in a fret for a variety of reasons. He was waiting to receive the King – and was not at all convinced that James would in fact put in an appearance; when he had last seen him, that afternoon, the monarch had mumbled merely that he *might* come, that he would see, that it was gey cold, and that he was busy working on a new ode to celebrate the forthcoming birth of an heir to the throne – all of which, from James

Stewart, might mean anything or nothing.

Moreover, Lennox, as yet, had seen no sign of the Master of Gray. After persuading Orkney to arrange this jollification, he had sent a trusted courier to Fast Castle, giving the details – and had since heard nothing of Patrick Gray.

If however, the two principal guests were thus doubtful as to appearance, there was one who was not, but whose presence added to the Duke's anxieties – Mary Gray herself. Mary, still suspicious of the entire proceedings, had insisted on coming from Methven for this occasion, to confront her father, bringing the baby with her. She was somewhere in this rambling building – and to have had to leave her unattended in this houseful of roystering, lecherous men, a young, beautiful and defenceless woman unfortunately with the reputation of a courtesan, was not a situation which Ludovick could contemplate with equanimity – despite the girl's assurances that she could well look after herself, having indeed lived in this household at one time, with the Master and his wife.

Finally, however much he tried, the Duke could not remain wholly unmoved by what was so frankly going on in a sort of open alcove flanking this door, designed presumably as a porter's lodge; quite unconcerned by his pacing and frowning presence only a few feet away, a young woman in there, of ripe charms, her clothing so disarranged as to be almost discarded, was generously, indeed enthusiastically, sharing her favours with two youths, who pulled her this way and that on an alternating basis, to a panting commentary, interspersed with her giggles. One of the young men was David Stewart, fifth or sixth legitimate son of the Earl, whilst the other was almost certainly one of his bastard brothers; and the lady appeared to be one of their father's latest mistresses. Ludovick found their antics a little upsetting; there was neither door nor curtain to the alcove, and try as he would he could not prevent his eyes from straying frequently in that direction. He wished that they would go and pursue their unseemly love-making elsewhere.

He debated with himself, not for the first time, whether or not he should go over to the palace, to discover the King's intentions. But he was reluctant, however foolishly, to leave this house with Mary in it; moreover he could not be certain that James might not come from the palace at all. It was all most irritating that he must hang about like this – especially since assuredly it was the host's duty to welcome the monarch, either in person or through one of his sons; but neither Orkney nor any of his crew had shown the least inclination to break off their various pleasures on this or any other account, and the Duke had felt bound to do the honours, for decency's sake. Not that decency was an attribute that anyone would look for in this house.

The inevitable clash of interests appeared to be coming to a head in the alcove, two more revellers arrived to watch and advise, and Ludovick, though not a young man normally much concerned with his dignity, was deciding that he could no longer linger here, when the clank of steel sounded from outside. Five men appeared at the door, two in front in half-armour and morion helmets and the colours of the Royal Guard, bearing halberds, two following in velvets and satins and a third guard bringing up the rear. Ludovick bowed low.

'Y'Grace,' he said briefly.

The King, stumbling over the steps up to the doorway, did not actually speak, although his thick loose lips were moving, shaping words. He may have nodded his head to his cousin – but James's head, much too large-seeming for his body, was always apt to loll and nod, especially when he walked. He came shuffling indoors, between the in-turned figures of his escort, tapping the worn flagstones rhythmically with the ferrule of a long white staff almost as tall as himself and decorated with a bunch of much tattered black ribbons. Clearly he was in the throes of composition.

James, King of Scots, was certainly an eye-catching figure. Now aged twenty-eight years, he looked a deal older, a slack-featured, slack-bodied, knock-kneed shambling man, ridiculously over-dressed in enormously high hat braided with silver and sprouting orange ostrich plumes, padded and stuffed crimson velvet doublet and trunks slashed with emerald-green satin, hose sagging about spindly legs, and high-heeled shoes of pale blue with huge bows and jewelled buckles. Around his neck was a great ruff, sadly stained and crumpled, and hanging about it a series of golden chains with crosses and charms, with over all a short purple cloak, lined with cloth-of-gold.

His companion was a big, burly man of similar age, high-complexioned, haughty-eyed, richly clad although his garb seemed quiet beside that of his liege lord – John Erskine, Earl of Mar, Captain of the Royal Guard, Keeper of Stirling Castle and the King's boyhood playmate. At James's back he nodded to Lennox, and grimaced.

The King may have been a poor physical specimen and unprepossessing as to feature, with a lop-sided face and a tongue too large for his mouth that caused an almost permanent dribble; but there was nothing wrong with his eyes. Indeed, they were his only good feature – great, dark, liquid eyes, almost feminine in appearance, expressive and with their own shrewdness however much they rolled and darted. And now, however preoccupied he appeared to be with his muse, his glance quickly perceived the performance in the porter's closet, and despite Lennox's attempt to usher him along the stone-vaulted corridor towards the main hall or refectory, he shuffled over, to peer in at the spectacle with keenest interest.

'Fornication and all uncleanness,' he mentioned thoughtfully. He poked with his long staff. 'Yon's Davy Stewart – a bonny lad, and strong. Strong. The other – houts, I canna just place him by the parts I can see!' James sniggered. 'Who is he, Vicky – who's this?'

'I do not know, Sire. Heed them not – they are all drunk. Will Your Grace come this way?'

'Drunken with wine, aye. Chambering and wantonness. Ooh, aye. On such cometh the wrath o' God. And they're gey young for it, I reckon. The lassie I dinna ken.' The King wrinkled his long nose distastefully when he perceived that the young woman at least had eyes for him there, and was indeed smiling up at him. 'She's a great heifer, is she no'? Shameless! Shameful!' He wagged his head, and his glance darted at Mar. 'Hech, aye – here's a right paradox, Johnnie, a conundrum. Can she be both shameful and shameless at the once? How say you – can she?'

Mar shrugged. 'I have not Your Grace's gift for words,' he said shortly. 'I'd name her a dirty bitch and h' done with it!'

'Shameless and shameful.' James muttered to himself. 'Aye, I could use that...'

'Sire – may I conduct you to my lord of Orkney?' Lennox

urged, and the King allowed himself to be escorted along the dimly-lit and echoing passage. In dark corners and recesses couples clung and wrestled and panted, and if James seemed disposed to linger and peer, his companions marched him along to the great hall from which light and music and shouted laughter streamed forth.

It was a lively and colourful scene that met their gaze, from the arched doorway of that abbey refectory. Three sides of the huge apartment, where hundreds of candles flared and wavered and smoked, were lined with tables where men and women sat or sprawled or clutched each other, amongst a litter of broken meats, flagons of wine and spilled goblets. There were many gaps at the tables, some represented by snoring figures who lay beneath. Dogs, great deerhounds and wolfhounds, were successfully taking over the remains of the repast unmolested either by the diners or the servants, themselves apt to reel, who still plied a proportion of the guests with fresh flagons. In the central space a group of gipsy fiddlers played vigorously, and to their jigging music a dark, flashing-eyed girl, diaphanously clad only in veiling, danced sinuously, voluptuously, to a great solemn dancing bear, which lumbered around her suggestively graceful posturings with a sort of ponderous dignity. And along the table-tops themselves, a man stepped and picked his way amongst the platters, bottles and debris, himself tripping a step or two of the dance now and again, skipping over some diner fallen forward with too much hospitality. He was a portly, florid, elderly man in disarrayed finery, who played a fiddle the while in tune with the gipsies, though occasionally using the bow to poke shrewdly at certain of the ladies below him – the Lord Robert Stewart, Earl and Bishop of Orkney.

It took the Earl – or anybody else, for that matter – some little time to notice the newcomers. When he did, he produced a great resounding crescendo of screeches from his fiddle, and flourished the instrument, to end by bowing low over it in an exaggerated genuflection which drew all eyes capable of being drawn in the direction of the doorway. What he said was of course lost in the general hubbub. He did not descend from the table-top. The lady and the bear continued to dance.

James had no eyes save for the bear, his expression registering a mixture of alarm and unwilling admiration. Indeed he backed a little against his companions each time the brute turned in his direction. Quite clearly he had no intention of advancing further into the hall until the creature was safely out of the way.

When, presently, the young woman reached a climax of hip-twisting, stomach-gyrating and bosom-shaking ecstasy, and thereafter slipped in close actually to embrace and rub herself against the burly upstanding shaggy animal, and its great fore-paws closed around her twitching, fragile-seeming form as the music sobbed away to silence, the King all but choked.

'Waesucks! Look at that!' he cried, in agitation. 'Look at the lassie! And yon horrid brute-beast. Och, foul fall it – the nasty great crittur! It'll . . . it'll . . . och, save us all – this isna decent!'

'It is but a ploy, Sire. There is no danger,' Mar assured. 'The gipsies tame these brutes from cubs. They come from Muscovy or some such parts. She'll come to no hurt – not from the bear, leastwise!'

James shook his heavy head. 'She shouldna ha' done that,' he declared, frowning. 'I didna like that. Na, na – it's no' right . . .'

With the musicians for the moment silenced, and the girl disentangling herself from the bear without difficulty and mincing off, the creature resuming all fours and waddling after her meekly enough, Orkney from his raised stance lifted his richly-seasoned voice.

'Our gracious lord! Most noble and revered liege and suzerain. Welcome to my humble house and board, Sire! Come, Majesty, and honour this poor company.' The Earl, whether deliberately or by accident, ended that with a notable belch.

With an eye on the disappearing bear, James nodded, and began to move forward. 'Aye, my lord – but no more o' yon, mind. No more wild beasts, see you.' Compared with his uncle, he had a singularly squeaky, and thick uneven voice.

Most of those in possession of their wits had got to their feet, or approximately so, though not without some stumbles and collapses. A place was cleared for the monarch and his two companions at the centre of the high transverse table at the head if the chamber, Orkney arranging this with the aid of his fiddle-bow. The officer of the Guard who had accompanied the King detached himself and made a circuit of the tables, knocking off the hats of such revellers as had so far forgotten themselves as to remain covered in the presence of the Lord's Anointed.

James had difficulty with his stave, as he sat down, not knowing quite what to do with it and apparently reluctant just to lay it on the floor. Eventually room was made for it to lie along the table itself – where unfortunately its bunch of ribbons lay in a pool of spilt wine. Lennox hoped that it was a good omen that the King had brought that staff tonight; it had been a present from the Master of Gray, brought on the occasion of his last return from banishment, as unauthorised then as now, five years before.

James, waving aside the food and drink set before him, drew out from within his doublet a crumpled bunch of papers, which he spread carefully on the table before him. At sight of them Orkney groaned, and hastily signed to the musicians to strike up once more.

'My new ode, my lord,' the King revealed, patting it proudly. 'More properly, an epode. Aye, an epode. To the new prince, Duke of Rothesay, Earl of Carrick and Lord of the Isles. Or, alternatively, to the Princess of Scotland, as the case may be. I'ph'mm. Just some wee bits of changes, here and there, will serve. Near finished, it is, but for a verse or two. Aye, and it goes excellently well, I warrant you. I have seldom wrought better verse. I will read it . . .' He looked up in annoyance as the gipsy players broke into full fiddle. 'A plague on that ill squawking!' he exclaimed, and flapped a paper at the musicians as one might shoo away a wasp. 'I say that I'll read it. I am prepared to honour this company wi' the first reading o' this most royal epode! Hush them, man – hush them.'

'Your Grace – perhaps later?' his uncle said urgently. 'When all is quiet. When the servants ha' removed the meats, the eating over.'

'Tush, man – am I, the King, to wait for scullions and lackeys? And these scurvy Egyptians wi' their caterwauling!'

'No, Sire – not so. I but suggested that it would be mair seemly suitable, to hear your verses later. After you've partaken o' my providing.' Orkney's voice was rich, thick, and just a little slurred. He was not drunk – he was seldom actually drunk; equally seldom was he sober.

'I'm no' hungry. Nor thirsty.'

'A pity, Sire. But the maist o'my guests are both! To read this . . . this effusion now, could be but casting pearls before swine, I say.' He had a little difficulty with that phrase. 'I had thought, later. When all are eaten. In a small privy room, maybe . . .'

'No' here? No' to a' the company? But I *came* to read it, man! It's a right notable rhapsody . . .'

'No doubt, Jamie – but it's no' a' folk who can take in the like, see you. There's a wheen o' them here'd no' appreciate it. There'd be no keeping them quiet. Better to have but a few. In a small room. Presently.'

The King was offended.'We are displeased. Much displeased,' he said. 'Vicky Stewart said I should read it.' He gathered up his papers, and pushed back his chair. 'Where's this room then, my lord?'

His uncle seldom allowed anything to upset him, but now he looked a little flustered. Then he shrugged, as James rose, and got to his own feet, beckoning a servitor to his side. All who were conscious of the fact, and able, must rise when the King rose, and in the confusion Orkney jerked a word or two to the servant. Then, picking up a candlestick, he conducted his nephew along behind the table, towards a door to an inner chamber. Mar and Lennox followed, and in some doubt not a few of the top-table guests left their womenfolk to do likewise. The royal guards took up positions at the doorway.

It was only a small room indeed into which the monarch was shown, containing a table, a few chairs and benches, and little else. There was no space here for much of an audience, and Orkney in fact turned back all at the door save Ludovick and Mar. James had promptly taken a chair, and was smoothing out the distinctly tattered and now wine-wet sheets of paper on the table, before he perceived how select was to be the company.

'What's this? What's this?' he demanded. 'Is this a', man? To hear my epode? Waesucks – but Vicky and Johnnie and your-sel'?'

'You'll no' want a rabble, Sire?' his uncle said. 'It's quality you'll want, I'm thinking – no' quantity.'

'Better this way, Your Grace,' Lennox assured. 'Here is no matter for the crowd, the multitude.'

Mar, who was not of a poetic turn of mind, muttered something unintelligible but resentful.

James, despite his disappointment, was already peering at the first lines of his precious work, lips savouring the opening words.

'You'll need mair light, Jamie. Bide a wee,' his uncle urged. 'I've sent for mair candles.'

'Aye, it's gey dark in here. Mind, I ken the most o' it by heart. But . . .'

They all looked up as another door opened at the far side of the room, and a cloaked figure came in bearing a silver-branched candlestick, unlit. This man came over to the table, and proceeded to light his candles from that already burning there. Then he set the illumination down beside the King, and stood back.

James promptly returned to the perusal of his papers without a glance at the newcomer. It was probably the other removing his dark cloak, and the consequent glow of light from that quarter, which caused the King to turn round – or it may have been the silence which had suddenly descended upon that little chamber and which could be felt almost like something physical – a silence which was broken by a choking sound from the Earl of Mar.

James stared, mouth open, jaw falling, at the resplendent vision which the candlelight revealed. A wavering hand, paper and all, came out in a part pointing, part holding-back gesture.

The newcomer, tossing aside the cloak, and running a hand over his carefully-cut long black hair, bowed deeply, with arm-flourishing elaboration. 'Your excellent and dearly-esteemed Grace's most very humble servant!' he said, smiling brilliantly.

James gobbled, clutching at his chair and half-rising, eyes rolling in alarm. 'P'Patrick!' he got out thickly. 'Patrick Gray! Guidsakes! Patrick, man – you! What's this? What's this? Mercy on us – you!'

'None other, Highness. Patrick Gray returned to your royal side, in love and duty. From far and foreign parts. Seeking your gracious clemency – and rejoicing to see you well. To see that I am in time. Aye – and bringing Your Grace an even more valuable token of my love and devotion than on . . . that last occasion!' The Master sank down on one knee beside the royal chair.

James continued to stare, slack lips working, long tongue licking. The suppliant looked quite the most splendid and immaculate figure seen in Scotland for long, dressed in white satin doublet and extraordinarily short trunks, slashed in gold, his spun silk hose sculpturing a lengthy leg as graceful as it was masculinely strong. The high upstanding collar of his padded doublet was edged with a chaste row of black pearls, and the Knight's Cross of the Order of St. Lazarus hung at his chest. High-heeled white shoes with jewelled buckles completed a dazzling appearance.

'This is an outrage!' Mar declared forcefully.

The monarch turned to look helplessly at Lennox and Orkney. 'But . . . but you canna do this, Patrick!' he quavered. 'It's no' proper. You're banished the realm, man! I've no' re-called you. The Council banished you. You behaved treasonably against me, Patrick – treasonably!'

'Only in the opinion of some men, Sire – never in my heart. That is not possible. Only in the prejudice and mistaken views of such as my lord of Bothwell and his friends.'

The King plucked at his lip. The name of Bothwell always perturbed him. 'Aye – but others too, Patrick. Maitland – my Lord Thirlestane, the Chancellor. He told me you were writing ill letters to Elizabeth o' England. Aye, and taking her gold. Plotting against me . . .'

'Never, Sire. The plotting and treasons are otherwise – as I have come to reveal to you. I left your realm because my enemies – and yours, Sire – had become too strong for me. I have re-turned to thwart them. And to save you,' Patrick had risen to his feet.

'Na, na – it's no' just that simple, Master o' Gray,' James declared, recovering himself somewhat. 'You canna just flout the decisions o' King and Council this way, I'd have you ken. Eh, my lords?' He looked round at the two earls and Lennox, all members of that Privy Council. 'Banished is banished, is it no'? Banishment canna just be terminate when the . . . the felon would have it so!'

'That is so,' Mar said heavily. He had never greatly loved the Master of Gray.

'Precisely, Sire. I am the last to dispute it. *You* only can terminate my banishment. You, the King. So I have come to you. If you will not do so, I abide the consequences. Either to return to outer darkness whence I came, from the sun of your presence. Or, if my presumption in coming here is too great, to pay the penalty for offending, with my life. But, to save *your* life, I had to come, Highness.'

'Eh? What's that? Save . . . save my life? What a pox . . .?'

'You are in deadly danger, Sire. From wicked and powerful men. I have uncovered a devilish conspiracy against you. But . . .' Patrick Gray glanced about him. 'As well that so few are here to hear me. Leal men. I'd be happier in even a more private place . . .'

'A cell in the Tolbooth, sir! Or better still, in the Castle!' Mar intervened grimly. 'Suitable enough for a forsworn traitor! As Captain of the King's Guard, *I* am responsible for His Grace's safety. And I'll see to it, never fear.'

'While you live, no doubt, my lord!' Gray returned briefly. 'Recollect that my lord of Moray was also Captain of the King's Guard!' That name upset both Mar and the King, as it was intended to do, for the Bonnie Earl of Moray's death had been horrible, and James could not wholly deny complicity. The Master pursued his advantage.

'It will require more than your Guard, my lord. The dagger even now points at the King's heart. Cold steel seeks his life's-blood – and swiftly. You do him no service to counsel that . . .'

He got no further. As he was well aware, the very words that he had used were enough to arouse the King to desperation. James was on his feet now, even though unsteadily. All his life he had had the utmost horror of cold steel, a terror at the sight or thought of spilled blood – believed to have been born in him when David Rizzio, his mother's Secretary, was savagely butchered in the Queen's presence a month or so before her son's birth. Now he was gabbling incoherently.

Patrick waited, as Mar cursed, Ludovick sought to soothe and reassure the King, and Orkney considered his son-in-law from

44

shrewd if blood-shot eyes.

'Out with it, Patrick,' the latter said, above the hubbub. 'What is this? What scoundrel thus dares to threaten the King's Grace? You'll no' make such charges without good cause, I'm thinking?'

'Indeed no, my Lord. Have I Your Grace's permission to proceed?'

James was still standing, and the others therefore had to be on their feet likewise. He had grabbed up his precious papers from the table, clutching them to him. Only after considerable coaxing by his uncle and Lennox, did he allow himself to be guided back into his chair. It was Orkney who signed to Patrick to continue.

The Master, amidst many interruptions and displays of royal horror, consternation and positive gibbering panic, recounted the gist of what he had told Ludovick at Fast Castle, with one or two elaborations relating to the scale of Spanish aid expected by the Catholics, the circumstances of the courier, George Ker's revelations to Patrick, and the names of other Catholic lords believed to be in the conspiracy – Seton, Sanquhar, Maxwell and Fleming. But he also made certain omissions, saying nothing about the proposed rape and remarriage of the Queen, and making only an oblique and disguised reference to the King's indiscreet letter to Philip of Spain, thus only hinting at the Kirk's blackmailing tactics on James – although, that the latter picked these up shrewdly enough despite his agitation and alarm, was evident by his quick, furtive and appealing glances at the speaker.

When Gray was finished his account of the plot, the monarch was reduced to tearful and hand-wringing impotence, a pitiful sight. Orkney was silent and very thoughtful. Not so the Earl of Mar.

'I do not believe it!' he cried. 'Bothwell is a crack-brained hothead – but he would never stoop to the death of the King! I would believe much of Huntly – but not this! He is your good-brother, my lord Duke. What think you of this tale?'

Ludovick shrugged in French fashion. 'I know not. But after Huntly's slaughter of Moray, I believe that little is beyond him. You will recollect that *I* did not choose him as my sister's husband!'

That had been James's doing, it was thought on the advice of the Master of Gray. The King chewed his trembling lower lip, blinking great liquid eyes.

'All this depends on the word of George Ker, does it not? That perjured rogue!' Mar went on. 'Should we believe such a renegade?'

'Not at all, my lord,' Patrick said. 'I made a most searching inquiry, when I heard of it. All of which confirmed the conspiracy. For instance, I have sure word that the Pope has promised Huntly a large sum in gold, to assist the project.'

Mar spluttered. A fervid Protestant, he was ever ready to pounce on the villainy of the Pope of Rome. '*That* I'll credit!' he said. 'But not this of murdering His Grace.'

'Whether or no they would go such lengths, the rest sounds like enough,' Orkney observed. 'This of seizing the child. Bothwell was but recently shouting it abroad that His Grace was of unsound mind. Declaring the same again, and holding the child, he could take rule in its name. And with the Pope's backing, the other Catholic powers, as well as Spain, would accept him. That would be an ill business, whatever else.' The old Earl was half-drunk and slurred his words slightly, but then that was his normal state, and presumably left his wits but little affected.

'God forbid!' James mumbled. 'We must take steps. Aye, steps. Forthwith.'

'Undoubtedly, Sire,' Patrick nodded. 'Stringent and vigorous steps!'

'Aye. But what, Patrick man – what?'

'That is a matter for the Council,' Mar asserted.

'Assuredly. The Council,' the Master agreed, 'Which is yourself. And the Duke, here. And my lord of Orkney. And, of course, amongst others, the Lords Bothwell, Huntly, Angus, Erroll, Seton, Fleming, Maxwell and so on! A notable company. May I wish the Council's deliberations most well?'

'No! No!' James cried. 'Folly! It's no' for the Council. There's no trusting the Council. Waesucks – who *can* I trust?' That was a wail.

'You can trust the Kirk,' Mar asserted. 'The Kirk will aid you.'

'Will it?' Patrick wondered.

At his tone, they all looked at him.

'Of course it will,' Mar said. 'The Kirk is as the King's right hand.'

'Then I think perhaps His Grace may be left-handed! Perhaps he writes his letters with his left!'

'Eh...?'

James stared at the Master in new and different alarm. 'Patrick, man...!' he faltered.

The other made a reassuring gesture. 'I refer to letters of which the Kirk should not know. Letters of state, which are no business of the godly divines!'

'You talk in riddles, sir,' Mar objected. 'To what end?'

'Patrick means letters . . . letters to the like o' my good sister o' England, Elizabeth,' the King intervened hurriedly. 'Eh, Patrick?' He could be as quick as any, on occasion. 'The like o' that, you mean?' There was pleading, there.

Gray smiled warmly. 'Exactly, Sire – the like o' that! I but point out to my lord of Mar that the Kirk's interests and those of the Crown may not always coincide. As in our Auld Alliance with France, for instance.'

'To be sure! Quite so. Just that. Precisely.' James babbled his relief. 'Patrick's right. Aye. The Kirk is no' to be relied on implicitly. No' in such-like a matter, Johnnie.'

'To whom will you turn, then, if not to Council nor Kirk?'

James tugged at his wispy beard. 'God kens! The Estates o' Parliament. Call the Estates. The folk, the lieges, will aye support their King!'

"How long will that take? Weeks. A month. And the child due any day.'

'The Chancellor. Maitland. He'll ken what to do ...'

'That whey-faced clerk! This will be no work for clerks – if the Master of Gray speaks truth!' Mar was no great lover of his fellowmen.

'Aye, but he has a good head on him, Johnnie,' James protested. 'Maitland's a canny chiel. Long-headed. He's no fool, Maitland ...'

'Perhaps my lord Chancellor may be just a little too long-headed for the present business,' Patrick intervened, mildly enough. 'For the normal affairs of state, I have no doubt he serves you admirably. But in countering violent men, armed uprising, as my lord of Mar says he may be something lacking. More especially as he is already linked with Huntly...'

'Huntly!'

'Maitland and Huntly! Never!'

'You jest, sir! That Calvinist capon and the Catholic rooster!'

This time his hearers were united in their incredulity. The Master had gone too far. To name the sober, Lowland, Protestant Chancellor in the same breath as the swashbuckling, arrogant Papist Cock o' the North, was almost to mock the intelligence of his companions. Ludovick, strangely enough, felt almost disappointed in his former friend and guardian.

'No jest – as Moray found out to his cost, my friends.'

'Moray? What has Moray to do with Maitland?' The King's voice quavered again.

'Your Grace does not know? Perhaps . . . perhaps, then, I should not have spoken? Forgive me, Sire. Forget my chance remark.'

James chewed at the back of his hand, eyes switching from one to another of the nobles, in most evident and unhappy quandary. The shocking and shameful murder of the handsome Earl of Moray, cousin of the King, by Huntly, had been the most unpopular act of the reign – for Moray had been the people's darling and beloved of the Kirk. James's jealousy of the sporting Earl, and his accusations of his tampering with the affections of the young Queen, were known to all, and his implication in the tragedy doubted by few. The sternly upright Chancellor Maitland however, had stood by the King, and with Patrick's help James had weathered that storm – even though Huntly had weathered it even more successfully. Now, it was clear that the unfortunate monarch was torn between his natural desire to have the whole wretched affair buried and forgotten, and to learn whether there were indeed aspects of it all which had escaped him and which in consequence might lighten his own burden of guilt.

James was of an inquisitive soul, and curiosity prevailed over apprehension. 'What's this? What's this, Patrick? Yon was a bad business. I was right displeased wi' Huntly. He overdid it

– aye, he much overdid it, yon time. But what's this o' Maitland? Out with it, man.'

'As Your Grace wishes. I would have thought that you would have been informed of this. The Chancellor was behind Huntly in Moray's death.'

'Why?' Mar jerked. 'What had Maitland to gain from that?'

'Much. Nor is he finished yet, my lord. All men, they say, pursue some quarry in their lives. With some it is pleasure; with some, knowledge.' Patrick made a small bow towards the King. 'With some, women; with others, position and power. Maitland pursues wealth. Already he has amassed much, gained great estates. But he seeks ever more. And these days, not in small handfuls but in great. Who are the wealthiest men in the land? Huntly, Angus, Hamilton and Argyll. The Gordons and the Douglases are too strong for Maitland. As are the Hamiltons. He has set himself to bring down Argyll, and gain the Campbell wealth.'

'He mislikes Argyll, yes. But what of that? What has it to do with Moray's death?'

'Moray's mother was old Argyll's daughter, my lord. Moray had the guardianship of young Argyll, the control of his great lands. Since his death, they have passed to the control of two of the young Earl's uncles – Sir Colin Campbell of Skipness and Sir John Campbell of Cawdor.' The Master snapped his fingers. 'I would not give that much for the lives of these two gentlemen!'

All gazed at him, with varying expressions of disbelief, perplexity and horror.

'This is but a conjecture, sir – a surmise,' Mar declared. 'Maitland does not have it in him to fly so high!'

'You think not?' Patrick turned to the King, smiling. 'Have you ever known my information amiss, Sire? This I am assured of.'

There was silence in that small chamber. Ludovick marvelled at the man. Since coming into the room he had managed to undermine almost the entire fabric of the realm. How much of what he said was fact, only time would tell; but meanwhile he had succeeded in creating suspicion and doubt about practically every powerful man and group in the land. It had been a masterly performance, such as only the Master of Gray could accomplish. And the immediate result was not hard to foretell.

'What is to be done then, Patrick?' Orkney demanded. 'You will have your notions as to that, I warrant!'

'Aye, Patrick – what am I to do?' James bleated. 'Maitland's my Chancellor! I need him, man. And the Council's no' to be trusted. And the Kirk . . . the Kirk . . . !'

The Master nodded briskly. 'Three steps, Your Grace. The Queen to be guarded surely night and day. In a strong place. What is your strongest castle? Stirling? My lord of Mar is Keeper thereof – also Captain of your Guard. Put the Queen in Stirling Castle under my lord's care, forthwith. So shall mother and child be secure. Eh, my lord? Thereafter you to be keeper of the young prince or princess until this danger be overpast.'

'That is wise, yes,' Mar nodded.

Ludovick almost found it in himself to smile. So the difficult Mar, who hated Huntly and despised Maitland, was won over.

'She's near her time, Patrick,' James mumbled. 'I misdoubt if she can travel to Stirling.'

'In a litter, Sire. With care, and well happed-up, she will do very well, I swear. There are a few days yet, are there not?'

'Aye. But . . . och, well. I'ph'mm.'

'Secondly,' the Master went on, 'we need men. Many men. And quickly. Not scores or hundreds. Thousands of men. Or the threat of them. Huntly and Bothwell and Angus have the largest followings – but there are others none so far behind. One is waiting, ready to hand – Argyll. He can field three thousand Campbells.'

'He is young. But a laddie . . .' the King pointed out.

'All the better. He will play your game with the less trouble. But he is nineteen – of an age with my lord Duke, here, almost. That's none so young. At nineteen I was . . . heigho – never mind! This way, you shall halt Maitland's scheming also. Give young Argyll some high appointment. He will be flattered, and grateful. You will have three thousand Campbell broadswords – that have been itching in their scabbards since Moray's death – for a start. To add to your Royal Guard.'

'Shrewd,' Mar acceded, judicially.

'Who is next, with numbers? Apart from the wilder Highland clans of the north-west, who would take time to bring to your side. The Kennedys. The King of Carrick – young Earl of Cass-illis. He can bring out two thousand, at least.'

'Hech – but he's younger still, Patrick! He'll be but sixteen.'

'His aunt was wife to my lord of Orkney, here. And his mother a sister of your Treasurer, the Master of Glamis.'

'Aye. Aye. But could we persuade the Kennedys to arms, man? They are an ill lot. And no' that kindly towards their King.'

'*I* could persuade them, Sire, I believe. And if you get the Kennedys, then you get Eglinton's Montgomeries and Glen-cairn's Cunninghams also! They are all linked by bonds and marriage. Another three thousand!'

Orkney chuckled, but said nothing.

'That brings me to my third step, Your Grace. Countermand my forfeiture and banishment, Sire, I pray you. Forthwith. That I may serve you in this matter. If you will so honour me, give me back my position of Master of the Wardrobe. It allows me to remain close to your royal person. An advantage. Which, h'm, is both my joy and my leal duty!'

Mar drew a long breath, and stared up at the groined ceiling.

James looked at the Master from under down-bent brows licked his lips, and then looked at the others. 'Aye,' he said. 'Ooh, aye. Let it be so, Patrick. Just that.'

It was as easy as that. Almost an anti-climax. No contrary voice was raised. Patrick Gray had anticipated accurately.

He had anticipated thoroughly also. From out of his dazzling white satin doublet, he drew a folded piece of paper and a neat little ink-horn and quill. Opening the paper he put all on the table before the King. 'Since it would be unsuitable to disturb the Chancellor at this hour of night, Sire – and since the Sec-retary is his nephew Cockburn – I thought it might be helpful to have this ending of my outlawry written and signed. By now, no doubt, not a few will know that I am here, in Edinburgh. So, if Your Grace will but add your royal signature to these few words . . . ?'

James, for whom the written word held an importance that was almost a fascination, was already scanning the paper, his lips forming the words as he read, '. . . restored to his former positions, privileges and offices . . .' he muttered.

'Modest and humble as they were,' the Master mentioned, easily. 'Including, of course, my Sheriffship of the shire of Forfar.'

'Ah! Umm. Well . . .'

'I thank Your Grace.'

With a sigh, the King fumblingly dipped quill in ink-horn and appended his signature, the pen spluttering.

By the time that the King's party came back into the hall, organised entertainment had been superseded by private, however much some of it might savour of public display. Pandemonium in fact reigned. Whether or not the host had been any restraining influence, his absence appeared to have removed all semblance of order. Two of his ladies, considerably underclad, had taken up his position on the table-top, and were attempting to emulate the bear-dancer's act, to the music of a gipsy fiddler standing on the King's chair, a young lordling, with one of the sheepskins from the floor around his shoulders, performing the bear's part with much pawing and embracing. Further down the table active love-making was in process, at various stages, to the uncaring snores of the sleeping or the encouraging advice of those too drunk to stand but not drunk enough to sleep. Horseplay of sundry sorts was going on all over the great chamber, guests, members of the establishment, entertainers and servants apparently equally involved.

The most popular activity, however, judging by the amount of attention received, was taking place on the raised dais at this top end of the room, behind the high table, where two gallants were fighting a spirited duel with naked swords over a young woman whom they had penned into a corner there, while a third young man egged them on with the King's white staff. Strangely enough, despite the vigour and drama of the sword-fight, and the shouted comments of the onlookers, it was the young woman herself who drew all eyes, so at odds was she with the scene around her. Seemingly wholly unconcerned with what was represented by the swording, the noise, and all else, she was gazing calmly over that chaotic hall, with a detached interest that had as little of shrinking alarm in it as it had of proud self-assertion. Even her dress was out-of-place – though by no means in the way that was the case with many women present; she was clad, not in any finery but in a plain dark pinafore-gown of olive green, that was almost prim, lightened by the white collar and sleeves of a linen under-blouse. For all her air of demure modesty and quiet reserve, she was the loveliest, proudest-borne and most alive figure in that room. She was Mary Gray.

The scene affected the royal party in differing ways. The King, at sight of naked, gleaming steel, blanched and flapped his hands wildly, exclaiming. The Duke of Lennox let fly an oath, and went striding forward. And the Master of Gray came to a halt, and stood completely still, staring at the girl, lips slightly parted below that crescent of moustache.

Mary turned her head and perceived the newcomers. Her dark eyes locked with those of her father. After a moment or two, she moved, coming straight towards him, even though her route inevitably lay close to the sparring, panting swordsmen. With quiet assurance she raised her hand a little to them, spoke a word or two, and without pausing came on. The duellists obligingly moved to one side, sensibly slackening the vigour of their clash, even grinning in drunken fashion. One of them was Patrick, Master of Orkney, the old Earl's heir, and the other the Lord Lindores, a son-in-law.

Mary reached Ludovick first, as he hurried to her, but though she held out a hand to him, touched his arm, she moved on. To the King she curtsied gravely, from a few paces off. Then she turned to her father, searching his face.

He had not ceased to gaze at her. So they stood, so uncannily alike. There might have been no one else in all that noisy, chaotic room.

Only Ludovick knew how last these two had parted. It had been in dire, tragic emotion in a garden-house of Bothwell's castle of Hailes in Lothian, twenty months before, with the girl informing her father that she had deliberately betrayed him, sent proof of his most treasonable activities to his prime enemy, the Chancellor Maitland, and warned him that he had only hours to get out of Scotland before the Chancellor would seize him on a capital charge, whereafter nothing could save him from the headsman's block. None had witnessed that scene between these two – but Mary had told Ludovick something of it, for it was for his sake that she had done it, to save him from the evil consequences of the Master's plotting. The distress of mind which forced that terrible action, long put off as it had been, had deeply affected and changed Mary Gray; it was to be seen whether it had in any way changed the man who at the age of fifteen had conceived her.

Patrick it was who acted. He did not move, but slowly his hands rose, open, towards her, arms wide. 'Mary!' he said, throatily, huskily.

She ran, hurling herself into those arms, to clutch him convulsively, to bury her dark head against his white padded shoulder. 'Patrick! Oh, Patrick!' she sobbed.

He held her to him and kissed her hair, eyes moist, hushing her like a child.

Watching, Ludovick bit his lip, frowning blacker than he knew.

The King, although somewhat preoccupied by the still naked swords so close at hand, and also by the insolence of a gipsy standing on his chair and one of Orkney's sons purloining his staff, could not find it consistent with his royal dignity to stand waiting in public while this private reunion was enacted, however touching. But he had a soft spot for Mary Gray, whom he conceived to be one of the few people who really appreciated his poetic outpourings, and was disposed to be lenient. He moved over, to tap her on the heaving shoulder.

'Mistress Mary,' he said. 'Waesucks, Mistress – I think you forget yoursel'. In our presence. Aye – this isna seemly, lassie.'

For a brief moment the Master's dark eyes blazed. But he restrained himself. As for the girl, she stepped back, raising her head, uncaring for the tears on her cheeks.

'As you say, Sire. I crave Your Grace's pardon. It has been a long parting.'

'I'ph'mm. No doubt.' And then, relenting. 'I've no' seen you for long, Mistress. How's the bairn? Vicky's bairn?'

'Well, Sire. Very well, I thank you.'

'You should be more about my Court, lassie. You and Vicky.

54

No' hiding away in yon Methven. I . . . I miss you. Aye, I miss you both. See to it, I say.'

'But, Your Grace . . .'

Patrick spoke quickly. 'Highness – this, I swear, is well thought of. That Mary should return to the Queen's side. She can no longer be a Maid-in-Waiting, it seems, as she was! But if Your Grace was to appoint her a Woman of the Bed-chamber, she could serve all notably well in this pass. Close to the Queen, at all times, and with a child of her own. She is quick, sharp-witted . . .'

'Aye, to be sure. She couldna be a Lady-in-Waiting, no. But an extra Woman o' the Bedchamber. Aye, we could have her that . . .'

'But I do not wish . . .'

'Wheesht, lassie – it's no' for you to wish this or that! This is our royal will, see you – for the good o' Her Grace and the realm. So be it. Aye. Now – come, Johnnie. Attend me back. I'm needing my bed. There's ower much clatter here. It's a right randy crew! Vicky – get me my stick. Yon ill limmer Robbie Stewart's got it. There's nae respect here. Come . . .'

'May I wait upon you in the morning, Sire?' the Master said. 'With plans. For your urgent attention?'

'Aye, do that, Patrick – do that. A good night to you. Aye – to you all . . .'

As they straightened up from their bows and curtsies, Mary signed to her father to follow her, while Ludovick trailed reluctantly after the King. At a side door she turned.

'This way, Patrick – I have a small room in the bell-tower.'

He climbed the narrow winding turnpike stair after her, up and up, to a tiny high chamber under the old abbey belfry, sparse and bare, and only large enough to hold the bed, a chest, the cradle, and little more. In it the gorgeous Master of Gray looked like a peacock in a henhouse. Arm around the girl's shoulder, he stepped with her over to the plain wooden cradle.

'Ha! A darling! A poppet!' he exclaimed, peering down at the wide-eyed, wakeful but silent child. 'And handsome! On my soul – he's not unlike my own self!'

'In looks, Patrick – only in looks, I pray!'

Soberly he looked up at her, saying nothing.

'How is Marie? Dear Marie?' she asked, then. 'And Andrew? He will have grown . . . ?'

'They are well. Both. And none so far off. In Northumberland. At the house of a friend – Heron, of Ford Castle. Marie is with child again, bless her! And young Andrew is a stout lad. Near eight. But not so like me as this of yours . . .'

'Patrick,' she interrupted him, with a tenseness which was not at all like Mary Gray. 'Pay heed to me. You have gained your way with the King again, it is clear – as I knew that you would. You are to be accepted back to Scotland, at Court, banishment past. Once more. I . . . I cannot be glad of it. I fear for us all.'

'Shadows, my dear – you imagine shadows, and start at them.'

'Aye, shadows, Patrick. Shadows of your casting. You are, as always, good to see, good to look upon. In one way, you warm my heart. But the shadows you cast are not good. They are cold.'

He sighed. 'Are you not a little unfair to me, Mary? I have made mistakes, yes – done certain things which I would wish undone. But I have done much otherwise. I have saved this realm more than once. Spared it from war and bloodshed. Preserved the King. I come to do so again . . .'

'Patrick – for sweet mercy's sake, do not palter and quibble! Not with me. Let you and I, at least, speak each other frank. We are too close to do other, too alike to make pretence. I know how your mind works – because my own works in the same way. But, pray God, to different ends! You . . . you learned that, when last we spoke, Patrick. To your hurt. And to my own. I crossed you then – sore as it hurt. I would do the same again.'

Slowly he spoke. 'Are you threatening me, Mary?'

'I am warning you.' Her hand reached out to grip his arm. 'Patrick – understand me. If I can understand you so clearly – then surely you must be able to understand me? We are of the same mould and stamp, you and I. Heed my warnings, then. For your own sake, and mine. And for Marie's, and Andrew's – aye, and Vicky's, and this child's also. For we have both great power to hurt and harm those we love!'

'Love!' he exclaimed. 'A strange love this, which knowing nothing yet threatens and counters me . . .'

'I know enough, knowing *you*, to feel already that cold shadow which you can cast, Patrick! I feared this, and would have stopped you coming, if I could. Although I longed to see you, God knows! No – hear me. Let me say my say. Now that you are here, I must give you my warning. Do not entangle Vicky in your schemes again. That before all. Do not injure or betray the poor silly King ...'

'God help me, girl – it is to save him that I am come!' the Master cried. 'Aye, and Vicky too. This conspiracy is against *them* ...'

'Aye – that I believe! But, Patrick – from what Vicky has told me of it, the same conspiracy is far too clever, far too deep-laid, far too intricate for my Lords Bothwell and Huntly to have contrived. Or any of their friends. Any man in all this realm ... save Patrick Gray!'

He drew a long breath, looking at her steadily. 'You believe that?'

'I believe that,' she nodded. 'Oh, some of it – much, perhaps – may be based on a true design of these wild and arrogant lords. They are capable of great villainy, great ambitions. But not of the cunning interweaving of artifice, the subtle stratagems, the close-knit scheming perfection of this master-plot! That would demand a mind infinitely more talented – with the evil talents of the Devil himself!'

'On my soul – I do not know whether to be flattered or affronted!'

She ignored that. 'This I see clearly. What I do not know is your object. Your main object, Patrick. Whether it is all just a device to win you back from banishment into a position of power, with the King much dependent upon you? And having gained this, little more will come of it? Or whether there is more than that? That you have worked up this conspiracy in order to betray it, so that there will be great upheavals, great troubles, which you may seek to control for your own ends? I wish that I knew.'

He swallowed. 'This is extraordinary!' he declared, turning to pace the two or three steps which was all that tiny chamber would allow. 'Are you out of your mind, Mary? What sort of creature did I beget on your mother those twenty years ago?'

'One too like yourself for your own comfort, perhaps! Or her own! One who can plot and plan also, if need be. And, as you have learned, betray! So heed me well, Patrick. For I have much more to scheme and fight for. More than formerly.'

'As . . . ?'

'Ludovick. Our son, John. John Stewart of Methven. All that Methven means to me . . .'

'You call that much, Mary? Mistress to Vicky, Duke though he be! To be cast off at will? Damme, child – I could make you better than that! With your looks and wits, and my influence, you could and should go far.'

'I desire no better than Vicky and Methven. His love – and its peace. These I have. I am secure in Vicky's heart. He would marry me – but I know this to be impossible. I know what I want, Patrick. I do not want position at Court. You will not make me one of the Queen's ladies again. For your own ends . . .'

'That is a royal command, girl. You cannot ignore or avoid it. You must obey – you have no choice.'

'I shall obey for a short time. Till the child is born. Then I shall take leave of the Queen. She will let me go. She does not love me greatly. Nor I her. So heed me. Do not seek to entangle Ludovick or myself in your schemes – or you will find me a more certain foe than Chancellor Maitland!'

'And what are you now?'

'Your daughter, Patrick, in bastardy and unacknowledged – who would love dearly to be your friend.'

Chapter Four

So Patrick, Master of Gray, returned to the left hand of the King of Scots – and it was not long before all Scotland was aware of it. The new hand bearing on the helm of the ship of state was not to be mistaken, a firm hand, assured as it was flexible – but flexible as is a Ferrara rapier blade.

The Chancellor, of course, remained the right hand of the Crown, the official agent of authority. That Lord Maitland of Thirlestane did not relish the return of his long-time foe went without saying: but he was too shrewd a man to fail to perceive that for the meantime he had been out-manoeuvred, and that he must bide his time if he would restore the situation. He made no secret of his distrust and dislike of the Master – but he did not deliberately put himself in the other's way or seek to provoke an open clash.

This situation was much facilitated by the immediate removal of the Court to Stirling. The very day after Patrick's arrival the move was made. James had always preferred Stirling to the Capital. He had been brought up there, in the castle of which Johnnie Mar's father had been Keeper; from there he was closer to his beloved Falkland, where this most unmanly of monarchs yet doted on the manly pursuits of the chase – hunting, hawking and coursing. Maitland, however, a Lothian man, had in the past years centred nearly all the agencies and offices of government, that were not there already, in the Capital; he was now more or less tied to Edinburgh – where also the Kirk leadership was ensconsed. All this the Master knew well, and had allowed for.

King, Queen and Court, therefore. travelled the thirty-five miles to Stirling, in the waist of Scotland, leaving the Chancellor and his minions behind. The young Queen, although nearly five years married, was still not nineteen, and looking somehow, with her great belly, even more physically immature than ever, however shrewd of eye and sharp of tongue. She rode, complainingly, in a horse-litter, with her ladies on palfreys all around her, a colourful, chattering, giggling throng. The King, all clumsy and excessive attention – for though he lacked enthusiasm as a husband, he had been anxiously awaiting this heir and proof of his manhood for years – kept close by. The Duke of Lennox also rode with the ladies, to be near Mary Gray, who carried her baby in a wicker pannier behind her. Mar, however, and most of his nobles, kept as far away as possible – with the Master of Gray circulating around all groups of the strung-out cavalcade, throughout the entire protracted journey like an elegant but genially authoritative sheep-dog. He was noticeably more welcome with the ladies than with the men. And he was very urgent that the escort of two hundred men-at-arms of the Royal Guard should maintain a tight circle at all times round the Queen's litter – although it seemed unlikely indeed that any kidnapping attempt could have been organised so quickly after this change of programme, and anyway it was notorious that members of the Royal Guard were usually the first to be suborned in any major conspiracy.

The journey was accomplished without either attack or premature birth, and the great fortress-castle of Stirling, towering above the climbing grey town and shaking its fist at all the frowning bastions of the Highland Line, received them into its security. But even before they reached it, Patrick Gray went to work, having a messenger despatched, in the King's name, to the young Earl of Argyll at his Lowland seat of Castle Campbell at Dollar, a dozen miles away, to summon him forthwith to his monarch's side. In the event, the young man was at Stirling soon after the King, and after being kept waiting for an hour or two was highly astonished to have James inform him in a fractious and preoccupied fashion – for he was distracted by the loss of a couple of sheets of his poem which must have been left behind at Holyroodhouse – that he was herewith appointed Lieutenant of the North, in the place of the Earl of Huntly, and was to be given a commission of fire and sword against that nobleman and his treasonable Catholic associates. More than this the bewildered youth could not get out of the King – whereupon Patrick took him in hand, explained the position privately and approximately, informed him that Maitland was plotting his downfall and the seizure of his lands, but that he, Gray, was his friend and had engineered this situation in order to bring to justice the murderers of the Earl of Moray, Argyll's cousin and guardian. This was the opportunity for which Clan Campbell had been waiting. MacCailean Mhor, to give him his proud Gaelic patronymic, set off for his West Highland fast-nesses there and then, eyes glowing, to raise the clan, on the Master's assurances that he would inform his Campbell uncles, his present guardians, of what was toward.

Next day Patrick himself set off south-westwards, for Ayr-shire, to inveigle, if he could, the Kennedys and their allies the Montgomeries and the Cunninghams, into the prompt armed service of the King. He promised that he would be back in three days at the latest.

Curiously enough, however, riding alone, once he was well clear of the Stirling vicinity, he turned his horse's head south-eastwards rather than south-westwards, towards the Border hills.

That same afternoon, whether as a result of the journey from Edinburgh or merely because of the fullness of time, Queen Anne's pains began. A strange young woman, she had had a number of false pregnancies, over which she had made the maximum fuss, setting her household by the ears; throughout the long period of this true pregnancy she had been difficult and demanding; but now, with the actual birth-throes upon her, she discarded all this, became calm and quietly assured, dismissed all her feather-headed and chattering ladies except the diffident young Lady Beatrix Ruthven who was her close friend and confidante, and Mary Gray whom she apparently trusted in an extremity, and sent for the midwife. To Mary she awarded the unenviable task of keeping her unsuitably interested and vocally anxious husband out of her chamber as much as possible.

Mary, therefore, spent much of the rest of the day and evening in an ante-room of the Queen's bedroom, discussing and indeed concocting poetry with King James, conceiving this to be the surest way of distracting his attention from what was going on next door. New stanzas were added to the natal epic – some of which pleased the royal composer so greatly that nothing would do but that they should be taken through forthwith and read to the labouring Queen, despite her evident lack of appreciation. James was also much interested in Mary's feeding of her own baby, which took place at intervals.

Inspiration in verse was still not quite exhausted when, at last, a child was born late that evening on the 17th of February 1594 – a son, somewhat weakly and small, but with none of the dire disabilities or deformities which the King, in moments of stress, had confessed to Mary as dreading, convinced as he was of the personal vendetta of Satan against himself, as Christ's Vicar and Vice-regent here upon earth.

James's relief and delight knew no bounds. Quite ignoring his exhausted wife, even before the child was properly wrapped and bound, he insisted on taking and parading the new-born Prince Henry throughout the castle, showing him to all whom he could find to look, courtiers, men-at-arms and servants alike, to the wailing not only of the infant but of the midwife and wet-nurse also. Mary, with Ludovick, accompanied the monarch on this tour, and indeed after some time she managed to prevail upon the exultant father to let her comfort the limp infant at her own breast. It demanded considerable dissuasion to prevent James from carrying out his heir to inspect the great bonfire which he had given immediate orders should be lit on the top-most tower of the castle, as signal to all the realm that a Prince of Scotland was born. If, throughout this perambulation, Ludovick was told once by his gleeful royal cousin that his eye was now put out, that he was fallen from high estate and no longer heir to the throne, he was told a dozen times. That the younger man was far from downcast, indeed even relieved, strangely enough did not commend itself to the other, either.

No one about the Court achieved bed until the early hours of the morning.

Next day brought to light a rift within the lute. James had had a nightmare. He had dreamed that the new prince had indeed been seized and spirited away from him, his mother playing a leading part in the abduction and going off with the kidnappers. Nothing would do now but that the precious infant should be delivered forthwith into the sure care of the Earl of Mar, to be kept in the most secure inner fastness of the fortress, with his wet-nurse. Queen Anne's indignation and protest at this decision was fierce but unavailing. She had already reverted from her excellent birth behaviour to the tantrums of the pregnancy period, and had taken a violent dislike to the wet-nurse, loudly declaring that the woman was a coarse and low-bred slut and that she should not be allowed to suckle the heir of a hundred kings. Mary Gray was to suckle the prince, she asserted, and although that young woman protested that she had her own child to feed and had not enough milk for both, the Queen was adamant. When confronted with James's fiat that the infant was to be put into Mar's keeping there and then, there was a major and unedifying scene, which ended with the King insisting on his decision, but agreeing that meantime Mary should act as foster-mother, despite the latter's objections.

So willy-nilly, Mary found herself in the situation, absurd as it was unwanted, of ostensible foster-mother to the new prince, temporary link between the indignant Queen and her offspring, and repository of the sovereign's confidences. A new wet-nurse was found for the infant, of course – for despite the royal desires, even commands, she would by no means agree to taking over the nursing of the prince herself and handing over her own son to another's feeding. James and Anne were more openly estranged than ever they had been, the Queen pouring out her troubles in the reluctant ear of the Duke of Lennox especially – whilst the nation, by royal decree, made holiday in public rejoicing, ringing church-bells, lighting beacons and composing loyal addresses.

This was the state of affairs to which Patrick Gray returned after two days – undoubtedly to his entire satisfaction. Whilst sympathising with everyone's problems, he had an air about him as though matters could hardly have been bettered had he arranged them himself.

All was well with the Kennedy project, he reported. While the young Earl of Cassillis was under age, and his uncle and Tutor, Kennedy of Culzean was unpopular, the leadership of that war-like clan had been assumed by the Laird of Bargany, head of the next most senior branch, a forceful and ambitious man who had readily responded to the Master's approaches on the royal behalf, on promise of pickings from the estates of the Catholic Lords Maxwell and Sanquhar. Moreover Bargany's sister was Countess of Eglinton, mother of the boy Earl, chief of the Montgomeries. This latter family was linked with the Campbells of Loudoun, the south-western branch of the great Clan Campbell. These also the Master had called upon. One thousand men of Ayrshire would be ready to march within the week, two thousand in a fortnight, and more if required. With Argyll's Campbells and the Border moss-troopers of the King's firm friends the Homes, a force was being born sufficient to meet the Catholic threat.

This news was well received – but the difficulty now was for anyone to maintain a belief that any such threat really existed. As the days passed and no action developed, no signs of subversion appeared, men began to doubt. The Chancellor had always pooh-poohed it all; now he sent messages to James declaring that it was all a fantasy, an alarum perpetrated by the wicked Master of Gray for his own ends. Indeed he strongly advised the King to forbid this unwarranted and dangerous assembling of armed men forthwith, as a menace to the security of the realm. Who could tell what ill uses they might be put to – especially the cateran and barbarous Campbells? It was always easier to raise the Devil than to lay him again.

Patrick smiled, unruffled, at all this. Was his information apt to be mistaken, he demanded? It would be ignored at peril. Let His Grace call a parliament, he advised, at which the Catholic lords should be summoned to appear for trial of treason, of conspiring against the realm with the King of Spain, and with plotting against the King's life. Since Bothwell was still ostensibly a Protestant, let him be summoned on a different charge – that of receiving English support against his liege lord, of accepting English money and arms to equip his forces illegally assembled. That, which was truth, Patrick assured, as he knew on best authority, should serve the case. The alleged conspirators, if they were indeed innocent, would come to the parliament to proclaim their innocence. If they stayed away, they as good as admitted their guilt – and anyway could be proceeded against as disobeying the King's summons. Even Maitland, who was a great parliament man, and the Kirk leaders whose policy was to strengthen their temporal power through parliament, could not disagree with this advice. It would take at least a month to organise and stage a meeting of parliament, because of the distances to be travelled and the arrangements to be made. Patrick privately assured the King that things would, in fact, come to a head before the parliament could meet, and urged that the forces which he had been conjuring up for the royal protection should be maintained in immediate readiness to move.

Maitland was commanded to proclaim an assembly of the Estates of Scotland in parliament, and send out the summonses in the King's name.

Chapter Five

It was, it is to be feared, a long time since Patrick Gray had
attended divine worship as authoritatively laid down by God's
true and Reformed Kirk – more especially in that temple and
citadel of the faithful, St. Giles' High Kirk of Edinburgh. Yet
not only had he gone to considerable trouble to attend there
that showery April morning, but it was solely because of his
efforts that the great church was crowded with so many other
worshippers, to hear Master Andrew Melville expound the
word of God, that hardly another could have been squeezed
inside – in that he had persuaded King James to come all the
way from Stirling for the occasion. He now sat, uncomfortably,
on a bare, hard and backless bench, to the left of the King's stall,
with Lennox on the right, and considered himself fortunate to
have a seat at all, for most of the attendant courtiers had to
stand, the Kirk being no respecter of persons. In a three-hour
service this could be an excellent test of faith. Every now and
again throughout the vehement and comprehensive praying of
Master Patrick Galloway, he raised the head which he should
have kept suitably downbent, and looked quizzically at the
soberly-clad, dark-advised and stern-featured man who sat so
rigidly upright in his accustomed place below the pulpit – John
Maitland, Lord Thirlestane, Chancellor of the realm. Only
once those steely eyes rose to meet his – and there was nothing
quizzical or remotely amused in their brief but baleful glare.

King James fidgeted. He always fidgeted, of course, but this
morning he excelled himself, for he was more nervous even than
usual. Matters had reached a thoroughly alarming stage, and he
doubted very much whether he ought to have allowed that
difficult and demanding limmer Patrick Gray, who was too
clever by half, to bring him here at all. Likely he should never
have left Stirling, where he was safe.

James, in his fumbling, dropped his high hat on the floor for
the third time, and the clatter of the heavy jewelled brooch that

held the orange-yellow ostrich-feather in place drew a quick frown from Master Galloway in his wordy assault on the Almighty. Picking the hat up, James scowled. He had a good mind to clap it on his head, kirk or none. Only in church, out of practically every other waking occasion, did he uncover. He even kept his hat on in his own bedchamber quite frequently, and had been seen by Mary Gray wandering into the Queen's boudoir, more than once, dressed in a bed-robe and nothing else but a high-plumed bonnet. All men must uncover in the King's presence; but here, in the kirk, the proud black-gowned divines behaved as though he, the King, was uncovering for *them?* James sighed gustily, and shuffled his feet. He nudged Lennox with his elbow.

'Is he no' near done yet, Vicky?' he whispered loudly. 'Man, I'm fair deeved wi' him!'

Master Galloway raised his harshly sonorous voice a shade higher, louder, praying for all sorts and conditions of men, especially those in high places who so grievously failed to recognise their responsibilities to God and man, who lived for their own pleasures, bowed down to idols, tolerated the ungodly wickedness of Popery, and hindered Christ's Kirk in the true ordering of His ways upon earth. He came to a thundering finish which certainly ought to have reached and affected the Deity.

With a sigh like a sudden stirring in the tree-tops, in profound relief the congregation straightened bent shoulders, relaxed stiff muscles, and eased their positions generally. Some of the women sat on stools which they had brought with them, but most of the great company stood upright on the flagstones, and now moved and stirred in their need.

The King looked along at the Master of Gray. 'Now?' he demanded. 'Will I do it now, Patrick?'

'No, no, Sire. Not yet. It must be *after* the sermon, to have fullest effect. The folk must go out with *your* words in their minds – not Melville's.'

'Ooh, aye.' That was acknowledged with a distinct sigh.

Patrick himself would have much preferred to get it over and to be able to escape the sermon – but that would not serve their purpose.

Andrew Melville came stalking to replace Master Galloway in the pulpit, black gown flying, white Geneva bands lost beneath his beard. Here was a man to be reckoned with - and none knew it more surely than Patrick Gray. Now in his fiftieth year, tall and broad, with a leonine head of grey hair and beard as vigorous as the rest of him, he had the burning eyes of a fanatic but also the wide sweeping brows of a thinker. Melville was indeed the successor and disciple of John Knox, but a man of still greater stature, mentally as physically. Like Knox he was an utterly fearless fighter for what he esteemed to be God's cause, but possessed of a bounding intellect and not preoccupied with the problem of women as to some extent was his predecessor. He had been regent of a French college at twenty-one and professor of humanity at Geneva a year or two later. At home, appointed Principal of Glasgow University at twenty-nine, five years afterwards he was Principal of St. Andrews. Now he was Rector there, Moderator of the General Assembly, author of the *Second Book of Discipline* and all but dictator of the Kirk of Scotland. He it was the hater of bishops, and not Knox, who had managed to establish the Presbyterian form of church government upon Scotland.

Patrick Gray had no doubts that he and Andrew Melville could never be friends; but certainly he was more than anxious not to have the strongest man in Scotland as his foe. Hence this visit to St. Giles.

After gazing round upon the huge congregation in complete silence for an unconscionably long time, to the King's alarm, Melville started by startling all and quoting as his text; 'But the thing displeased Samuel when they said, Give us a king to judge us. And Samuel prayed unto the Lord.' He could not have known that James was to be present, for no word had been sent from Stirling. Whether therefore he totally altered the subject of his discourse for the occasion was not to be known, although it seemed that way; certainly what he had to say was very much to the point, suitably or otherwise. He preached on the position of temporal princes in God's world.

From unexceptional beginnings, mainly historical, he traced the sins and follies and limitations of the kings of the earth from earliest recorded times, to the Israelites' demand for a monarch, on through the degenerations of the Roman emperors and the barbarities of the Dark Ages, to the glittering vanities of the Renaissance and on to the religious interference of the princes of the present-day – with many a shrewd swipe at the bastard and Anti-christian kingship of the Popes of Rome in the by-going. It took him a long time, but even so he held the great concourse enthralled, by the flow of his knowledge, his eloquence, his unerring sense of drama, his sheer story-telling. Even James was absorbed enough in the brilliantly selected sequence and exposition to apparently swallow for the moment the consistent implication of tyranny, malpractice and disobedience to God's ordinances of his own order of kings throughout the ages. He had dropped his hat again early on, but thereafter let it lie.

And then, after a full hour of it, Melville abruptly changed his entire tone, manner, and presentation. Throwing up his hand to toss back the wide sleeve of his gown, he suddenly pointed his finger directly at the King – who shrank back in his stall, eyes rolling, as though he had been struck. There sat the King of Scots, he cried, his voice rasping, quivering with power, to whom belonged the temporal rule of his vassals, under God. But woe to him who misused that rule. For King James himself was only God's silly vassal. There were two kings and two kingdoms in Scotland. There was Christ Jesus and His kingdom the Kirk, whose subject King James was, and of whose kingdom not a king, nor a lord, but a member. And they whom Christ had called and commanded to watch over His Kirk, and given his spiritual kingdom, had sufficient power from Him and sufficient authority to do so, which power and authority no Christian king nor prince could or should control.

James, under this abrupt and unexpected attack, gobbled and gasped, half-rising in his seat, and holding up a trembling hand before him, as though he would hide the preacher from his sight. All around him his courtiers stared, frowned, and murmured. Somewhere a woman giggled hysterically, although the mass of the congregation stood as though electrified, their eyes riveted on the speaker. The Master of Gray sat forward on his bench, admiration, assessment and concern struggling within him. To an anxiety about the time – for he had relied on the fact that of late years Melville's preaching had tended to become comparatively brief, in contrast to that of most of his colleagues – was added anxiety about the effect of it all on the King, and the direction which the man might take from here.

Master Melville seemed to be incensed by James's feeble rising in his seat. Both hands raised now, he declared in a terrible voice that he spoke from the most mighty God. Where the ministry of the Kirk was once lawfully constituted and those that were placed in it did their office faithfully, he cried, all godly princes and magistrates ought to hear and obey their voice, and reverence the majesty of the Son of God speaking in them. But did King James so do? Did he not rather accept and solicit devilish and pernicious counsel, desiring instead to be served with all sorts of men, Jew and Gentile, Papist and Protestant? Melville glared now, not so much upon the open-mouthed monarch but upon the angry, embarrassed or perturbed men around him – and, it seemed, most especially upon the Master of Gray.

Patrick looked back at him, and gravely nodded. But he was more tense than he looked. Much depended upon the next words – and on James not becoming so flustered and upset that he forgot his part.

Leaning forward, Melville altered his demeanour and attitude once more. Now, while still authoritative, dominant, he was understanding, forgiving, even confidential. The King was young. Those who advised him were the greater sinners. He paused, for moments on end. Urgency charged that eloquent voice. The inevitable consequence of the King heeding such corrupt counsel was upon him, upon the realm upon them all. This day, this very hour, the hosts of Midian were on the march. The Papists, the legions of the Whore of Rome, were in descent upon the faithful. He had sure word that those sinful and violent lords, Huntly, Erroll and Angus were even now on the march south from their ungodly domains, with a great army. Nearer still, just north of the Forth, was the young Earl of Argyll, hot-headed and misguided son of a pious father, with a heathenish Highland host. Worst of all, that apostate son of the Kirk, the Earl of Bothwell, was reliably reported to have ignobly forsworn himself and turned Papist, and was marching north from the Border, with English aid, to the scathe of the realm and the Kingdom of Christ. The Devil himself was this day abroad in Scotland.

As alarm, almost panic, swept the congregation, the great voice quelled and overbore the rising disturbance, as the preacher lifted clenched fists high above his head.

'Now is the time to draw the sword of the Lord and of Gideon!' he thundered. 'Time for the Kirk and all the men to arise and put their armour on. Let them gird their brows with truth, and don the breastplate of righteousness! Let them take the shield of faith and wear the helmet of salvation! Let them draw the sword of the Spirit! In the name of God the Father, God the Son and God the Holy Ghost!'

Something like a sobbing wind arose throughout the great church as he finished, a wind that set the tight-packed ranks of worshippers swaying like a cornfield. Voices rose, men shouted, women screamed. A form of bedlam broke loose – while the man who had provoked it gazed around and down at it all, stern, alert but confident, assured that he was wholly in command of the situation even yet.

Strangely enough of all that excited throng, Patrick Gray was probably the only other man as calm as the preacher. Whilst others stormed and exclaimed, he sat back now, relaxing. All was well. It was better, much better even than he had hoped. His planning and manipulation had succeeded. One day he would preach his own sermon on the snare of the fowler!

King James was on his feet in much agitation, his hat clapped back on his head. He was wringing his hands. 'What now? What now, Patrick?' he demanded. 'Och, man – all's awry! They'll no' heed me now. He's ca'd the ground frae under me...'

'Not so, Your Grace,' the Master assured. 'Far from it. Rather has he prepared the ground for you. Now is your opportunity. Do as we agreed. Proceed, Sire, as arranged. All will be well.'

'But... but, they'll never hear me in this stramash! It's ower late...'

'They will hear and heed you,' Patrick turned, to catch the eye of one of the trumpeters who accompanied the King on all public occasions, and signed to him. 'I pray Your Grace to remember well the words we decided upon,' he advised, but easily. 'And to recollect your royal dignity.'

The high blaring summons of the trumpet neighed and echoed, piercing the hubbub like a knife, even as Melville raised his own hands to regain control. The sudden surprise on the man's face was noteworthy. Everywhere folk were galvanised by the authoritative sound. Men stilled, voices fell. By the time that the last flourish had died away there was approximate silence in St. Giles once more. Into it the Master of Gray's voice, so musical, so pleasantly modulated, after the vibrant harsh intonations of the preachers, spoke calmly, almost conversationally, but clearly enough for all to hear.

'Pray silence for His Grace. King James speaks.'

'Aye,' James quavered. 'That I do. That *we* do,' he amended, to use the royal plural. 'We would speak to you. We are much concerned. It's a bad business – bad! We are sair grieved. He's right, the man – Master Melville's right. In this. No' about my lord of Argyll, mind. But the others. There's revolt and rebellion afoot. It's yon Bothwell's doing. He's an ill man – I aye said he was an ill man. I had him locked in my castle o' Edinburgh here, yon time. He was let out, some way . . . I was right displeased . . .'

Patrick coughed discreetly, and glancing along at him, the King swallowed, and wagged his great head.

'I'ph'mm. Well – Bothwell's joined forces wi' the Catholics, foul fall him! He's been colloguing wi' the English ower the Border, this while back. We've kenned that. Now, yesterday, he crossed back into our realm o' Scotland in insolent and audacious rebellion. Wi' many Englishry. And a host o' his own scoundrelly folk frae Eskdale, Liddesdale and the like. To attack his lawful prince. That's . . . that's treason maist foul!'

A murmur swept the congregation. All eyes were fixed on the awkward, overdressed figure of the Lord's Anointed.

'We have instructed my Lord Home and the Laird o' Buccleuch to hold him. Meantime. At Kelso. To gie us time. The Earl o' Cassillis marches frae the west wi' his Kennedys, to intercept. But it's a gey long trauchle, frae Ayr and yon parts. He'll likely no' be in time, at Kelso. The Homes and the Scotts will no' hold Bothwell that long, I doubt. So . . . so, my friends, I jalouse we're like to hae the wicked rebels chapping at the gates o' Edinburgh-toun in two-three days' time! Aye . . .'

James flapped his hands to quieten the surge of alarm which gripped the concourse. His voice squeaked as he raised it to counter the noise.

'You'll no' want that limb o' Satan and his wild moss-troopers rampaging through your bonny streets! Like Master Melville says, it's time for a' true and leal men to arise. Aye – that's the Kirk, and the toun, the train-bands and the guilds. A' sound men. And mind, no' just to guard the toun's walls. Na, na – to issue forth. A great host, to contest Bothwell's wicked passage. Wi' my Royal Guard to lead it. And cannons frae the castle. The sword o' the Lord and Gideon, right enough!'

Quite carried away by this unaccustomed belligerence, James had difficulty with the tongue which, always too big for his mouth, tended to get grievously in the way in moments of excitement. Master Galloway and one or two other divines had moved over to Chancellor Maitland's stall below the pulpit, and were holding a hurried whispered consultation, Melville bending down from above to take part.

Patrick touched the King's arm. 'Excellent, Sire,' he encouraged. 'A little more Protestant zeal, perhaps! Assail the Catholics. A, h'm, holy crusade! And explain Argyll.'

James raised his voice again, but could be no means make himself heard against the hubbub he had aroused. Patrick had to signal the trumpeter to sound another brief blast, before the royal orator could resume.

'Wheesht, now – wheesht!' he commanded. 'I'm no' finished. I canna hear mysel' speak. Aye, well – that's Bothwell. But there's the others – the main Catholic host. Coming frae the North. Geordie Gordon o' Huntly, Douglas o' Angus, and the rest. They're further off, mind – still but in Strathmore, I hear. No' at Perth yet. But there's mair o' them – a great multitude. Aye, a multitude o' wicked men. Descending upon us, the . . . the Lord's ain folk!' James stumbled over that; he was not entirely convinced that the Kirk held open the only clear road to salvation, nor yet that the Lord personally sponsored men, or groups of men, subjects, others than His own anointed Vice-Regent the King. 'They tell me there's eight or ten thousands o' them. Wae-sucks – we'll no' need to let them join wi' Bothwell! That's

73

the main thing. That's what Argyll's at, see you. He's brought his Campbells frae the Highlands. They're moving into Fife, the now. Like Master Melville said. That's to keep Huntly frae crossing Forth. They're on my side, *our* side, mind – they're to stop Huntly. If they can. So . . . so . . .' His thick voice tailed away uncertainly.

'The crusade, Sire,' the Master prompted, in an urgent whisper. 'Your royal oath!'

'Ooh, aye. Here's work . . . here's work, I say, to do. The Lord's work. It's a crusade, see you – a crusade against violent and wicked men, Satan's henchmen. To that crusade I, James Stewart your liege lord, call you. I . . . I will lead you, and all true men, in person. Aye, in person. Against the troublers o' the realm's peace. Rally you, then – Kirk, tounsfolk, gentle and simple all. I say – rally to me, and I . . . I . . .' The King, swallowing, in an access of enthusiasm, raised his hand on high. 'I swear to God Almighty, on my royal oath, if you'll a' arm and march wi' me to the field, I'll no' rest until I have utterly suppressed and banished these limmers, these ill men, these rebellious Catholic lords and traitors, frae my dominions. On my oath – so help me God!'

Patrick Gray was on his feet almost before the King finished. 'God save the King!' he cried. 'God save the King!'

All around, the cry was taken up in a roar of acclaim. Everywhere men stood and shouted. Even Ludovick, who had been a somewhat cynical spectator of the entire performance, rather than any participant, found himself on his feet, applauding. The ministers, though clearly concerned by the way in which the initiative had been taken from them, could not but approve of this public royal commitment to their cause, whatever the underlying meaning. Only one man in all that church seemed to remain unmoved, stiffly unaffected by the dramatic proceedings – Chancellor Maitland. He sat still in his stall, frowning, while the din maintained. Patrick Gray caught his steely eye for a moment, before noting Melville's preliminary attempts from the pulpit to restore order, he turned to make for the great main doorway. He waved to those around the King to do likewise, and nothing loth they began to move in the same direction. James was not going to be left behind, and seeing the King going, most of the congregation felt impelled to leave also. Everywhere a surge towards the various doorways commenced.

Andrew Melville, a man practical as he was eloquent and able, raised a hand and pronounced a hasty benediction.

Outside, in the jostling, milling throng in the High Street, Patrick found his sleeve being tugged. A rough-looking, sallow-faced man in dented half-armour, had pushed his way close – Home of Linthill, one of Logan of Restalrig's cronies.

'Fiend seize me – I've been trying to get to you this past hour!' he jerked. 'Restalrig sent me with word. From Fast. Bothwell has jouked my lord and Buccleuch at Kelso. Coming down Teviotdale from the West, he cut ower by Bowden Muir and Melrose, and up Lauderdale. He camped on the south side o' Soutra last night.'

'Damnation!' Patrick exclaimed. 'By now, then, he'll be in Lothian! Within a few miles . . . !'

'Nearer than that! I came in from Fast by way of Haddington, Musselburgh and Duddingston. I saw the tails o' his rearguards.'

'His *rear*guards, man . . . ?'

'Aye. He was making for the sea, folk said. For the Forth. At Leith.'

'Slay me – Leith!' The Master clenched his fists. 'The fox! It's Huntly. He's driving through, to link with Huntly. With all haste. 'Fore God – he's much cleverer than I thought! Or somebody is! But . . . at this speed he cannot have his entire host? You cannot move an army at such pace.'

'No. He left his main force in the Borders, to front my lord and Buccleugh. He has but the pick o' his horse. Moss-troopers frae the West March dales – Armstrongs, Elliots, Maxwells. Cut-throats and cattle-thieves. Six hundred o' them. But bonny fighters.'

'Aye. So that's it! Here's a pickle, then. Six hundred of the keenest blades in the land to face – and only the Royal Guard and a pack of townies to do it. But we've got to keep him from joining Huntly. Either crossing Forth himself, or holding Leith, for Huntly to cross.' He frowned as a new thought struck him. 'But . . . why Leith? If he's for holding Leith it could be that Huntly's sending part of his force by sea. It could be, by

God! He has all the fisher-craft of Aberdeen and Angus to use. Sink me - could it be that? We shall have to have Bothwell out of Leith...!'

'What's this? What's this?' King James was plucking at his other sleeve. 'Here's the Provost, man. I'm telling him he's to assemble the toun. Forthwith. We...we march the morn. That's what you said, Patrick...?'

'That is what I said, Sire,' the Master nodded grimly. 'But I was wrong. We march sooner than that, I fear. Much sooner.'

'Eh...? Hech – what's this, man? What's this?'

'I have just had word, Sire, that Bothwell is at Leith. He has eluded Home and Buccleuch, in the Borders. Ridden hard, with six hundred men, over Soutra, and is even now at the port of Leith.'

'Leith! Waesucks – *Leith*, d'you say?' James wailed. 'Bothwell at Leith! Guid sakes – it's but two miles to Leith, man! It's no' possible. I'll no' credit it! No' Leith...'

'I fear it is true, Sire. We shall have to act accordingly. And swiftly...'

'Stirling!' James ejaculated, thickly. 'I must get back to Stirling. Aye, to Stirling. I should never ha' left Stirling. This is your doing, Master o' Gray. You shouldna ha' brought me here. I told you it was dangerous. It was ill done, I say...'

'It was necessary, Sire. Necessary that you won the Kirk and the town of Edinburgh to your side. There was no other way. Just as it is necessary now that you stay here. That you do not flee back to Stirling...'

'Wi' yon Bothwell but two miles off! And him ettling to murder me!'

'He is not attacking the city, Your Grace. Not yet. It is Leith that he has made for. It must be to take the port. To hold it. Perhaps Huntly is sending a force by sea. We must not let him land at Leith. Bothwell must be driven out. He has but six hundred men, I hear. A few minutes past you swore your royal oath before all in the church that you would lead them, and all true men. In person, against these rebels...'

'Aye – but that was different, man. Different. That wasn't to-day. That was for the morn. To march for the Border. To join Home and Buccleuch and other lords. Wi' their host. Och, I'd march wi' them, mind. Some way. Ooh, aye. But . . . no' this! No' a battle wi' Bothwell today. At Leith. On the Sabbath . . .'

'Someone must needs do battle with Bothwell today, Sabbath or none, Highness – or your cause is lost!'

'Aye – but no' me mysel', Patrick! It's no' safe. No' seemly . . .'

'His Grace is probably right,' the Duke of Lennox intervened, from behind the King. 'He ought not to be hazarded in this. He would be safer back at Stirling. If someone is required to lead a force against Bothwell, I will do it. In the King's name . . .'

'Don't be a fool, Vicky!' Patrick snapped – a very different man this from the languid and ever-amused courtier. 'Can you not see? Only the King's presence can muster a force out of these townsmen. There are but two hundred of the Royal Guard – and half of them are left guarding Stirling Castle! Kennedy of Bargany has three hundred riders outside the city, at Craigmillar – but that is all. Save for what the Kirk and the town can give us. Cassillis and the main body of the Kennedys are somewhere crossing the Border hills from Ayr. Argyll's Campbells are at Loch Leven, entering Fife. Both too far off to be of any use to us in this pass. Only the presence of the King himself will produce a host to attack Bothwell. And attacked he must be.'

'God save us a' . . .' James cried.

'What's to do, Your Grace? What's amiss?' a new voice interposed, sternly, strongly, as the powerful and authoritative figure of Andrew Melville reached group around the King, after cleaving his way through the press. 'What's this talk of Bothwell that I hear?'

'Wae's me – he's at Leith, man! Leith, d'you hear!'

Other voices broke out in amplification.

Patrick Gray, looking at the confident, dedicated and commanding man before him, made a swift decision. A gambler by nature, he assessed all in a moment, and staked the entire issue on a single throw. 'Sir,' he said, touching the other's black sleeve. 'We must act. Without delay. Or the Kirk's cause is lost equally with the King's!'

'I had not known, Master of Gray, that you were concerned for the Kirk's cause! Indeed I esteemed you Papist!'

'I have been esteemed many things, sir – even by those who should have known better! But that we can discuss on another occasion. I am concerned for the Kirk's cause because it is identical with the King's cause today, the realm's cause. To all of which you are committed, Master Melville, as much as am I.'

The other eyed him steadily for a little, ignoring the royal gabblings and the other voices upraised around them. 'Well, sir?,' he said at length. 'What would you?'

In terse clear fashion the Master briefly outlined the position, paying Melville a compliment by neither elaborating or explaining. The divine heard him out in silence.

'You desire, then,' he said slowly, 'that the Kirk joins forces with you and such as you, in violence and strife?'

'I do. The Lord whom you preach used violence and strife to cleanse the temple, did he not? And joined forces with publicans and sinners against those who threatened *His* cause. You said back there, sir, that now was the time to draw the sword of the Lord – for all true men to arise. I believe that you meant that, and did not but mouth empty words. As do some. I do not believe that you are a man of words only, not deeds. Or that the Kirk will stand by and watch Bothwell, for his own ends, seek to turn this realm Papist again.'

'In that you may be right. But the Kirk's action, and mine, may not be as your action, sir.'

'Only one sort of action will prevail to drive Bothwell out of Leith this day!' Patrick returned strongly. 'Drawn swords in the hands of resolute men. Or do you believe that words, mere words, will turn him?'

Melville inclined his lion-like head. 'No, I do not. So be it. This once. What is required?'

'Every able man and youth who can handle a sword or a pike, to assemble in the King's park of Holyroodhouse, forthwith. Or as swiftly as may be. Two hours – no more. We cannot spare more. In the name of the Kirk. And the King. Bellmen and criers through the streets, with your ministers. To tell the folk. The kirk bells to ring. Royal trumpeters. To get the folk out. You, Sir Provost – the Watch. Have it out. The Town Guard. The train-bands. The guilds. Have the bailies and magistrates out, to lead the townsfolk. In the King's name. Armed to

the fight. Before Holyroodhouse. You have it? In two hours —
no more.'

The little stout Provost of Edinburgh began to stammer his
doubts, but Melville cut him short. 'How many men are required?'

'Every man that we can muster. Bothwell has only six hundred, I am told – but they are seasoned moss-troopers, cattle-
thieves who live by the sword.'

'Very well. And you, sir?'

'I go to the castle. His Grace agreeing. There is the garrison.
And cannon. The Royal Guard is at the palace – such as is not
here. Vicky – my lord Duke – ride you to Craigmillar, where
Bargany and his Kennedys lie. They had to be kept out of the
town. Bring them to Holyroodhouse. Provost – riders out
hot-foot to all nearby lairds, Protestant lairds. In the name of
King and Kirk.'

Melville nodded. 'The Kirk will be there,' he said levelly.
'What of the King?'

'His Grace has sworn his royal oath before all men,' Patrick
said, with entire confidence. 'To lead in person. It is unthinkable that any should doubt the King's word.'

All looked at the unhappy James. Not meeting any glance, he
stared down at the cobblestones of the High Street, fiddling
with the buttons of his doublet. 'M'mmm. Eh, eh. I'ph'mm,'
he mumbled. 'Ooh, ay. Och, well...'

'Exactly, Sire. No other course is consistent with your royal
honour. I shall not leave your side...'

Melville smiled thinly. 'Just so, Your Grace. Thou hast said!
Master of Gray – I will await the King at Holyroodhouse. In
two hours.'

Patrick inclined his head – but his eyes held those of the other.
Here was a man with whom he could work; or do battle.

Chapter Six

'A great host, Sire,' the Master of Gray said, striving to sound enthusiastic. He had been seeking to edge the King further away from the solid phalanx of Bargany's contingent of three hundred tough Kennedy horsemen, who insisted on making loud and ribald comments on the appearance and fighting qualities of the rest of the assembly spread over the green meadows at the foot of towering Arthur's Seat. 'They have mustered well. Many men.'

'Iph'mm,' James acceded doubtfully. 'Many men, aye. But . . . will they fight? Eh? *Can* they fight, man? Against Bothwell's limmers!'

'It is for that they have assembled. To fight they must intend, at least! And . . . I sense much holy zeal!'

'D'you no' reckon the zeal's more for the Kirk than for me, Patrick? I dinna like the looks o' some o' them.'

'Let us hope that Bothwell will think the same, Sire! What matters it who the zeal is for, so long as they fight Your Grace's battle?'

Andrew Melville and his clerical colleagues had certainly proved persuasive recruiters. A vast, if far from disciplined mob milled and seethed between the grey palace and the abrupt slopes of the hill, armed with almost as much variety as was the range of age and appearance – with pikes, swords, daggers, billhooks, sickles, axes, staves and knives bound to poles. Half the city appeared to be present – though which were volunteers and which mere spectators was difficult to ascertain. There was much brandishing of these weapons and much shouting, it being doubtful how much of it was Godly exhortation and acclaim and how much native quarrelsomeness, high spirits and horseplay. There was, and could be, no real order of formation maintained – although the many black-gowned ministers who pushed everywhere amongst the crowd, seemed to be trying to impose their own ideas of military, or at least militant, comportment.

Women and children permeated the assembly, and looked as though they were by no means going to be left behind when the time came to march.

The Duke of Lennox had been urging for some time that such order should be given forthwith. A certain amount of internecine strife had already broken out between the warlike townsmen and their traditional oppressors, the Town-Guard, and Ludovick had been seeking to aid the Provost and magistrates to restrict this within modest limits; the apprentices, who were out in force, clearly had other ideas, and, grievously outnumbered, the Town Guard had now formed a tight square around the civic dignitaries, and the Duke had been sent to beseech the King either to send his own Royal Guard and the Kennedys to their aid, or to order an immediate march on Leith as distraction.

Patrick Gray had demurred. Let the Town Guard solve its own problems, he argued; the last thing that they wanted was for the King's Guard to make itself unpopular with the populace. Moreover, they must await the arrival of the cannon from the castle, which should make for a great access of enthusiasm and aggressive spirit. Also, so far, very few parties of retainers and men-at-arms had appeared from lords and lairds near the city and they, being horsed, were badly required.

Andrew Melville came striding up to the royal party, beard, white Geneva bands and black gown all streaming in the breeze. 'We must up and move, Your Grace,' he declared strongly. 'The good folk get restive. Let us wait no longer.'

'Aye. But . . . the cannon . . . ?' James, nibbling his nails, looked at the Master.

'A little longer, Master Melville,' Patrick said. 'We would be foolish not to await the cannon. The sight of them, I swear, will greatly encourage these people of yours. Also, the garrison from the castle who brings them are to bring with them all the armoury of pikes and halberds. Hundreds of them. These we much need. They should have been here by this but the oxen that draw the cannon are slow . . .'

There was a diversion, as the thunder of hooves drew all eyes eastwards. Round the foot of the hill, from the higher ground at that side, came at the gallop a gallant cavalcade, about one hundred strong, banners flying, steel glinting, armour clanking. The great leading banner showed the famed Red Heart of Douglas.

At sight of that dread emblem there was next to panic amongst much of the crowd, for the Douglas reputation was as savage as it was ancient and the Earl of Angus, one of the chief rebels, was head of the clan. But the knowledgeable sighed with relief, recognising the ensign of the Earl of Morton, from Dalkeith five miles away, of the Protestant branch of the house.

Morton himself, elderly, portly and purple, clad in magnificent and old-fashioned gold-inlaid armour, led his superbly equipped and mounted cohort up to the King's position, scattering lesser folk, volunteers, guild-members and ministers alike, right and left, his men roaring 'A Douglas! A Douglas!' in traditional fashion. James shrank back before the flailing hooves of Morton's charger, as the Earl pulled the beast back in an abrupt, earth-scoring halt, on to its very haunches.

'You need Douglas, I hear, my lord King?' the old man bellowed. 'I came hot-foot with these. Twice so many follow. What's to do, eh? What's to do?'

'Aye. Thank you, my lord. Aye, my thanks,' James acknowledged from behind Patrick. 'It's Bothwell . . .'

'Bothwell! That bastard's get by a Hepburn whore!' Morton cried, caring nothing that the bastard involved was one of the King's own uncles. He dismounted heavily, throwing his reins to an attendant, and clanked forward, roughly pushing aside the two divines, Melville and Galloway. 'Out o' the way o' Douglas, clerks!' he barked.

'Sir!' Master Galloway protested. 'Have a care how you go . . .'

'Quiet, fool!' the Douglas standard-bearer ordered, coming behind his lord.

'But . . . I am minister of the High Kirk of St. Giles . . . !'

'I carena' whether you're the Archangel Gabriel, man! No daws squawk where Douglas is!'

Andrew Melville stroked his beard, but said nothing.

Patrick hastened to close the breach. He had helped substantially in bringing low the previous Morton, the terrible one-time Regent of Scotland, and had no love for the nephew. But this unexpected adherence now was a major access of strength. 'My lord,' he cried. 'You are welcome, I vow! A notable augury – Douglas joins the King and the Kirk! Master Melville here has nobly rallied the faithful. Brought out this great host of the people, to assail Bothwell . . .'

The Earl snorted. 'That rabble!' He spat. 'Clear them out of the way, I say! Before Bothwell does. They encumber the decent earth!'

'My lord of Morton,' Melville said, quietly but sternly. 'I mislike your words and your manners. You speak of the people of God! Fellow-heirs, with yourself, of Christ's mercy. By the looks of you, you will need that mercy more than most. And sooner than some!'

'Devil burn you!' Morton swung round, to stare at the other. 'You . . . *you* dare speak me so! God's Passion – I'll teach you and your low-born like to raise your croaking voice in Douglas's presence! By the powers . . .'

Patrick was tugging at the King's sleeve. 'Quickly!' he whispered. 'Stop him, Sire.'

'Eh, eh! Hech, me! My lord! My lord o' Morton – ha' done. We . . . we command it. Aye, command it. You also, Master Melville. Ha' done, I say. This'll no' do, at all.' James's thick voice shook, but he went on. 'It's no' suitable. In our royal presence. Eh . . . ?' Patrick was prompting at his side. 'Aye. We need you both – greatly need you. Our cause is one. We canna have bickering and brabbling . . .'

A commotion to the north drowned his words. Shouting arose, there and was taken up by the huge concourse, as with a great groaning and squealing of wooden axle-trees, three massive iron cannon, bound and hooped, each drawn by a train of a dozen plodding oxen, lumbered from the cobblestones of the Canongate on to the grassland of the park. Such a thing had not been seen since Flodden. Everywhere men surged forward, to admire and exclaim. Even Morton forgot his spleen, to stride off to inspect the monsters. Folk were shouting that here was Mons, good buxom Mons, the most famous piece of ordnance ever forged.

Gratefully Patrick seized the opportunity. He slipped over to Melville's side, spoke a few sympathetic words, and urged immediate superintendence of the issue of the garrison's hundreds of pikes and halberds to the people. Then he besought the King to mount his horse and have the Royal Standard unfurled above his head, to a fanfare of trumpets. No speeches this time – for not one in a hundred would hear him. Then, the move to Leith at last.

So, presently, that strange, discordant, sprawling horde set off on its two-mile march, surely the most unlikely army ever to issue from the Capital behind the proud Rampant Lion of Scotland. First rode an advance-party of fifty Kennedys, to clear the way and act as scouts. Patrick had been anxious about the Kennedys and the Douglases coming to blows, and conceived this useful and honourable duty as in some way countering Morton's arrogant assumption that he and his must remain closest to the King. Then came the hundred of the Royal Guard, preceding the King's Standard-bearer and the Lord Lyon King of Arms. James himself followed, with Morton only half a head behind on the right and the Duke of Lennox on the left, flanked by Douglas horsemen, four deep. Next a motley group marched on foot – including, strangely enough, the Master of Gray, despite tall riding-boots and clanking spurs; when he had discovered that Andrew Melville and the other Kirk leaders intended to walk all the way to Leith, refusing to be mounted where there followers were not, he promptly handed over his horse to a servant and marched with them. The little fat Provost also puffed and panted with this party, as did certain deacons of guilds, magistrates and other prominent townsfolk. Then came Bargany and his remaining two-hundred-and-fifty horse, followed by a mixed assortment of mounted men to the number of another hundred or so. Thereafter the castle garrison, with the ox-drawn cannon, followed by the great mass of the people, starting with companies and groups which kept some sort of order, armed with pikes and bills, but quickly degenerating into a noisy and undisciplined mob, to tail off eventually in a vast following of onlookers, women, children and barking dogs. How many the entire strung-out host might add up up to it was impossible to guess – but it could be computed that there were over five hundred horse and perhaps a thousand footmen who might generously be called pikemen, with three or four times that of miscellaneous approximately armed men, apart from the hangers-on who far outnumbered all.

This straggling multitude progressed – since it could hardly be said to march – in a general northerly direction, by way of the Abbey Hill, the flanks of Calton Hill, the village of Moutrie, the Gallow's hill where the bodies of offenders hung in chains, and on down the long straight track of Leith Loan past the hamlet of Pilrig and the outskirts of Logan's property of Restal-rig. The bare two miles took the best part of two hours to cover, largely because of the desperately slow pace of the plodding oxen drawing the heavy cannon over the churned-up mud of the un-even route. Indeed, the impatient apprentices, who started by helping to push the lumbering artillery at bad patches, presently took over from the oxen altogether, and the last part of the journey was completed at a slightly better pace. By which time the entire incoherent column had spread and strung itself out sufficiently to make it barely recognisable as a unified force.

The Kennedy outriders kept the leadership posted as to the situation ahead. Quite early on scouts came back with the word that Bothwell, after taking Leith with little or no resistance – for the town walls, once stronger than those of Edinburgh itself, had been broken down during the religious wars of Queen Mary's reign and never rebuilt – had now moved out of the port itself to the east, to take up a defensive position amongst the fortifications in the open area outside the town known as Leith Links. Later information confirmed that he was still there.

The news could be both good and bad. He was evidently not sallying forth to challenge the King's force; on the other hand, he was not retreating – and these fortifications, earthworks thrown up to protect Leith and the Capital from an expected English landing by sea fifty years before, were defensively very powerful.

As the leaders of the royal force neared the broken walls of Leith, James became ever more agitated. He was a good horse-man, strangely enough, although his slouching seat was decep-tive, but, though twice the man mounted that he was on his shambling feet, he was still no warrior-king. Without Patrick Gray at his side to sustain him, and unappreciative of Morton's bellicose confidence, he kept looking back wistfully, most clearly desiring to be elsewhere. Ludovick Lennox presently fell behind to speak to the Master, to declare that if he did not come forward to take the King in hand again, there was likely to be a crisis.

So, his usually immaculate appearance notably soiled and mud-spattered, Patrick took to horse once more and resumed his nursing of the monarch's slender militancy.

In sight of the town's belatedly closed gates and gapped walls, they swung away right-handed, eastwards. They could see the green mounds of the earthworks on the Links, now, about half-a-mile away, between them and the sea. A few figures could be distinguished on the summits of the ramparts, but there was no sign of an army. Bothwell's troops could be hidden behind the grassy banks easily enough.

The King's relief at not being able to see his enemy was comic. Patrick was more concerned at not being able to see the sea, which the banks and the town between them hid.

'We must send a party to keep watch from the Signal Tower, Sire,' he declared. The environs of Leigh were flat, with no hills to offer vantage-points, and a tall watch-tower was a prominent feature of the harbour works, for observing the approach of shipping. 'If Bothwell is waiting here, it may well be to help in the landing of a force coming by sea. We must be warned of any such.'

'Aye, Patrick – Aye.' James obviously had an idea. 'I could do that, man. *I* could watch in the auld Signal Tower. Fine I could. And keep you informed here . . .'

'No doubt, Sire. But your royal presence with this host is entirely necessary. All would be at each others' throats without you, I fear – or away home to Edinburgh! Others we can spare – not the King!'

Silent, James rode on.

They were about four hundred yards from the first of the ramparts when the scene was suddenly and most dramatically transformed. All along the summit of that lengthy line of earthworks horsemen appeared, in a well-concerted movement, to stand there, side by side, upright lances glistening in the sun, pennons fluttering. The line was only one man deep but it was almost half-a-mile long, and the effect was impressive in the extreme – and daunting to more than King James. The advance of the royal horde came to a ragged halt.

Seeking to soothe the sovereign's near panic, Patrick pointed out that there was no immediate danger. The ground between the forces was cut and scored by trenches and holes, out of which the soil for the ramparts had been dug – now mostly filled with water. No cavalry charge across this was a practical proposition, from either side. Bothwell could not come at them, in his present formation, any more than they could get at him – save with footmen, who were certainly not likely to be anxious to throw away their lives in any head-on assault. And the range was too great for musketry. They had one advantage, however, denied to Bothwell. They had artillery. When the cannon came up, the situation would be changed.

Only slightly reassured, James was in a fret for the arrival of the guns. Confusion prevailed along the royal line – if line it could be termed. Some bold spirits pressed forward, to shake weapons and fists at the long still array of horsemen quarter-of-a-mile away – but more pressed back. There was a deal of shouting, some unauthorised and wild musket-fire, and considerable prayer, both offensive and defensive. Morton, without consulting anyone else, ordered his Douglas horsemen into a spectacular earth-shaking, lance-shaking, gallop, up and down the front, back and forward, shouting slogans, banners flying – but not coming within three hundred yards of the enemy. The main mass of townsmen, still coming up, kept pushing in amongst those in front, and then, discovering the situation, pushing back again.

In contrast to these highly mobile and fluid tactics, the enemy remained rather alarmingly motionless, grimly sure of themselves. Only in the centre of the long front was there any movement at all, where, under the red and white banner of Hepburn a small group of dismounted men were clustered.

Kennedy of Bargany, a stocky, bull-necked middle-aged man, and veteran of innumerable feuding affrays in his own lawless Carrick, rode up to Patrick, and after hooting his contempt of the King's force in general, and disparaging Morton's antics with his Douglases in particular, suggested that he should seek to outflank Bothwell with as much of the cavalry as could be spared. The fortifications ended at the very walls of Leith on the west, and nothing could be done there; but they must peter out somewhere to the east, amongst the open sand-dunes, and the enemy line could be turned from that side.

Patrick agreed – although the riding away of a large part of the cavalry might have a disastrous effect on the foot. On the other hand, to wait there doing nothing in the face of that grim line of moss-troopers was equally bad for morale. Bargany's move might at least cause Bothwell to break his threatening frontal formation.

Andrew Melville, from a consultation with some of his clerical colleagues, came to announce that the shepherds of Christ's Kirk had not marched all this way to stand inactive before the Philistines. The Lord's battles were not won so. Let them advance and come to grips. The Kirk would lead if the King would not.

Both these proposals appalled James. Patrick however saw virtue even in the latter, suitably modified – since almost any action, in the circumstances, was better than this inaction, which was in danger of turning their unwieldy host into a useless panic-stricken mob. Something to keep the crowd interested and occupied, whilst they awaited the cannon, was essential. Any head-on assault would be suicidal – but if part of the cavalry riding off to the east was balanced by a movement of foot to the west, order might be maintained and the impression given of some assured strategy. He urged Melville to lead some portion of his Kirk following in a flanking move to the west, towards the point where these ramparts joined Leith town walls. The said walls were broken and tumbled, and it ought to be possible to infiltrate through the streets and possibly work round the back of the enemy line. This, taken in conjunction with the Kennedy move, should at least worry Bothwell – whilst leaving the front clear for the cannon when at length they could be brought to bear.

Melville conceded the sense of this, and he and his fire-eating clergy went to harangue their more fervid supporters, while Bargany, with his own people and the miscellaneous horse, rode off eastwards, to the jeers of Morton's breathless warriors, now returned from their exercises in the full face of the enemy.

As the faithful surged off to the west, quite a proportion of the main body electing to trail after them, Morton transferred his scorn and abuse to these, asserting that they were deserting the field as he had known they would, but that honest men were well rid of riff-raff of the sort. The King's Grace was in a bad way when he had to call on such to fight his battles for him – and Westland Kennedy bogtrotters little better! Let His Grace but wait until the Douglas reinforcements arrived, and they would sweep Bothwell and his scoundrelly Borderers into the sea without more ado.

The Master of Gray gravely acknowledged that this, of course, would be the ideal consummation, and to be looked forward to by all. But meantime they must be content with less epic gestures – and if his lordship would be so good as to use some of his horse to go back and help expedite the arrival of the dilatory cannon . . .

Whilst King, Duke and upstart courtiers were being informed in no uncertain terms of the unsuitability of any suggestion that Douglas should be looked upon as agency of any sort of haulage and traction, a substitute for draught-oxen, happily a rumbling and creaking from the rear announced the arrival of the ordnance at last. The effect upon all was extraordinary. The crowd seemed to forget its fear of that ominous waiting rank of steel-clad horsemen fronting them. Everywhere men actually pressed forward as the pieces were trundled up. Even James himself was partially transformed. He dismounted, and went to pat Mons Meg, the largest of the monsters, stroking the great barrel as though it was a restive horse. His well-known hatred of cold steel did not seem to apply to forged iron. Perhaps something of his great-grandfather James the Fourth's strange and ill-rewarded enthusiasm for artillery – and James the Second's before that – had descended to their unlikely successor.

The cannon were set upon the nearest thing to an eminence that could be found thereabouts, and the castle garrison set about the laborious process of loading, priming and preparing to fire. James himself was eventually proffered the burning, spluttering rope, to have the honour of firing the first shot from Mons – but he preferred to leave it to the master gunner, and retired a fair distance back and to the side, clapping his beringed hands over his ears and tight-shutting his eyes.

The report thundered out with a most satisfactory crash, shaking the earth, belching forth flame and black smoke, sending echoes chasing amongst the tall lands of nearby Leith, and setting the sea-birds screaming and Morton's horses dancing. A great cheer arose from the throng – despite the fact that the ball smashed into a ditch fully one hundred and fifty yards short of the enemy, throwing up a huge fountain of mud and water. The second piece did not go off properly, most of the blast seeming to blow backwards rather than forwards, to the alarm of those nearby, and the ball only went a short distance in a visibly drooping arc. The third however went off with another tremendous bang, and though nobody detected where the shot went – certainly no enemy were seen to fall – enthusiasm was restored.

The loading and priming process recommenced.

Whilst they waited, the crowd continued to cheer. At the same time, activity was to be observed in the centre of Bothwell's line, with men mounting and riding here and there. Patrick spoke low-voiced to Ludovick.

'We have stirred up Francis Hepburn at last, Vicky. Now we shall see some action. If he elects to come straight at us, see you to the King. He cannot charge us, over that broken ground – but he could ride through in column. He far outnumbers Morton's horse. I do not think that he will do it, mind – although he would only have to face one salvo of cannon, for he would be on us before they could be recharged. But if so, get the King out of it swiftly, eastwards to Bargany. At all costs he must not be captured, whatever else happens.'

"I'd prefer some stouter role . . .'

'Don't be a fool, Vicky! The King is the ultimate prize. Lose him and all is lost in this unfortunate realm . . .'

Mons roared once more. Earth and sand flew up from the base of the green rampart on which the Borderers were ranked. Horses could be seen to rear and plunge. Loud and shrill was the delight of the onlookers.

A trumpet neighed tensely in the middle distance in front. And like puppets pulled by a single string, the entire extended array of Bothwell's moss-troopers turned around to drop away out of sight behind the embankment, as suddenly and completely as they had first appeared.

'Now how do we get at them?' Lennox demanded. 'Our shots cannot reach them behind yonder.'

'No. But he cannot just sit there, with our two forces working round behind him. Moreover he throws away his great advantage, in his cavalry . . .' Patrick stopped, to raise a pointing finger. 'See there!' he cried.

Although the height of those ramparts hid men and horses both, they were not quite high enough to hide something else – the proud red-and-white banner of the Hepburns. The top half of this could still be seen, clearly outlined against the pale blue of the sky over the sea. And it was streaming out, not hanging limp – moving fast, eastwards. And not only the banner; keen eyes could just distinguish, behind it, lesser movement in the same direction, small pennons and the tips of lances, going at an equal pace.

'What now, Patrick? What now?' the King wondered, as voices shouted these tidings.

'Bothwell moves east, Sire. Fast.'

'Aye. But where, man? And why?'

'That we must wait to discover. The Kennedys are there.'

'He'll no' round on us, that way?'

'Not without Bargany warning us. Have no fear, Sire. There is no lack of time. And my lord of Morton will guard you well!'

There was a distinct unease now amongst the royal host, with nothing for the cannon to fire at, and Bothwell on the move, while much of their own strength was dispersed. When, presently, a single horseman came galloping towards them from the east, in obvious urgency, something like alarm gripped a large proportion of the concourse. There was a notable tendency to drift in the other direction.

The messenger, one of Bargany's men, panted out his news in his singsong West Country voice. Bothwell was gone! He and his whole company had ridden out of the fortification area at a point where he had been able to avoid the Kennedys, and headed south by a little east, at fullest speed. Bargany was following, keeping him in sight – but there seemed to be no likelihood of his turning, of seeking to make some circling attack on the King's rear. He gave every sign of being in full flight.

At first it seemed as though nobody took it in. Only gradually did it begin to dawn. The Battle of Leith Links was over. Without a drop of blood shed, without a single casualty on either side, as far as it was known, the day was won and lost. The forces of the Lord had triumphed. They had blown the trumpets, and down had come the walls of Jericho. Patrick Gray began to laugh softly to himself.

King James was the last to be convinced that the immediate danger was over. He was sure that it was all a cunning stratagem on Bothwell's part to take him unawares. And then, when presently another messenger from Bargany arrived to say that the enemy were now past Restalrig and fleeing due south on a line to take them east of Arthur's Seat, the King was prepared to accept that the threat for the moment was over, he nevertheless became convinced that this merely meant that Bothwell intended to attack Edinburgh itself, while its protecting forces were absent and thus cheaply win the Capital. While Patrick doubted the likelihood of this, not believing that Bothwell's mind would work in that way, he had to admit that it was a possibility, however much Morton scoffed and others expressed more polite disbelief.

Few here were indeed to take fears seriously now. Most people there at Leith Links went slightly mad, in their relief, laughing, singing and dancing. Some even remembered their previous praying, and one or two went so far as to get down on their knees on the grass and thank the Kirk's God for this happy reward for their valour and petitions – which reminded Patrick to send a messenger to inform Andrew Melville's company of the changed situation.

The King refused to be impressed or lulled by the general jollification. That Devil-possessed man Frances might be yammering at the door of Holyroodhouse, or planning to take over the castle that lacked its garrison, he claimed. Nothing would do but that they hasten back to Edinburgh forthwith. The problems of getting the excited and now carefree crowd in hand again, of collecting the missing Kirk contingent, and of re-establishing connection with Bargany, did not concern him. Patrick must see to that.

Patrick pointed out that the threat from the sea, which presumably was behind this business of Bothwell, was still to be faced. He proposed that the cannon and their crews should be left to take up a good position guarding the entry to the harbour of Leith, to prevent a landing, and that the Kirk's leaders suitably instigate their followers in the port to rise in arms to defend the town. Melville could see to that and then come on after the King to Edinburgh. Meantime fast couriers should be sent off to the south to try to find Lord Home and Scott of Buccleuch, to inform them of Bothwell's movements. Home of Linthill, Logan's messenger, had told Patrick that he understood his chief and Buccleuch to be hurrying north, on hearing of Bothwell's original sortie. By this time they might not be far from Edinburgh. They might just possibly catch Bothwell between them.

All this took longer to arrange than it ought to have done, against the holiday mood of the vast majority; but presently the faces of most of the host were turned towards the Capital, whilst on in front making no attempt to linger with the many, Morton's Douglases with the small remainder of the mounted men and courtiers, rode hard and fast, and, strangely, in the lead and most urgent, was now the newly victorious King of Scots.

Another line of battle, another confrontation of armed forces – this time on the long ridge of Edmonstone, south of Edinburgh and near to Dalkeith, in Morton's territory indeed, and much more the traditional battlefield than Leith Links. More professional and military, too, the loyalist array. The King's hard-riding party could see them lined up along the ridge in reassuringly solid-looking formation as they themselves rode out of the valley behind Craigmillar, somewhat wearily. That these others up above must be a deal more weary did not strike all. These were Home's and Buccleuch's men – not the main force, but a strong detachment of perhaps a thousand horse under the Lord Home himself, who had hastened up from the Borders after Bothwell, and had now, almost by accident, come face to face with their quarry as he returned south towards his own main army.

Bothwell, it seemed, had not in fact designed to attack Edinburgh. Now he stood at bay on this flat ridge of Edmonstone, so near where greater battles had been fought earlier in that troubled century, at Pinkie and Carberry, the latter indeed where his predecessor, the former Bothwell, had taken his last leave of the lovely Queen Mary nearly thirty blood-stained years before. James's company after having rejoined Bargany and his Kennedys on the Borough-muir of Edinburgh, had been brought this information, and now rode to join Lord Home.

But on this occasion, also, actual hostilities, the clash of arms, was to elude the diffident monarch. His column reinforced by another two hundred Douglases, met in Leith Loan, was barely half-way up the long sloping farmlands of Edmonstone when a convulsion seemed to seize the ranked men on the skyline. Abruptly the solid phalanx broke and scattered, chaos and confusion succeeded comforting and substantial order, shouts and trumpet-calls and clangour came thinly down on the breeze. King James drew rein in haste, only to resume his advance again, with caution, when the sounds of strife were clearly receding over the brow of the hill.

Arrival at the summit revealed no fighting, but a deal of disarray. Also an angry and discomfited Lord Home, whose greeting to his sovereign was somewhat perfunctory in consequence. Bothwell, it seemed, after having shown every sign of riding off the field, as though to continue his retiral southwards, had suddenly swung round and made a flanking attack on Home's force from the side, at speed, his manoeuvre hidden by a slight rise in the ground. Thus he had been able to bring almost his whole force to bear against only part of Home's. With sad results. A dozen men were dead – all on Home's side – more were wounded, and Home himself had had a narrow escape, so narrow indeed that his personal trumpeter, close at his side, had been captured. Surprise achieved, Bothwell had returned to his former position half a mile away. Home did not say so, but probably a glimpse of the King's force, approaching up the north side of the hill, had caused him to draw away. Added to all this distressing mishap was, apparently, the fact, vouched for on all hands, that Bothwell's men had fought shouting as slogan 'For God and the Kirk!' The enemy, clearly, was not lacking in initiative when he did not have to face artillery.

While Morton was authoritatively describing to Home how *he* would have dealt with the situation, and Patrick was assessing the military possibilities, a diversion occurred. A small party, under a white flag rode out from the now familiar extended front of the Bothwell line, and came to just within hailing distance of the loyalists. A trumpet blared.

'My lord Earl of Bothwell's compliments to my Lord Home,' a voice called. 'He has, by inadvertance and chance, collected a poor cornet and his trumpet, who claims to be the property of the Lord Home. Not being in need of so sorry a fellow he returns the creature herewith, and two rose nobles in generous recoupment. If the Lord Home considers this to be insufficient indemnity, my lord requests that they meet, alone, in personal match, here between the arrays, to settle the matter.'

Out from the little party then rode, distinctly sheepishly, the missing trumpeter, towards his own folk.

King James, now feeling comparatively safe with some fifteen hundred horsemen around him, actually began to tee-hee with mirth at this sally – to the grave offence of Lord Home, who was after all his most senior and experienced soldier. Home's answer of a salvo of musket-ball shot through the white flag was probably fair enough.

'Bothwell was ever a madman,' Ludovick commented. 'What does such a caper serve?'

'It serves two purposes, I think,' Patrick answered. 'For time, first – time to observe our strength, and to assess. He is no man's fool, is Francis Hepburn Stewart. And his spirit, it seems, is nowise damped.'

'Perhaps. Should we not therefore now attack? We must outnumber him by three to one...'

'I wonder, Vicky? Contrary to the opinions of some, I am a man of peace. I am but little fonder of bloodshed than is our liege lord. It would be better to end this day without actual blows, if it may be so. And if I interpret this latest gesture of Bothwell's aright, he now intends to retire. He would not have thought of it, I believe, had he intended to attack. It allows him to leave the field with a flourish – and who would deny him that, so long as he returns south whence he came?'

'But . . . our task is to roundly defeat him, to bring him low, not to let him go unscathed!'

'We shall not roundly defeat him, by any means, Vicky, if he does not intend to fight. In this situation, commanding some of the finest horsemen in this land, and in open country, he has but to signal them to disperse – and that will be the end of it. With foot it is different, but cavalry in open country cannot be defeated if they choose not to fight. Home, I think, will reckon the same.'

Whatever Lord Home's assessment of the situation – and he showed no signs of preparing to attack – was little to the point. Almost immediately after the return of his white-flag party, Bothwell's trumpets rang out, to be followed by rounds of mocking cheering from his moss-troopers. Then, unhurriedly and in perfect order, the long line of horsemen swung round and merged into a column-of-route formation, and so trotted off southwards behind the Hepburn banner in most final fashion.

Home sent scouts to the highest vantage-points around, to ensure that there was no circling back – but that is as far as his counter-measures went. No major protest was raised from the loyalist ranks at this policy of strategic inaction, least of all from the King of Scots.

A party of Douglas horse were despatched to trail the invaders southwards, to make certain that they left the district – which, being Morton's domains, he did not contest. In an access of relief, James thereupon dramatically knighted Kennedy of Bargany for courageous service on the field of battle. On this happy note, horses' heads were turned towards Edinburgh, the sunset and supper.

It had been a momentous Sabbath. Patrick sent a messenger ahead of them to proclaim victory and to have the church-bells acclaim the King's triumphant return to his rescued Capital.

Chapter Seven

The Chapel-Royal at Stirling Castle was packed tight as any barrel of Leith herrings. A small place, built only a few years before by King James to replace one that had fallen into ruins, it had been designed only for the devotions of the monarch and his suite, and was quite inadequate and unsuitable for any major ceremonial. But here the ceremony must be, for still, on no account would the King permit that his precious son and heir be carried over the heavily-guarded threshold of Stirling Castle. So willy-nilly, into this meagre space must be packed not only much of the Protestant aristocracy of Scotland, but the host of special envoys and representatives of the Courts of Europe invited for the occasion – for James was, these days, much uplifted with satisfaction, pride and self-esteem, and was determined that the world should not be backward in recognising the good cause he had for it.

Despite all this, however, and her lowly status, Mary Gray had one of the best positions in that seething crowded church, up at the chancel steps, between the altar and the font. This was not so strange, for she held in her arms the principal and centre of interest of the entire affair – the scarlet-faced and distinctly puny Prince of Scotland; by the King's command, if not the Queen's.

The trouble was that Mary had already held the infant for over twenty difficult minutes. James had insisted that his son should be in good time for his christening, that all might have the opportunity of admiring him – an understandable paternal ambition had, in fact, the crowd in the chapel been of a density to see anything other than their nearest neighbours; or had he ensured that the ceremony started approximately up to time. As it was, the situation was on the verge of getting out of hand, and deteriorating rapidly.

In the heat of that August day, the Chapel-Royal was like an oven. Even Mary, normally so cool and fresh, was pink and breathless. The baby, in its tight swaddling clothes, was turning from scarlet to crimson, and seemed to be near apoplexy with bawling – even though, with the noise made by other people, the child's cries were next to inaudible.

Mary, exhausted, limp, and isolated by the throng from all assistance, almost fell on his neck when the Duke of Lennox came, elbowing his way through the crush to her side.

'Oh, Vicky,' she gasped, 'God be praised that you have come! The child – he is all but crazed. The heat! The noise! This long waiting...'

'I am sorry, my dear. It is the Queen. She is beside herself. She forbids that the christening goes on if the child is not baptised Frederick first, after her father of Denmark. And only then Henry. The King insists that it be Henry first, as compliment to Queen Elizabeth, after *her* father. That the boy may one day be King in England also. Elizabeth must be conciliated, he says. Neither will yield – Henry Frederick or Frederick Henry!'

'The folly of it! They are no more than stupid wilful children themselves! They care nothing how the bairn suffers! Tell the King that the child will be ill, Vicky. Endangered. They must delay no longer...'

'Already I have tried,' he told her. 'But you know Anne!'

'Can Patrick not help?'

'Patrick is soothing the Kirk. And Elizabeth's special ambassador, Sussex. He esteems this an insult to his Queen.'

'Ask Patrick, nevertheless.'

Whether Patrick Gray's doing or not, a flourish of trumpets sounded from outside, fairly soon after Lennox's departure, the signal for the royal entry. Obviously, however, it was quite impossible for the procession to come in by the main door and up the aisle, as arranged. Instead, the small vestry door near the chancel was thrown open, and through its narrow portal the official retinue had to squeeze – with a certain forfeiture of dignity. The Lord Lyon King of Arms, his heralds and trumpeters, preceded the other high officers of the realm, who bore the Sword of State, the Sceptre, the Spurs and so on. Then came Lennox as Lord Chamberlain, followed by the youthful Earl of Sussex, resplendent in pearl-sewn velvet, and carrying a towel with which most evidently he did not know what to do. At his back and jostling to see which could be hindmost, and therefore senior, came two clerics, one in sober black and Geneva bands, one in gorgeous cope, alb, stole and mitre – Master David Lindsay, the King's chaplain, and Cunningham, Bishop of Aberdeen. Two young women then appeared, edging through side by side, one nervously giggling, the other red-eyed with weeping – ladies in waiting.

There was a space, and then the Queen sailed in head high, set-faced and frowning blackly, the two pages who held her train having to follow at the trot. She was a small creature, slim as a boy, with sharp-pointed features, reddish hair, and a darting eye. She had had a certain pert prettiness when first she came from Denmark five years before, but at nineteen this was no longer apparent. She was clothed in royal purple, which went but doubtfully with her red-brown hair.

King James came in with the two pages – indeed he all but trotted with them, looking anxious, clad in sufficient magnificence for three men. The Master of Gray slipped inside last of all, to close the door. After only a moment or two, however, he turned back and opened it again.

Queen Anne, ignoring the Lord Lyon's indication of where she should stand, made straight for Mary Gray, to snatch the protesting infant from her, glaring.

Although this was not the arrangement, Mary gave up her burden with relief, curtsying. It distressed her that the Queen should look upon her as an enemy nowadays, as one of those who kept her from her baby. The fact that Mary had no wish to act as a sort of governess to the young prince, and indeed longed only to get back to her own life with Ludovick and her son at Methven, did not help her with Anne, who saw her now only as the woman who was supplanting her with her child.

The King, gobbling with apprehension, hastened forward to remonstrate. He actually laid hands on the child – whereupon the Queen clutched him the tighter, suddenly became a tigress with her whelp. It looked as though a tug-of-war might develop, when the Master of Gray sauntered up, smiling, to murmur soothingly to the King and then to turn his fullest charms upon Anne. What was said could not be heard by others because of the baby's yells and the chatter of the congregation. But somehow Patrick convinced the Queen, however reluctantly, to hand over the squirming, yelling bundle to the young and far-from-eager Earl of Sussex, who held it gingerly, dropping his towel in the process. James himself stooped to pick this up, hovering around Elizabeth's envoy in agitation. Hurriedly Patrick signed to Lyon, who nudged the nearest trumpeter. The blast of the instrumentalists thereafter drowned all other sounds in that constricted space.

As the reverberations died away, with only the baby unaffected apparently, Master Lindsay, having taken up his position in front of the altar, but facing the congregation, made it very clear whose service this was by plunging into headlong and vigorous prayer. Unprepared for this, it took a little while for the assembly to adopt an attitude of silent devotion, especially those visitors from furth of the realm unused to Scottish customs. The King it was, waving his towel and shushing loudly, who succeeded in gaining approximate quiet from all but his son.

It was a long prayer, a monologue adjuring the Deity to be on watch and take particular care for this infant from the fell dangers of idolatry, heresy, Popery, Episcopacy, witchcraft and other like devilries, to which the bairn looked like being most direly exposed. That neither the Almighty nor anyone else make any mistake about the danger, he went into considerable detail on the subject. Sussex squirmed with his burden, and shot agonised looks all round, which met with only darts of sheer venom from the Queen, whilst James punctuated the praying with vehement amens – which, if they were intended to bring it to a premature close, were notably ineffective.

At length Master Lindsay had to pause for breath. The Bishop seized his opportunity. Straight into the baptismal rite he swung, his voice sonorous but mellifluent after the other's vibrant harshness, presently holding out his arms for the child. Never did a proxy godparent deliver his charge more promptly.

Thus started, things went with a swing, almost a rush, Bishop Cunningham apparently being unwilling to surrender the initiative even for a moment. Responses were taken for granted, inessentials jettisoned, and the office repeated at a pace which could scarcely have been bettered or even equalled, yet without a single slip of the tongue or scamped intonation – a piece of epis-copal expertise which was much admired.

The Bishop was slightly less successful, however, at the actual moment of christening when, after a quick glance at the Queen and then the King, he signed with the holy water and rather mumbled. Many there were, including the monarch himself, who declared stoutly thereafter that he enunciated 'Henry Frederick – Frederick Henry'; but Mary Gray for one was quite sure that he in fact said 'Frederick Henry – Henry Frederick'. But then, the Bishop of Aberdeen was susceptible to young women; moreover he was near enough to the Old Faith still to consider Elizabeth Tudor a dragon and her father Henry the Eighth as Antichrist himself.

If it was possible, the Bishop actually quickened his pace. Dexterously balancing the infant between the crook of his arm and the edge of the font, he dived a hand within his cope, to produce a small silver phial, to the accompaniment of a rich flood of words, and proceeded to anoint the child's head with oil therefrom, in the name of the Trinity. King James's dark eyes gleamed triumphantly, there were gasps from certain of the congregation, and Master Lindsay started forward, hands up-raised. But it was all over too swiftly for any intervention, and the episcopal eloquence slowing down, the Bishop handed the prince back to Sussex, and sinking his mitred head towards his breast, tucked ringed hands within the wide sleeves of his cope and, reverently contemplating the floor, sank his voice away into private whispered intercession.

Thereafter, as the Queen suddenly darted forward to snatch the child from Sussex, the much more assuredly Reformed Master Lindsay sternly, angrily, took over again, and after more resounding prayer and a lengthy reading from the Scriptures, showed every sign of being about to preach a sermon. Mary Gray looked desperately at her father, who nodded, and signed to the Lord Lyon. At the first opportunity thereafter the trumpets blared out once more in joyful and sustained flourish. The trumpet, Patrick reflected, was the undoubted prince of instruments.

Not waiting for any benediction, the Queen turned and hurried for the open vestry door, baby in her arms, taking her train-bearers and ladies by surprise. But not her husband. Moving with unusual swiftness, James reached the door first, and with a sort of dignity bowed, and quite firmly took the infant from her. Holding the prince proudly if inexpertly, he shambled out first into the sunshine. He hurried round to the front door of the Chapel-Royal, to display his son to the congregation as it emerged.

The move to the Great Hall thereafter was not a stately procession, as planned.

The King, still clutching the baby, was entering the Hall, one of the noblest apartments in the land, where refreshments were laid out for all, when he remembered to give orders for the firing of the cannon.

This martial touch, a subtle reminder of James's recent successful campaigning, was on a scale hitherto unknown in Scotland. Pieces had been brought specially from Edinburgh to reinforce the local artillery, and the resultant uproar was breathtaking. The castle, Stirling itself, the entire Carse of Forth shook and trembled to it, and the mountain barrier of the Highland Line threw back the echoes. Inside the Great Hall, as time went on, women grew pale, rocked to and fro, and neared hysteria, while strong men held heads in hands and stared glassily ahead – for of course no conversation was possible, no two consecutive words were to be distinguished. The great cannon and culverins, the smaller sakers and falconets, and the host of lesser pieces, skilfully synchronised, ensured that not for one second was there a pause in the assault upon the eardrums – a triumph of the cannoneer's art, undoubtedly.

The heir of Scotland screamed on and on, while his mother wept, and Mary Gray, after having pleaded in dumb show with Ludovick and Patrick to try to have the hellish din halted somehow, slipped away to her own quarters of the castle, to soothe young John Stewart of Methven.

Eventually James, who had taken the precaution to bring woollen plugs for his ears, grew tired of it, and sent a thankful messenger to halt the clamour – to the great relief of the Lord High Treasurer, the Master of Glamis, amongst others, who though now somewhat deaf could still count the cost of such expenditure of costly gunpowder.

To the dizzy and all but concussed company, the monarch then gleefully announced that although the main celebrations were being reserved for the evening, when there would be a banquet with masque and guizardry, withal of deep moral meaning, present delights were not quite completed. He thereupon turned to the Lord Home, who had carried the Sword of State, demanding the said weapon – which caused some small upset, for it was of the awkwardly huge two-handed variety, suitable only for heroes like the original owner, Robert the Bruce, and Home had left it standing in some corner. When produced, James found it exceedingly difficult to handle, his wrists not being of the strongest, but refusing proffered alternatives, and tucking it under his arm like a lance, he advanced upon his son held in his mother's shrinking arms – to the alarm of more than the Queen. Poking at the infant with its enormous blade, approximately on the shoulder, he cried out,

'I dub ye knight, Sir Henry! Aye, Sir Henry Stewart! That is . . . Henry Frederick. You'll no' can arise, my wee mannie, as a knight should – but no matter. Aye. Now, Johnnie – Johnnie Mar. The spur, man.'

The Earl of Mar stepped forward, holding out one of the symbolic spurs. As he bore down upon Queen and babe, Anne made as though to hide the child from him, for she had conceived a great hatred for Mar, the prince's governor. The touching with the spur, therefore, was only a modified success, especially as its spikes got entangled with the infant's christening robe, to the mother's loud protest.

The Lord Lyon, however, came to the rescue by making impressive announcement of the new knight's styles and titles, crying.

'See here the Right Excellent, High and Magnanimous Henry Frederick, Frederick Henry, by the Grace of God, Knight, Baron of Renfrew, Lord of the Isles, Earl of Carrick, Duke of Rothesay, Prince and Great Steward of Scotland!'

This over, and the child's health and well-being pledged by all, James suddenly wearied, as he was apt to do, and began to look around him.

'Mistress Mary,' he called, querulously. 'Where are you? Vicky – where's your Mary Gray? Where is she, man?'

'She has gone, Sire. To see to our own child, I think.'

'Then she shouldna ha' done, Vicky. She hadna our royal permission to leave. We are displeased. Aye, right displeased. Fetch her back. Here to me.'

'As you will, Sire.'

'No – wait, now. We havena the time. It's no' suitable for us to wait on the lassie. Take you the bairn to her, Vicky.'

Ludovick, faced with the unenviable task of abstracting the infant from its mother's embrace, went about the business but hesitantly. Seeing which, James himself hurried over, took his son from his wife's protesting grasp, and handed him to Lennox.

'Off wi' him. And watch him well, mind. The bairn's no' to be wearied, see you. I'll no' have him unsettled.'

'As you say, Sire.'

'Aye. Well – I shall retire. I'll need to prepare for the masque. Anne! Fetch Her Grace, Patrick man. Lyon – your trumpets . . .'

'How does it feel, Patrick, to sit and watch all dancing to your tune? To move men like pawns in a game? To watch all that you have contrived come to pass?'

'Not all, my dear. Most perhaps, but not all,' the Master amended lightly.

'Does it make you happy?'

'Happy? What is happiness, Mary? If you mean am I contented – I am not. Nor elated. Nor proud. Say that I see a good beginning, and am encouraged and hopeful.'

'I think perhaps that you even deceive yourself, Patrick – as well as others!'

'But not Mary Gray! Eh? Never Mary Gray!'

She did not answer that. Father and daughter were sitting together in quite a lowly position at the banquet in the Great Hall – Ludovick being required to take his due place up at the dais table near the King, amongst all the ambassadors and chief guests. The Queen was not present, pleading a headache – and undoubtedly James was in better fettle for her absence.

'You accuse me of deceit, Mary,' her father said conversationally. 'Because, on occasion, I do not tell *all* the truth – all that I know. But where is the virtue in a surfeit of truth? Look around you this August night. What do you see? The King merry, and safe. The new prince secure. The realm as near at peace as it has been all this reign. Bothwell abandoned by Queen Elizabeth and skulking a fugitive in his Border mosses. Indeed Elizabeth godmother to the precious child, her cousin Sussex bringing rich gifts and sitting at the King's side – and the English succession that much the nearer. All this, and more, that might not have been. And you see naught in it but deceit!'

'The English succession!' she took him up. 'That, to you, is all-important, is it not? Paradise! The Promised Land itself! Why, I have never understood.'

'I should have thought that wits so sharp as yours would require no telling. Only when the two realms are united under one king, will our land have settled peace, Mary. Only then will Scotland open and flourish as she should, with hatred past and opportunity before her. Always, the threat of England's might has constrained us, hedged us in. Always there has been an English party in Scotland, betraying the nation...'

'*You* say that! You who have betrayed so much and so many? Who have accepted so much of Elizabeth's gold...!'

'Aye. I say it. For I have chaffered with Elizabeth for Scotland's sake, not to line my own pockets, girl! As do the others. What you name my betrayals have been done that Scotland might survive. Always I have laboured and contrived that this realm should survive in the face of all that would tear it apart, sufficiently long for King Jamie there to be accepted also as King in England...'

'And Patrick Gray a power in two kingdoms!'

He sighed. 'You are hard on me, lassie. In some ways, those bonnie eyes of yours, that see so much, are strangely blind. You see me as crazed for power. That I have never been. As hungry for wealth. That I do not seek, save to carry out my purposes. As pursuing vengeance on those who counter me...'

'I see you as a puppet-master, Patrick – with men and women as your puppets. Aye, and kings and queens and princes. Even Christ's church! Puppets that you discard at will, caring not that they have hearts and souls! The puppet-show alone matters to you, not the puppets. Can you deny it?'

He was silent, then, for a little, his handsome face without expression.

As so often was the way it went, Mary could not withhold her love and pity – although pity was scarcely a word that could be used in respect of the Master of Gray – from this extraordinary sire of hers. Her hand went out to touch his arm.

'I am sorry, Patrick. Sorry that I should seem to think so ill of you. But . . . I cannot forget what you have done.'

'You speak out of ignorance, Mary. You do not know one tenth of the circumstances.'

'Perhaps not. But the tenth is more than sufficient. I would not wish to know more.' She paused. 'Though that, I think, is not wholly true. I would much like to know, Patrick, how your present triumph was achieved?'

'I do not take you? You have seen what has been . . .'

'Do not cozen me, Patrick. Credit me with some of those wits you spoke of! Do not tell me that much of all that has happened was not planned months ago. Before ever you came to Fast Castle. Someone planned it, surely. And neither Bothwell nor Huntly has the head for it. Moreover it has worked out only to *your* advantage . . .'

'And the King's.'

'Perhaps. But King James did not plot it, that is certain. Was any of it true, Patrick? Was the realm ever in real danger? Did Bothwell ever really design the King's death? And the capture of the prince? This move to Stirling – was it not all that you might draw the King away from the Chancellor Maitland? Did Bothwell ever intend to attack Edinburgh? Was the threat no more than a device that you might gain the Kirk to your side? You that I think are a Catholic at heart! I think that I see your hand behind Bothwell in all. But Bothwell is now a fugitive – whilst you, that was a banished outlaw, now guide the King's hand!'

'On my soul, girl, you attribute me with the powers of a god!'

'Not a god, Patrick!'

'Are you finished, my dear?'

'You have not answered any of my questions.'

'Save to say that all are nonsense. Something has disordered your mind, I fear. Childbirth, perhaps?'

'Is it nonsense that you devised this threat to the prince, for your own ends? To separate him from his mother? In order that the King and Queen should be thus at odds – and you have the greater hold over both?'

''Fore God, girl – you are bewitched! Spare me more of this, for sweet mercy's sake! You are, I think, clean out of your mind!'

Mary uttered a long sigh. 'Perhaps I am, Patrick. It may be so. Sometimes I tell myself that I am. Indeed, I would wish with all my heart that it is so. And yet . . .' She shook her head, and left the rest unsaid.

He considered her, and then patted her hand. 'There is ill and good in all of us,' he said, more gently. 'Allow me some of both! Even the Kirk is prepared to do that! Is my daughter less generous than Master Melville and his crew?'

'The Kirk! The Kirk would be wise to take care with the Master of Gray, would it not?'

'The Kirk must learn who are its friends. I have spent much time and labour this day aiding the Kirk. Convincing the King that he must allow the Kirk some part in the christening – for he would have had only the Bishop. Ensuring that the Bishop was discreet – and swift. Soothing Master Lindsay over the anointing oil. It is only because of the shameless and heretical Master of Gray that the righteous representatives of the Kirk are sitting here tonight.'

'And is that greatly to the Kirk's advantage? Or just to your own?'

'To the Kirk's, equally with the realm's. And therefore mine. And yours. In this pass the Kirk must be seen to act with the King. If that fails, they will go down both.'

'Is that true, Patrick? Is there any true threat remaining? Was there ever? Are not the Catholics everywhere held? Their day done?'

'Lassie,' Patrick lowered his musical voice to a murmur. 'Believe me, the Catholic threat is not gone. Was never so great, indeed.'

'You mean Huntly, still? The Catholic North. And Bothwell?'

'A greater threat than Huntly or Bothwell. Not a word of this to others, Mary – for none know it yet. Not even to Vicky, I charge you. But I have sure word that the King of France has turned Catholic.'

'Henry! That was Henry of Navarre? The Protestant lion!

Champion of the Huguenots! Never! That I do *not* believe.'

'Be not so sure, girl. Henry is under great pressure. He must unite his France – and the Catholic party is much the stronger. The Emperor, the Pope, Philip of Spain – all are pressing him hard. France, weakened by internal wars, needs stronger friends than little Scotland.'

'Even if this was true – why need it threaten Scotland?'

'Because it is only France that has restrained Philip. From doing as Huntly pleads, and invading Scotland. He cherishes an old claim – that Mary the Queen left him the throne of Scotland. He has feared France and our Auld Alliance – that France would attack Spain if he attacked Scotland. But should Henry turn Catholic, will he hurt Catholic Spain in favour of Protestant Scotland?'

Mary was silent. At length she spoke.

'You have known this for long? This of Henry?'

'For only a few days. But . . . I was expecting it.'

'How is it that Patrick Gray always knows such things before his King and the Council?'

'Because, my dear, I make it my business to know. Information, knowledge, is valuable. Especially in this game of statecraft. I have always paid much silver that I could ill afford in order that I might know of important matters a little sooner than do others. Many times I have proved the money well spent.'

'Even when it was Elizabeth's money? As when, at Falkland five years ago, you knew even before the French ambassador that the previous king had died? I remember that – and how you turned the knowledge to your own advantage. It was then, I think, that I first began to perceive what sort of man was the Master of Gray!'

He smiled thinly. 'I shall forbear to thank you for that! But I was right then, was I not? As I shall be proved right now . . .'

A commotion turned all heads towards the great main doorway. Through this was entering an astonishing sight, a magnificent Roman chariot, painted white, drawn by a single gigantic Moor, naked but for coloured ostrich plumes, ebony skin gleaming, mighty muscles rippling, and a grin all but bisecting his features. The chariot was heaped with fruit of various kinds, and standing amongst it were six divinities most fair. These were young women of most evident charms, garbed significantly but scantily, to represent Ceres, Liberality, Faith, Concord, Perseverance and Fecundity – the last as naked as the Moor save for three tiny silver leaves no larger than those of a birch-tree. This, the Lady Lindores, formerly the Lady Jean Stewart, Orkney's second legitimate daughter and Patrick's sister-in-law, had always been a warm and roguish piece, like most of her kin; now she was grown into a most voluptuous young woman, challenging as to eye, body and posture. She held in one hand a cornucopia which seemed to spill out the fruits to fill the chariot, and cradled in her other arm a doll fashioned in pink wax, baby-sized, with open mouth towards her full thrusting breast.

The King's cry of delight was undoubtedly mainly for the Moor and the fact that he could alone draw the chariot – for James was never really interested in women. He shouted, and clapped his hands, jumping to his feet – which meant that every-one else must likewise rise.

'Your work, I think?' Mary said. 'It has all the marks of your devising.'

'You are too kind,' Patrick told her. 'It was His Grace's notion. As his Master of the Wardrobe, it falls to me to, h'm, interpret the royal wishes in such matters.'

'I do not believe the King would have thought of displaying the Lady Jean so – who has been four years married and still no child!'

'A small conceit!' he nodded. 'You are not jealous, my dear? Would you rather that I had chosen you?'

'Even you, Patrick, are insufficiently bold for that! Perhaps you might more aptly have used me as Perseverance!' She smiled faintly.

He laughed. 'I should have thought of that. I vow you well earn the part, where I am concerned! Why, Mary? Why do you do it?'

'Because I am your daughter. Does that not answer all?'

'And so you must reform me? A hopeless task, I fear, my dear.'

'Say that I seek to out-persevere my sire.'

'You are a strange creature, lass.'

'Bone of your bone, Patrick. Blood of your blood.'

The Moor was drawing the chariot round all the tables of the Banqueting Hall, whilst the ladies thereon handed out fruit to all who would partake. Few refused such fair ministrants; many indeed sought more than their fruit. The King rewarded the Moor by feeding him sweetmeats, but after a sidelong askance glance, he ignored the lovely charioteers altogether.

Soon James was gesturing vigorously towards the Master of Gray, who in turn nodded to a servitor near the door. Shortly afterwards a thunderous crash shook the entire castle, guests, tables and plenishings alike leapt, and black smoke came billowing in at the open doorway. There were cries of alarm and some screaming – until it was seen that the King was rubbing his hands and chuckling gleefully. Then a great ship surged in, a true replica of a galleon, a score of feet long, all white and gold but with the muzzles of ranked cannon grinning black through open gun-ports. The tall masts had to be lowered to win through the doorway, but once inside they were cunningly raised, the central one to a full forty feet, to display a full set of sails of white taffeta, emblazoned with the Rampant Lion of Scotland and finished with silken rigging. No men were in evidence about the vessel, but when it was approximately in mid-floor out from beneath it emerged, with a swimming motion, no less a figure than King Neptune himself, complete with crown, trident and seaweed hair, who after a few capers, turned to bow deeply towards the ship.

King James cheered lustily.

'This, I may say, is *all* His Grace's devising,' Patrick mentioned. 'Spare me any responsibility. It represents his triumph over the sea, no less. And his epic Jason-like quest to claim a sea-king's daughter. Now he lauds the voyage rather than the bride!'

An anchor was cast to the floor in realistic fashion, and out from the entrails of the vessel streamed a dozen boys, entirely unclothed save for caps of seaweed, bearing all sorts of fish and shellfish moulded in sugar and painted in their natural colours, for the delectation of the guests. Neither sweetmeats or boys lacked appreciation.

'I go now,' Patrick whispered. 'To prepare for what follows. If you are wise, my heart, and can tear yourself away from this spectacle, you will brave the royal wrath and come with me. You will not regret it, I swear!'

'How so...?'

'Our liege lord is not finished yet! Come.'

They were not quite in time. Slipping out behind the tables, father and daughter were nearing a side-door when the cannonade started. The model ship could only support comparatively small pieces firing blank shot, but even so, within the four walls of the Banqueting Hall, and only feet away from the crowded tables, the noise was appalling, causing the earlier bombardment to seem like a mere pattering of hailstones. Thirty-six consecutive detonations crashed out, the chamber shook, bat and bird droppings fell amid clouds of dust from the roof-timbers, and acrid smoke rolled and eddied everywhere, while men cowered and cringed, women stuffed kerchiefs into their mouths, threw skirts over their heads or merely collapsed, and even Neptune's youthful assistants scuttled from the scene as their fine vessel shook itself to pieces.

Up at the dais table, James was on his feet again – but this time nobody noticed, or rose with him. He was slapping his thigh and shouting his merriment – having of course come provided with his ear-plugs – a picture of uncouth mirth.

'Since Leith,' Patrick bellowed in Mary's ear, 'Majesty has become aware of the delights of gunpowder. Would that I had realised the price of victory!'

The girl nodded. 'I go to soothe my child. And his!' she cried, and fled.

When Mary returned to the Hall some time later, it was to find the King absent but armed guards permitting no guests to leave the chamber nevertheless, anxious as were many to do so. A sort of dazed torpor had come over most of the company – although some determined drinking was going on, as a form of elementary precaution, no doubt, against promised further regal entertainment. The air was still thick with throat-catching fumes.

Ludovick hurried to Mary's side.

'Would to God we could escape from this madhouse!' he

groaned. 'Oh, for Methven, and you alone! And Johnnie, of course. This is Bedlam, no less! James grows ever the worse. You are all right, my dear? I saw you go out...'

'I went to Johnnie. And the little prince. Patrick knew what was to come, and advised that I go. Both bairns were awake, the prince screaming but Johnnie quiet. They are now asleep.'

'You were wise to go. And fortunate! It was beyond all belief So sore was my head that I could not see. Besides the smoke. I was blind. Nor I only. Young Sussex was sick. All over the Countess of Northumberland – though I think she scarce noticed it. He is but a frail youth. And James has been paying him attentions, stroking him like a cat, which must alarm him. What tales he will take back to Elizabeth, the good Lord knows! He asked permission to retire – but James would have none of it. None must leave. He has quick eyes, even though they roll so! He even saw you leave, my dear, and would have had you brought back. But I told him that you would be going to see to the prince. He is but a step from madness, I do believe.'

'Hush, Vicky!' Mary laid a finger on his lips, glancing around them. 'Such talk is dangerous. You know it. We learned that before. Nor is it true, I think. The King is not mad. He is strange, yes. And capricious. But he is clever too. Quick with more than his eyes. Shrewd after a fashion. And frightened – always frightened. He was born frightened, I think – as well he might be! We owe him pity, Vicky – compassion. As well as loyalty.'

'Always you were generous, Mary. Kind-hearted. I still think him mad – or nearly so. After the cannons, he read us this poem that he has been writing for the christening – that you have been aiding him with. Even so it was a purgatory! And endless! Save that it was better than the guns.'

'He means kindly...'

'Does he? I think otherwise. He is but puffed up with foolish pride. And he shows scant kindness to his wife. The Queen sent for me to attend her, a little back – but James would not hear of it. I must wait, we must wait, to witness his next triumph! It is a great secret. Has Patrick told you what it is?'

'No. He but said that the King aimed to surpass himself. You know how Patrick would say that. But little of this night's doings are his work, I think.'

'Do not be so sure, my love...'

A fanfare of trumpets cut the Duke short. There was the clatter and stamp of hooves on the stone floor outside, and then into the Hall itself pounded three riders in wild career, scattering servitors right and left.

The wildness was not confined to the canter of heavy horses indoors; the riders were wilder still. Amazons they were intended to represent, undoubtedly, complete with long streaming hair, brief green skirts, and great flouncing breasts in approximately the right positions. Nevertheless, these were most obviously men, and identifiable men – indeed Scott of Buccleuch had not troubled to shave off his red beard, and with his long black wig and massive hairy limbs, made a fearsome sight. The other two were younger and less fiercely masculine – the Lord Lindores, formerly Prior of the same, Lady Jean's husband, painted and powdered with lips red as cherries, and Orkney's favourite illegitimate son, lately made Commendator-Abbot of Holyrood in place of his father, a graceful hairless youth adorned with the largest bosom of all.

Round and round the Hall this trio rode their spirited steeds, to mixed affright and acclaim, colliding with tables, upsetting furnishings, scoring and splintering the floorboards with iron-shod hooves. Armed with short stabbing spears, they made playful jabs at all and sundry, uttering eldrich whoops and falsetto cries. The Abbot's breasts, phenomenally nippled but unstably anchored, slipped round until he was able to hold them securely, one dome on either side of his left shoulder. Even the pale Lord Sussex smiled faintly.

A second blast of trumpets heralded more hoof-clatter, and in at the door rode, less precipitately, a figure in full armour, helmeted and visored, splendidly mounted and couching a long lance. This anonymous paladin was clad at all points as a Christian Knight of Malta, wearing no blazon and carrying no banner. But there was something familiar, even under the unbending armour, about the slouching seat and lolling head. Moreover, he was mounted on one of the King's favourite Barbary blacks. The Earl of Mar led a dutiful cheer, and everyone rose to their feet.

James trotted round the great room, graciously waving his

guests to their seats. The circuit made, he turned his attention to the Amazons, digging in his spurs.

As has been indicated, James was at his best on a horse, despite his peculiar posture. He rode straight at the Laird of Buccleuch. There was little room for manoeuvre in that place, and a high standard of horsemanship was demanded to remain even in full control of the beasts. In the circumstances, Buccleuch's avoidance of the royal lance-tip was masterly, especially as he made it seem a very close thing, and his return gesture with the short stabbing spear hopelessly wide of the mark.

This set the tone of the encounter. The Amazons dodged and jinked and ducked, however much their mounts slipped and slithered on the timber floor, and ferociously as they yelled and skirled, their counter-attacks were feeble and ineffective, even allowing for the inadequacy of four-foot spears against a twelve-foot lance. Not that the said lance was always accurately aimed either, but at least James wielded it with all the vigour of which he was capable.

It became evident that the object was to defeat the Amazons by separating them from their bosoms. That this was not entirely achieved by the royal lance-point was neither here nor there. To the plaudits of the company the trio were reduced to huddled shame and abasement – whereupon the enthusiastic monarch set about removing their long tresses also, a still more ambitious and hazardous procedure which soon had the demoralised Furies dismounted and running from the Hall, casting all trace of their femininity from them in shameless panic.

Thereafter, left victor, the King threw up his visor, and pantingly launched into a lengthy harangue and explanation. Because of his excitement and his breathlessness, and the hollow boomings of his helmet, his words were even less clear than usual, his Doric broader. But it seemed that what had been witnessed was an allegory of much significance and moral worth. The Amazons, it appeared, as well as representing undisciplined and assertive womanhood in general, also were to be identified as the evil harpies Witchcraft, Heresy and Treason, from whose grasp he, James, with God's help, was in process of freeing his realm. As the Viceroy of Christ, with the armour of faith and the lance of righteousness, he would smite these daughters of Satan hip and thigh.

James was warming to his theme when a servitor pushed his way to where Ludovick was standing, with Mary.

'I come from the Queen's Grace,' he said, low-voiced. 'She orders that you attend her forthwith, my lord Duke. By her royal command.'

'Command . . . ?' The young man bit his lip. 'James will not like this. Why should she want *me*? But – I cannot refuse her command.'

'No. You must go. The poor Queen – I am sorry for her. But she has her own dangers, Vicky. Be careful with her . . .' '

Patrick returned soon after Ludovick had left the Hall.

'You are elevated and informed, I hope, Mary?' he murmured.

'I am a little weary,' she answered.

He looked at her quickly. 'I don't think that I have ever heard you admit as much, before. Do not say that our puissant monarch is too much for Mary Gray! But it is near done now, lass. And the final act will revive you, I swear!'

'There is more to come?'

'A last tit-bit. That only His Grace would have thought of. Meanwhile, let us see if we may anywise shorten this homily.'

Patrick waited until the King's next needful pause for breath. Then he nodded to his man at the door. Just as James was about to recommence, music struck up from outside, fiddles, lutes and cymbals. A protesting royal gauntlet of steel was raised, but it was too late. In filed a column of sweet singers, the former Neptune's acolytes, now decently clad in black, reinforced by a number of older vocalists and instrumentalists. They were chanting the hundred and twenty-eighth Psalm, in fourteen-part harmony.

The King, whom life had made a realist of sorts, accepted the situation, and switched from declamation to lusty psalmody:

For thou shalt eat of the labours of thine hands
O well is thee, and happy shalt thou be . . .

he boomed from within his helmet, waving to all his astonished guests to raise bodies and voices in vigorous worship.

'James, by the grace of God, King. Protector of Christ's Kirk here on earth!' the Master of Gray observed. 'Look at Master Melville, my dear! And Lindsay. And Galloway. They are smiling, all. For the first time this night. The day is saved. The True Faith triumphs. King and Kirk are one, after all!'

'*You*, then, did have a hand in this, also?' Mary charged him.

'I? I do not even know the words of the psalm,' he said.

> The Lord shall bless thee out of Zion: and thou shalt see
> the good of Jerusalem all the days of thy life...

the King shouted, strongly if tunelessly:

> Yea, thou shalt see thy children's children, and peace
> upon Israel...

Chapter Eight

Falkland was the smallest of the royal palaces, and the little grey-stone, red-roofed Fife town which huddled round it, beneath the green Lomond Hills, as ever when the King was here, was bursting at the seams, every house, cottage, room even, taken up and overflowing with the host of nobles, envoys, courtiers, ministers, their families, retainers and servants. On this warm evening of early September, everyone seemed to have surged out of the crowded houses into the narrow streets and wynds, the gardens and pleasances and encroaching woodlands, for air and space. Ludovick Stewart, hot and tired after his long ride, pushing his way through the throng with only a groom in attendance, frowned at the milling crowds distastefully, wrinkled his nose at the stink, and cursed again the fate of birth which enforced on him a life for which he had no desire, amongst people with whom he had little sympathy, when all that he wanted was to live quietly, simply, at Methven with Mary. It was all wrong, and the sort of grudging affection he had always had for his cousin the King was suffering under the strain. He had hoped and expected that now that there was a prince, and he was no longer heir to the throne, the situation might have improved. But things were in fact worse, with James demanding ever more of his time and company – whilst yet finding fault with him constantly.

Just across from the palace gates, he was held up by a herd of bullocks being driven down to the slaughter-houses by the waterside, and further congesting the already crowded streets of the little town. The feeding of the Court here was ever a major problem, for Falkland was a hunting palace, set down in an area of forest, marsh and wilderness with no farming country nearby, and the influx of hundreds, even thousands, presented great difficulties of commissariat. Yet it was James's favourite house, and once the stags were in season and the threat of attack apparently receded, nothing would do but that the move from the confining fortress of Stirling twenty-five miles away must be made. But not for the prince; that precious babe's safety was not to be risked outside the castle walls. Therefore Mary Gray must needs remain at Stirling also, plead as Ludovick would. Hence his almost daily rides of fifty miles, and his monarch's oft-expressed complaint.

Before ever he reached his modest room in the palace, Peter Hay, Ludovick's page, met him.

'The Queen again, my lord Duke,' he announced. 'You are to go to her. At once, she says. For hours she has been having me seek you.'

Lennox groaned. 'What ails her now? What does she want with me, this time?'

'I do not know. But she is most strong. I was to bring you to her forthwith, she said. She is in her bower...'

'She can wait until I have washed, at least,' the Duke growled. 'Where is the King? Still hunting?'

'Yes. Since morning.'

When, presently, Ludovick presented himself at the Queen's apartments however, Anne had him kept waiting for a full half-hour in an ante-room, making the stiffest of talk to her ladies and ill concealing his impatience – for he was both hungry and tired. At length a bell tinkled to admit him to the presence.

The Queen stood with her back to him, facing a window of her boudoir looking out on the palace gardens. 'You have been long, Ludovick,' she said, without turning. 'Too long. On my soul, you pay a deal more respect to that by-blow of Gray's than you do to your Queen! I have been left alone all this day. Must you be off to Stirling all and every day, sir?'

'Had I not gone to Stirling, Ma'am, I would have been required to go hunting with His Grace.' That was gruffly said, it is to be feared.

'Aye – chasing stupid deer! The folly of it. Always chasing deer!' Anne's voice, still with traces of its guttural Danish accent, was accusing, petulant.

Lennox did not comment on that. 'You sent for me, Your Grace?'

'Yes, how is my child? How is the Prince Frederick?'

'Well, Highness. Never better.'

'Is that all you have to tell me? To say to me? His mother!'

Ludovick was not a hard-hearted young man and he did sympathise with Anne in her unhappy situation with regard to her baby. He cleared his throat. 'The child seemed happy. Contented.' Perhaps that was not the right thing to say to the deprived mother? But what could he say about an infant, that was merely a bundle of swaddling clothes and a pink screwed-up face? 'He is fatter a little, I think. Mary looks well to him.' That also might not be what she wished to hear? 'You need have no fears for the child, Highness.'

She did not directly answer that. When she spoke, however, her voice was quite changed. It had become soft, girlish, almost playful. 'Ludovick,' she said, 'come and sit here by me. I have tidings for you.' She sat down on a cushioned window-seat.

Without enthusiasm he had moved forward obediently before she half-turned towards him on the seat, and he perceived how she was dressed. Embarrassed, he faltered.

The Queen wore a long bed-robe of blue silk, but underneath it she was bare to the waist, below which there was some sort of underskirt. The robe was hanging open, and Anne was making no attempt to hide her body. Always she had had a figure more like a boy's than a woman's; but motherhood had developed her breasts. They were still small, but pointed. It seemed that she was proud of them, for the rest of her remained slender to the point of thinness.

When she saw the young man hesitate, Anne smiled. 'Come, my lord Duke,' she urged. 'Have you no compassion for me, left alone all the day?'

'I ... I am sorry,' he said.

She sighed. 'I am sorry also. I am no less a woman for being a queen, see you.' When still he stood irresolute, she pointed, imperiously now. 'Sit!' she commanded.

He lowered himself, almost gingerly, on to the very edge of the window-seat. This however brought him very near to the Queen's person. He sat back, therefore, into the corner; but even so, they were very close together.

Now that she had him there, Anne herself seemed to know discomfort, and turned to stare out of the window. She was less than a practised charmer. She had recently celebrated her twentieth birthday, although in manner and outlook she was old for her years. Sharp-featured, with darting pale blue eyes beneath her reddish-brown hair, with a determined small chin and tight mouth, she could lay few claims to beauty. But Ludovick perceived that she had indeed taken some pains with herself this evening, for as well as the sudden flush over her normally pale complexion, there were distinct traces of deeper colour on her cheeks, there was a dusting of dark shadow at her eyes, and her lips were carmined – as indeed, he realised, were the nipples of her breasts. Nothing of this recognition added to the man's ease.

They seemed to have nothing to say to each other now. Small talk had never been Ludovick Stewart's speciality. To look at her he found upsetting; to stare out of the quite small window brought his head altogether too close to the Queen's; so he gazed stolidly into the room – which, littered about with women's things, and with the door open to her bedroom beyond, failed to soothe likewise.

'Your Mary,' Anne jerked, at length. 'Mary Gray. She is very fair. And sure of herself. For such as she is.'

'She is . . . Mary Gray!' Ludovick answered briefly.

'She is like her father. Perhaps too much like her father.'

He did not answer.

'Your wife. Who died. Gowrie's daughter – the Lady Sophia Ruthven. She was a poor creature, was she not?'

She had roused him now. 'She was not my wife,' he answered hoarsely. 'I scarce knew her. We never lived together. We were forced to wed. But that did not make us man and wife. It was but a device. Of . . . others.'

She nodded. 'Many marriages are so.' Anne sighed. 'Queens' in especial.'

He cleared his throat. 'Perhaps, yes. You said that you had tidings for me, Ma'am?'

'But yes. They will interest you, I think, Ludovick. I have today had word, sure word, that Maitland is ailing. The Chancellor.'

Lennox looked at her now. 'Ailing? You mean, seriously?'

'Very ill. A sick man – and like to remain so. To worsen. He has left Edinburgh for his house in Lauderdale. And is never likely to come back again.'

'So-o-o!' The young man thought rapidly. He could not remain unaffected by the news, any more than could almost anyone else in Scotland – even though it was not necessary to be so undisguisedly gleeful as was the Queen. Maitland was not a popular figure, cold, sour, dry; but he was the most effective administrator Scotland had known for generations, and he had had the day-to-day running of the country in his hands for so long that his removal must needs in some measure concern all.

'You are sure? He is none so old a man. Fifty? No more . . .'

'The word is sure,' she nodded. 'Maitland's day is over.'

'His Grace? What says His Grace to this?'

'James does not yet know.'

Lennox raised his eyebrows. Who would inform the Queen before the King? And why? All knew that Anne hated Maitland. She had disliked him from the first, when he had accompanied James to Denmark to fetch her to Scotland. Then there was the business of Musselburgh. The rich regality of Musselburgh, with its revenues from coals, fisheries and salt-pans, had been given long ago by David the First to the Abbey of Dunfermline. Maitland had managed somehow to get these detached and into his own hands soon after the break-up of the old church lands. The Abbey of Dunfermline had been conferred upon Anne by James, as a wedding-present – but Maitland had clung to Musselburgh despite all her attempts to regain it. Lastly, since the Master of Gray had returned, it was whispered on all hands that Maitland had been behind the murder of the Earl of Moray by Huntly – and Anne had been fond of the bonnie Earl.

'Your Highness is sure that this is truth? If the King has not been told . . . ? It may be but some tale. Mere idle talk.'

'The Master of Gray's tales, Ludovick, are seldom idle, I think!'

'Ummm.' So here was Patrick's hand again. He might have guessed it. In which case the matter was serious, whether strictly true or not. And Patrick had come to tell the Queen; for some good reason of his own, no doubt. And the Queen had sent for himself. 'His Grace will be much concerned,' he said.

'His Grace will be better served, lacking Maitland! He is an evil man. Hard and cruel. The realm has too long suffered under his grip, Ludovick.'

'At least his grip was firm, able. As Chancellor he was strong. Who will succeed him?'

'Need any succeed him? Meantime. Should not James take more the rule into his own hands? Lest another become too strong. The Kirk – the Kirk would clamour that the new Chancellor should be of that party. Possibly the man Melville himself! Then the Kirk would indeed rule the King, as well as the kingdom. The King must rule. To that he is born. Should not the chancellorship be left in . . . in abeyance?'

Thoughtfully Lennox considered her. These words, these deliberations on a new problem of state, were not those of the twenty-year-old Anne herself, that he was sure. They could only be Patrick Gray's, using the Queen. Which meant that he was on the move once more. And it was not very difficult to perceive his direction.

'I see,' he said.

'My lord of Mar also would wish to be Chancellor,' the Queen went on. 'That would not be wise. He is not the man for it, and too greatly sways the King even now.'

That was true, of course – despite the fact that Anne looked on Mar as almost as much her enemy as was Maitland, since James had put the young prince in his keeping.

She reached out suddenly, to touch the young man's arm. 'Ludovick – it is our opportunity,' she said eagerly. 'To aid His Grace in the proper rule of this realm. James is timorous. He lacks judgment in many things. He is foolishly trusting. He needs our aid, Ludovick. Together, and with one or two others of goodwill, lacking Maitland we could take the rule in Scotland. For its good. And His Grace's good. Do you not see it?'

He drew back as far as he might into his corner. He could not well shake off the Queen's hand from his sleeve, any more than he could rise and leave her without permission. He was as uncomfortable over her intimacies as he was over her suggestions. Seldom, if ever, had Ludovick Stewart been so embarrassed.

Anne tightened her grip. 'Do you not see it, Ludovick?' she repeated, her voice a strange mixture of coaxing caress and impatience. 'Maitland has so long managed this realm that none other is ready to take his place. Save only Melville and the Kirk. That must not be, or there is an end to the Throne, to us all. But Queen and Duke acting together, behind the King. With others to aid us. With the Prince Frederick back in my care. Against such the Kirk could not prevail. Nor any other faction.'

'All this, Your Grace, according to the Master of Gray?'

Anne hesitated, searching his blunt features. 'The Master would aid us, no doubt...'

'Aye, no doubt. Or we should aid him. Or serve to shield him, rather...'

'But... he is your friend, is he not? Your Mary's father. You assisted him to return, after banishment.'

Heavily Lennox sighed. 'All true,' he admitted. 'But...' He shrugged. 'Let Patrick be. But myself – I am not your man for this, Highness. I wish the rule over none. I have no love for statecraft...'

Quickly she caught him up. 'Then, is not your love for me, your Queen, sufficient, Ludovick? Will you not aid me, for true love's sake? And therefore, of course, James.' She moved closer, so that her knee now pressed against his. 'Always you have been my friend. When others were not. When boorish lords and haughty clerics scorned me, a weak woman, you were kind. Always you were kind.'

'Majesty, it was but... it was but...' He swallowed. 'I am your friend, yes. Your true servant. But...'

'You like me well enough? Not only as a princess, but as a woman?'

He was intensely aware of her nearness – as well he might be. She was leaning forward, her gown hanging open, so that her pointed breasts were within inches of his hand, the perfume and faint woman-smell of her in his nostrils, the warmth of her leg against his own. He was no prude, nor cold, nor afraid of women; but Anne held no appeal for him. Yet, even had she not been the Queen, he could not have told her so, could not so grievously have wounded any woman.

'Your Highness is very fair. Very comely. And kind also –

most kind. I am honoured by your regard. But this of rule and power is not for me.'

'You were Viceroy of the realm once, were you not? When James was in my country?'

'Aye – in name. But only that. Patrick Gray decided all. He it was who ruled. I but signed my name to his edicts. And liked not all of them! I swore that never again would I do the like!'

'You are older now, a man, when then you were but a youth. A notable man, and strong – born to high things. You would not fail me? I need a man on whom to lean, Ludovick. James . . . he is scarce a man, I sometimes think! No woman, queen though she be, can stand alone. Even Elizabeth Tudor! And, God knows I am more woman than ever she was! This heart that beats in my breast, is it not a woman's heart? A frail and tender woman's heart that must needs serve a queen – and needs the more a strong man's sure support. Hold it, Ludovick, and see, feel . . .' She reached for his hand, and drew it to her left breast, holding it there. 'Tell me – does it say naught to you?'

Into Lennox's embarrassment and alarm flooded a great pity. He did not snatch his hand away – although neither did his fingers move to fondle her warm flesh. The recognition flashed upon him that here was a woman denied, starved of that dual love that was her due, the true love of both her husband and her child. That she had never before seemed to be a passionate woman – as Mary Gray, despite her inherent serenity, was passionate – might but mean that she had not been fully awakened. For she was young, his own age exactly, although he had been apt to think of her as older. He would not hurt her if he could help it. Yet . . . how to free himself of this tangle?

'Your Grace's heart is warm. And true,' he got out, hoarsely. 'It beats . . . it beats stout and sure, I vow, for those you love. For His Grace. The child. Your friends. Even myself, perhaps. I . . . all must rejoice in it. As I do. But – my, my devotion, my support, must be in humbler things than you ask, Highness. For affairs of state I have no inclination, no aptness. You named me strong – but I am not strong. Save only in my thews and sinews. In joust and tourney, or even battle – then I'd be your champion, with sword or lance . . .'

'And that you shall be, Ludovick!'

'But this other is not for me. If Patrick Gray again would steer the ship of state, let him . . .'

He broke off as upraised voices sounded beyond the boudoir door. The Queen still clung to his hand, but she too had her head turned and raised. A woman's voice rang out high and clear.

'Your Grace . . . !'

Lennox was just in time to jump to his feet, pulling his hand free, and taking a stride or two forward, when the door was thrown open and the King came in, his mud-spattered riding-boots scuffling.

'Annie! Annie – a white hart!' he cried. 'White – all white. We killed at yon Hainingshaws. Far out. A great bonnie beast, wi' a notable head. Never have I taken a white hart. I ran it miles – och, miles . . .' James's excited thick voice faltered and died away as he saw Ludovick. Then his great rolling eyes darted to his wife, and he screwed them up against the evening light that flooded in at the west-facing window. He perceived how the Queen was dressed – indeed she made no attempt to hide her comparative nakedness nor to draw the bed-robe closer. 'What's this? What's this?' he gobbled.

The younger man bowed. 'Your Grace,' he jerked. 'You have had a good day?'

'Vicky! Anne, woman! What's this? What's to do here?'

'Nothing is to do, James', the Queen told him coolly. 'Save that you stamp into my bower as though you were still hunting your deer! In mud and . . .'

'Wheesht, woman! What is Vicky Stewart doing here? Eh? And you this way? Look at yoursel', Anne! You're no' decent! Cover yoursel' up, woman – cover yoursel', I say!'

She stood up, drawing the robe around her, but turning a disdainful shoulder on her husband. 'Ludovick and I have been discussing the illness of the Chancellor – that is all,' she said.

'Wi' your paps hanging out!' he cried. 'Fine that! You'll no' tell me . . .' James paused. 'Eh? The Chancellor, did you say?'

'The Chancellor, yes. Maitland. He is an ailing man. He has gone to Thirlestane, and is not like ever to leave it.'

'Waesucks! Maitland! Hech, hech – sick? Sick to death? Na, na – it canna be. No' Maitland.'

She shrugged. 'Believe it or not.'

'Why . . . why was I no' informed, then?'

'You were away chasing your deer! All the day. The Master of Gray came from Edinburgh. At midday. Since you were not to be found, he came to me.'

'Patrick! It's *his* word?' The King tugged at his wispy beard. 'This is bad, bad. The Chancellor's the chief minister o' the realm. If Maitland has to yield it – who then? There's no' that many could play Chancellor! Guidsakes – here's a right coil!'

'Need there be a Chancellor? Always? Could not you rule your own realm? Are you dependent on such as Maitland to manage the kingdom?'

'Eh? What's that? No Chancellor?' James stared at her. 'Well, now . . .' He shook his head. 'Where's Patrick? I maun see him. Vicky – fetch you Patrick here.' Then James recollected. 'But . . . hech, hech! Bide a wee! No' so fast, man. First tell me – aye, tell me what you were doing here? Wi' Anne yon way. In her bower. The two o' you. Aye. Vicky Stewart – tell me that!'

'There is nothing to tell, Your Grace. The Queen summoned me here, on my return from Stirling. To tell me of this. This matter of Maitland. Yourself being absent . . .'

'Aye – absent! There you have it, Vicky! Mysel' being absent!'

'I but meant that the tidings being notable, Her Grace would discuss them with someone. Someone close to you, yourself being away . . .'

'Aye, close. Gey close! My being away! So she takes off her clothes, the better to discuss the matter wi' Vicky Stewart! Ooh, aye – fine I understand!'

'Not so, Sire. You greatly err, I swear!'

'Na, na! I'm no more a bairn than you are, Vicky. And there's nothing wrong wi' my eyes, mark you!'

'You are wrong nevertheless, Sire. On my honour . . .'

'Your honour? Och, well – your honour could be no' that reliable, Vicky! I've had a notion o' this, mind, this while back. Aye, I've seen you slipping off to Anne. Many's the time. Colloguing together.'

'I have been the Queen's friend, yes . . .'

'Friend! Aye, more the Queen's friend than the King's, I

jalouse!' The more Ludovick protested, the more furious James grew. 'I'll teach you to cuckold your liege lord!'

'James – a truce to this! You ill serve your own honour when you so assail the Queen's!'

'Say no more, Ludovick,' Anne urged. 'Here is only folly. Madness.'

'*You* would name me mad, woman!' James all but screamed. 'You, now – who bore my bairn!' He gulped, slobbering, seeking to win under control the tongue which was too big for his mouth. 'If . . . if it *was* my bairn! Aye – whose bairn was it? Was it mine, or his?' A trembling finger pointed from one to the other of them, as the King sobbed out his dire question.

The Queen swung round abruptly, without a word, and almost ran to her bedroom. The door slammed shut behind her.

The bang of it seemed to bring James more or less to his senses. He stared at the shut door in silence for a few moments, and then glanced sidelong at Ludovick, from under down-bent brows. 'Aye,' he said. 'Och, well.'

'Have I your permission to retire, Sire?' the younger man asked stiffly.

'Ooh, aye. Go. Aye, leave me.'

'I ask permission further, Sire, to leave the Court. To retire to Methven. Forthwith.'

'Eh . . . ? Methven? Na, na – wait you, man. That's another matter.'

'Your Grace cannot desire my presence here, believing me false. Nor do I wish to remain at Court.'

'*Your* wishes are no' the prime matter, Vicky. You're High Chamberlain, I'd remind you. On my Privy Council. Aye, and Lord Admiral o' this realm. At my pleasure.'

'It is my pleasure, Sire, to resign these offices.'

'Ha – hoity-toity! No' so fast, no' so fast! I'll maybe ha' need o' your services yet, Vicky Stewart. If Argyll finds Huntly ower much for him, likely the Admiral o' Scotland will need to go aid him!'

'And gladly, Sire. That would much please me. As you know, I would have gone north with Argyll two weeks ago had you permitted it.'

'Umm. Well – we'll see. But you're no' to retire from Court

lacking my permission, mind. And you're no' to take your Mistress Mary away from Stirling. I require her there. Mind that, too. You understand, Vicky?'

Lennox bowed stiffly, curtly. 'Is that all, Sire? Shall I send the Master of Gray to you?'

'No. No' now. I would be alone.'

Ludovick went storming through the palace to his own room.

'A fresh horse,' he shouted to Peter Hay. 'And food. Ale. In a satchel. I ride for Stirling forthwith.'

'Stirling? But . . . you are new here from Stirling!'

'Back to Stirling I go, nevertheless. See you to it – and quickly.'

'Yes, my lord Duke . . .'

Chapter Nine

The King of Scots sat in the Hall of Scrymgeour the Constable's castle of Dudhope, in Dundee town, biting his nails. Down either side of the great table the members of the hastily called Council sat, looking grave, concerned or alarmed – those who were sober enough to display any consistent expression. Eight o'clock of an October evening was no time to hold a Privy Council.

Alone, down at the very foot of the table, sat a beardless youth almost as though he was on trial, drumming fingers on the board – Archibald Campbell, seventh Earl of Argyll. James glowered everywhere but at him.

'They slew a herald wearing my royal colours!' the King muttered, not for the first time: This, of it all, seemed most to distress him. 'Huntly killed my herald! That's more than treason, mind – that's *lèse-majesté*!'

'It is the work of wicked and desperate men, fearing neither the ordinance of God or man, Sire!' Andrew Melville declared strongly. 'They must be destroyed. Rooted out, without mercy. In the past Your Grace has been too merciful.'

'The destroying and rooting-out would seem to be on the other foot!' the Lord Home snorted. 'Who will now do the rooting, Master Melville? The Kirk?'

'Aye, my lord – the Kirk will root right lustily! Have no fear. Pray God others may do as much!'

'If Argyll's six thousand Highlandmen ran before Huntly, how does the Kirk propose to destroy him, sir? By prayer and fasting?'

'My lord!' young Argyll protested from the foot of the table. 'My Highlanders did not run. They stood their ground and died by the hundred. Cut down by cavalry – Huntly had horse in their thousands. And mown down by cannon – Your Grace's cannon, which Huntly held as your Lieutenant of the North!'

'Ooh, aye,' the King said vaguely. 'The ill limmer!'

'We shot his horse under him. We killed his uncle, Gordon

of Auchindoun. Also Gordon of Gight. We sore wounded Erroll...'

'But you lost the day, man – you lost the day!'

'My lord of Forbes, with the Frasers and Ogilvies and Leslies, was to have joined me. They were but a day's march away. We were waiting them at Glenlivet when Huntly attacked. With cavalry and cannon...'

'Hear you that, Master Melville? Cavalry and Cannon!' Home taunted. 'That is what you face. On, the godly ranks of the Kirk!'

'Curb your tongue, scoffer – ere the Lord curbs it for you!' Melville thundered. 'Christ's Kirk will triumph!'

'Undoubtedly,' the Master of Gray intervened soothingly. 'So pray we all. Meantime, the Council must advise His Grace on his immediate action. May I ask my lord of Argyll if he knows whether Huntly pursues?'

'I think not. But how can I tell, sir? When all was lost, I was ... Tullibardine and others dragged me off the field. By main force. My Uncle Colin of Lundy was sore wounded at my side. Campbell of Lochnell my Standard-bearer, dead. I would have stayed – I would have stayed...' The young man's voice broke.

'Surely, surely, my lord,' Patrick nodded. 'None doubt your hardihood. We but would learn if Huntly is like to descend upon us here at Dundee. Whether he follows close? Or at all?'

'No. No – I do not believe it. Huntly lost greatly also. My Uncle John said he must surely lick his wounds awhile. And with Forbes and the others only a day away. We withdrew northwards after, after ... towards Forbes. My people were scattered. I sent to gather them. Sent Inverawe back to Argyll for more men. Left my uncle, Sir John of Cawder in command. Then hastened south to inform and warn His Grace.'

'Then, no doubt, were Huntly indeed hot on your heels, Sir John would have sent word. We should put out picquets to watch all approaches from the north – but I think we need have little fear of surprise. We can therefore plan how the situation may be retrieved.'

'That is so, Patrick,' James nodded sagely.

'We must back to Edinburgh,' the Earl of Morton roused

himself to declare, hiccuping. 'This is when that mis-miscreant Bothwell will strike. Back, hic, to Edinburgh, I say!'

'Not so,' the Earl Marischal countered. 'The capital is well enough defended. Most of the realm's cannon is there. Your Grace should advance, and raise the loyal north against the Gordons and Hays. Aye, and against the Douglases of Angus!' Keith, the Earl Marischal's estates, of course, were in the north; whereas Douglas of Morton's were south of Edinburgh.

'The north is more loyal to Gordon than, hic, to the King, I think,' Morton sneered. 'How many men will my Lord Marischal provide?'

'A thousand – given time to raise them.'

'We'll no' can go north, Your Grace,' the Master of Glamis, the Treasurer, protested. 'If Huntly can defeat six thousand Campbells how shall we face him wi' this? We should remain here, at Dundee. Mustering our strength. All leal men to assemble here. Within the month. Then, in strength, march against Huntly. Not before.' The Glamis lands lay close to Dundee.

'Wait a month and let all Scotland see Huntly set King and Kirk at naught!' Melville cried. 'Here is craven counsel, I say! In a month Bothwell could have railled again – raised new forces in the Border. The King of Spain could send men instead of gold. Papists everywhere would rise, acclaiming Henry of France's apostacy and Huntly's victory. Delay, my lords, can only hurt our cause, Christ's cause. The King set out on this progress to show the north who ruled in Scotland. I say let him continue. Let us march north tomorrow, trusting in God and the right! Take the bold course, Sire – and led by the Kirk your people will support you.'

Into the hubbub of challenge and mockery, Ludovick Stewart raised his voice. It was his first intervention. 'I agree with Master Melville,' he said. 'To go back now would be to concede defeat before all. This battle will have cost Huntly dear. Let us strike now while he is still not recovered. We can confront him within two days. From here.'

James plucked his thick lower lip. He did not look at Lennox, any more than he did at Argyll. In the month which had elapsed since the scene in the Queen's boudoir at Falkland, there had been a notable stiffness between the cousins. The King would not allow the other to retire from Court, but he behaved towards him almost as though he was not there. On his part, Ludovick was rigidly, coldly correct, and that was all – at the Court but not of it. All knew the cause of the trouble – the Queen's ladies-in-waiting left none in doubt – and whispers inevitably magnified the entire business dramatically, so that most had come to assume that Anne had indeed been Lennox's mistress; indeed the English envoy wrote to his own Queen to that effect. This progress to the north had, in consequence, come as a most welcome break to Ludovick.

'Aye, well,' James said. 'Maybe. I'ph'mm.'

The Master of Gray nodded. 'There is much in what all have said, Your Grace. I would humbly suggest that something of all should be done. Have my lord of Morton, and perhaps the Laird of Buccleuch, return south to strengthen the defences of Edinburgh. Call a muster here at Dundee. No doubt the Treasurer will be glad to remain here and see to it.' He raised a single eyebrow in the direction of the Master of Glamis, an old enemy. 'Although I think it need not take a month. For the rest, let us march north forthwith, as Master Melville advises. Before Huntly rallies again after this battle. My lord Duke is right – Huntly cannot fail to be ill prepared for us at this juncture. His victory was dear won, it seems. Erroll is out of the fight. Auchindoun, the best of the Gordon leaders, is slain. Angus is a weakling. Moreover, my lord of Forbes and the loyal northern clans have not yet been engaged. With my Lord Marischal and his Keiths, and the reassembled Campbell host of my lord of Argyll, we should outnumber Huntly three to one.'

'But not his cannon!' Home pointed out.

'Our strategy must be to give him no opportunity to use his cannon, my lord. We all know that cannon have their drawbacks. They are cumbersome, slow to move, and require a set target. At Leith, once Bothwell moved, our cannon were of no service to us. We must offer Huntly no target, seek not to bring him to battle, but to harass him at every turn. Attack not Huntly himself, but the Gordon and Hay lands of his lairds and supporters. So that they leave him to go defend their houses. Thus, too, shall we provision ourselves whilst cutting off *his* provisions.'

That was shrewd pleading. At the thought of the easy pickings, under royal license, of a hundred fat Gordon lairdships, many eyes gleamed and lips were licked. Only the Treasurer's voice was raised in opposition.

'How does the Master of Gray, Sire, ensure that his old friend Huntly obliges us thus kindly?'

'Your Grace – if we play our cards aright, he has no choice. He cannot move the Gordon lands and castles, that have been his pride and strength. Nor can he defend them all, or any number of them. We shall make them his weakness rather than his strength. We shall not fight my lord of Huntly and his host, we shall fight his broad provinces of Aberdeen and Buchan and Moray and the Mearns – and watch his army melt away like snow in the sun! I assure you...'

He was stopped by the great shout of acclaim.

Ludovick Stewart had great difficulty in making himself heard. 'I had not meant, Sire, that we should go to war against a land, an entire countryside. These are your people, as well as Huntly's. Your Grace's subjects...'

'They are rebels, young man!' Melville declared sternly. 'And Papists to a man. In arms against both God and the King! They must be rooted out, as were the Amalakites...'

'They are Christian men and women, sir. Fellow-country-men, fellow-subjects of your own.'

'We are well aware, my lord Duke, that Huntly is your sister's husband!'

'To my sorrow and hers! That was a marriage arranged otherwise!' He shot a glance from the King to the Master of Gray. 'On Huntly I would make war, yes – but not on the homes of his people!'

James frowned. 'Aye, but it's no' you that's making the war, Vicky Stewart! It's me. I, the King, make the war.' He wagged a finger. 'Me it is they rebel against, mind – no' you! They slew my herald, Red Lion. That's tantamount, aye tantamount, to an attack on my own royal person. It's no' to be borne.'

'Then we march, Sire? Northwards?' the Earl Marischal demanded.

'Och, well. I'ph'mm. Aye, it seems so, my lord, does it no'?'

'God be praised!' Melville exclaimed.

Patrick Gray caught Lennox's eye, and almost imperceptibly shook his head.

Perhaps two-thirds of the way up the long, long ascent of Bennachie, Ludovick of Lennox drew rein, to rest his weary sweating horse, and behind him his straggling column of something like one hundred men-at-arms thankfully did likewise. All Aberdeenshire seemed to slope up, from every side, to this thrusting central isolated cone of Bennachie, and if the Duke's magnificent Barbary black was weary and flagging, the lesser mounts of his followers were all but foundered. And not only the horses; the riders also were drooping with fatigue. Few would elect to go campaigning with the Duke of Lennox again, were they given the choice.

This land of Aberdeenshire was vast. so much more widespread, richer, populous and diverse in aspect than Ludovick had realised. They had been in the saddle since daybreak, and now it was mid-afternoon, and most of the intervening hours they seemed to have spent climbing, climbing towards this green rock-crowned pinnacle of Bennachie. There had been distractions, of course, diversions, turnings-off from the line of general advance; but these, in the main, Ludovick would have preferred to forget – if he could.

This was the second day of the advance into the great Gordon territories, and they were not yet within twenty-five miles of Huntly's inner fastnesses of the upper Don basin, of Strathbogie, Formartine and the Deveron. But yesterday, whilst still south of the River Dee, Ludovick had had his bellyful of the royal progress, and had urgently sought permission to lead instead one of the scouting forces which probed ahead of the main army, seeking contact with the enemy – since he could by no means bring himself to recognise as the enemy the occupants, men, women and children, young and old, of the innumerable houses, towers and castles, small and great, which were the object of the kingly wrath and the Council's policy, rebels as they might be named. Sickened, after witnessing the fate of a dozen such lairdships, belonging to Hays and Douglases and other lesser allies of Gordon, on the mere outer fringes of Huntly's domains, and finding his protests of no avail, he had chosen this scouting role of the advance-guard, hoping for clean fighting, honest warfare, in place of sack, rapine, arson and pillage, in the name of Kirk and Crown. Allotted a company mainly of Ogilvy and Lindsay retainers from Angus, with a leavening of more local Leslies and Leiths, his task, along with other similar columns, was to ensure that there was no unknown enemy threat ahead of the more slowly advancing and widely dispersed main punitive force of the King. The high pass between the two peaks of Bennachie, and its secure holding for the King, had been his day's objective.

Their route here had been devious indeed, despite the way that all the land rose to this proud landmark – for in this vast rolling countryside it was not sufficient just to press ahead; always they had to scour the intervening territory to left and right, to ascertain that there were no concentrations of men hidden in the far-flung ridge-and-valley system, with its spreading woodlands, and to link up regularly with other columns similarly employed. Groups of armed men they had encountered now and again, and some had even shown tentative fight – but these were small parties and obviously merely the retainers of local lairds, concerned to defend their homes. Although it was no part of his given orders to do any such thing, the Duke had further used up considerable time and effort in seeking out the towers and mansions in his area of advance, which might be linked with the Gordon interests, to warn their occupants of the fate which bore down upon them so that they might at least have time to save their persons, families, servants and valuables by fleeing to some hiding-place. These warnings had not always been well received nor acted upon; nor had Ludovick's men-at-arms considered the giving of them a suitable and profitable employment.

Now, turning in the saddle and gazing back eastwards and southwards over the splendid landscape which sank, in the golden October sunlight, in great rolling waves of tilth and pasture, moor and thicket and woodland, between Dee and Don, to the level plain of the distant, unseen sea, Ludovick stared, set-faced. From on high here, the fair land seemed to spout smoke-like eruptions from underground fires. There were the dense black clouds of new-burning brushwood and thatch;

the brown reek of hay and straw; the murky billows, shot with red, of mixed conflagration well alight; and the pale blue of old fires, burning low. All these smokes drifted on the south-westerly breeze to mingle and form a pall of solid grey that hung like a curtain for endless miles, as though to hide the shame of the land. Directly behind themselves, the fires did not start for perhaps five or six miles – though even so, it meant that the main force, still unflagging in its enthusiasm, was closer than Ludovick had imagined; but elsewhere the smokes were considerably further forward, almost level, if more scattered – indicating that not all of the advance-parties were, like his own, failing to further the good work in their necessarily more modest way.

Lennox, by now, well knew the significance of those different-hued burnings. The thick black represented thatch torn from cot-house roofs and laid against the walls of stone towers. These little fortalices of the lairds, with their stone-vaulted basements, gunloops and iron-barred small windows, were almost impossible to reduce without cannon, even for a large force, short of starving out the occupants; but they could be rendered untenable by the knowledgeable. Masses of dense-smoking material, heaped all around the thick walls almost as high as the narrow arrow-slit windows to vaults and stairways, and set alight, would soon produce, with the fierce heat, a strong updraught of air. This, sucked through the unglazed or broken windows into the interior of the house, especially the winding corkscrew stairways, could in a short time turn any proud castle into what was little better than a tall chimney. No occupant could endure this for long; all must issue forth for fresh air, or suffocate. The yellow and brown smoke was corn and hay barns burning. Other fuels produced their own coloration.

Silently the Duke pointed to where, perhaps eight miles south by east of them, in the area of their own march, a fire larger than the others was spouting dense black-brown clouds at the foot of the lesser Hill of Fare. The dark young man beside him, John Leslie, Younger of Balquhain, appointed as his guide and local adviser, nodded.

'Midmar Castle,' he said. 'Where we were at noon. Gordon of Ballogie's house. An old man. He said he would not leave, you'll mind. He would have done better to heed your warning, my lord.'

'He gave us food and drink. His wife was kind. And there were two girls, bonnie lassies . . .'

'Aye, his son George's daughters. Janet is . . . friendly. George is with Huntly. Yon will bring him home, I warrant!'

Ludovick said nothing. His thoughts went back to the only other occasion, three years ago, when he had viewed a castle in process of being smoked out – that grim February night at Donibristle on the north shore of Forth. Then Huntly himself had been the incendiary, and the victim, the Earl of Moray, unable to stand it longer, had leapt from a window, hair and beard alight, to run to the sea, and on the beach had been overtaken, run through by Gordon swords, and slashed across his handsome face by Huntly's own, Ludovick helpless to restrain it. Some would therefore call this but justice – save that it was not Huntly himself who now bore the brunt of it, but old men and girls, his innocent people.

Sighing, the Duke turned away. 'We shall move on up to the pass between the hill-tops,' he said. 'We shall secure that, and plan its defence. Then send out parties beyond, to ensure that there is no enemy near. To inquire also the whereabouts of my Lord Forbes's force. Is there a house convenient nearby where we may pass the night?'

'There is Balfluig, my lord,' Leslie answered. 'A Forbes house – but it is five miles beyond the pass.'

'Too far. We must be close at hand. Encamped, if need be, in the pass itself. An enemy column stealing through here could play havoc amongst the King's scattered forces.'

'Aye. But we need not all spend a cold night on the hill, my lord. I have just minded – there is a house nearer, *this* side of the pass. The House of Tullos. It lies yonder, maybe a mile or so more to the north, unseen in a fold of the hill. A snug place.

'Seton is laird – and married to a daughter of Gordon of Tillyfour!'

'Gordon!' Ludovick frowned, biting his lip. He was coming to dread the sound of the name. 'Another of them?'

'Aye – and Papists all.'

The Duke sighed. 'Then, they fall to be warned. But first the pass.' He looked wearily up the hill.

'Send a party up there, my lord. To the pass. No need for you to go. It has been a long day. Let us to Tullos. Our lads will soon inform us if there is aught amiss up there.'

'No,' Ludovick decided. 'That pass is important. Of all this country, there alone could Huntly slip through a force unobserved. I cannot leave it to others to see to. I must go prospect it. You, Leslie, go to this Tullos. My compliments to its laird. Take a score of the men. Say that we come peacably – but that tomorrow he would be wise to seek some sure hiding-place for his people. This night, if he will have us, we'll bide with him – and pay for our entertainment. If not, we shall spend the night in the pass well enough. It is for him to say, in his own house ...'

'But they are rank Papists, my lord!'

'I was born a rank Papist, sir – as, little doubt, were you! So speak them fair. I want no trouble. Remember our task – not to punish Catholics but to seek out Huntly. See to it, friend. I will come later.'

So Ludovick rode on up the long hill, with the majority of his men, whilst Leslie and a lesser company trotted northwards over the slantwise sheep-dotted pastures.

The pass between the Mither Tap and the Millstone Hill of Bennachie was a narrow defile of bracken, heather and rocks, one thousand feet high, breaking the long barrier of hill which so effectively divided the great shire of Aberdeen, the largest single area of fertile land in all Scotland. Because of its situation, with the land dropping away steeply on all hands, a comparatively few determined men could hold it against an army. Ludovick approached it very cautiously, quite prepared to find it held. But it proved to be clear. Also the onward slopes seemed to be devoid of life save for the scattered peacefully-grazing cattle which obviously had not been disturbed for long.

There was no lack of cover in the place, with great boulders and outcrops littering the sides of it, and Ludovick chose positions for his men, strong positions. He was not concerned with hiding their presence. Better indeed that the enemy should know that the pass was held against them, and so not attempt any passage thereof. Ludovick was by no means looking for trouble. He gave orders therefore that his men should gather fuel – dried heather-stems, roots, bog-oak, anything which would burn – to light fires and if possible keep them burning all night, so that they might be seen from afar. He sent pickets out to spy out the land ahead and appointed watchers and sentinels on the actual flanking hill-tops and ridges. Not until all was to his satisfaction did he leave, to ride back downhill towards the House of Tullos.

He saw the smoke almost as soon as he came out of the defile, and recognised that it came from the direction Leslie had taken. Set-faced, he spurred his jaded horse.

He never doubted that the fire was at Tullos. The smoke rose out of a sort of corrie, or fold in the hill – and Leslie had mentioned only the one such house. This was thick black smoke – like thatch again. It could scarcely be that – but whatever it was boded no good. Smoke, to Ludovick Stewart, now represented only sorrow and shame.

As he neared the cleft in the hillside he could hear the crackle of fire, interspersed with shouting. The quality of that shouting, coarse laughter, taunts and jeers, darkened the Duke's features.

Riding over the lip of the corrie, Ludovick saw that it was altogether a bigger and better place than he had anticipated. In a wide green apron on the lap of the hill sat a pleasant white-washed house backed by trees. Flanking its sides and rear was a farm-steading, barns and cot-houses, while an orchard slanted down in front to where a fair-sized burn was dammed to form a duck-pond, the whole looking out south by east over the prospect of a quarter of Aberdeenshire. The house itself was quite substantial, of two storeys and an attic, L-shaped, with a circular stair-tower in the angle and squat round corner-turrets at the gables. It had a stone-slated roof – but the roofs of the outbuildings and cot-houses were reed-thatched. It was this that was burning.

The shouting came from behind the house. Hastening there, Ludovick came to a cobbled yard between house and farmery. It was thronged with people, mainly his own men-at-arms, their horses feeding on heaps of hay thrown down at the windward side of the burning buildings where the drifting smoke would not worry them. The men were much and noisily engaged. None even noticed the Duke's arrival.

Ludovick spurred forward to see what went on within the circle of shouting troopers. Apart from these, there were two groups of people in the centre of the courtyard. One contained a middle-aged, heavily-built man, a buxom woman, a boy in his teens and a girl still younger. These, plainly but decently dressed, were all held fast by soldiers, being forced to watch the proceedings. One of the man's eyes was practically closed up by a blow. The other group was larger, obviously servants and farm-hands huddled together in cowering fear. The women's clothing was noticeably disarranged and torn. They stared at what went on in the centre.

There, a peculiar proceeding was being enacted, whither was directed all the shouting. Two people were being forced to kneel on the cobbles, gripped by men-at-arms – a comely young woman and facing her a young man in rent and soaking blood-stained shirt, with blood trickling down from his hair. These were notably alike in feature, and looked as though they might be brother and sister. Between them, on a stone mounting-block, stood a carved wood crucifix perhaps eighteen inches high. Nearby was a half-barrel of water.

The young man and woman were being forced to fill their mouths with the water, and then to spew it out over the crucifix. At least, that was their tormentors' intention. In fact they were spilling and ejecting it anywhere but upon the cross. For their obstinacy they were being kicked, their arms twisted and mugfuls of the water thrown in their faces, to mingle with the girl's tears and the young man's blood.

Appalled, seething with anger, Ludovick drove his black horse straight into the press of the men. 'Fools! Oafs! Animals!' he exclaimed. 'Stop! Enough! Have done, I say!'

Leslie came pushing towards him, gesticulating. 'My lord, my lord!' he cried. 'I couldna help it. They'll no' heed me. I've told them . . .'

Ludovick ignored him, shouting at the men around the crucifix. He in turn was ignored.

Leslie reached for the black's bridle, and held on to it. 'They'll not heed me,' he insisted. 'I can do nothing with them. But it's Seton's own fault. He resisted us. They're all stiff-necked, insolent. One o' his people drew a sword on us . . .'

'I told you. You were to speak him fair. There was to be no trouble. You were in command. You are responsible.'

Leslie looked half-frightened, half-defiant. 'They are not *my* men. I never saw them before this day. They scoff at me. One in especial – yon red-headed stot Rab Strachan . . . !' He looked very young and inadequate there amongst all that passion and violence – although he was possibly a year or so older than Lennox.

'Here – take my horse!' Ludovick threw him the reins, and leapt down. He pushed his way through the throng, elbowing men aside. He came to the central space.

'I said stop that!' he snapped. 'Unhand these two – d'you hear! At once.'

Men turned to stare now, and the shouting died away. But the comparative quiet only emphasised the crackling roar of the burning roofs, with its own inflammatory effect on the tempers of men. Even the heat engendered inner heat. Lennox himself was affected by it. He could hardly control his voice.

'You . . . you louts! Sottish numbskulls!' he yelled, when none answered him. 'Do as I say.'

None moved. None released their grip on the unfortunate pair at the crucifix, or on those forced to watch. Then a big and burly red-haired man deliberately stooped, to scoop up a mugful of water from the barrel and throw it hard in the girl's face.

Blazing-eyed Ludovick strode up to the fellow, and slapped him across the face, twice, right and left, with the palm and back of his hand. 'Brute-beast!' he jerked. 'Miscreant! Obey, fool!' He swung round, to grasp the shoulder of one of the troopers who held the young woman, and flung him aside. 'I said unhand her, scum!' He stooped, to take the girl's arm.

It was the warning in the kneeling young man's eyes that saved him. Ludovick twisted round, just in time to avoid a savage, swinging clenched-fisted blow from the red-headed Strachan.

He side-stepped, rage boiling up within him, his hand dropping to his sword-hilt. Then he mastered himself somewhat, and drew back a little in distaste. The last thing to be desired was for him to become involved in a brawl with his men. 'How

141

dare you!' he cried. 'Stand back, man! All of you – do as you are told. Back to your horses. Back, I say!'

'No' so fast, your Dukeship – no' so fast!' the man Strachan declared thickly, standing his ground and scowling. 'Why so hot? Eh? What ill are we doing, sink me? We're but justifying thrice-damned Papists!'

'Aye,' one of the others supported him. 'Where's the harm? They're a' doing it. The others, Shauchlin' Jamie, the King, himsel'! Why no' us? Doon wi' the sh-shtinking rebels, I say!' Like the other, he spoke indistinctly. Obviously they had been drinking; presumably they had found liquor in the house.

There were hoarse shouts of agreement from all around.

'Silence! You dare to raise your voices to *me*! Lennox!' Ludovick glared round at them all. He reached for the young woman's arm again, and raised her up. She stood trembling and sobbing at his side. He twitched off the short riding-cloak that hung from one shoulder, to drape it around her near nakedness – at which mocking laughter rose from his men.

The red-head pointed. 'See – that's it!' he hooted. 'He wants the bitch for himsel'! Our Dukie wants her ...'

'Hold your idiot tongue! I am Chamberlain and Admiral of this realm. You will obey my orders. And without question. Or die for it! 'Fore God – this is the work of felons! Savages! And dolts! Leslie – here! Take this girl, and this young man. Into the house. Forthwith. And release the laird and his lady. I will deal with these fools. Come ...'

As without enthusiasm John Leslie came forward, some of the soldiers barred his way. An angry murmur arose. Leslie was fairly easily dissuaded.

'Here's idolatry!' Strachan shouted. 'They're Popish idolators. Bowing down to idols. The Kirk says we're to root them oot. Aye, and the King, too! He says it. If the Duke o' Lennox doesna ken better, he needs teaching, I say!'

There was a great shout of acclaim.

'Would he have us bear wi' images and idols? Eh?' The man spat in the direction of the crucifix. 'We'll teach him ...'

'You imbecile! You ignorant clod!' Ludovick turned, and snatched up the cross. 'This is no idol. This is the simple symbol of your Saviour. Of Christ, who died on such a cross.

For you and for me. For this girl and this man likewise. For Protestant and Catholic alike. We are all Christians, are we not? Christ died on the cross for all men – not just for some. For the mistaken, for sinners – aye, even for fools like you! And you spit on His cross!'

'It's an image!' Strachan insisted heavily. 'Made wi' men's hands. A graven image...'

'It is a symbol. As is the King's crown. As is that blazon you wear.' He pointed to the blue and white fesse checky, the arms of the House of Lindsay, painted on the man's breastplate of steel. 'A sign. Of something that means much. If you spit on Christ's cross, you spit on Christ Himself!'

'Talk! Just talk – and accursed Papist talk at that! You'll no' cozen us, laddie, wi' your ill talk – Duke or nane! Images are images, and them that bow doon to them, damned! They've to be rooted oot...'

'Likely he's a Papist himself!' a small dark man shouted shrilly. 'They say his sister's married on Huntly!'

'Aye, like enough. Sold to the Whore o' Rome!'

'A buidy Catholic – like a wheen ithers aboot the King!'

'Doon wi' the fell Papists!'

As the uproar mounted, Ludovick handed the crucifix to the wounded youth who now stood at his side. Then grimly, silently, deliberately, he drew his sword from its sheath. The weapon came out with the creaking shrill of steel. It was but a thin high sound, but it seemed to cut through the hubbub of angry voices as though with the slender blade's own keenness.

The shouting died away, to leave only the roar and crackle of fire and the jingle and stamp of restive horses.

Lennox gestured to the brother and sister to follow him, and moved forward directly towards the house, sword-point extended before him.

In the face of that flickering steel men fell back. When one, bolder than his fellows, seemed to hold his ground, the blade leapt out like a striking snake, and the fellow jumped aside cursing – but discreetly.

The Duke, with the two youngsters close at his heels, came up to where Seton of Tullos, his wife and the other two children were held fast.

'Free them,' he jerked at their captors, reinforcing his command with a flick of the sword. To Seton himself he bowed briefly. 'My apologies, sir. I am Lennox. All this is directly against my orders. Madam – believe me, I am sorry.'

Neither the laird nor any of his household made any reply. They stared from angry hostile eyes, in hatred.

'Into your house,' Ludovick directed tersely. 'All of you. Take your people. Lock your doors. Quickly. But . . . be gone by morning, if you value your lives! To some hiding-place. When the King comes.'

As they turned to go, without a word, it was the bloody-headed youth again who warned Lennox. 'Sir . . . !' he said, glancing back urgently.

Ludovick swung round. The man Strachan had drawn his own sword, and was advancing upon him menacingly.

When the fellow saw that he was observed, he raised his voice. 'Hey, lads – come on!' he yelled. 'We'll teach this Romish duke to name us names! To call us fools and savages. God – we will!'

He gained much vocal support, and a few of his companions crowded behind him, but only one actually drew his sword.

Ludovick smiled now, thinly, grimly, his blunt boyish features much altered. Flexing his blade purposefully, he moved in to meet them.

The red-head, nothing loth, came at him fiercely, heavily, at one side, his colleague, the same dark wiry man who had announced Lennox's relationship to Huntly, dancing in in bouncing fashion on the other. Ludovick made a swift assessment. He seemed to make directly for Strachan, but just before they closed he swung abruptly to the left and lunged at the small man. Taken by surprise his opponent skipped backwards, and a second quick feint by the Duke sent him further back still, blinking. Ludovick swung on Strachan.

This one had not half the speed of his friend, but he had a furious determination. His vicious slash at Lennox would have cut him down there and then, and for good, had it struck home – and indeed the Duke only avoided it by instants and inches. The backhand sideways stroke which he flashed in return only rang upon the other's steel breastplate.

Ludovick leapt clear, his glance darting round the circle of the other men-at-arms. He saw no sympathy for himself in their eyes – but none had drawn their swords. Reassured, he turned his full attention on his two immediate assailants.

He allowed Strachan to rush him, almost scornfully side-stepping and warding off the jabbing thrust with a parry and twist of the wrist. Then, as the man stumbled past, he beat him insultingly across the back with the flat of his blade, and in a single complicated movement switched to the dark fellow, his point flickering and flashing about like forked lightning. Before even this agile customer could win clear, his sword-hand wrist was slashed and spouting blood and only the tough leather sleeve of the hide jerkin he wore beneath his breastplate saved his entire arm from being ripped up. With a yelp of agony he dropped his weapon, and stumbled back clutching his wounded wrist.

Lennox turned back to the red-head. That individual, though still gloweringly angry, was wary now, as well he might perceiving something of the quality of the Duke's swording. Ludovick had learned the art, from boyhood, at the hands of the Master of Gray – who was possibly the finest swordsman in all Scotland. Not for him the lusty but crude cut-and-thrust of men-at-arms. Moreover his blade was much lighter and more manoeuvrable than that of the heavy cavalry sabre used by the troopers. Strachan's only advantage was in his slightly longer reach and the fact that he wore leather and steel against the Duke's mere broadcloth.

Ludovick undoubtedly could have dealt with the big man, alone, in a very short time. But his intentions were otherwise. He was not merely fighting Strachan; he was concerned to re-impose his authority and control over his mutinous soldiery. So they should be taught a lesson, through this over-bold red-head.

Therefore he sought to play with the man, and to make it obvious to others that he was so playing – a dangerous game for both of them. Round Strachan he skipped and gyrated, flicking, darting, feinting with his sword, pinking the leather jerkin, tapping the steel breastplate – and avoiding the other's ever more wild rushes. What he was doing must have been apparent to all – he hoped with the desired effect.

There was one effect, however, which Ludovick had not bargained for. Strachan, perhaps, had a close friend amongst the watchers; or it may have been the dark man's friend. A shout from Leslie, in the background, saved the Duke – but only just. A thick-set bull-necked man had picked up the wounded trooper's sabre, and now sprang at Ludovick with this held high.

It was almost disaster. Flinging himself out of the way of the descending blade, the younger man all but impaled himself on Strachan's sword. The point of it indeed ripped through his doublet at the back of the shoulder, to come out again at the front, fortunately merely grazing the skin. Not so fortunate was the fact that for the moment it transfixed him, skewering through his tightly-buttoned doublet. He lost his balance, toppling.

Although this mischance had the effect of temporarily disarming Strachan, it also left the Duke wide open to the other man's attack. Desperately he took the only course left open to him – he hurled himself down at the red-head's knees, encircling them with his left arm. The force of his unexpected attack and the other's own impetus, brought them both to the ground with a crash. The third man, unable to halt his advance in time, cannoned into and fell headlong over them.

Great was the confusion. Ludovick, however, had the small but significant advantage in that he was not taken by surprise. He had done what he did deliberately. While the others scrabbled and floundered he, despite the handicap of the sword through his doublet, was purposefully wriggling himself free. He still clutched his own sword, and as the stocky man, on top, struggled up, the Duke, with a great effort twisted himself into a position where he could reach up and bring down the pommel of the weapon hard on the back of the other's neck. Grunting, the fellow sagged, and slewed sideways.

Somehow Ludovick got himself out from under them – and staggering to his feet abruptly found himself in command of the situation. Strachan now had no sword, and on top of him the other man was dazed, moaning. Panting, Lennox tugged out the skewering blade from his shoulders, and so stood, a weapon in each hand.

He stared round at the circle of watching faces. None of the others had drawn sword. No eye met his own. All gazed fascinated at their two colleagues helpless below him.

Ludovick's sigh of relief was lost in his deep breathing. For long moments he stood; there was no hurry now.

Then he sheathed his own sword, making something of a play of it. But as the stocky man was unsteadily rising to his feet, the Duke quite leisurely leant over and brought down the flat of Strachan's weapon on the man's wrist, not hard enough to break the bone but enough to make the unfortunate drop his sabre with a cry of pain. Ludovick kicked the weapon out of the way, and then, stepping forward, slapped the man across the face and pointed peremptorily over towards the horses. He stood blinking for a moment, and then turning, tottered away, mumbling.

A sort of corporate sigh issued from the ranked spectators.

Strachan was now on all fours, looking up at the younger man with fear in his eyes.

'You I should kill,' Ludovick said slowly. 'You are not fit to live. Can you think of any reason why I should spare you?'

The man gulped, but found no words.

'Speak, oaf! Can you, I say?'

'N'no, lord.'

'Nor can I. Save, I suppose, that Christ died for you, as I said! Is that sufficient that *I* should spare you?'

Hope dawned in Strachan's eyes. He began to gabble. 'Aye, lord. Ha' mercy, lord. Aye – spare me, for sweet Christ's sake! Spare me, my lord Duke!'

'If I do, it is not I who spare you, but Christ's cross. Which you spat upon! Yoo hear? Christ's cross. Remember that, always.' He looked up. 'And you all. Remember it, and take heed.' Then he held out his hand. 'Here is your sword, man.'

The other stared at the sabre proffered him, scarcely comprehending. He did not even put out his hand to take it.

Shrugging, the Duke tossed the weapon to him, and turned on his heel, ignoring him thereafter. 'Leslie,' he called. 'Have all men mounted forthwith. Then up with them to the pass. Do not wait for me. I go speak to Seton.'

There was a general move towards the horses almost before Lennox had finished speaking. The incident was over.

Another house, another godly assault, more faith, fervour and fury. And again Ludovick Stewart groaned in spirit. But this time he had to restrict himself to groaning, and that inwardly. For the assault was by no means confined to unruly men-at-arms; the highest in the land were involved, from the monarch downwards.

It was two days after the affair at Tullos – and no battle had taken place. There had been isolated scuffles between small parties on both sides, but the main forces had not been engaged. It seemed evident now that Huntly dared not attack the King, indeed did not even dare to take vigorous defensive action. For this house which was now being assailed was none other than his own great Castle of Strathbogie, for centuries the headquarters of Gordon power in the North.

At first, on arriving at Strathbogie, there had been a sort of constraint about everyone, despite the sense of jubilation and assurance, ever growing, which these days possessed the King and his army. Strathbogie was so vast a place, so proudly assured itself, as to daunt even the boldest – although Ludovick's advance-party had duly sent back word that it was not in fact even occupied much less being defended, and there was no sign of an enemy force within a dozen miles. It had taken some little time, when the royal force came up, for the sense almost of awe to wear off, in the face of this mighty establishment which spoke so eloquently, however silently, of enormous wealth, entire authority, almost unlimited power, in a way that none of the royal castles and palaces seemed to do. This was no military fortress, towering on top of a frowning rock like Edinburgh or Stirling; it was not even in a notably strong position within the spreading parkland and water-meadows at the junction of Bogie and Deveron – and the very lack of these obvious defensive precautions spoke of the complete confidence of the Gordon chiefs, Cocks o' the North for centuries, that here amongst their Grampian foothills in the centre of a million acres of Gordon-dominated territory, they were entirely, perpetually secure. This Strathbogie was not so much a castle or palace as a city in itself, surrounding and building up to the great central mass of masonry which was the citadel, tall, commanding, serene. That all this should be utterly devoid of life this October day only added to the sensation of eeriness, as of something wholly assured, infallible that but waited to strike.

James himself, these last days, had become a man transformed, as the certainty grew upon him that his coming had changed Huntly from being a rampant and ever-present menace to something like a wary fugitive. Strathbogie abandoned before him had seemed like the crowning of his efforts. Nevertheless, when he had walked through the empty halls and corridors of the Gordon citadel, he had been much affected, doubtful again. Even the riches littered there in such profusion – plenishings and furnishings, tapestries, plate, pictures, gold and silver ware – although they had him licking his lips and ordering all to be packed up and sent to Holyrood, Falkland, Stirling or Linlithgow, nonetheless made him uneasy. That any man could go and leave all this behind him, wealth grievously unsuitable for any subject, somehow oppressed him. It must argue vastly more elsewhere, to be sure.

But now James was confident again, restored in spirit. The first blasts of gunpowder had done that; there was something so positive and vigorous about gunpowder, and the King had developed an extraordinary faith in it. Not that it was proving very effective at Strathbogie as yet. Many of the surrounding buildings were tumbling down nicely – but the main central range was altogether too massively built, with walls ten to twelve feet in thickness, with iron-hard cement; it would require ever greater charges of explosive, ever bigger bangs. But meantime there was ample good work to be done on a different scale, much faithful effort requiring direction.

The Kirk needed no egging on, at all events. Led by Andrew Melville, the covey of ministers who accompanied the army and acted as local recruiting-officers, had all along marched and campaigned like troopers, fighting vehemently where opportunity offered, strong in the Lord's work. Melville had actually borne a pike throughout. Now he was zealously demonstrating to an admiring group how that horror of horrors, the Popish chapel of Strathbogie, could be demolished with greatest effect.

The King was more concerned with the castle itself. As well as cavities to be made in the great walls, for the explosive charges, there were battlements and parapets to be toppled, windows to be torn out, stone carvings to be defaced. He had to keep an eye also on the unending stream of men who emerged from the castle, ant-like, bearing idolatrous images, shrines and pictures, as well as doors, panelling, tables, benches and other non-valuable plenishings, to feed the flames of two huge bonfires which burned in the large main courtyard – for of course it was necessary to ensure that nothing of real worth was destroyed.

Ludovick, already roundly rebuked as faint-heart, backslider and appeaser of evil, who had been pacing restlessly, unhappily, to and fro near the King, turned to go and seek the Master of Gray whom he had noted earlier entering the castle pleasance. He found him, stretched out in a garden-house, making the most of the October sunshine, a picture of relaxation and ease.

'Patrick,' he cried, 'can you not do something to halt this folly, this destruction? This senseless violence. It is like a plague, a pestilence, sweeping the land!'

The Master yawned. 'My dear Vicky,' he said, 'why fret yourself? What's a little burning and knocking down of masonry? It relieves feelings which might well burst forth in worse things.'

'You sit there and say that? When the King himself leads the folly, pointing the way for others. And when on you lies much of the responsibility!'

'On me? Shrive me – how could that be?'

'Was it not you who advised James to this course? Destroy the Gordon homes, you said, so that Huntly's army may melt away. Do not fight battles, you said – burn roofs instead, and Huntly cannot strike back. Well, you were right. Huntly is beaten without a battle. But not without cost. The price paid is a king and people with the lust of destruction. Are you proud of your handiwork, Patrick?'

The other shook his handsome head. 'On my soul, Vicky, you astonish me! Since I made your education my own concern, I must indeed be at fault. I would have thought that your judgement would better this. Has it not occurred to you that in this sad world we cannot always have perfection? That ill exists and will not be wished away – so that the wise man makes the best that he can out of it, and does not weep and wail that all is not excellence...'

'Spare me a homily, Patrick – from *you*!'

'Someone else said that to me, not so long since. Our Mary, I think. The saints forbid that Patrick Gray should take to preaching! Could it be a sign of premature age? I shall have to watch for this! Nevertheless, may I point out, my good Vicky, that I feel I scarce deserve your censure, for seeking to make better what might have been infinitely worse. Is it not infinitely more desirable that stone and lime should be dinged doun, wood and gear burned, than that men should be slain? That was the choice. Huntly had to be defeated if James's crown and realm was to be saved. Enough blood has been spilt at Glenlivet – but that would have been as nothing to the bloodshed that must have followed had this course not been taken, whoever won. I do not like bloodshed, Vicky, however ill my reputation. And of all bloodshed, civil war is the most evil . . .'

'What do you name this? Ludovick swept an eloquent arm around to encompass all smoking Aberdeenshire. 'Is this not civil war most damnable?'

'No, lad – it is not. I have seen civil war. In France. The same weary, sad folly, between Protestant and Catholic. And it is much . . . otherwise. The dead choking the rivers, men, women and children, stinking to high heaven! Cities in ashes. Forests hanging with corpses. Disease and famine rampant. By the Mass, I will do much to keep such from Scotland! This . . . this is a mere punitive expedition by the King. A corrective display, that serves to enforce the royal authority, and at the same time leads to the disintegration of the Gordon host. Only material things are being destroyed in this. They can be replaced. New houses will go up, new sacred carvings be contrived . . .'

'You name it but material things when men and women are forced to deny their faith at the sword-point? When terror is called God's work? When the price of safety is to renounce belief?'

'Would you prefer that it should be battle, then? Slaughter and blood? Thousands dying for these same beliefs? Is my way not the better?'

The Duke was silent.

'These days will pass, Vicky, and men will be but little the worse for the heat and fury. But dead men will not live again. It is ever the way with religion . . .'

''Fore God – you, a Catholic at heart, talk so! I noted you swore by the saints and the Mass, back there. I cannot understand you, Patrick.'

'Am I a Catholic at heart?' the other wondered. He waved a lazy hand around. 'Might I suggest, lad, that you moderate your voice, if not your words? The phrase could almost be construed as a charge of highest treason hereabouts! Let us not add fuel to the already well-doing fire! Say that I am an undoubted but doubtful Christian, and leave it at that! That I value the substance higher than the form – unlike most alas!'

'So you will do nothing to halt this wickedness? You, who are as good as Chancellor of the realm, and can sway the King more than any other man!'

'You flatter me now, I vow! And I am not convinced of the wickedness. This Strathbogie is but a house, when all is said and done. Huntly is the richest lord in all the land – much richer than our peculiar liege lord James. He has enriched himself at the expense of many. Even at *my* humble expense, when he cost me Dunfermline Abbey! A little wealth-letting will hurt only his pride – of which he has over-much. And pride is a sin, is it not? So we do him little disservice . . . !'

'On my soul, you are impossible!' The younger man swung about and went stalking back whence he had come.

After a few moments, the Master rose unhurriedly and went sauntering after the other.

Back at the courtyard the work went merrily, enhanced by the infectious enthusiasm of Andrew Melville, who, having seen the demolishment of the chapel well under way, had now turned his attentions to the secular challenge. He was attacking the citadel walling with intelligence and vigour, as an example to feebler folk. Using an ordinary soldier's halberd, he was picking and probing shrewdly at the mortar around the masonry of a gunloop, an effective method of making a cavity large enough to take a major charge of gunpowder.

James was examining a handsome carved-wood chest which he appeared to have rescued from the bonfire. Beside him stood a protesting black-robed divine, comparatively youthful, his gown kilted up with a girdle, and long dusty riding-boots showing beneath. A group of grinning lords stood around, watching.

'It's a bonny kist, man,' the King insisted. 'Right commodious. It could be put to good and godly use.'

'It is stained with the marks of idolatry.' The minister pointed to a carved panel containing the intials I.H.S. flanking a cross. 'Evil cannot be countenanced in the hope of possible good to follow, Sire.'

'Ooh, aye. But this is no' a' that evil, maybe! Just the letters and a bit cross. There's ... ha ... there's a cross in your own coat-armour, Master Melville!'

'I do not use or acknowledge such vanities, Sire!' the young preacher declared. This was James Melville, nephew of Andrew, and no less positive in his views. 'There must be no truck with sin. Idolatry is sin, and these things are idolatrous.'

'Oh, no' just idolatrous,' James contested. 'A thing's no' idolatrous until it's worshipped, man.'

'No! No Sire I say! An idol is an idol, whether you or I worship it or no! It should be hewn down and broken in pieces and utterly destroyed, according to the word of the Lord!' The utter blazing-eyed authority of the statement set the King biting his nails – but still tapping at the oak chest with the toe of his boot.

From the rear Ludovick spoke up. 'You, a minister of Christ's Kirk, then name the cross of Christ an idol?' he demanded.

'Christ's true cross, no sir. Vain and paltry representations of it, yes!'

'That true cross exists no more. Is not its symbol to be reverenced?'

'The only honest symbol of Christ's cross is in the hearts of his elect, sir! No other is to be acknowledged. All images are false.'

'Yet you reverence the image, the symbol, when it represents the reality which is absent, do you not? Even you and your like! You acknowledge the signature on a letter, do you not? It is not the reality, only the symbol. The seal on a document, proving it valid. On your ordination papers, sir. That also you acknowledge, do you not? Representing due authority. His Grace, here – his crown. The image of that crown represents

the King's power when he is absent. Much is done in its name –
must so be done. Do you spurn the royal crown?'

'Aye, Vicky – you have the rights o' that!' James said – one
of the few words of commendation addressed to the Duke in
weeks.

'I do not worship crown, seal or signatures!' James Melville
declared stiffly.

'And I do not speak of worship. Only reverence. Respect. You,
who name yourself reverend, should know the difference.'

There was a murmur of amusement from the listening lords,
few of whom loved the ministers.

'These are different, quite,' the other jerked. 'I deal with
God's affairs, not men's.'

'Then I think you are presumptuous, sir! God made you a
man, and set you in the world amongst other men. Is it not said
that the sin of presumption is grievous? Almost as grievous as
idolatry?'

The King all but choked with a sort of shocked delight.

'Sir – beware how you mock the ministers of the Lord!'
James Melville exclaimed hotly.

'I do not mock,' Ludovick assured. 'I am full serious. More
serious than you, I must believe, when you name this poor
block of wood God's affair!'

James slapped his knee, and hooted. 'Man, Vicky – I didna
ken you had it in you!' he cried – though with a quick glance over
towards Melville senior, who was still picking away at the
Strathbogie masonry.

'My lord Duke is a man of hidden depths, of many surprises,
Your Grace,' the Master of Gray observed conversationally.
'He has been opening my eyes to a number of things! He takes
Holy Writ seriously! An uncomfortable habit – eh, Master
Melville?'

'Such jesting is unprofitable, sir.'

'Ah, but I do not jest. Nor, I think, does the Duke. I could
almost wish that he did, indeed! He actually believes in the
practice of mercy – as distinct from the mere principle thereof!'

Warily both the King and minister eyed him. Ludovick himself opened his mouth to speak, and then closed it again.

'He has been telling me, Sire, that he considers that with the triumph of the fall of Strathbogie, the policy of spoiling the Gordons has reached its peak and pinnacle. He holds that when this good work is finished . . .' The speaker raised a single eyebrow at the Duke in warning. '. . . When this is finished, further spoliation will but set back Your Grace's cause. A view which may possibly hold some truth, perhaps. Further measures against these people, after the notable downfall of Huntly's principal stronghold, might well savour of the futile, of flogging a dead horse. Moreover it might turn the folk sour – all the North-East. They must fear the King, yes; but the Duke's point, I think is that they should not *hate* Your Grace.'

Ludovick stared, at a loss.

'Eh . . . ? You mean . . . ? No more?' James looked from one to the other.

'So my lord Duke proposes, Sire. And he may well be right.'

'Would you leave the task half-finished, man?' the Earl Marischal demanded.

'Aye, why hold your hand now? When all the North is as good as ours?'

'Because a king is a king to all his subjects – not just to some few,' Lennox asserted strongly.

'But these are rebels, my lord – the King's enemies.'

'They are all His Grace's subjects, nevertheless. However mistaken.'

'The man, be he king, lord or common, who sets his hand against evil and then turns back, is lost, condemned in the sight of God!' James Melville exclaimed. 'Remember Lot's wife!'

'Ooh, aye,' James said.

'From such fate you must pray the good Lord to preserve us, my friend!' Patrick Gray agreed, smiling. 'But may it not turn on the question of what is evil?'

'There you have it!' Ludovick said strongly. 'A king who pursues vengeance on his subjects, even rebellious subjects, instead of showing mercy, I say does evil. Master Melville, I think, will not deny *his* own Master's words. "Blessed are the merciful, for they shall obtain mercy!" '

The young divine raised a declamatory hand. 'Mercy on sinners, yes! But on their sin, never!' he shouted. 'The sin must be rooted out. This Northland is full of the sin of idolatry, heresy and all uncleanness.'

He drew a greater measure of growled support for that than was his wont – from lords growing rich on Gordon pickings.

Perhaps it was his nephew's upraised voice which reached Andrew Melville. He left his labours at the wall-face and came striding over to the group around the King, still clutching his halberd, dust and chips of mortar further whitening his beard and flowing hair. All there were the less at ease for his arrival – save for Patrick Gray, who hailed him in friendly fashion.

'Well come, Master Melville,' he greeted. 'Yours is the wise voice we require, to be sure. Like dogs at a bone we worry and snarl, discussing good and evil, expediency and mercy. We deeve His Grace with conflicting views. My lord Duke of Lennox holds that mercy will now best become King and Kirk. Others say ... otherwise.'

'To halt now, with Popery still rife in the North, would be weakness,' the younger Melville asserted, with certainty.

'Yet the Duke holds rather, does he not, that mercy is a sign of strength?'

'I do not play with words!' Andrew Melville announced shortly. 'What is debated?'

'Simply, sir, with Strathbogie fallen, whether His Grace should go on after lesser and lesser things, as though unsure of victory? Or proclaim victory to all by calling a halt here. By offering mercy to all who return to the King's peace and the Kirk's faith. Not to flatter Huntly by chasing him further into the trackless mountains; but to show him to all as no longer a danger, his teeth drawn. To turn back at the height of victory rather than to go on and possibly, probably, fail to catch Huntly. This I conceive to be the Duke's advice.'

As his nephew began to speak, Andrew Melville held up his hand peremptorily. 'The Duke, sir – but what of your own? The Master of Gray is not usually lacking with advice. What say *you*?'

'Aye, Patrick,' James nodded. 'What's your counsel, man?'

'This exchange was between the Duke and Master James Melville, Sire. I only interpolated, perhaps foolishly. But if you would have my humble advice, it would be somewhat other. A mere matter of degree. I would say neither go on nor go back. Turn aside, rather, to the good town of Aberdeen. It has long had to bear Huntly's arrogance; let it now know the King's presence and clemency. The Kirk there has suffered much. Hold a great service of thanksgiving, I say, in the High Kirk there, for victory over Huntly and the Catholic threat – the provost, bailies and all leading men to attend.' Patrick, though ostensibly speaking to the King was looking at Andrew Melville. 'Some days of rejoicing, feasting, and then Your Grace returns south in triumph.'

Melville was considering the speaker keenly, calculatingly. Here was strong pressure. Of all Scotland's major towns Aberdeen was weakest for the Presbyterians. Not only was the old religion still well entrenched here, but even amongst the Reformèd, episcopacy was strong, reinforced by the University with its pronounced episcopal tradition. The Bishop of Aberdeen was no lay lordling, no mere secular figure enjoying former church revenues, as were so many; he was the most powerful prelate remaining in Scotland – and the Kirk had not forgotten his anointing-oil at the christening of the infant prince. Any opportunity to advance the Kirk's prestige and power in Aberdeen was not to be dismissed out of hand.

'A service of thanksgiving, sir, would be apt and suitable,' he said slowly. 'Provided that it was performed in meet and worthy fashion.'

'Who more able to ensure that than the esteemed Moderator of the General Assembly of the Kirk? And, h'm, the Rector of the University of St. Andrews!'

Since Andrew Melville held both of these offices, the matter was unlikely to be challenged in present company. The master-stroke, of course, was the anticipation of St. Andrews University being in a position to lord it over its upstart rival in Aberdeen itself. This could do no less than clinch the issue as far as the Kirk was concerned.

'It would appear, Sire, that such a course is worthy of consideration,' Melville advised, with dignity.

'Aye. But... to leave Huntly. At large. Undefeated...'

'In all that matters, Sire, he is defeated now,' Patrick as-

157

sured. 'We know that he has retired into the mountains. Your Grace cannot follow him there. We cannot bring him to battle now, even if we would. October is almost past. You cannot campaign in the mountains in winter. Indeed the campaigning season is all but over.'

'That at least is so,' the Lord Home agreed.

'So Aberdeen will serve you well in all ways, Sire. Deny it to Huntly. When you return to the south, leave it well garrisoned. Huntly will miss its protection this winter. There will be near-famine, I think, in this land, for the corn is everywhere un-gathered and wasted, and the beasts scattered. If Aberdeen is held for the King, where can he shelter and feed his men? And if its port is denied him, and other smaller havens along the coast, he can receive no help from Spain or the Pope. Is that not so, my Lord Marischal?'

Grudgingly the Earl agreed.

'Aye, well,' James sighed. 'Maybe you're right.'

'It is important that Your Grace returns south shortly, before the hard weather. When the passes may be closed by snow and flood,' the Master went on. 'It will, of course, be necessary to appoint some wise and sober royal representative, Sire, who may govern here in your name. My lord of Argyll is still Lieuten-ant of the North in room of Huntly – but he is returned to his Argyll, er, licking his wounds. Some other will be neces-sary.'

'Eh? Umm. Aye.' James looked vague. 'Argyll could be fetched back.'

'He requires time to recover himself, I think. He is young. Glenlivet hit him sore.'

'My Lord Marischal then, maybe . . . ?'

'An excellent choice, Your Grace – save in that the Keiths are the inveterate enemies of the Forbeses. My Lord Forbes, I fear, would not supply men for my Lord Marischal. Which men Your Grace sore needs. I suggest that the wisest choice would be my lord Duke.'

'Eh? Vicky . . . ?'

'I have no wish for such a position,' Ludovick announced shortly.

'Have you no' . . . ?'

'No, Sire. I wish to return south as soon as I may.'

'Aye. Aye, Vicky Stewart – I dare say that you do!' James's eyes narrowed. 'That I could well believe.'

'If the Duke has pressing interests in the south, Sire, on which he is set, I of course withdraw the suggestion,' Patrick said. 'Now who else might serve . . . ?'

'You may withdraw or suggest as you will, Master o' Gray – but *I* decide!' the King declared strongly. 'Mind that. There's times you are presumptuous – aye, presumptuous, Patrick! The Duke o' Lennox will bide here if I say so. As I do. He'll take rule in the North, here, when I go. Wi' the Earl Marischal to aid him. And my Lord Forbes too. That will be best. We shall hold a right Council to confirm these matters, sometime . . .' His voice trailed away. Then he turned to the castle. 'Aye, when we've dinged doun Geordie Gordon's house! This Stra'bogie still stands! There's work to do here. We're no' just finished yet! Master Melville had the rights o' it – Master Andrew! To work, my lords and gentles. We've had enough o' talk. Aye – and this oak kist, here. Lay it aside. A' Gordon's gear's confiscate to the Crown. *I'll* decide what's to be burned and what's no'!'

All bowed low, and none lower than the Master of Gray.

It was some time before Ludovick had opportunity for a word with Patrick Gray alone, amongst the fury of destruction which followed.

'Mary says that you have a devil,' he charged him. 'I say that you *are* one! What you did, back there, was devilish!'

'I think you . . . exaggerate,' the other replied, easily.

'Could I?' Ludovick considered him heavily. 'To use others, so cynically, so shamelessly, you can have no respect, no regard, for them, for anyone. Are men and women nothing to you but pawns to be moved on a board?'

'Tush! The state, this realm, consists of men and women, Vicky. There is no steering it save by moving them.'

'But not as you do it. Not by esteeming men as less than animals.'

'Here is wild talk. Who have I ever used so?'

'Myself. The King. Even Melville – although I would scarce

have thought it possible. Any and all you manipulate. Strip naked of all dignity, to win your own way . . .'

'*My* way! Shrive me – has it not been your way that I have been winning, this day?'

The Duke shook his head. 'Never that. Always your own. You but used my desire to have done with this burning and destruction, to smooth your own way. You had decided this of Aberdeen long before – that was clear. You twisted Andrew Melville round your finger for the same ends. James you made a mock of, as ever. And then you persuaded him to appoint me Lieutenant here in the North!'

'And who better? That your own policy of mercy be carried out . . . ?'

'Do not seek to cozen me with such talk, Patrick. I am no longer a child. You want me to be kept here. You want to take Mary away from me – that is your aim. So you would keep us separate. So you entangled me with the Queen! Think you I did not know you were behind that? So I am to be as good as exiled here . . .'

'On my soul, Vicky – this is too much! Even from you. You do not know what you say! I warn you – do not try me too hard! Others have done so, and regretted it.'

'Think you I care for your threats? I tell you this, Patrick. You will not part Mary and me. You will not, I say! We love each other. We are as one, belonging one to the other. It is not something which you will understand. But it is true. None shall part us. You hear?'

The other was moments in answering. 'Do you think that only you understand what love means, boy?' The Master's voice, normally so assured and controlled, actually quivered as he said that, 'Great God in His heaven – if you but knew . . . !'

Without another word, Patrick Gray swung abruptly about and left an astounded Ludovick Stewart standing there amongst the smoking ruins of Strathbogie.

Chapter Ten

Mary Gray came to Castle Campbell soaked, her hair plastered about her face, her riding-cloak heavy sodden with rain. But it was warm rain, and for this she must be thankful. At least the winter's snow and frost and sleet seemed to be over at last, and the passes to the North would be clear, or at least clearing. Although floods also could cut off that mountain land.

She urged her reluctant mount up the steep climbing track between the wooded ravines of the twin burns of Care and Sorrow towards the tall, frowning castle. It was not any lengthy and punishing journey from Stirling – a mere dozen miles – but the beast was a poor broken creature, though the best that she could hire secretly, out of her slender resources. She was less conspicuous so mounted, anyway, than on a horse from the royal stables, and she believed that she had escaped notice, at least as anything but a countrywoman returning home from Stirling market.

She was challenged, of course, at the outer bailey gatehouse, and here she had to play a different role.

'I am the Mistress Mary Gray, daughter of the Master of Gray,' she called to the porter. 'Seeking my lord of Argyll.'

That gained her admittance with little delay – for it would have been a bold man who would have risked offending un-necessarily the Master of Gray that spring of 1596, in Lowland Scotland. The drawbridge was already down, and Mary rode across it, having to withstand nothing more daunting than the speculative stares of men-at-arms and murmured asides as to her chances with their peculiar lord.

The inner bailey was not even guarded and she rode straight under the archway into the main courtyard. The rain had driven everyone indoors, and the place seemed to the girl as cheerless and unwelcoming as its name and reputation. When the first Earl had bought it, exactly a century before, on appoint-ment as Chancellor of Scotland and requiring a house nearer

Stirling than his traditional seat of Inveraray on far-away Loch Fyne, it had been called Castle-Gloume, or just The Gloom. Set on a spur of the Ochils above the township of Dollar, sometimes spelt Doleur, and set between these burns of Sorrow and Care, even its wide prospect of the Carse of Stirling and the Forth estuary, and the change of the name to Castle Campbell, did not altogether counteract the sombre feel of the place.

The girl was ushered into Argyll's presence, not in any of the main chambers of the great beetling central keep, but in a small room in a flanking tower of the courtyard, where he was writing letters before a blazing log fire. Archibald Campbell, seventh Earl, was a strange, studious, unsmiling young man to be chief of so pugnacious and influential a clan, dark, slight and wary – and his experiences at the Battle of Glenlivet almost six months before had by no means heightened his spirits. Mary Gray he knew slightly, as must all about the Court.

His surprise at seeing Mary there was not lightened by any access of gallantry. Far from a lady's man, he tended to avoid women. Clearly he would have preferred to be undisturbed at his writing.

'I am sorry if I trouble you, my lord,' the girl said. 'I would not do so, you may be sure, were the matter not urgent.'

Belatedly he laid down his pen, nodding. 'How may I serve you, Mistress Gray?' he said briefly.

'By hearing me out, my lord,' she told him frankly. 'A hard thing perhaps to ask of any man, with a simple woman!'

He blinked at that, eyeing her more warily than ever. Mary Gray was ever a problem and challenge to men, even to those not attracted to her physically; her modest quietness of dress and manner were so much at odds with the innate assurance and calm authority of her whole bearing, so unlooked-for in a young woman of her age and in her peculiar position. 'I would not name any of the Master of Gray's kin simple!' he returned. But he waved her to a settle near the fire. 'You are wet. Your cloak . . .'

'It is nothing. I am no fine Court lady to shrink at a little rain,' she assured him. But she laid her cloak across the end of the settle, to steam in front of the blaze, and deftly touched up and tidied her soaked and wind-blown hair. Without sitting down, she turned to him. 'My Lord – I learned only yesterday that you had come back from the West, from Argyll. At last. I came as quickly as I could.'

He frowned. 'Why, Mistress?'

'Because I have been waiting for you. For long. Months. To come from Inveraray. I know that the passes have been closed ... but the waiting has been weary work.'

'You waited for *me*?' Argyll was not the man to make the obvious jests over her avowal.

'Yes. Since you are the King's Lieutenant of the North.'

He waited, searching her lovely face. 'What of it?' he said, at length.

'My Lord – the Duke of Lennox has been held at Aberdeen all these long months. Acting for you. He would be home. And I would have him home.'

Argyll stared at her. 'You are ... you are ...!' He coughed.

'I am the Duke's concubine, yes. His mistress,' she agreed calmly. 'No more than that. I can make no claims upon him. But still he wishes to return. And dearly I would have him back.'

The very simplicity of that set the young man's dark head shaking. 'But ... this is the King's business!' he protested. 'A matter of the state. Not for, for ...'

'For such as myself to meddle in? It may be so. Perhaps I am remiss. But I know the Duke's mind in the matter.' She sighed. 'I have indeed spoken to the King.'

'You have!'

'Yes. And the Duke has written letters. But he will not heed.'

Argyll picked up the pen again, and nibbled at its feathering. 'In that case, why come to me? The Master of Gray? Your ... your sire. He now all but rules in Scotland. He is the man to petition, to be sure.'

'My father, I fear, considers the Duke well placed in Aberdeen!'

'M'mm. Indeed! Well, dear God – what can *I* do?' the other demanded. Despite his sober and serious manner, he seemed very young – at nineteen, a year younger than herself, and in all but years infinitely her junior.

'You can do much, my lord – if you will. You can go there. To Aberdeen. To take up your rule there.'

Argyll threw down his pen and got to his feet, to pace about the little room. 'That is not possible,' he said. 'What you ask is not possible, Mistress Mary. I could not go there now – even if I wished it. I was made Lieutenant of the North a year ago, in name only. Well I knew it. In order that my Campbell broadswords could be used against Huntly. It was an appointment of the Master's – your father. The King would never have thought of it. A scratch of the King's pen made me Lieutenant – at Gray's behest. Another scratch made the Duke Lieutenant in my place.'

'If you will pardon me – no, my lord. Not so. The Duke's position is only as *acting* Lieutenant. *You* are still Lieutenant of the North. He writes to me that his commission appoints him until you, my lord, resume your duties. Why my father planned it so, I do not know. But no doubt he had his reasons.'

The young man shook his head. 'I cannot go. But even if I could and would, it is clear that the Master – and therefore the King – would not have it so. I would be stopped forthwith.'

'Not if you went quietly, swiftly, secretly. As you have right to do. You are Lieutenant, the Duke but your deputy. You could be in Aberdeen in two days – and the Duke back here before the King and Council knew aught of it.'

'God be good – and to my cost! Do you know what you ask? You would have me to offend the King and your father! For what? For the sake of your fond lust for Ludovick Stewart! Does he esteem me fool enough so to pander to him . . . !'

Calmly, quietly, the girl spoke. 'Ludovick did not send me, my lord. He knows nothing of my coming to you. Nor would he approve, I think. Before you say more ill of him, I pray you, hear me out – as first I asked. None would esteem you fool, my lord – least of all myself. There is more need for you to go north to Aberdeen than merely to allow the Duke to return to his son and mistress!'

He paused in his pacing at that, to peer at her. 'I cannot go, I tell you – be it for one reason or another. I have other and pressing work to do. But . . . what is it you speak of? This need that I go to Aberdeen?'

It was the girl's turn to pause, and move a little. She turned to face the fire. 'My tidings will hurt and displease you, my lord,' she said slowly. 'I am loth to tell you. But you ought to know them, I judge. And you cannot know them – or you would scarce be here at Castle Campbell this night!' She looked at him over her shoulder. 'You were betrayed at Glenlivet, my lord.'

'What ... ? What do you say? Betrayed?'

'Yes. Shamefully betrayed. That you should lose the battle.'

'Christ God! What is this? What do you mean, woman? How betrayed? And by whom?'

'By those you trusted. By your own people – some of them. Aided by ... others. You were not intended to win that battle, my lord.'

Appalled he gazed at her. 'It is not true ...' he got out, thickly.

'I fear that it is,' she assured him sadly. 'I would not lie to you.'

'Who, then?' he demanded.

'I do not know all the names. But ... too many of them were Campbell!'

'No!' he cried. 'Never! That I will not believe.'

She went on steadily, if unhappily. 'All the names I do not know. But some I do. Campbell of Ottar. Campbell of Lochnell ...'

'That is false, at least! Lochnell was my own kinsman. My Standard-bearer. And he died by my side.'

'By a chance shot, my lord. He nevertheless was one of the ringleaders in selling the battle to Huntly. He was near enough kin, was he not, to see himself as Earl in your place? His death, perhaps, was just – since he caused many others to die. Then there was Campbell of Glenorchy ...'

'Another cousin. He commanded the van. Here is folly!'

'Aye – folly! Campbell of Ardkinglas, too. Others were Campbell of Inverliver and MacAulay of Ardincaple. Likewise John, Lord Maxwell, who is linked to you in some way. All conspired that the battle should be lost. That Huntly should attack early. That my Lord Forbes should be misinformed, and fail the rendezvous. That one of your arrays – I know not which –

should take the wrong glen and so miss the onset ...'

'That was Glenorchy, yes. Leastwise ...'

'All was arranged, my lord. Huntly was not to be beaten. Only checked. Your own life was to be forfeit – but something miscarried. Probably the chance death of Lochnell at your side ...'

'Lord have mercy! But why? Why, woman? Why should men act so? My own people?'

She shook her head. 'Can you not better answer that? Why do men do these things? Lie and cheat and betray? For gain, or for power, is it not? Most, no doubt, desired to see your great Campbell lands and wealth differently divided! Under a new lord. But others, behind them, would be playing a deeper game. The game they call statecraft – which is of all sports the most evil! The balance of power! In that sacred name, all wickedness may be allowed, all vileness accepted!'

'How could Huntly achieve this?'

'It was not Huntly's achievement, my lord – though Huntly benefited. It is all a balancing, see you. Huntly must not be brought too low, and the Catholic cause fail utterly, lest Campbell and the Kirk grow too strong! The scales must ever balance!'

Argyll was considering her wonderingly now. 'How do you, who are a mere girl, know all this?' he demanded. 'Did Lennox tell you?'

'The Duke does not know, I think. Besides, I have not seen him for six months and more. Few indeed know this. For if the Kirk had learned of it, all would have been lost.'

'Aye – the Kirk! The Kirk would have given much to know this, I warrant! But *you* know it! If you did not learn it from the Duke, it could only have been ... !' He left the rest unsaid.

'My lord,' she said steadily, levelly, 'how I learned this matter is my affair only. You I have told, that you might be warned. Since your life is still in danger, I think. But I ask that you keep my secret. For not only I might suffer, in consequence.'

He nodded, sighing. 'I understand.'

'So you must go north. For some of these men are still in Aberdeen, with your Campbell host, are they not? Glenorchy and Ardkinglas? Moreover, your uncle, Sir John Campbell of

Cawdor, is threatened, I understand. He is in command there, is he not?'

'Yes. But why should my Uncle Cawdor be threatened?'

'Because he is your Tutor, your lawful guardian, is he not, until you come of full age? And if you were to die, my lord, it is thought that he would have next claim to the earldom.'

'Fiend seize me!' Almost as alarming to Argyll as these revelations themselves was their quiet, factual enumeration by this young and innocent-seeming girl. He stepped close to her. 'Tell me,' he said tensely, 'is it Maitland who is behind all this? The Chancellor? As they say he was over the death of my cousin Moray, my former guardian.'

She shook her head. 'I think not. He would be useful, to take the blame of it, if need be. But he is a sick and dying man. Maitland's is not the hand, I think.'

'Then . . . ?' He eyed her from under down-drawn brows, and all but groaned. 'Mistress Mary,' he whispered, 'you frighten me!'

'That I can understand,' she agreed. 'I also am frightened. Will you go, then? To the North?'

'I cannot!' he cried, turning away again, and clutching the loose furred robe which he wore. 'Not now. It is impossible. I return to Inveraray tomorrow.'

'But . . . you only came from there two days ago!'

'Yes. But I must go back. I have received word of trouble, sure word. Only today. I must return to my own country at once. In the morning. That is why I write these letters.'

Mary sought to swallow the flood of her disappointment. 'Is it so urgent? This trouble. More so than the other?'

'Aye, it is. The Clan Donald is on the move. From the Isles. There was some word of it before I left, but I did not esteem it serious. Now I hear that it is. There is something much amiss. A great fleet of MacDonald galleys is moving south from Skye, growing as it comes. I am Sheriff of Argyll, as well as Earl. Also Justiciar of the Isles. I must go. Indeed, I am recalling my host from Aberdeen. I may need my broadswords nearer home!'

'Why should that be? The MacDonalds – it is not you they move against? Who do they threaten?'

'When the war-galleys sail from the Isles, there is no saying where they will attack! I do not think that they intend war with me. But my lands of Islay and Jura and Kintyre are on their road, and they may be tempted to raid them in the by-going.'

'On their road to where, my lord?'

'To Ireland. To Antrim. This is the word I received this morning. Donald Gorm of Sleat and the other chiefs of the Clan Donald Confederacy have decided to take part with the Irish in their revolt against Elizabeth of England's power. You will know that the Earl of Tyrone and O'Donnell have risen in Ulster, and are seeking to throw off the English yoke. Now this host from the Isles is sailing to their aid, it seems.'

'But why? The Islesmen have never loved the Irish. They are all Catholics, but ...'

'They have been bought. With gold. From Spain and the Pope. That rogue Logan of Restalrig is with them. He brought it. The gold. So Maclean of Duart writes me ...'

'Restalrig! Robert Logan!' Involuntarily Mary Gray's hand rose to her mouth. 'This is ... this is ...' She bit off her words thereafter.

'Aye – that forsworn scoundrel! A Papist and as big a rascal as any in this realm – although he is banished the realm, and outlawed! If he is in it, the matter is serious. It's an ill day when that one crosses the Highland Line!'

The girl stared into the fire. 'This could not be linked with Huntly?'

'No. I think not. Huntly is still in the glens of Mar. A hundred miles and more from our Western Sea. Moreover, the Islesmen hate him. As Lieutenant of the North he has borne hardly on them for long years. Clan Donald would not readily play Huntly's game, I swear!'

'All this, then – the Isles and the remote Highlands of the North-West – comes under the rule of the Lieutenant of the North?'

'Why, yes. In so far as it can be reached and ruled, at all! The North is all the North, not only the North-East. All the Highlands and Islands should be his concern.'

'I had not understood that.' She looked thoughtful. 'So meantime Vicky – the Duke – could be held in some measure responsible for this of Clan Donald?'

'Eh? Responsible? No, no – that would be beyond reason. No man can control the Isles from Aberdeen. But it is in his bailiwick.'

Mary hardly seemed to be listening. 'This MacDonald host. This fleet of ships. It is now at sea? Making for Ireland?'

'No – that is not the way the Islesmen work. Or there would be little danger to the Campbell lands. They move down the islands, gaining strength as they go, drawing in others, extorting tribute, lifting cattle and victuals, taking women. It is a sport, with them. Then, when they are ready and their enemy has grown careless, they sail across the narrowest seas to fall upon them. It may take them months. They will aim to win more than Spanish gold, if I know them!'

'I see. You go to halt them, then, my lord?'

'Halt them? Not I! As well seek to halt a torrent in spate! I go to protect my lands and people. From the plague that may strike them. Meantime, I write my news to the King. To my Uncle Cawdor. And . . . ' He paused. '. . . to my Lord Maxwell! Whom you say betrayed me!'

'Yes.' It would have been dark in that room now with its small window, without the flickering firelight, as the wet March evening closed down around Castle Campbell. 'My lord,' she said, 'it is time that I was gone. It will be full dark soon, long before I can reach Stirling. I am sorry that you cannot go to Aberdeen. But at least you are warned. Of what was done against you, and what may still be planned.'

'Yes. I thank you for that. I would aid you if I could.'

'I understand.'

'You came alone? I will provide an escort, at least, for your return.'

'It is not necessary. Indeed I would rather not . . . '

'A woman, riding alone? At night? And the country unsettled thus?'

'Very well. But they must leave me before Stirling. I came secretly and I would return secretly.'

'Why?'

'Would you not agree that the fewer who know that Mary

Gray rode to visit the Earl of Argyll in his castle, the better?'

'M'mmm. Aye, perhaps you are right, Mistress.' He held up her cloak for her. 'The Master, then, does not know that you are here?'

'The Master is at Forfar, where he is Sheriff. Holding justice ayres.'

'Ah. Your cloak, I think, is near dry ...'

The Master of Gray did not lodge within Stirling Castle, which might have had its inconveniences on occasion, tightly guarded as it was. He rented instead a modest house in the Broadgait of the town, where it climbed the hill to the castle. It was here that Mary Gray presented herself later that same wet night, asking of the astonished servant to see the Lady Marie.

She was shown into a warm and comfortable room, mellowly lit, where before a cheerful fire a woman rocked a wooden cradle with the pointed toe of her shoe while she knitted something in white wool. It was a homely and domestic scene indeed for the house of the notorious Master of Gray.

The woman, who had been crooning gently to the cradled baby, looked round smiling as Mary was announced – and then rose quickly, grey eyes widening, at sight of the girl's bedraggled and mud-spattered appearance.

'My dear, my dear!' she cried, starting forward. 'What is this?' What's amiss?'

'Nothing, Marie – save a little mud and rain! Leastwise ...' Mary kissed the other. 'It is shame to be troubling you. So late.'

'You coming is never trouble. Not to me. You know that, Mary, my sweet. But this is an ill night to be abroad. Come to the fire ...'

Firmly but without fuss, the younger woman was taken care of and cherished, her wet clothing removed, things of her hostess's given her to wear instead, a hot posset sent for, and food provided – all before Mary was allowed to declare the object of her untimely visit.

The Lady Marie Stewart, Mistress of Gray, was like that. Only recently returned to her husband's side from Ford Castle in Northumberland with her new baby, she was a person as practical and forthright as she was fair. Now in her early thirties, well built and fine-featured, with her broad brow, grey level eyes and sheer flaxen hair, she was a very beautiful woman – an extraordinary daughter for Robert Earl of Orkney, though less extraordinary niece for the late and lovely Mary, Queen of Scots. Eldest legitimate child of the Earl, she seemed to be not only quite untainted by all the peculiarities of her Stewart ancestry, but by her upbringing in the raffish Orkney establishment. For that matter, she was almost equally unlikely a wife for Patrick Gray.

'Now,' she said, when she had Mary settled and cosseted to satisfaction. 'I'll have your explanation, young woman!'

'I have been to Castle Campbell, Marie,' the girl told her. 'And to no avail. My lord of Argyll will not go to Aberdeen.'

'You went, Mary? That was rash. But who am I to talk, who would have done the same myself! But . . . Argyll then, was not to be moved? Even by what you told him? Of the treachery?'

'I told him, yes. He was much distressed. At first would not believe me. But there is no winning him to Aberdeen. He returns to his own Argyll tomorrow, Marie – there is more trouble. More wickedness. More than we knew. Much more.'

The Lady Marie searched the younger woman's lovely face, and said nothing.

'Have you heard Patrick say aught about the Isles? The Hebrides? And Clan Donald – the great Clan Donald Confederacy?'

'No, I think not. It is a far cry to the Hebrides, Mary.'

'Yes. But I fear . . . I greatly fear it may not be too far for Patrick! Marie – Argyll has word that thousands of MacDonald clansmen are making for Ulster, to aid the Irish rising against Queen Elizabeth. Paid by Spanish gold. And the gold was brought to them by Logan of Restalrig!'

'Robert Logan!'

'Yes. Had it been almost any other . . . ! Marie – you told me that he was here, some time ago? Secretly.'

'It was a month ago, perhaps. Yes, soon after I returned here. He came one night. He was closeted with Patrick most of the night. And gone by morning. You think . . . ?'

'How much of Patrick's ill work has Logan done for him?

He is the tool most apt to Patrick's hand. Did you learn anything of what he was here for, that night?'

The other gave a small laugh – but with little of mirth in it. 'Aye – you may be sure I asked Patrick! And for once he told me, with seeming frankness, secret as it was. He was in excellent spirits was Patrick that morning! It was gold that Logan had brought! Much gold!'

Mary Gray let out her breath in a long quivering sigh.

'Wait, my dear,' Marie told her, in a tight voice. 'It was not Spanish gold that Logan fetched – at least, so Patrick said. It was from Elizabeth! English gold pieces!'

'Elizabeth! English gold! For Patrick? Not the King's pension, at last?'

'Not the King's pension, no. James knows nothing of this.'

'Then what . . . ?'

The two young women stared at each other across the cradle wherein the Master of Gray's infant daughter gurgled contentedly, to the hiss and splutter of the burning birch-logs.

'Oh, no – not that!' Marie said, at length. 'Even for Patrick! Not so bare-faced as that!'

'You think not? No other would think of it – but Patrick might well. Playing his eternal game of balancing the scales of power. He saves Catholic Huntly from the Protestant host which he himself assembled. He could use Protestant Elizabeth's money to hire legions to aid the Catholic cause. It would all be of a piece.'

'But why aid the Irish? Will that not only inflame Elizabeth's ire against the Scots? Which cannot be Patrick's desire. All he works for, he says, is the English succession.'

'That I do not know. But it may be that it is not for Ireland that the MacDonalds make, at all. That could be but a feint. Suppose they were really to aid Huntly? Coming south, merely to turn to march east. To move in behind the King's forces, and cut off the North – all the North. Ludovick would be trapped!'

'How would that advantage Patrick, my dear? He does not want the Catholic threat to be wholly lost, I think, for fear that the Kirk grows too strong, and silly weak James goes down before it. But it is the Protestant cause which he upholds in the end, surely? He must, because of the English succession.

Only a Protestant prince will ascend the English throne after Elizabeth.'

'With Patrick, who can tell his true aims? At heart, I am sure that he is more Catholic than Protestant.'

'At heart, Patrick is only . . . Patrick" his wife said, heavily.

'That is true. But it serves us little here . . .' The girl leaned forward. 'Marie – together we have halted some of Patrick's wickednesses before. We must do so again, if we can. For his own sake, as well as others'. Will you do me a notable great favour? Only you could do it – and only you could I ask. Will you take the Prince for me? And my Johnnie too? So that I may go to Vicky?'

The Lady Marie swallowed, seemed about to speak, and then changed her mind.

Mary went on. 'I know how much I ask. It will be a great burden to you, with your own baby, and little Andrew, to look to . . .'

'That would be the least of it, my dear! The King . . . !'

'The King will be angry, yes. But he admires you, is a little afraid of you, I think. And you are his cousin. And the Master of Gray's wife. He will at least agree that I left his child in good hands! You can face him, Marie, as none other could.'

'And face Patrick, too!'

'All Patrick needs to know is that I have grown weary of my separation from Vicky, and have decided to end it. Patrick contrived that separation, and knows that I would have gone long ere this had the King allowed it. Time and again I have asked His Grace, pleaded with him. But he will not hear of it. I must stay with Prince Henry. Patrick it was who had me appointed to this position, for his own purposes, against my wishes. He need not be surprised that I rebel, at last.'

'His surprise, I think, will be that his wife aided you in your rebellion!' the other said, a little ruefully.

Mary bit her lip. 'I am sorry,' she said. 'Selfish. But . . . so much hangs on it.'

Marie sighed. 'So be it. But have you thought of the difficulties, my dear? How it is to be contrived? With the Prince close-guarded in the castle.'

'You will do it, then? Oh, Marie – you are good, good!'

'I will do it, yes – for you. There is not much that I would not do for sweet Mary Gray.'

'I am not sweet.' That was levelly said. 'I am a hard and sinful woman – and near as great a schemer and plotter as my sire.'

'My dear – that you say so makes you sweeter still!'

Mary shook her head. 'No. It is true. But . . . as to tonight, I have thought of how it may be done.'

'Tonight? Mercy, girl – *tonight*, you say?'

'Yes – it must be tonight. Every hour is precious, now. And only at night could it be done as I plan it.'

'But, Mary – a night of wind and rain, like this! And late . . .'

'So much the better for my purpose. Wind and rain are kindly things compared with what we fight against, Marie.'

The other considered the young, eager but strangely assured and authoritative creature before her for a few moments. 'You are your father's daughter, of a truth!' she said. 'Go on.'

'I plan it thus. You come back with me to the castle. With a servant. This child under your cloak. We tell the guards that you accompany me because of the hour, and the rain. Your cloak should be kenspeckle, if it is possible – different from mine. That the guards may recognise it later. Letting all know that you are the wife of the Master of Gray. So we gain my lodgings in the Mar Tower, where sleep the Prince and my Johnnie. There should be no trouble – the guards know me well. Then I leave you with the bairns, wearing your cloak. I am smaller than you – but only a little. The rain will well excuse me being close-hooded. The guards will look to see you return, and with your cloak and your servant, in the dark and rain none will question me, I wager. I return here – and then take my journey north.'

Marie drew a long breath, and then nodded. 'Yes. It will serve, I have little doubt. I must needs take up my quarters in the castle, then? Leave this house. Until you return.'

'No, Marie dear – not until I return. I do not intend to return! Not to being governess to the Prince. The King must find another governess. Why not the Countess of Mar? She lives there, in the same tower. She sees the child each day. Her husband is his governor. Henry is weaned now. There should be no difficulty in a change. If Lady Mar will not, there must be many others the King could call on.'

'So, as well as offending the King, and my husband, I must needs now find a new governess for the Prince, before I can return to my own house, and the said husband's side!'

Mary bit her lip, and did not answer.

Marie leaned over to touch the girl's arm. 'Never fear,' she said. 'I will brave them all! But I am still suckling my baby. That may cause difficulties. If I could but bring the two bairns here...'

'I think the King would never permit that the Prince should leave the castle. He so greatly dreads an attempt to seize the child.'

'We shall see. But you – what of yourself, Mary? This talk of journeying to the North. Who is to take you?'

'I need no one to take me. I can well look to myself, Marie – have often done so. If I may borrow one of Patrick's horses, to take me to Castle Huntly? There, Davy Gray will set me on my way to Aberdeen. If I start by daybreak, I shall be at Perth by midday and Castle Huntly before evening. Then another day to Aberdeen.'

'Alone?'

'Why, yes. I have gone far alone, many times. Have no fear for *me*. I was reared a land-steward's daughter, you'll mind – not a dainty lady!'

'I do not think Davy Gray will let you ride alone to Aberdeen,' the other said. 'Davy Gray! It is two long years and more since I saw him. You will tell him of my, my devotion, Mary?'

The girl nodded. 'That I will. He will rejoice to hear of it, I know well...' She smiled. 'You are very fond of Davy Gray, Marie, are you not?'

'Yes,' her hostess said simply.

'I know that he is ... like-minded. Sometimes I think ...' She paused.

'Do you, Mary?'

Again she smiled. 'Yes. Sometimes I think that I may think too much! But, Marie – the time! It is late. There is much to do...'

'Very well, my dear. I am at your service. First, let me find a cloak...'

Mary Gray's plan worked without a hitch. The guards, well knowing the Prince's governess, admitted her and her two companions to the castle without question. With most of the Court having to lodge outside the fortress walls, they were used to much coming and going. The baby hidden under the Lady Marie's handsome white riding-cloak fortunately did not cry or whimper and attracted no attention. The only remarks passed were disgusted comments on the wretchedness of the night. In Mary's quarters at the top of the Mar Tower, the tire-woman who aided with the little Prince was dismissed to bed. Within half an hour Mary was returning as they had come, wrapped in the white cloak, with the old servitor, after a sore-hearted parting from a calmly sleeping Johnnie Stewart of Methven – their first real parting. The guards at the gatehouse made no remarks, and Mary came without incident back to the house in Broadgait.

Well before daybreak, well mounted and equipped for the road, she was on her way north. The rain had stopped.

Chapter Eleven

David Gray, land-steward to the fifth Lord Gray, rode quietly, almost stolidly, at Mary's side, saying little but listening to the girl's talk and nodding occasionally. He was a stocky, plain-featured man now in his late thirties, rather taller than he seemed because of his width of shoulder. Hair showing no grey above his somewhat heavy brows, strong-jawed, muscular, simply-dressed, he looked very much of a man of the people – and a strange man for the lovely, delicately-built and patrician-seeming young woman to be calling father, in aspect as in age.

Always Mary Gray had called him father, an address she had never used to her true sire. David Gray, eldest child, though bastard, of Lord Gray, and only six months older than his legitimate half-brother Patrick, had at sixteen married Mary's mother bearing Patrick's child when the latter would and could not. He had brought up Mary as his own – and indeed, in his undemonstrative way, loved her even more deeply than the three later children of his own begetting. Mary Gray admired him above all men.

'They are no closer, then?' the girl was saying. 'No less at odds? I had hoped, prayed, as time passed, that they would come together. Slowly, perhaps, at first. But as Granlord grew older...'

'No,' the other said. 'It is not so. If anything the breach is wider, deeper. I have sought to do what I could. But it is of no avail. My lord will hear no good of Patrick. And Patrick will make no move towards his father. There is a hardness as of steel that nothing will break.'

'It is so wrong, so stupid! They are like foolish, wilful bairns. Patrick is much to blame, of course – but I believe that Granlord is more at fault. Patrick once would have come to terms with his father.'

'Aye. But the terms were to be his wn! My lord will never

forgive him for his betrayal of the Queen. Of Mary Stewart. Never!'

'Nor will you, I think, Father?'

He shook his head. 'Who am I to forgive or not to forgive? To judge at all? I failed the Queen also. If I failed her less than Patrick, it was because I had less opportunity.'

'No! No – you must not speak so!' she told him. 'It is not true. You might fail in your task – as might all men. But you would never fail anyone who trusted you. Especially Mary the Queen. Not Davy Gray!'

He was silent.

'So now,' she went on, 'Patrick and his father hide from each other in separate castles a dozen miles apart, frightened that they may cross each other's paths! Have ever you heard such folly!'

That was indeed the position between the Lord Gray and his heir. While Patrick was holding his justice ayres in this his sheriffdom of Forfar, he stayed in his strong castle of Broughty on its jutting rock in the Tay estuary, while his father abandoned his house of Castle Huntly a few miles away to retire to Foulis Castle amongst the Sidlaw Hills. That the son had been granted the sheriffdom in place of his father, some years before, by no means assisted amity.

Mary herself, of course, was also avoiding the Master of Gray this breezy spring morning, keeping well clear both of Broughty Castle and of Forfar town in her ride north. She could scarcely hope that her sire would be as understanding as was her foster-father over this expedition of hers.

David Gray, though scarcely approving of the girl's project, had done what he could to aid her in it. He and her mother, Mariota, had welcomed her warmly to her old home at Castle Huntly the previous evening, and knowing their Mary had made no major attempts to dissuade her from her chosen course. The Lady Marie had been right, of course; David Gray would not hear of his daughter riding to Aberdeen alone, and now accompanied her himself on the seventy-mile journey.

They went by Auchinleck and Guthrie and Brechin, through a bare treeless land of rolling pastures, heath and isolated grassy hills, and they were thankful that the weather had improved, for it would have made grim travelling with no cover from wind and rain. By midday they were back to the coast at Montrose, and thereafter were never far from the white-capped sea. In the late afternoon they passed near the Earl Marischal's great castle of Dunnottar on its thrusting promontory, before riding down into Stonehaven. After that it was barely two hours more to the Dee, through a cowed and ravaged country, with Aberdeen town rising beyond. Saddle-sore and weary, and depressed by the evidences of men's passions and savagery which they had ridden through, the travellers were thankful indeed to reach the end of their journey.

And now Mary had reason to be grateful for David Gray's presence – for Aberdeen in 1595 was something of which she had had no experience, an occupied city in a conquered country-side. The place was full of soldiers and men-at-arms with not enough to do, men but little amenable to centralised authority and discipline, being in the main the retainers of individual and often jealous lords and the clansmen of fierce Highland chiefs. A woman riding alone through the crowded evening streets of Aberdeen would have been fair game indeed; even with David's masterful dourness they made a difficult and sometimes alarming progress. Only by dint of much shouting of the name of the Duke of Lennox did they gain passage.

The Duke's headquarters were in the Bishop's palace in the Old Town, and this being to the north of the city, reaching it presented the greater problem. When eventually they arrived, it was to discover that Lennox was away investigating some disturbance in the Skene district, but was expected to return before nightfall. Fortunately Master David Lindsay, the King's Chaplain, one of the group of ministers appointed to the Council of Lieutenancy, well knew Mary in Stirling – he it was who had conducted the Prince's baptism service, and was now much enjoying occupying the hated Bishop of Aberdeen's palace; while strongly disapproving of ducal concubines, he recognised that Lennox would expect the lady to be well treated.

When Ludovick duly arrived, therefore, himself somewhat tired and travel-worn, it was to find his visitors washed, fed and refreshed. At sight of Mary sitting in smiling anticipation at the table in his private room, he was quite overwhelmed. Never one for ducal dignity or any sort of public or private pose, he shouted aloud his joy, and ran across the chamber to pick her up bodily out of her chair and hug her to him in an embrace which would have done no injustice to any bear, gasping incoherent questions and exclamations in the process of covering her face and hair with kisses. It was some time before he even realised that David Gray was also in the room.

That sobered him only a little, although from boyhood he had always been slightly in awe of this strangely humble man with the almost legendary reputation for competence and effectiveness, the only man of whom Patrick Gray was said to be afraid. Still clutching Mary to him, he more or less carried her over to where David stood, to take the other man's hand and wring it warmly.

David Gray was no more enamoured of Mary's peculiar relationship with the Duke than was Patrick or other members of the family – than indeed was Ludovick himself; but he recognised that they loved each other deeply, in fact looked upon each other as man and wife in the sight of God. He knew that any such unsuitable marriage for one so close to the throne would be immediately annulled by King and Council, undoubtedly. Faced with this fact, therefore, and out of his great love for Mary, he had accepted the situation with the best face possible, and sought to disguise his heartache for the girl.

After the first brief and disconnected explanations, and while Ludovick ate the meal which the servants brought him, Mary told him of the treachery to Argyll, and how she had sought to use her knowledge of it to persuade the Earl to come and take up his still official appointment as Lieutenant of the North. Long before she was finished this part of her story, Ludovick had his chair pushed back, his food forgotten, and was striding about the room in indignation and near-despair.

'I need not ask you,' he interrupted the girl, at length, 'whose hand was behind this infamy! There is no lack of dastards and betrayers in this Scotland of ours, sweet Christ knows! But only one, I swear, who would think of such a thing as this! Of such extreme perfidy. It is his doing, I say, as though all signed and sealed with his own hand!' He swung on David Gray. 'You, sir

– have you any doubts as to who was responsible? For this evil betrayal of Argyll?'

'None,' the other answered gravely. 'Although no doubt my brother would justify it to you in most convincing fashion!'

'Aye – for the King's and the realm's weal! Necessary, for the good steering of the ship of state! That, to Patrick, is justification for all. Hundreds may die, men behave worse than brute beasts, good faith be spat upon . . . !'

'I do not excuse any of it, Vicky, God knows,' Mary interrupted, 'but Patrick *does* care about bloodshed. Of that I am sure. I think that he truly believes that much of what he does is to spare worse things. Worse bloodshed. It may be folly, but it is his belief.'

'Aye, I have heard him at that, Mary! He is the chirurgeon! A little judicious blood-letting, here and there, to save a life! But it is ever Patrick who wields the knife, who chooses the victim!'

'Yes – but Vicky, had he not arranged the betrayal of Argyll, had he allowed the battle to go on, would there have been less bloodshed or more? Might there not have been a great deal more? In a full battle between two armies, as was planned, might not thousands have died? Instead of a few hundreds. Not only Gordons. As many and more Campbells might well have been slain in a true battle as in that rout which he contrived.' She shook her head, as the men stared at her. 'Oh, I may be wrong, wicked, to think such things. I may be too like Patrick, my own self! But – if we would contain and counter him, halt him in any way, we should at least seek to understand how he thinks, *why* he acts as he does! Is that not so?'

Ludovick did not answer, but David Gray nodded slowly.

'There is something in that,' he conceded. 'Your understanding of Patrick's mind, lass, might well be the strongest weapon that can be brought against him.'

'Not against him, Father! I do not fight against Patrick,' the girl asserted strongly. 'Patrick himself I love, despite all. I have no choice. It is his schemes and plots and acts that I hate.'

'Is a man to be judged apart from his actions, then?' the Duke demanded.

'I think so, yes. We can see and judge of his actions. But the man himself, what is in him, what he fights against, what moves him – do any of us know? And if we do not know, how can we fairly judge?'

'Save us, Mary – you are as bad as the ministers! As Melville and his kin!' Ludovick complained. 'If a man does evil, again and again – that is enough for me.'

'Do we not all do evil, again and again, Vicky? In some degree. In the judgment of different people. I know that I do. I am doing it now, in being here at all ...'

'Enough, Mary – enough! This is hair-splitting! When *you* accuse yourself of evil-doing, enough nonsense has been talked! I am a practical man. Actions to me speak louder than words. What are we to *do*? That is important.'

'No more hair-splitting then, Vicky. For it is action that has brought me this long road. The dire need for action. The betrayal of Argyll is bad, but it is past – whatever may yet come of it. There is more than that to concern us. A matter more urgent. There is trouble in the North-West. In the Isles. I believe Patrick to be behind this also. And so long as you act Lieutenant, it is your responsibility also, is it not?'

Puzzled, he eyed her. 'What do you mean? Trouble in the Isles ...?'

'Sit down and eat, while I tell you,' she said.

Once again, long before Mary was finished her account of the bribing of Clan Donald – or he was finished his repast – Ludovick was up and pacing the floor. He could not sit, or for that matter stand still, over what he heard. Continually interrupting exclaiming, demanding, he made so much poorer a listener than had David Gray the day before.

'You think, then,' he charged, at length, 'that Patrick does this to aid the Catholic cause? To hold his damnable balance? To spite Elizabeth? Or what? Where's the reason for it? The Argyll treachery is simple, compared with this.'

'Who knows? Patrick's reasons are seldom simple or straightforward. There may be a number not all evident.'

'If this is indeed Patrick's work?' David put in. 'That is not yet certain.'

'If Logan is in it, I'll wager it is!' the Duke said. 'Logan carrying gold! Who else would he be working for?'

'If it was Spanish gold, as the rumour has it, he might be working for the Catholic party itself, rather than Patrick. For Huntly. Or more possibly Bothwell, since he comes from the Borders.' The other turned to Mary. 'You say that the Lady Marie knew naught of this? Had heard nothing?'

'No. Save only that Logan had been to Patrick's house in Stirling secretly, a month ago. Bringing *English* gold. Or so Patrick said.'

'It looks damning,' Ludovick said. 'And whether it is Patrick or other, the position is full of danger. It must be dealt with. When the Clan Donald Confederacy is on the move, and the war galleys sail, it behoves all men to take heed. Especially the Lieutenant of the North!'

'So thought I,' Mary agreed. 'Whether they move to aid the Irish, assail the Campbell country, or turn east, leaving their galleys, to cut you off here in Aberdeen, they signify peril. Peril for you, Vicky – if not for all Scotland.'

He nodded. 'I must find out what is intended. What is behind it all.' He looked from one to the other. 'How is it to to be done? Who can I turn to? The Western Highlands and Isles are a world to themselves, speaking a different language. Who can tell me what goes on there?'

'Who sent the word of this to Argyll?' David asked. 'Did he tell you that, Mary?'

'Yes. It was Maclean, he said. Maclean of Duart.'

'Maclean? Sir Lachlan? Why, he led one of Argyll's arrays at Glenlivet! The man who came best out of that sorry business.' Ludovick paused. 'Unless . . . ? Save us – this couldn't be linked to the other? More treachery? I do not know the man. He was gone back to his own country before I came here. Is he another false knave, another Judas?'

'I did not know that he was at Glenlivet . . .' the girl faltered. 'You think . . . you think that this could be some further device? Against Argyll? Part of the same conspiracy?'

'I do not know. How can we tell? It may be all lies. A plot to entangle Argyll. On my soul, I am so confused by plots and trickery and deceits . . .'

'Wait you,' David Gray interposed. 'Lachlan Mor is a fighter, not a schemer, I think. You say that he came well out of Glen-livet? It is what I would expect . . .'

'You know him, then?'

'I have met him, yes. In the old days. He is a man to be reckoned with. No cat's-paw. He is chief of his name, and a giant of a man. Some would name him rogue, no doubt – but it would be roguery in no petty fashion. Patrick told me once that he received a pension of four hundred crowns each year from Queen Elizabeth to keep the narrow Hebridean seas open to her ships, and to recruit Highland mercenaries for her armies in Ireland.'

'Plague on it – and you call him no schemer! Is he not but another traitor . . . ?'

'I think he would not consider himself that, my lord Duke. These island chiefs scarce look on themselves as vassals of the King of Scots. They esteem themselves to be petty princes, all but independent. You'll mind it is less than a hundred years since James the Fourth put down the Lordship of the Isles – in name, at least. Before that, these chiefs held their charters and paid their tribute to the MacDonald lords, as sovereign, not to the King. They allied themselves to whom they would. Some still think so. Sir Lachlan will go his own way. But he fought bravely against the King's enemies at Glenlivet, did he not? With Argyll.'

'It may only have seemed that way. Foul fall them all – I do not know what to think!'

'This at least you may be sure of,' the older man told him. 'Lachlan Mor hates the MacDonalds. They took from the Mac-leans the island of Coll and part of the Rhinns of Islay. They have been at bloody feud for years. Indeed, he and Angus Mac-Donald of Sleat were both forfeited by the King for refusing to obey his orders to make peace. Still are, I should think. So, since this news concerns the MacDonalds, I think it will be true, and no mere lying device. He will make it his business to know what the MacDonalds are doing, you may be sure. What they intend. That he may counter them. Not for the King's sake. Nor the Protestants'. Nor Argyll's. But for his own. If you would know what goes on in the Isles, my lord – send to ask of Sir Lachlan Maclean.'

'Aye. You are right. But – better than that,' the Duke said, grimly. 'I shall go myself.'

Mary nodded. 'That is what I would say also, Vicky. Go yourself.'

'Is that wise?' David asked. 'Can you do it, my lord? Can you leave here for so long? It is a far road to the Isles. You rule here, in the King's name . . .'

'I rule there also, in the King's name, do I not? Supposedly, at least. Rule, action, may be required. And swiftly. If I must wait here whilst couriers make the journey to and fro, I may be too late. This authority which I have, and do not want, might there serve some good purpose, I think. Here the Marischal and Forbes and the ministers, the Council of the Lieutenancy, have power and authority in plenty. They do not need me. Indeed they would liefer have me gone, I know well – for I restrain them grievously! They consider me weak, afraid to act, over merciful. I have had months of them . . .' He clenched his fists. 'All winter, month after month, I have been held like a trussed fowl in Aberdeen. I have had enough. Here is opportunity to win free. If James does not like it, he may appoint a new Lieutenant!'

'Well said, Vicky! And I shall come with you.'

They looked at her askance.

'My dear, this is no work for a woman,' Ludovick said 'Journeying over the roughest bounds of the realm. Amongst the wild clans . . .'

'Are the clans and the Islesmen like to be more wild than the rude men-at-arms of proud lords? Has journeying ever troubled me?' she demanded. 'Besides, this is best for me. I came to be with you, Vicky. I hazarded much to be so. I cannot go back to Stirling meantime. Nor to Methven. The King would soon hear of it. He will be very angry. He may even send for me, here. Better that I should be gone where he cannot reach me, until his wrath is cooled. It may be that he will have cause to be grateful to us hereafter, Vicky, when he may forgive.'

The Duke could never out-reason Mary, even when he desired to do so. He part shrugged, part nodded. 'You may be right. And Heaven knows, I would be loth to lose you now!' He turned to David Gray. 'And you, sir? Do you come with us?'

The other shook his head. 'I am a man *under* authority, not having it, my lord. I cannot come and go as I please. I must return to Castle Huntly tomorrow.'

'Must you, Father?'

'You know that I must, lass. I cannot spend days, weeks, stravaiging amongst the Highland West. With my lord at Foulis, Castle Huntly and half the Carse of Gowrie is in my charge alone. Besides,' he smiled, faintly, 'you came all this long way to be with my lord Duke – not with me!'

In the morning, then, leaving the Earl Marischal in command at Aberdeen, they rode across the Brig o' Dee and took the road south, as they had come, now a party of a dozen – for though the Duke would have preferred to have ridden alone with Mary, it was inconceivable that the King's Lieutenant of the North should range unescorted about the land; he took a group of tough Campbell gillies, under young Campbell of Ardoran, conceiving these to be of more use in the Gaelic-speaking West than any larger troop of conventional men-at-arms. Like them, he and Mary were mounted now on shaggy, short-legged Highland garrons, essential for the country they would have to cover.

At Brechin, nearly forty miles to the south, they parted from David Gray in mid-afternoon, to turn west, by Tannadyce and Cortachy, making now for the great mountain barrier that frowned down upon these Braes of Angus. Their more direct route, of course, would have been up Dee, through Mar, and over into Speyside and so down Laggan into Lochaber and the Western seaboard – but Huntly, after a fashion, held all the upper Dee and the hill country of Mar. Hence this more southerly route.

They could have spent the first night at Cortachy Castle, whose laird, Ogilvy of Clova was a loyal supporter of the King, and kinsman to the Lord Ogilvy; but Ludovick had no wish for his identity and whereabouts to be known and reported, and was determined to avoid all castles and lairds' houses, even though this was bound to add to the discomforts of the journey. Mary would have been the last to complain. So they passed well to the south of the castle, and pressed on into the sunset, climbing steeply now into the skirts of the high hills, to pass the night in the great Wood of Aucharroch at the mouth of Glen Prosen. The Campbells, experts at living off the land, produced a couple of fine salmon out of the river to add to the provender they had brought with them. Eating this by the light of the flaring, hissing pine-log fires amongst the shadowy tree-trunks, sitting at Ludovick's side, Mary felt happier than she had done for many a long month. They slept, wrapped in plaids, in great contentment.

In the morning they started really to climb, and went on climbing all day, with only occasional and minor descents into the transverse glens of Isla, Shee and Ardle, through the vast, empty, trackless heather-clad mountains which formed the towering backbone of Scotland. Even though the sun did not shine and the going was hard, it was a halcyon day wherein fears and anxieties could be dismissed, if not forgotten, banished in the limitless freedom of the quiet hills. The larks trilled praise without end, the grouse whirred off on down-bent wings, and high above them eagles wheeled their tireless circles in the sky. The air was keen, but heady with the scent of heather and bog-myrtle and raw red earth. The world could once again be seen as a clean, simple and uncomplicated place. Although the travellers covered less than half the mileage of the previous day, by nightfall they were in Atholl, lodging in the hut of a cowherd high on the roof of the land between Garry and Tummel. Save for this silent but smiling man, they had not spoken to a soul in thirty miles.

Two more days they took to cross the breadth of the land, climbing, descending and climbing endlessly, skirting great lochs, fording foaming torrents, ploutering through bogs and peat-hags. Young Ardoran was invaluable as guide, leading them heedfully to avoid the settled haunts of men. This was not only to avoid recognition of the Duke, but was a normal precaution for Campbells travelling clan country where they could be by no means certain of their reception. The next night they bedded down on a sandy island in the middle of the rushing, peat-brown River Orchy. On the afternoon following, the second day of April, they smelt salt water and the tang of seaweed on the westerly breeze, and presently came down to the great sea-loch of Etive, to gaze out over the magnificent prospect of the isle-strewn Sea of the Hebrides.

Mary sat her garron enthralled. Never had she dreamed of anything so lovely, seen so much colour, known such throat-catching sublimity of beauty. The sea was not just all of a single shade of blue or grey, as she had known it hitherto, but as though painted with a hundred delicate variations of azure and green and purple and amber, reflecting the underlying deeps or shallows, the banks of gaily-hued seaweeds, multi-coloured rock and pure white cockle-shell sand. Into or out of this thrust mountains and headlands to all infinity, dreaming in the sunlight under sailing cloud galleons; and everywhere were islands, great and small, by the hundred, the thousand, proud peaks soaring from the water, cliff-girt and sombre, smiling green isles scalloped with dazzling beaches, tiny atolls, abrupt stacks, scattered skerries like shoals of leviathans, weed-hung reefs and rocks ringed with the white lace of breaking seas. No one had prepared the girl for all this wonder. She drank it all in, lips parted, speechless with delight. Even Ludovick, less susceptible, was affected. The Campbells merely hailed it as signifying journey's end.

Ardoran led them down to the very shore of the wide Firth of Lorne where, on a jutting promontory a tall castle stood – Dunstaffnage. They were in Campbell country now, with need for anonymity over, and Campbell of Dunstaffnage was close kin to Argyll himself; indeed the place ranked as one of the Earl's own strengths, and its keeper was hereditary captain thereof rather than true laird.

They were well received, and slept in beds for the first time since leaving Aberdeen – even though the master of the house seemed less impressed by the presence of the King's ducal Lieutenant than by his comely young woman companion.

He was full of anxieties and rumours about the Clan Donald activities. They were swarming south like locusts, he declared, eating up the islands as they came. Donald Gorm of Sleat, Angus of Dunyveg and Ruari Macleod of Harris, were said to be leading the sea-borne host; but now Clanranald had joined the enterprise, with MacDonald of Knoydart, MacIan of Ard-namurchan, and other mainland branches of the clan, and was ravishing and plundering his way down the coastline by land. Much of Lochaber and the Cameron country was already overrun, as were the Maclean lands of Ardgour. Only the Appin Stewarts lay between them and Campbell territory. MacCailean Mor, Argyll himself, was back at Inveraray, calling in men fast. It was to be hoped that he would make haste to send some of them, many, north here to Dunstaffnage, for it lay full in the route of the MacDonalds, the first major Campbell stronghold which they would reach.

In the circumstances, the Captain was disappointed that his visitors were set on moving on across the Firth of Lorne and the Sound of Mull – for even such small reinforcement would be welcome if the MacDonalds came. He tried to put them off by warning them of the dangers of the narrow seas, of freebooting MacDonald galleys, of strange winds and currents. When he saw that they were determined, however, he provided them with a boat – not his one galley, which he could by no means spare at this juncture, but a seaworthy, high-prowed fishing-craft for eight oars, which Ardoran's gillies were competent to handle.

That night Mary Gray saw her first Hebridian sunset, and laughingly but determinedly denied Ludovick's urgent arms until its last fiery glories died in smoking purple.

In the sparkling morning they put to sea from the little haven under the castle walls. Their course was due west, and with a southerly breeze they were able to hoist the square sail to aid the oarsmen. They bowled along in fine style, at first, the boat dipping spiritedly to the long Atlantic swell. The rowers chanted a strange endless melody as they pulled, age-old and haunting in its repetitive rhythm. Soon Mary found herself joining in, humming and swaying to the lilt of it. This bright morning, it seemed scarcely to be believed that their journey was being made against a threat of war, bloodshed and treachery.

The Maclean territory was the large island of Mull, third in size of the Hebrides, and Sir Lachlan's seat of Duart Castle perched on a rock at the end of a green peninsula thrusting into the sea at the north-east tip of it, dominating all the narrows of the strategic Sound of Mull, the Firth of Lorne and the Linne Loch, so that no vessel might sail the inner passage of the islands should Maclean seek to challenge it. Queen Elizabeth never paid her pensions for nothing.

Duart Point lay some nine sea miles from Dunstaffnage, no

lengthy sail. But there had been something in their late host's warnings as regards tides and currents at least, for amongst all these islands and peninsulas, representing really the tops of sunken mountain ranges, the tide-races, over-falls and undertows were quite phenomenal. The rowers presently found that once they were clear of sheltered waters, the incoming tide, sweeping down the Sound of Mull and circling the tip of the Isle of Lismore, was largely countering their efforts and the effect of the sail. They had to pull even harder to make any substantial headway, and Mary and Ludovick soon were doing most of the chanting, the oarsmen's contributions being reduced largely to gasps. The mountains of Mull seemed to keep their distance.

Never did nine miles seem to take so long to cover. Not that Mary, at least, could arouse any impatience, so well content was she to feel herself part of that fair painted seascape. She could not really conceive the continuous scanning of the horizon by Ludovick and Ardoran, for the menace of Clan Donald galleys, to be more than play-acting. After leaving a few inshore fishing-boats behind, no single other vessel was to be seen in all that sun-filled prospect – although admittedly, as Ardoran pointed out, a hundred might lie hidden behind the myriad islands.

At last the towering rock of Duart, with its castle perched high above the waves, became distinguishable from its background of the blue mountains of Mull. But barely had they descried it than out from behind the tip of Lismore, the long low green island which had formed a barrier to the north of them for hours, swept another vessel at last. A groan went up from the straining Campbells as they saw it.

'Is that . . . a galley?' Ludovick demanded, a little breathlessly. He had never seen such a craft.

Ardoran nodded, grimly. 'A galley it is, God's curse on it! Och, they have been just lying in wait for us.'

Certainly the ship appeared to be making directly for them. It was a long, low, dark, slender vessel, with soaring prow and stern, rowed by double banks of lengthy oars and having a single raking mast set amidships supporting a huge square belly-ing sail. It was the centuries-old pattern of the Viking-ships, scarcely altered, which had terrorised these same northern waters then and ever since, lean greyhounds of the sea, the fastest craft that sailed. At either side the blue water boiled, leaving clouds of drifting spray, where the double lines of oar-blades lashed it in urgent oscillation.

'How many oars?' the Duke asked.

'Each side a score. To each oar, two men. On this. Larger galleys there are than this.'

'What do we do now?' Mary wondered.

'What *can* we do? That craft can move five miles to our one,' Ludovick said. 'We can only wait, and parley.'

'Parley!' Ardoran snorted. 'Much parleying will the Mac-Donalds be offering us! Strike first, and parley with the corpse – that is the style of them, whatever!'

'They may not be MacDonalds . . .'

'That is a war-galley. Whose else would it be if not Clan Donald? Or their friends.'

The long-ship came up on their quarter at a great speed, with a notable bow-wave snarling in disdain at either side of her lofty prow. A device was painted in bold colours on her huge sail, but because the wind was southerly and the galley bore down on them from the north-west, the sail was aslant and the device undecipherable. Ranked warriors lined her sides, steel glinting in the sunlight. If there were eighty oarsmen, there must have been at least as many fighting-men.

The galley swung round the smaller boat in a wide arc, fierce faces inspecting them.

Ludovick stood up. 'We must put some face on this . . .' he muttered. Raising his voice, with as much authority as he could muster, he shouted. 'Who are you? And what is your business? Answer me!'

There was a general throaty laugh from the larger vessel.

A young man spoke from the prow, in good English. 'We but come to meet and greet you, my lord Duke. You are welcome to the Isles.'

Ludovick all but gasped his surprise. 'A pox! How . . . how knew you? What is this? Who are you?'

'My name is Maclean, lord – and little takes place in all the Isles that Maclean does not know. Especially so important a matter as the coming of the King's Lieutenant, the Duke of Lennox – God preserve him!'

'Maclean?' Ludovick frowned. 'You mean – from Duart?'

'None other. Where my father waits to receive you.'

'You are Sir Lachlan's son?'

'Lachlan Barrach, yes.'

'But, how . . . ?' The Duke stopped. There was no sense in shouting his questions at such range, to the hurt of both throat and dignity. The young man, although his words were polite enough, had a fleering note to his voice. He was dressed in a long tunic of untanned calf-hide, brown and white, which almost covered his kilt, and he carried his broadsword on a wide shoulder-belt studded with silver-work and jewels which glittered in the sun. A single tall eagle's feather adorned his bonnet. He made a tall, swack figure, and knew it.

'Come aboard, my lord,' he invited, all but commanded. 'A poor craft that is to be carrying a duke. And his lady. We'll take you to my father.'

Something of mockery in his tone made Ludovick refuse, although the other's suggestion was sensible. 'We are very well in this,' he gave back. 'But you may take us in tow.'

They were near enough to observe the quick frown on young Maclean's darkly handsome features. Ludovick chuckled. He thought that would touch the fellow. For a proud galley captain to have to return to port towing a small and humble fishing-boat would be a tough mouthful to swallow.

The other hesitated, pacing the tiny foredeck as his men with their oars skilfully held the great vessel almost stationary against the tide-race.

'Well, sir?' Ludovick shouted. 'Are you unable to tow the King's Lieutenant?'

With what looked like muttered cursing, the other turned to give curt orders. The galley spun round almost on its own axis, to present its pointed stern to them, and a long rope came snaking over to the smaller craft. Grinning, Ardoran tied it fast.

Mary, dark eyes dancing, touched Ludovick's arm. 'That was well done, my lord Duke!' she murmured. 'Another word that may be whispered round these Isles!'

'Aye. But how did they know? About me? How *could* they know?'

'That I cannot tell you. But . . . no harm is done. As well that your coming should create a stir, surely?'

If Lachlan Beg Maclean felt in some measure humiliated, he sought to make up for it in his own way. Despite the contrary tide, he most obviously called for the very maximum of the galley's speed, urging his rowers to their most vehement efforts. The vessel positively leapt over the sea – and the small boat behind seemed to alternate between almost leaving the water altogether and plunging its nose deep into the waves of the other's creaming wake, in crazy career. Never had any fishing-boat moved at such a pace before. Tossed about like peas in a pan, the Duke's party were quickly soaked by the water they shipped and by the continuous clouds of spray which enveloped them from the galley's oar-splashing. Unable to make their protest heard above the lusty chanting of nearly two hundred throats in front, they were glad to run down their sail and huddle together beneath its canopy.

In such fashion, they came to Duart.

Chapter Twelve

Maclean's castle of Duart which, because of its position and site might have been expected to have certain affinities with Logan's Fast Castle, had in fact no similarity. Where the latter stronghold, clinging precariously to the Berwickshire cliffs, was a harsh and savage place, a secret, almost furtive, this Hebridean fortress was proud, assured, open flaunting itself indeed on its rock in confident challenge. It was much larger also, something of a citadel, its lofty retaining walls enclosing all the summit of its rocky knoll, the great square keep within massive and towering high to lofty battlements, the stonework rude but impressive. An enormous banner streamed in the breeze from its topmost tower. And inland from the castle, nestling below it on the low-lying greensward of the peninsula, was an entire town of cot-houses and huts, over which hung a blue haze of peat-smoke.

Young Maclean had to moderate his pace on nearing his landfall, and the newcomers were thankful to be able to emerge from beneath their sail and relax somewhat. Indignation was fairly quickly submerged in wonder at what they saw.

Most castles had a portcullis, included in their gatehouses, to raise and lower a drawbridge over a moat; Duart had its version of this device facing not towards any approach road but to the open sea, its massive double chains plunging directly down into the water itself. Ardoran explained that these great chains were anchored to a projecting reef far out, and though they hung slack just now, could by a pulley system be drawn taut to stretch just above the surface of the sea right across the intervening channel, and so effectively bar to shipping the only passage round the east of the great island of Mull – for the deep water channel here ran close in around Duart Point, and beyond the reef referred to was perilous shoal water strewn with rocks and skerries. The fate of any vessel reaching this upraised barrier and refusing to pay Maclean's toll, could be envisaged very clearly; the black snouts of cannon thrusting from the crenellations of the castle parapets were very eloquent.

There were other evidences of Maclean's persuasiveness. What at first had looked like a forest of bare tree-tops rising from behind a spur of the castle-rock, as they rounded the Point proved to be the masts of over a score of galleys anchored in neat rows in a sheltered little bay tucked in to the north-west. On the boat strand behind this possibly a hundred small craft were drawn up.

The visitors were not unimpressed.

It was the sound of piping which drew their attention from these indications of naval strength up to the high castle-keep itself. There a group of kilted musicians paced round and round the battlements, blowing lustily. It was not at these, nevertheless, that Mary pointed mutely. Projecting from the keep's sides, just below parapet-level, were booms, long poles of wood. From these hung things that swung and twirled in the breeze – men. There were three hanging from one pole, four from another, two from a third. Altogether the girl counted sixteen corpses dangling there – and that did not include any who might hang at the unseen sides of the building.

The sight affected more than Mary. The Campbells eyed each other uneasily, and Ludovick fell silent.

His silence was neither here nor there a few moments later, when galley and tow turned into the haven behind the castle. This evidently had been a signal. Cannon fire crashed out from the battlements above, to set the seabirds screaming and the mountains around echoing and re-echoing. How many guns were fired, and how often, was uncertain in all the reverberation, and by King James's standards it was no doubt quite a modest bombilation; nevertheless it was as the greeting of one prince for another. After Davy Gray's observations, Ludovick did not fail to recognise the significance of it.

Ardoran cast off the tow-rope so that they might row to the shore with some dignity – the maintenance of dignity being obviously of prime importance amongst these people. They were watched in silence from the anchoring galley.

Men came hurrying down a path from the castle, led by an enormous young man with a shock of fiery red hair, dressed in full Highland finery of great kilt and plaid. Despite all his magnificence however he strode straight into the sea as the Campbell boat grounded forefoot in the shallows, and came splashing out to its side, careless that the skirts of his kilt floated wide on the water. Reaching the boat he extended great arms over the side to grasp Mary where she stood waiting, and with no more greeting than a wide grin, swept her up as easily as though she had been the merest child. He turned to carry her ashore under one arm, before she or anyone else could make effective protest. Seeing others wading out to the boat, Ludovick, sensing their intention, hastily lowered himself over into the water. It came well above the tops of the thigh-length riding-boots which he wore. So he splashed to land, his own man still.

The red-head, who yet clutched Mary's arm, laughed aloud. 'You should have waited, my lord Duke!' he cried. 'Necessary it was, of course, to bring the lady first. If you had but had patience...'

'I have been having patience for the past hour, sir!' Ludovick told him grimly. 'So you also know who I am? How comes this? I sent no word.'

'That is nothing,' the other said, still laughing. 'We know here at Duart what Dunstaffnage, or any other Campbell, dreams on his bed of a night! How much more when the Duke of Lennox comes seeking boat to the Isles!'

'I see. You keep spies in other men's houses, sir! And presumably fast boats to carry their tales through the night?'

'Spies...?'

'Informants then!'

'To be sure, informants is a better word, entirely. Information is an excellent thing, is it not, my lord?' The big fellow chuckled – a cheerful soul it seemed. 'Och, we can never be having sufficient of it, to be sure. Holy Writ says something of the sort, does it not? It is information, I think, from some good informant, that brings the King's Lieutenant here to Duart, this day?'

'H'mmm.'

Mary gently disengaged herself from her captor's grasp. 'You also are a Maclean?' she asked, smiling a little.

'Are not we all, lady? But I am Hector. Hector Ruari Younger of Duart. And you... you are very fair, whatever!'

'I thank you,' she said gravely, although Ludovick frowned. 'For your information, I am Mary Gray, mistress to my lord Duke.'

Grinning, the big man looked from one to the other assessingly. 'Come,' he said. 'I'll be taking you to my father.'

He turned and led them up the steep climbing path to the castle, gallantly offering Mary his arm – and when she declined its aid, masterfully taking her own. There was only room for two abreast on that track, so perforce the Duke had to come up behind, water squelching about inside his thigh-boots unpleasantly. By half-way, the martial figure of Lachlan Beg had come up and taken his place at his side, no word spoken.

So they came to the outer bailey, crowded with armed clansmen who watched, silent, a distinctly daunting company. Here two more pipers met them, and turned to escort the little party, marching before them and striking up a lively air. Thus they crossed the slantwise naked rock to an inner bailey, where other men stood waiting. These were more elaborately dressed in finer tartans, and bore themselves proudly – obviously gentlemen and minor chieftains of the clan. They offered no sort of greeting, but fell into place behind the four and the pipers, to pace across the inner courtyard.

In the open arched doorway of the central keep itself, directly below those hanging figures high above, a single man stood, tall deerhounds at his side. It was quite a lofty arch, but even so this man stooped slightly, and not from age or infirmity. He was quite the largest individual that either Ludovick or Mary had ever seen, dwarfing even the burly Hector Ruari, as all others there. He must have been at least seven feet tall, and broadly built in proportion, with huge shoulders and a great barrel of a chest. His features were leonine and ruddy, his blue eyes keen but strangely pale, and his plentiful hair which had been notably blond and was now silvering, fell to his shoulders. He wore a red tartan doublet, a long embroidered waistcoat, and tartan trews cunningly cut on the slant to clothe his tremendous thighs and calves close as a glove right to the ankle. His expression was stern, but he smiled gravely as his eldest son came up with Mary, to step aside and allow Ludovick to approach him first.

The bagpipe music died away in bubbling groans, both above and below, and only the screaming seabirds continued their accompaniment.

'Duke of Lennox – I rejoice to see you,' the chief said, his voice curiously light and musical for so vast a man. 'I bid you welcome to my humble house. A pleasure it is to receive the representative of King James.' He turned to Mary, and bowed a little – thus emphasising that he had not bowed to the Duke. 'And you, lady – all that is mine is at your service.'

Ludovick cleared his throat, and spoke almost as carefully as did the others. 'Sir Lachlan – your fame is known to me, to all. I have come far to see you. *I* rejoice to have reached Duart safely. I have noted your . . . arrangements for my reception!'

'Had you sent word of your coming, Duke of Lennox, I would have received you more fittingly! But perhaps King James's Lieutenant must be discreet in how he visits one whom King James and his Council have seen fit to forfeit!' The English was as perfect as his every word was significant, however gentle the slightly sing-song intonation of the North-West.

The other schooled his features to expressionlessness. 'Your services to His Grace, I am sure, will outweigh any such unfortunate edict, sir,' he answered slowly in turn. 'I came secretly for other but good reason. That others should not know of my visit, and that I might travel the faster. The matter that brought me is urgent.'

The big man nodded. 'The matter of Clan Donald, I have no doubt. I can think of no other that would bring the representative of James Stewart to Duart, Duke of Lennox!'

Ludovick inclined his head. 'That is the reason, yes. And is it so strange that the King's Lieutenant should be here – when, Sir Lachlan, I understand that you receive Queen Elizabeth of England's representative almost yearly!'

There was silence then as they eyed each other, and all others watched and waited. Now at last they knew where they stood. Lennox had served notice that he knew of Maclean's English pension, and indicated clearly the chief's duty and service to his own monarch; the other had evidenced his resentment at the sentence of forfeiture passed upon him over his feuding with the MacDonalds, and hinted at his refusal to acknowledge overlordship of any sovereign by his persistent use of the term King James instead of the King. Notable also was his refusal to accord the customary my lord to Ludovick – or, no doubt, to any man.

The giant seemed in no hurry for further speech. For his part, the Duke bit back the words that sprang to his lips, and instead raised his head to contemplate the corpses hanging there against the blue of the sky.

'Mainly MacDonalds!' the chief observed, briefly. Then he turned to Mary again. 'This lady – how do I receive her, Duke of Lennox?' he asked, in a different tone.

'As my wife, sir.' That was crisp.

'Very well. Her sire is known to me. The Lady Grizel awaits her. I bid you both enter my house.'

Involuntarily, Ludovick heaved a sigh of relief, as possibly did others. The pipers took up their refrain once more, but remained to pace and blow outside as Sir Lachlan led his visitors into the echoing vaulted corridors of Duart Castle.

Mary was delivered into the motherly charge of the Lady Grizel Cunningham, who greeted her in friendly fashion. Maclean was unusual in this also, that he had married a Lowland wife, a daughter of the Earl of Glencairn, from Ayrshire. Undoubtedly she pined for the gossip of her own kind. Ludovick was taken to a chamber on the second floor, where three Highland servants awaited him. One was a plump, sonsy smiling girl, and after the merest flickered glance at his guest Maclean dismissed her casually.

'A meal awaits you below, when you are ready,' he mentioned. 'Anything which you require, these will serve you. They speak your tongue.'

'I thank you, Sir Lachlan. You are ... thoughtful!'

The magnificent meal over at last, Maclean filled a great drinking-horn with amber liquor, sipped it, and then passed it to the Duke. 'Your good health and good fortune, sir,' he said. 'And now – to our business.'

The Lady Grizel rose, at her cue, glancing at Mary Gray. But though that young woman smiled and nodded, she did not rise in turn.

'If it is permitted, I would remain, to listen,' she said, greatly daring. Her expression was modesty itself, however.

Maclean and his sons stared – although Hector Ruari, who had hardly taken his eyes from the girl's face throughout the repast, looked well content, as did the youngest of the family, Ian Ban, a lanky lad of eighteen. There seemed to be no Maclean daughters.

'The Lady Mary is much interested in affairs. Interested – and wise,' Ludovick said. 'She is, h'm, the Master of Gray's daughter!'

'Ah!' Maclean nodded and shrugged in one. 'I have met the Master.' He made no other comment.

A little uncertainly the Lady Grizel left them.

Ludovick barely touched his whisky although the others, even the young Ian Ban, were drinking deeply. 'Sir Lachlan,' he said, 'the Lady Mary it was whom my Lord of Argyll told of your message. Regarding the Clan Donald. At Stirling. Conceiving it my business, she rode hot-foot north to Aberdeen, to inform me. I set out for Duart the very next morning.'

'Then you have not come from Stirling? From King James and the Council?'

'No. *I* am the Lieutenant of the North. The responsibility is mine. To discover the truth of this matter. To learn what action may be necessary.'

Keenly the other searched his face. 'James Stewart does not even know that you are here?'

'No. Leastways, not of my telling.'

'And the Master of Gray? He knows naught of this, either?'

'The Master has his own sources of information. Who can tell what he knows or does not know? But . . . he has learned nothing of this from me.'

The big man looked at Mary.

She shook her head. 'I have not seen my father for two weeks. He is at his justice ayres. At Forfar.'

'You would pass Forfar, would you not, riding to Aberdeen, lady?'

'I did not turn aside to call on him, sir.'

Maclean stroked his clean-shaven chin thoughtfully. 'That is what you meant, then, Duke of Lennox, when you said that you came secretly?'

'In part, yes. This matter is so uncertain, so delicate, that we decided that none should know of it until we learned the truth.'

'God be good!' Lachlan Barrach burst out. 'There is little uncertain or delicate here, I swear! Donald Gorm and Angus of

Dunyveg are at Rum and Eigg and Coll and Tiree, sword in hand! And Clanranald and his kin ravage Morvern and Ardgour – Maclean lands. They all but surround Mull, in their arrogance! What is delicate there, sir . . . ?'

His father signed him to silence. 'If the Duke of Lennox esteems it delicate, Lachlan, then no doubt he has good reason?'

That was a question, and Ludovick felt that too much questioning was coming from Lachlan Mor. 'Sir,' he said, 'you are well informed. It is clear. Have you learned where this Mac-Donald thrust is aimed? Is it to aid Huntly? Against the King? Or against Argyll, perhaps? Or even yourself . . . ?'

'I believe it to be aimed at Ireland. To aid Tyrone and O'Donnell.'

'That is the word you sent Argyll, yes. But is it so indeed? Why should Clan Donald aid the Irish?'

'For gold. Spanish gold.'

'Aye. But . . . even so? Would the Spaniards be so eager to spend their gold for that?'

'They ever seek to weaken England. A great uprising in Ireland would force Queen Elizabeth to send ever more men to hold down that country. And so weaken England.'

'M'mmm.' Ludovick glanced at Mary. He could scarcely declare that they in fact believed the gold to be English, not Spanish, and so demolish the other's theory.

'Spanish gold might be equally well spent, might it not, aiding Huntly in place of the Irish?' Mary suggested diffidently. 'If Scotland could be turned Catholic again, would that not serve Philip of Spain no less?'

The big man looked at her consideringly from those pale eyes. 'I think not. That would take a deal longer. Besides, Donald Gorm is assembling more and more galleys in the havens of Coll and Tiree. From all over the Isles. What purpose would these serve were he aiming at the mainland, to aid Huntly?'

'He is? You are certain of this?' Ludovick demanded. Coll and Tiree were the outermost isles of the Inner Hebrides, and surely would never be selected as an assembly place for any attack on the mainland.

'Think you that I would not know such a thing!' the chief gave back haughtily. 'That I am not watching them like a hawk?

I have men, galleys, fishing-boats, watching every move that they make.'

'Yes, yes – I understand. But why do they need more and more galleys? Out there?'

'To carry the mainland branches of the Confederacy to Ireland – Clanranald, Glengarry, Knoydart. Keppoch, and the rest. These, being mainly inland clans, have no galleys – or but a few. They gather there for a swift descent on the Irish coast – where no word may reach the English fleet. Small craft can bring out the others to Coll and Tiree. These galleys are for the open sea crossing. And the assault on the Ulster coast.'

'I see. Yes, it could be so. The English ships – where are they? Of that, no doubt sir, you are equally well informed?'

'Naturally. Save for a small squadron, off Dublin, they are massed in the south. Elizabeth fears aid to the Irish from Spain and France – not from Scotland. I have sent word – but it has a long road to travel. It could be weeks before the main English might can reach these waters.'

Mary drew a quick breath, as though to speak, and then changed her mind.

'Then what is to be done?' Ludovick demanded. 'Such an attack on Ireland could be almost as ill a blow at Scotland as at England. It would anger Elizabeth against James. It would enhearten the Catholics everywhere. And if it was successful, France and Spain and the Pope could use Ireland to invade Scotland just as readily as England. More so, i' faith! Possibly to attack England through Scotland.'

'I rejoice that the Lieutenant of the North perceives it so!' Lachlan Mor said grimly. 'Argyll, and those others I have warned, but consider the danger to their own lands, it seems, should the MacDonalds turn eastwards against them. Naught else concerns them.'

'And you? You take the longer view, sir? You see the danger to the realm? And would act, if need be?'

'I shall act, Duke of Lennox. Even though your King James and his Council proclaim me forfeit. Though I act alone!'

'You would so act, I think, not out of love for the realm, Sir Lachlan, but for Queen Elizabeth! And out of hatred for Clan Donald! Is it not so?'

The other looked at Ludovick steadily, unwinking, but did not answer.

'Maclean acts as Maclean sees fit!' Lachlan Barrach declared strongly. 'In the Isles, that is enough.'

'Does it so greatly matter *why* the MacDonalds are halted, so long as halted they are?' Mary Gray asked. 'Maclean's cause, the King's cause, even Queen Elizabeth's cause, could all be at one in this.'

'Well said!' Hector Ruari approved. 'The lady has the rights of it.'

His father nodded. 'So I see it. So I act. My galleys lie ready, beneath these walls. Throughout Mull my people wait. I could strike tomorrow But . . . what can King James do? Can he lend a single blow to the onset? The cause may be one - but effecting it would seem to be all for Maclean!'

'That is it, by the powers!' his younger son cried.

Ludovick spoke slowly, carefully. 'There is much, I think, that the King may do - through his Lieutenant of the North. I hold fullest powers to act in the King's name. To raise men, to command service, to exact provision, gear, arms, horses. To take over houses, shipping. All in the King's name.'

Lachlan Barrach's snort and his father's level stare demonstrated how much they thought of such powers, and how much attention would be paid to them in the Highlands and Islands.

But the Duke leaned forward over the table urgently. 'Wait before you scoff!' he charged. 'What if, in the King's name, I lift the sentence of forfeiture? If I accredit Sir Lachlan Maclean of Duart to act in the same King's name against the still forfeited Clan Donald, now in open revolt? If I authorise Maclean to demand men, seize boats and take victuals, commanding the aid of all leal subjects of the realm, under pain of treason? Does that not play a different tune?'

He had their attention now. The turning of the forfeiture into a royal commission of fire and sword against the MacDonalds, which was what Lennox's proposal amounted to, was a dramatic and notable inducement. The royal power in this area was negligible - but Maclean acting in the name of such royal power was a different matter altogether.

'Would King James and the Council agree to such?' Lachlan Mor demanded shrewdly.

Ludovick considered his finger-nails. 'Is that important?' he asked, in turn. 'They might not, I admit. From prejudice and lack of knowledge of the true position. They might seek to repudiate what I had done afterwards – were we unsuccessful. They would not, if we were successful, I think. But either way, that need not trouble us now – for it would take much time for them to hear of it, and then to do aught concerning it. Meantime, I am the Lieutenant, and have full and undoubted powers to act as I think best in the King's name and service. The responsibility is mine, Sir Lachlan.'

The older man eyed him steadily. 'There is much in what you say, Duke of Lennox,' he admitted at length. His glance slid over to Mary. 'This, I say, is uncommon like the work of the Master of Gray!'

'Like, may be – in some measure,' Ludovick conceded. 'But it is not, sir, nevertheless. I propose what I believe is best for the King and the realm. Do you agree to it? Your forfeiture cancelled? And you to act to prevent the Clan Donald's descent on Ireland – or anywhere else indeed – in the King's name?'

'Aye. But on one condition. You must act with me. At my side. For I will not act under King James's authority. *With* his authority – that I can use. Maclean will act with King James's Lieutenant – not *for* him!'

'I understand. It shall be as you say. If you will bring me paper and pen, I shall write it so, that there be no mistake. We can agree the words together.'

'Aye, so. Duke of Lennox, I think we may work well together!' The big man smiled faintly. 'And while you use pen, sir – write you to MacCailean Mor, to Argyll, commanding men and galleys. Not to sit close defending Campbell lands, but out here, to assail King James's enemies! And quickly. A score of galleys and two thousand men, shall we say, for a start?'

Ludovick drew a hand over his mouth. 'That is . . . apt!' he said. 'I shall do that. There are others too that we can summon?'

'To be sure. MacDougall of Lorne. MacNeil of Barra. MacQuarrie of Ulva. Stewart of Appin. And lesser men.'

'Very well. Let us to work. There is no time to be lost . . .'

'I am proud of you, Vicky,' Mary said. 'You have done splendidly. You have held your own all day, in the face of this proud and wily chief. And you have gained what you set out to gain, and more.'

'What we set out to gain, Mary. I could not have done it without you. As well you know. Yours is the mind behind all this. And I think that Maclean knows it likewise! Often when he seems to be speaking to me, it is you that he watches. I have seen it. He is no fool.'

'And you have shown him that you are not, either, Vicky. You have achieved much – more than I had looked for. If only we are in time.'

'Aye. There's the danger. Time. Will the MacDonalds give us time? Time to assemble these forces that I have written for? Time to bring them to bear?'

'Sir Lachlan believes that Donald Gorm and his main force will wait for Clanranald and the others. The inland clans. And these are still on the mainland. To carry them out to Coll and Tiree will take time – thousands of men.'

'Yes.'

They lay on their bed of plaids laid on layer upon layer of the shaggy hides of Highland cattle, and tried not to listen to the creaking of the chains that hung two storeys above, with their grisly burdens, swinging in the night wind. It had been a taxing, busy and eventful day. Sleep eluded them.

Tossing, Ludovick sighed. 'I still cannot see Patrick's purpose,' he said. 'In this of Ireland. Granted that he seeks to hold a balance between Catholic and Protestant. In Scotland. Where is the sense in using Elizabeth's money to send forces to Ireland? To aid Huntly, I could have understood. Even to assail Argyll, and so weaken myself and the King's forces at Aberdeen. But . . . Ireland! This is to aid the Catholic cause at large – the Pope, Spain, France. Why should he do that? We know that, Catholic though he may be at heart, his concern is with Scotland. That his abiding aim has always been to see James succeed to Elizabeth's Protestant throne, to rule one united kingdom. How can this serve that aim?'

The girl did not answer for a while. When she did, she spoke very thoughtfully, picking her words. 'I have much considered this. Sought to put myself inside Patrick's mind. Remembering that his mind is never simple, never obvious. I think that I may have found an answer. I may be wrong, but at least there is sense in it. To hold the balance between Catholic and Protestant will be a matter of much delicacy. We know that. Because of the betrayal of Argyll, we are apt to assume now that Patrick must be ever working against the Protestants. But it could be otherwise. It could be again Huntly's turn to be worked against. Wait, Vicky – hear me! Suppose that Huntly himself had been seeking the aid of the MacDonalds? It could be. They have not been friends – but then neither have the Irish and the Mac-Donalds been friends. They are all Catholic, and the Clan Donald Confederacy is the greatest single force left in Scotland, is it not? Suppose that Huntly offered Donald Gorm the Lord-ship of the Isles back again, if he would aid him in gaining the power in Scotland? But for King James the Fourth, Donald Gorm *would* have been Lord of the Isles, would he not – an independent prince in all but name? Might he not swallow that fly?'

'M'mmm. Perhaps. Go on.'

'Suppose, then, that Patrick learned that such was planned. And decided that the combination would make Huntly too strong – as it well might. How could he stop it? While still having MacDonald think that he was acting in the Catholic interest, against the Protestants and King James? Why – by this very thing! By paying him with gold, said to come from Spain. To go to the aid of the Irish Catholics. Against Protestant Elizabeth. If the MacDonalds are fighting in Ireland, they cannot be aiding Huntly.'

'Dear God! But . . . to use Elizabeth's gold for it! If he did . . .'

'That would please Patrick more than anything, I swear! And since this of Ireland is unlikely to lose Elizabeth her throne, he may consider the money well spent on James's behalf! A patriotic duty, no less!'

'Save us, Mary! This is too fantastic!'

'Is it any more fantastic than so many other plots and intrigues that Patrick has devised? Only on a greater scale . . .'

'No. It is too much! But the wild imaginings of your mind, my dear . . .'

'Perhaps.' She was suddenly quiet-voiced, lying back. 'But remember, Vicky, that I heired part of that mind from Patrick Gray!'

It was long before they slept, that night.

The day that followed was a strangely idle one, considering the urgency of the situation. Having written his letters, and despatched them by Maclean couriers, to Argyll and other chiefs, there was nothing more that Ludovick could do meantime save await the response to his summons. As for Maclean, he was all poised for action anyway, and only awaited tidings, information, from his many and far-flung scouts and spies. So there was little to be done in the great castle on Duart's rock. After all the travelling of the last days, Mary especially would have been glad of the interval, to rest and relax – but the atmosphere was not conducive to relaxation. There was a tension in the air, a waiting as for something to explode, a sense of violence on leash in all around, save only the Lady Grizel, which precluded rest and ease.

Maclaine of Lochbuy, chief of the most important subsidiary of the clan, sailed in in a galley that afternoon, a fiery-seeming and harsh-spoken man of early middle years, who had very little English and made no secret of the fact that he was but little impressed by the Duke of Lennox. He brought word that he had eight galleys, as well as smaller craft, lying manned and ready in Loch Buy, and that MacQuarrie of Ulva was assembling his small clan.

All that day Hector Ruari Maclean was hardly away from Mary's side. While his father and brothers, and Ludovick with them, spent most of the time down amongst the men at the township and about the galleys, he made it clear that he was more interested in the entertainment of their guest than in warlike preparations. Mary, however, who had had much experience of admiring and pressing young men, forceful as they might be, had no difficulty in looking after herself and keeping the jovial Hector approximately in his place.

The news which reached Duart late that evening was unexpected. Clanranald and the mainland MacDonalds had turned back, to north and west, leaving south Lochaber and the threatened Appin area, and streaming back into Morvern and Sunart – to the relief and congratulation of the Stewarts and Campbells. Lachlan Mor was very thoughtful at hearing this, dismissing scornfully any suggestion that it could be on account of any menace to the rampaging MacDonalds posed by the said Stewarts of Appin and the Campbells. He interpreted it as meaning changed plans on the part of Clanranald – which probably meant urgent instructions from Donald Gorm.

The air of tension was by no means lessened when Mary and Ludovick retired for the night.

They were awakened early and rudely. Horns were bugling loudly, alarmingly, above them, presumably from the castle battlements. It was apparently just dawn. Even as they sat up, questioning, young Ian Ban Maclean opened their door excitedly to announce that his father required the Duke of Lennox's presence below forthwith. He added that it was action, at last.

Wisely dismissing any offence at this peremptory summons, hastily Ludovick threw on some clothing. Mary, wrapped in a bedrobe, insisted on accompanying him. Down in the Great Hall, they found Lachlan Mor, his sons, and some of his chieftains, already assembled and in urgent discussion. Maclean made an even more striking, almost awesome, figure than usual, clad now in a long coat of antique chain-mail, which made him seem taller and more massive than ever, a huge two-handed sword slung behind his back with its hilt thrusting up at the back of his silver-blond hair, his head being covered with a great winged helmet. He had the appearance of some ancient semi-legendary hero of centuries before.

There was nothing legendary or theatrical about his manner or voice, however, as he swung on the new arrivals. 'Duke of Lennox,' he jerked, his sibilant voice crisp. 'The time for talk is past! Clanranald goes too far! He has had the insolence to set foot on my territory – on Mull. Yesterday, late, he and part of his host sailed from Loch Aline, in Morvern. In small craft. To join Donald Gorm at Coll. This north-westerly wind that has blown up has much hindered their passage up the sound.

Last night they turned in to land. But not to their own side. Not to Sunart or Ardnamurchan. To mine! They are landed at Tobermory Bay – a thousand of them, and more. On Maclean's land!'

The whereabouts of this temporary landing seemed of less significance to Ludovick than was Clanranald's ultimate destination. 'On their way to join Donald Gorm? At Coll? You are sure of this? That must mean, then, that they are ready. To cross to Ireland. For all these thousands, on small islands like Coll and Tiree, would soon starve.'

'No doubt. But . . . we shall see that they never reach Coll and Tiree, to starve there!'

There was a growl of agreement from the others.

'You do not wait for Argyll and the others, then?'

'I do not! Here is an opportunity not to be lost, whatever! I strike at once. Clanranald's force is split. There are not boats enough to carry them all out to Coll, at once. He can have few galleys – only birlinns and small craft. We sail as soon as my men are embarked. If you would come with us, hasten.'

Ludovick nodded. 'I shall not delay you.'

If the Duke did not get away quite so quickly as he anticipated, it was mainly, strangely enough, because of Mary. She was all arguments and pleas to be taken also. From protests as to unsuitability and inexpediency, he had to progress through prophecies of encumbrance and danger, to firm refusal, before she yielded her claims that she would be perfectly safe, in no man's road, and would keep hidden in the ship. But for once Ludovick overruled her vehemently. She would remain in Duart Castle, he declared. She might think like a man in some things, travel like a man – but when it came to warfare she must remember that she was a woman. When Mary saw that he was determined, she gave in with good grace – but nothing would prevent her from coming down with the men to the boat harbour, to see them off.

They sailed, just as the first lemon-yellow bars of the sunrise sent slantwise rays between the purple-tinged night clouds above the eastern mountains.

Chapter Thirteen

Ludovick Stewart, though essentially a man of peace, with
no love for strife and clash, could by no means deny the excitement and elation of that early morning dash up the long Sound
of Mull. Twenty-three galleys in all, long, dark and menacing
in the strange half-light, unhampered by any smaller and slower
vessels, slipped out of Duart Bay and headed due north-west,
directly into a stiff and steady wind. No sails were raised, in
consequence, and the host of oarsmen strained at their long
sweeps with fierce and sustained vigour, to send their leanly
sinister craft surging against wind and seas. Fortunately the tide
was nearing full ebb, for otherwise, in the narrow two-mile-wide
sound, twenty-five miles long, even these greyhounds would
have been held as though in leash. As it was, vying with each
other – although none ever drew ahead of Lachlan Mor's galley
– they raced up the dark mountain-girt channel at a stirring
pace, each craft's position picked out by the stark white of its
bow-wave, the steady lines of oar-splashes, and the creaming
wake. Snatches of the panting, moaning chant which rose
rhythmically from each vessel could be heard between the gusts
of the wind.

It was cold out on the water thus early, and the breeze searching. Ludovick almost envied the rowers their task and exercise.
He stood on the tiny forecastle of Sir Lachlan's craft, with Ian
Ban and two or three of the clan's chief men, Hector and Lachlan Barrach captaining their own ships. A film of salt spray and
spume stroked his face continuously, for these vessels seemed
not so much to ride the seas as to cut through them.

There was twenty miles of narrow seas between Duart and
Tobermory, from the south-east to the north-west tip of Mull,
and the galleys raced to cover it in ninety minutes or less. It
was Maclean's aim to reach Clanranald before the other put
to sea again. This breeze would be apt to delay the departure.

'But would you not better wait until they *are* at sea? In their small boats?' Ludovick put to his host, with vivid memories of their own helplessness, in the Campbell fishing-boat, before the swift might of Lachlan Barrach's galley. 'At sea, you would scatter them like a flock of sheep before wolves.'

'Scatter them, aye. But that is not Maclean's intention, my friend! I go to smite and destroy the MacDonalds, not to scatter. Once they are in their hundreds of small craft, there will be no bringing them to battle. Some we would hunt down, to be sure, but most would escape us amongst the islands. Eagles cannot fight finches!'

'How do we do, then?'

'We smite them by land as well as by water,' the big man said grimly. 'I will teach the Sons of Donald to take heed for the Sons of Gillean!'

By the time that the sun was fully risen clear of the Argyll mountains, and dazzling all the sound behind them with its sparkling brittle radiance, Sir Lachlan was scanning the Mull coastline on his left front keenly. Many small headlands thrust out from it but, well ahead, there was one taller and more massive than its neighbours.

'Yonder,' he pointed to Ludovick. 'Rudha Seanach. There we land. Behind it opens the bay of Tobermory. One mile.'

'You attack overland?'

'Aye. My main strength. The galleys will land us. Then go on. Tobermory bay is wide – but its mouth is all but closed by an island. Calve Island. A sheltered anchorage – but I will make it a trap! The main entry, to the north, is but a quarter-mile wide. That to the south is much narrower – a mere gullet. Stop these with my galleys, and Clanranald is bottled up. He must stand and fight.'

'I see. Yes. But . . . would it not serve to scatter and disperse the MacDonalds? To spare his, and your own, men? This battle and bloodshed. I say that would serve our purpose. There is no need for a great slaying.'

The chief considered him coldly. 'Maclean does not engage in play-acting, Duke of Lennox!' he said briefly. 'In especial against Clan Donald.' And he turned away abruptly, to speak to his shipmaster.

As they neared the headland of Rudha Seanach, keeping fairly close in-shore now, a single small boat put out from the shadow-slashed coast there to meet them, making straight for Sir Lachlan's own galley. It brought Maclean of Tobermory himself, a dark, wiry man in stained tartans, who swarmed up a rope into the larger vessel with the agility of a monkey. He it was who had sent Lachlan Mor the news in the first place. Now he came to announce that the MacDonalds' camp was astir but that they were not yet embarking, no doubt giving time for the strong wind to subside – as he prophesied it would. They might, however, be awaiting the next tide. Himself he had offered no resistance to the invaders the previous night. In fact, on word of the host of craft approaching, he had slipped quietly away from his house, leaving servants to say that he was from home. Clanranald, he was sure, was unsuspicious of attack.

Lachlan Mor was well satisfied. He turned his ship directly into the little bay beneath the high headland.

Skilfully steered and rowed, the leading galley gently grounded its forefoot on the shingle of the beach, and Sir Lachlan, despite his years and heavy chain-mail, was first over the side and into chest-high water. Ludovick could not do other than follow, gasping at the cold.

Soon armed men were streaming ashore by the hundred. All save a few of the galleys' fighting-men, as distinct from the oarsmen, were landed, to the number of some seven hundred. Sir Lachlan, with Hector Ruari and Ian Ban, Maclean of Tobermory and other notables, was already striding up the rugged hillside of the ridge which lay between them and Tobermory's bay. Ludovick was thankful for the exercise, at least, to set the blood flowing in his veins.

The galleys were still all lying huddled close in the inlet below, when the climbers neared the top of the ridge. Lachlan Barrach had been left in command of the ships.

Cautiously the Maclean leaders approached the crest, the main mass holding back. Utilising the rocks and bushes, they crept up, to peer over.

The basin of the bay of Tobermory was still half in shadow. It was large, as Maclean had said, fully a mile across, with fairly steep sides heavily wooded, curving round to two headlands. Between these lay a long, low, green island, substantially blocking the entrance. To the south, the passage looked little wider than a river; to the north it might be four hundred yards, but was narrowed by a thrusting sand spit.

The entire area, land and water, presented a scene of activity this early morning. The bay itself was full of craft, mainly small but with two or three galleys and birlinns amongst them. There was much coming and going of rowing-boats out to these. On land there was considerable movement, mainly down to the shore. It looked as though camp was now being struck.

'Good! This is well!' Lachlan Mor declared. 'We shall leave them a little longer. There is no hurry now, at all, at all! Signal your brother to wait, Hector.'

The red-head slipped down below the skyline, to stand up and wave his plaid in the direction of the galleys below, a prearranged notification.

'You wait? For more men? Further aid?' Ludovick inquired.

'No. Not that. Clanranald has more men than I have, yes. I but wait for more of them to embark. So we shall lessen his advantage.'

They lay watching while the sun rose higher, and more and more of the MacDonalds transferred from the shore to the boats. Obviously they were not going to wait for the tide. As had been foretold, and as often happens, with daylight the night wind was dropping. At length Maclean was satisfied.

'Now!' he said. 'Sign him to start, Hector.'

Lachlan Barrach, below, was quick to recognise his brother's second signal. It was only a few moments before oar splashes could be seen, and the galleys began to move seawards.

As soon as he saw the leading vessel rounding the point of Rudha Seanach, with a bare mile to go to the south channel and Calve Island, Lachlan Mor rose to his feet, right on the skyline as he was. Reaching back over his shoulder, he drew the great two-handed sword strapped there in a single magnificent sweep, to hold it aloft.

'Brothers!' he shouted, in the Gaelic. 'Sons of Gillean! There is your prey. Come and kill!' And he flung the sword round in a flashing arc, to point northwards, downhill.

A roar rose from hundreds of throats, as the impatient multitude surged forward.

After that, as far as Ludovick was concerned, all was chaos and confusion, in an onset totally unlike anything he had experienced hitherto. In that yelling, shouting rush downhill, he was quickly overtaken and passed by more enthusiastic and lighter-clad runners, broadswords held high – though even so, mail-clad as he was, Sir Lachlan with his vast strides kept the lead. No doubt the continuous shouting, since it was led by the chief, was more than just barbarous sound and fury, and intended to confuse the enemy as to numbers; it certainly had the effect of confusing the Duke, its rageful uproar preventing him from thinking, from using his brain coherently at all. It was only later that he could piece together the happenings of the next hour or so into any comparatively clear pattern.

Clanranald and the other leaders of the MacDonald host were still on shore when the Macleans appeared on the skyline to the south and came charging down upon them. With most of their men embarked, it was obviously their best policy to embark likewise, rather than to stand their ground. This they were proceeding to do when the topmasts of the galley fleet were perceived above the low sandhills and grass banks at the southern end of Calve Island, most evidently blocking the south channel. A general movement of boats towards the north channel followed, in consequence.

But it was too late. The Maclean galleys were there first, and all escape by sea was precluded. Clanranald's horns bugled the recall.

Getting his scattered host back to the shore again, however, and in fighting trim, was no easy task. It demanded time – and time was a commodity in short supply indeed that morning. Their numbers much masked by the woodland, but sounding a fearsome array, the Macleans bore down on the beach at a furious pace.

Clanranald could only turn now and face the onslaught as best he might, with a bare third of his force, hoping that others would reach him quickly. But this was to reckon without Lachlan Barrach. Only a comparatively few of the Maclean galleys were required to block the entrances to the bay; with the others, braving the hazards of navigation in the confined and shallow waters, he drove in and bore down upon the trapped craft, large and small, his cannon crashing out their dire contribution. The MacDonald boats darted hither and thither in complete disorder.

No real battle eventuated, however many minor skirmishes developed. The MacDonalds were brave and indeed terrible fighters, but in the circumstances they could make no coherent stand, no unified defence. In the face of Lachlan Mor's headlong charge, those around Clanranald were borne back, overwhelmed and driven into the sea.

Ludovick's own part in it all was scarcely glorious. By no means in the front rank of the Macleans, after having tripped over tree-roots, fallen in a burn and floundered through bog, he found himself carried down over the shingle of the beach and into the water itself. There, in a wild melee of struggling men, he was knocked over by combatants, much at a disadvantage over keeping his feet on the slippery wet stones in his heavy riding-boots. He was staggering up when he was attacked by a black-bearded MacDonald wielding a dirk which already dripped blood. Trying to shorten his sword for in-fighting in the crush of men, Ludovick defended himself as best he could, whilst seeking space to use his weapon to fuller effect. Before he could succeed in this, the MacDonald's steel struck sparks on the simple breastplate which Ludovick wore, and slid along it to rip open the left shoulder of his doublet and the skin beneath it. As the man stumbled forward with the impetus of his blow, Ludovick desperately smashed down the hilt of his sword on the fellow's back neck. He collapsed into the water.

Reeling, the Duke was carried along in the press of struggling fighters, dazed now and not very certain who was friend and who was foe in the tartan-clad and largely bare-chested throng. Recognising both his danger and his uselessness, he turned to try to force his way back to dry land – and was promptly knocked down by a furious Maclean in consequence, fortunately with only a random blow from the flat of the sword. On all fours thereafter he dragged himself up on to the shingle of the beach and so crouched, clutching at his shoulder.

He was still huddled thus, unheeded flotsam on that beach of battle, when horns beginning to bray from near and far announced Clanranald's surrender and the end of hostilities. All fighting did not cease forthwith, especially out amongst the boats and on Calve Island where many of the MacDonalds had landed to offer a more effective defence than in swaying small boats. But all major resistance collapsed, and the day was lost and won.

If it was not a great battle at least it was a most notable victory, and Clan Donald's pride, the fiercest in Scotland probably, took its greatest humbling for centuries. As well as Clanranald's, Lachlan Mor accepted the surrendered swords of three of his uncles, of Donald Gorm's brother, of MacDonald of Knoydart, MacIan of Ardnamurchan, and other celebrities. Undoubtedly not a few MacDonald clansmen escaped into the interior of Mull, but some eleven hundred were taken prisoner. Of corpses there were astonishingly few, considering the noise, cannonade and fury – although the sea might have hidden some; but there were large numbers of wounded, most of whom bore their injuries with astonishing philosophical calm.

Ludovick's own inclusion in this total seemed to raise him greatly in the estimation of all. Happily, although painful, his was merely a surface cut and far from serious. Yet even Sir Lachlan appeared to consider that he had gained much stature in consequence.

Maclean, indeed, was in fine fettle altogether, giving praise to his people, courteous to his captives, genial towards all. Not wishing to burden himself with large numbers of prisoners, he appropriated the weapons, equipment and anything else which his people fancied of the bulk of the MacDonald fighting-men, and then turned them over in batches of one hundred or so to his various galley captains, with orders to take, land and release them in isolated parts of the Clan Donald coastline of Ardamurchan, Moidart and Morar. All chieftains, lairds and gentleman, of course, he held for ransom. Keeping the captured galleys and birlinns for himself, he distributed the small craft amongst his clansfolk. All this seen to, he re-embarked, with his principal prisoners, for Duart.

Scudding down the Sound of Mull with sails set and the wind behind them, they made a swift and triumphant return. Ludovick took the opportunity to speak with Donald, tenth Captain of Clanranald, a fine-featured youngish man of proud carriage, who bore his humiliating defeat with dignity. His line, although it had never been that of the later Lords of the Isles, claimed nevertheless to be the senior stem of the great Clan Donald and of the dynasty of the mighty Somerland. He acknowledged Donald Gorm of Sleat as *de facto* leader of the Confederacy, but by no means as his chief.

Whilst he was far from voluble or forthcoming, Clanranald did admit, in response to Ludovick's questioning, that this Clan Donald adventure was indeed aimed at Ireland and the aiding of Tyrone and O'Donnell. Without conceding that he personally had soiled his hands with money, he agreed that gold was involved, gold from Spain. When the Duke suggested that the gold was in fact from England, the other showed that he was slightly better acquainted with the specie than he had indicated by acknowledging that the actual coins were English gold crowns, for convenience, but that they had of course come from the King of Spain. No other source, obviously, had occurred to him. He also admitted that Logan of Restalrig had acted as intermediary, and had in fact recently called upon him at Castle Tiorrim on his road south from Donald Gorm in Skye. Ludovick could get no more out of him, save that his captors need not imagine that this small reverse would seriously upset Clan Donald plans, for Donald Gorm had a force of at least eight thousand men assembled out there amongst the Isles, and would avenge this day's work in suitable fashion.

So they came back to Duart Castle, with cannon firing and cheering. For the ceremonial entry, the captive chiefs were chained together like felons, and their banners dragged in the mud behind them – although, as soon as they were safely inside the castle walls the chains were taken off and they were treated almost as honoured guests. Apparently there was a Highland form to be observed in such matters.

The Lieutenant of the North, the only member of the castle party to have been wounded in the engagement, found himself elevated to something of the status of hero, a situation which, after due modest disclaimer, he found it best to accept with good grace – especially from Mary, who cherished him with a concern worthy of a man at death's door.

In the midst of it all, Maclean's courier to Argyll arrived

back from Inveraray. He brought word from the Earl that he would answer the Duke's call for men and ships as effectively and quickly as possible – but that he was much exercised over another and more personal matter. His uncle and former guardian, Sir John Campbell of Cawdor, had been murdered – here in his own Campbell country. On Argyll's instructions he had been bringing the remainder of the Campbell host back from Aberdeen, to face this MacDonald threat, and the journey nearly over had ridden ahead to his own house in Lorne, where he had been shot dead through a window.

Ludovick and Mary eyed each other sombrely at this news. The cold hand of fear reached out to touch them again.

It took two weeks and more to assemble the force and fleet which Lennox had called for to assail Donald Gorm, largely on account of continuing high winds from the north-west which made navigation on this beautiful but dangerous seaboard hazardous indeed – but also, of course, because of the lack of enthusiasm on the part of the chiefs involved. For this latter reason too, the host which did eventually gather was a deal smaller than had been hoped for, amounting to no more than four thousand men in all, with some twenty more galleys and a number of birlinns.

Fortunately the same unfavourable winds had been equally so for Donald Gorm and his MacDonalds, out in the further isles, holding up his reinforcements likewise as well as precluding his sailing for Ireland. Clanranald's prophesy that the defeat at Tobermory and consequent loss of support would not dissuade him from the enterprise, appeared to be confirmed; the advance was only being postponed.

Maclean was for immediate action, despite odds – but Ludovick insisted that they should wait for Argyll. There were above a thousand Campbells in their company, but Argyll himself delayed, intent on discovering who had slain his uncle. Urgent messages went from Duart that he should leave this inquiry until later.

In the end, coincident with a marked improvement in the weather, the long anticipated tidings arrived. Strengthened by a further contingent of Macleods from the Outer Isles, Donald Gorm had sailed from Coll and Tiree, south by west, in a great fleet of some sixty galleys as well as many other craft. And as, furiously, Maclean ordered his host to prepare to put to sea, a flotilla came sailing up the Firth of Lorne, led by a galley with its sail painted with the bold gold-and-black gyrony-of-eight of the Campbells and the proud banner of MacCailean Mor himself flying at its masthead. Argyll had come at last, with five hundred more broadswords.

The Earl, it turned out, had brought more than that. In his own galley, specially fitted up with comfortable cabin-space fore and aft, came his lady-mother, the Countess Agnes. Also his young brother, Colin Campbell of Lundie. It was an indication of the state of mind prevailing in this proud house, in this era of treachery and murder, that the Earl had not dared to leave mother and brother behind, even in his castle of Inveraray. The death of Cawdor, after all the others, left only this young Colin as sure heir to the earldom and chiefship. One by one those close to Argyll had been eliminated. He was now taking no risks.

Mary Gray, of course, had been agitating to be taken on this important voyage also, the more so as it might well be a prolonged one. Hitherto her pleas had been unsuccessful. The arrival of the Countess Agnes however put a different complexion on the matter. Argyll would not hear of his mother being left behind at Duart, a young man now trusting no one but himself; and if the Countess was to sail with them, Mary claimed that there was no valid reason why she should be forbidden. Argyll, grateful to the girl for what she had revealed to him that day at Castle Campbell, and seeing her as company for his mother, backed her plea, offering to take her in his own vessel. Ludovick, actually delighted to have her company, could not refuse, however much Maclean might scoff at the idea of women in war galleys.

When the combined fleet, therefore, sailed from Duart only a couple of hours after Argyll's arrival, Mary shared the stern cabin of the Earl's galley with the Countess and her maid, while Ludovick, as before, accompanied Lachlan Mor. In the event of battle, it was agreed that Argyll himself would transfer to another Campbell galley leaving this craft to keep well out of danger's way.

They drove down the Firth of Lorne, a magnificent sight in

the gold and shadow of the evening sunlight, the largest fleet seen in these narrow waters for many a long day – over forty galleys and a dozen birlinns, but nothing more slow such as might hold them back. The MacDonalds had a sizeable start, but they had somewhat further to sail, and would be delayed inevitably by the craft, slower than the galleys, which they were having to use as additional transports. Almost certainly they were making for the Irish rebel stronghold area of Ballycastle in Antrim, and Maclean hoped and anticipated that they would keep fairly close in to the Scottish coast, amongst the islands, until opposite the northern tip of Antrim, lie anchored in some remote and sheltered bay overnight, and then in the early morning make a swift dash across the North Channel, the shortest direct crossing – this in order to avoid losing any of their slower vessels during the night, and also to avoid being spotted by the watchdogs of Elizabeth's navy which patrolled these Irish waters continuously. The one great danger which Donald Gorm had to fear was to be caught by a squadron of English ships of war and galleons, in a position where his superior speed and manoeuvrability could not save him – for compared with these the galleys were cockleshells and could be sunk with ease by the others' vastly greater fire-power and longer range. Sir Lachlan was going to take the risk of sailing all night, even through these dangerous reef-strewn seas, in order to steal a march on his enemy.

The wind, though much moderated, was still north-westerly. This, for the sake of speed, meant that Maclean should take the most southerly course possible, once out of the Firth of Lorne – that through the narrows of the Sounds of Luing and Jura. Donald Gorm, who would probably reach the same waters via the Sound of Islay – and it was no part of Lachlan Mor's strategy to engage in a stern-chase and open battle with sixty MacDonald galleys as against his own forty. He required surprise to aid him outnumbered as he was, and planned accordingly. Emerging therefore from the comparatively sheltered waters of the Firth, instead of south he swung round almost due west, half into wind and seas – to the immediate reduction of their speed. Passing to the north of the jagged fangs of the Garvelloch Isles, dipping and tossing and leaving behind a drifting cloud of spray from a couple of thousand lashing oar-blades, they made directly for the open sea.

Nearing the long island of Colonsay, and night coming down, Maclean signalled for all his galleys to close in, reef sails, and reduce speed. From now on the most intense care was demanded of every captain. Few commanders would or could have risked this endeavour, for there was still some twenty miles of rock- and skerry-infested waters to be covered, including the far-flung menace of the Torran Rocks, before the final isolated reefs of Dubh Heartach were reached and they could turn due south in clear deep sea. For over fifty ships to thread this vicious maze in formation, in darkness, demanded a discipline and standard of navigation ill at odds with the wild appearance of this clan host. Led by Sir Lachlan's own galley, the vessels must proceed three abreast and only one ship's length behind the trio in front, each guided by the white splashes of its leaders' and neighbours' oars. Course-changing would be ordered by a code of signals blown on horns and passed back from ship to ship. Hector Ruari and Lachlan Barrach alone were exempted from these strict commands; almost as expert as their father, they were to act as sheep-dogs for the convoy, to watch for stragglers, round up and warn off, as necessary – an onerous task indeed in the darkness.

Ludovick, fascinated by it all, could by no means curl up in a plaid and sleep, as advised by Maclean, but stood hour after hour on the heaving forecastle of the leading ship, chilled as he was, while admiration for the older man's brilliant seamanship, swift decision and uncanny instinct, grew upon him. Time and again his heart was in his mouth as sudden spouting seas to left or right hissed and snarled dire danger. But not once did Sir Lachlan show hesitation, alarm, or even anxiety. The lives of up to five thousand men depended upon his sole and instant judgment, but he revealed no hint of strain or excitement.

Mary, for her part, was no more prepared to sleep, whatever the comforts available. She found the Countess a proud and haughty woman younger-seeming than might have been expected considering that, before she had married the Earl's father and former Chancellor, she had been the widow of the famous

Earl of Moray, Regent of Scotland and eldest half-brother of Mary the Queen – a child-wife she must have been, surely, for the Regent was dead twenty-five years. She was a Keith, daughter of the fourth and sister of the present Earl Marischal. Full of her woes now, she was apparently more outraged by the blows to Argyll pride than distressed by loss or danger. Mary discovering the more sympathy for the Earl and his brother, preferred their company up at the galley's prow. Their vessel, of course, was deep in the centre of the flotilla, sandwiched between others, with responsibility only for maintaining position – but even so the situation absorbed the girl. She knew no fear, but recognised the danger, savouring the spice of it. Peering into the blackness ahead and around, and seeing only the vague outline of the ship in front and the wan white of oar-thrashed water, listening to the hissing rush of the waves, the whine of wind in cordage, the creak of timbers and oars, and the gasping refrain of the rowers, she knew a strange exhilaration that desired only that this should go on and on, that it should not stop, a feeling that she and the sea and the night were one. Even when young Colin Campbell, shivering, went below, and Argyll urged her to do likewise, she shook her damp head and remained standing at his side, wrapped in a wet plaid, hair plastering her face, licking the salt spray from her lips. Although they scarcely exchanged a word throughout, some affinity developed there between the girl and the restrained, sombre, dark-browed young man, an affinity unexpressed and unstressed, yet which would hold Archibald Grumach Campbell, in some measure, for the rest of his life. Frequently, inevitably, with the lurching of the ship, they staggered against each other; sometimes she grasped his arm for support, sometimes he held her firmly.

It was nearly midnight before an eerie winding of horns from front to rear of the fleet proclaimed that they were past the unseen pillar of Dubh Heartach and its savage outliers, and a change of course of almost ninety degrees was ordered. No more navigational hazards now lay between them and the north coast of Ireland, sixty miles south. The same formation was still to be kept, but with much more space allowable between ships. Sails were hoisted and speed picked up, reliefs of rowers taking over. Tension relaxed everywhere.

Just before she went below, Mary turned to the silent Argyll standing by her side. 'My lord,' she said, 'that was good for us, I think. Clean danger, not foul. That was living, was it not?'

He nodded, wordless.

'All men are not betrayers,' she added. 'There is courage and strength and honesty in men. Aye, and faith – much faith. Deceit and treachery – these, in the end, must fail. The good, the true, *must* prevail. I know it. Something . . . something in this night tells me so.'

For a little he stared straight ahead of him. Then slowly he inclined his head. 'It may be so. I hope so. I thank you, Mary Gray.'

She touched his arm briefly, and left him there.

As she lay in her dark bunk thereafter, it came to her that this unsmiling lonely youth, whom men already were calling The Grim, had not asked her why and what made her speak as she had done, how she had come to her conclusion. He had somehow understood and accepted. Which was more than Ludovick Stewart, for instance, would or could have done.

Chapter Fourteen

Probably it was the comparative quiet and the lack of motion which wakened Mary. The Countess and her maid still slept. She rose, tidied herself, and slipped out into the grey light of early morning.

It was a strange sight that met her gaze. All around her, men slept, slumped over their oars, curled on every bench, littering every inch of space in the crowded galley. And on every hand the galley's sister-ships lay sleeping also, tight-packed in neat rows in a small bay, gunwale to gunwale, stem to stern, a concentrated mass of timber and armour and sleeping clansmen, motionless save for the slight sway that was the echo of the Atlantic swell. Close by, to the south, a rocky beach rose in broken redstone cliffs, backed by grassy hills of an intense greenness, even in that dove-grey morning light. The bay was sheltered, irregularly shaped, and perhaps half a mile at its mouth, and of approximately the same depth. Seaward, perhaps five miles to the north, on the edge of the slate-grey horizon, the long black line of a low island showed.

The girl's impression that all the Highland host slept, exhausted, was soon corrected. On their own ship's forecastle two or three men stood, wrapped in their plaids, silent – and when she looked around her, she perceived that on every vessel men thus stood, on watch. She perceived also that all these seemed to divide their attention between two points – or rather, three – forward, where Sir Lachlan's galley lay broadside on to the bows of the first row of ships, giving it greater opportunity to manoeuvre, and east and west to where on the green summits of the headlands which enclosed the bay, two dark columns of smoke rose high in the morning air. That these were signals of some sort could hardly be doubted. They were obviously preoccupying the attention of the silent watchers.

Mary could by no means make her way forward to the forecastle over the sprawled bodies of some hundreds of Campbells, but she climbed the ladder to the after-deck which roofed in the Countess's cabin. There, amongst more sleeping men, including the galley's captain, one man sat, hunched in a corner but awake – Archibald, Earl of Argyll, MacCailean Mor himself. He might have been there, waking, all night by the set look of him.

'My lord,' she whispered, 'Do you not sleep?'

He shook his dark head. 'I am no great sleeper,' he said. 'Besides, we shall have more to do than sleep presently, I think.' And he nodded towards the smoke signals.

'Where are we? Is this Ireland?'

'Aye. A small bay to the west of the great bay of Ballycastle, on the north coast of Antrim. Yonder, to the east, is Kinbane Head. Here we await Donald Gorm. But . . . it seems we have been discovered.'

'Those smokes? Are they to warn the MacDonalds that we are here?'

'Who knows? But they are surely to warn someone. O'Neill and O'Donnell have sharp eyes, it seems. For we crept in in darkness. The fires have been lit but a score of minutes.'

As they watched those ominous black columns that drifted away on the north-west breeze, there was a certain stir amongst the watchers on each vessel nearby as a small rowing-boat wove its way in and out amongst the closely-ranked galleys, a man therein shouting up to each one, in the Gaelic, as it passed.

'What does he say, my lord?' Mary demanded, as it came near.

'That Maclean orders all captains to be ready to sail at his signal. He has sent ashore a party to deal with those fires.'

As the bustle of waking men stirred the fleet, a single man came climbing up from the small boat into Argyll's galley. It proved to be the Duke of Lennox himself. Embracing Mary frankly, openly, he turned to the Earl.

'I came to apprise you of what is toward, my lord,' he said. 'It would be wisest, I think, if you would now move to another ship of your array, and keep close to Maclean, so that this galley with the women may remain hidden and secure. There may be fighting shortly.'

The other nodded. 'Are Donald Gorm's ships sighted?'

'No. Not that we may see from here. But perhaps from the high ground. These smokes may mean that watchers on the headlands have seen them, and seek to warn them of our presence. Or it may be only that the warning is for Tyrone and O'Donnell themselves, inland. Ballycastle, their main stronghold, is but some five or six miles south by east of here. That is why here it is that the MacDonalds must come.'

'Then . . . it may not be a warning at all?', Mary put in. 'If these watchers look for a Highland fleet, will they not be likely to take us for the MacDonalds? So these signals may be but a sign to the Irish chiefs that his friends are come.'

'Yes. It could be so. We cannot tell. Maclean has landed a party to go up there and discover the matter. When we have their report, we may have to move swiftly.'

'Move from this bay?'

'Aye, if need be. This place, though it hides us well from sight from the sea, could be a death-trap for us. As was Tobermory Bay for Clanranald. We are here to hide from Donald Gorm, to sally out and attack him when he is unready, approaching Ballycastle Bay, and knowing nothing of our presence. But if he is warned that we are in here, he could bottle us up. We would be lost.'

'Maclean did not foresee this?' Argyll demanded.

'He did not look to be observed so soon. Not in this remote bay of Kinbane. He knows this coast well. There is empty moorland and bog behind here, for miles, he says – savage, waterlogged country where no men live. It is strange that it should be watched, guarded.'

'It may be only because the Irish look for Donald Gorm?'

'How could they know when he would come? He has been many weeks preparing . . .'

While they were discussing it, a considerable outcry developed from the detachment which Maclean had sent ashore. They had climbed up the rising ground of the eastern horn of the bay, Kinbane Head itself, making for the nearest fire, and had reached an intermediate summit, a spur of the headland. Here they had halted suddenly, and begun to wave and gesticulate wildly, their shouts sounding thinly on the morning air. Obviously they had seen something which excited them greatly.

'Donald Gorm! They have spied his fleet!' Mary cried.

'I think not,' Argyll said, in his unemotional, factual way.

'They would have shouted before this, in that case. If they can see the MacDonald ships now, they could have seen them before – for they have but moved on to a knoll yonder. They would not have waited. No, it is because they can now see down beyond. Eastwards, into the next bay. Into the main Ballycastle Bay, or whatever lies beyond that cape. It is something down there that they have seen.'

'You are right,' Ludovick nodded. 'It must be that. Perhaps it is an encampment, there. Of the Irish . . .'

Whatever they had seen, the scouting party considered it of sufficient importance to abandon their mission to the hilltop. They came hurrying downhill again, sending two racing emissaries ahead.

Argyll, anticipating trouble, went below to arm and to inform his mother and brother that he would be moving to another Campbell galley meantime. Ludovick waited, for the small boat to come back for them.

While still they waited, the word flew like wildfire round the fleet, from ship to ship, that it was not Donald Gorm at all that was spied – it was the English! A large squadron of English ships of war were in the main bay, just around the headland. So said the running scouts.

Men's excited discussion of these tidings was interrupted by a peremptory blaring of horns from Maclean. Sir Lachlan, waiting for no one, had his oarsmen pulling already, and was signalling all craft to make for open water immediately. Even as they wondered at his precipitate haste, eastwards they saw the topsails of the first English ships appearing above the thrusting base of the headland.

There was no question now of Lennox getting back to Maclean's galley, or of Argyll transferring to another meantime. Already there was urgent movement all around them, with ships manoeuvring for space and position in the constricted space.

More English ships appeared as the leading galleys headed for the mouth of the bay. Argyll's vessel, delayed until it had space to use its oars, had just begun to move when a cannon crashed out its angry message. A great spout of water rose out of the sea just ahead of Lachlan Mor's ship.

'God be good – the knaves! The fools!' Ludovick exclaimed.

'What do they think they are about? We are their allies . . .'

'No doubt they also mistake us for the MacDonalds,' Mary said.

'But they cannot know about Donald Gorm.'

'Even so, they must esteem us foes . . .'

Unswerving, Sir Lachlan drove his galley straight ahead. His urgency to get his ships out of that trap of a bay was now vindicated and explained.

Six English ships were now in view, large ships all, one of them a great galleon, a proud sight with all sails set. Even as they watched, this tall ship, with its rows of black open gun-ports, swung round directly into the north-west wind, and suddenly seemed to explode in orange flame and black smoke, as a tremendous broadside thundered out.

Undoubtedly this was intended as a demonstration of might and authority rather than an actual attack, for the galleon was the furthest away of the English ships, and all the shot fell well short of Maclean's craft, throwing up a vast wall of water, scores of feet in height.

Sir Lachlan, now in the mouth of the bay, could have swung hard to port, to the west, and drawn clear away – for, sailing into a wind, of course, his galley, with all its oars, had possibly three times the speed of the fastest English ship dependent wholly on sails. But he did not do so. He continued on his course, directly towards the Englishmen – though from his stern he signalled for the remainder of his fleet to veer to port, westwards out of that corner of the bay.

'He will be blown out of the water!' Ludovick cried to Argyll, who had now reappeared, in armour. 'He is sailing right into their guns.'

Lachlan Mor was no suicide, however, determined as he might be to give his fleet every opportunity he could to win out of the trap. He hoisted a large white flag to his masthead, part of an old sail – surely the first time that any vessel of his had worn so sorry an emblem – and for good measure draped another approximately white sail over his sharp prow.

No further broadsides were fired from the English vessels, but the leading ships turned a few points more north by west, to cut across Sir Lachlan's bows, clearly attempting to head off and draw within range of the escaping galleys beyond. Three more tall ships had now appeared round the headland, making nine in all.

'My lord,' Ludovick exclaimed, to Argyll. 'Direct your captain to sail us after Maclean. Not with the others. I must get to those English fools!'

'Even in this women's galley?' the Earl asked, thin-voiced, brows raised.

The Duke bit his lip. 'Aye – even so,' he said. 'I must, man! They may not heed Maclean, a Highlander. But they must surely heed me. The King's cousin! The Lieutenant! Sweet Jesu – am I not Lord Admiral of Scotland?'

'Aye. But how to let them know it, my lord Duke?'

'Only by going to them. There is no other way. It is necessary.'

The Earl nodded. Turning, he shouted the required orders, in Gaelic, to his captain.

The big galleon, obviously the flagship of the English squadron, was now moving in to meet Maclean, although the other craft were making what speed they could against the wind to head off at least some of the galley fleet. The leading two fired the bows cannon, but these were lesser guns with shorter range than those of the galleon, and their shot fell far short.

It was clear that most, if not all, of the Highland ships would escape.

Because Argyll's vessel was, as it were, going against the tide, by having to cross diagonally the route taken by the other galleys, its progress was infuriatingly slow – at least to Ludovick Stewart. He paced the after-deck impatiently, urging speed.

'Do not fret, Vicky,' Mary soothed. 'The big ship is not firing on Sir Lachlan.' She had been told to go below, but with good sense had spiritedly declared that if their ship was going to be shot at and sunk, she would much prefer to be on its open deck than trapped beneath.

'One shot, now, is all that is needed, and Maclean is finished!' he told her. 'Those great cannon could smash his galley, at such distance, like an egg-shell.'

'Sir Lachlan knows that. But still he goes on. The English are not savages. They will respect his flag-of-truce.'

'I hope so. I pray so.'

'Even though they believe us to be MacDonalds they will surely parley . . .'

'Why should they believe us to be MacDonalds? How could they know of the MacDonald threat, Mary? How could they have learned of this?'

'That I cannot tell you.'

'And how is this great squadron of ships up here? Maclean said that all the English ships of war were being kept in the south, for fear of an invasion from France or Spain. That only small scouting craft kept watch in these waters. And Maclean should know. He deals with Elizabeth, and makes it his business to know all that goes on in these waters. Yet . . . here are these great ships. Nine of them. Come this day, of all days!'

Wordless, Mary shook her head.

The galleon had now hove to, and Lachlan Mor's galley was almost up with it. Most of the Highland fleet had made good its escape from the bay and was fanning out north-westwards into the open sea; but some few vessels were trapped, and were in fact turning back into the bay under the threat of the English guns.

Argyll's craft, also with a scrap of sail hoisted as a white flag, now bore down fast on the two leaders' ships. Ludovick could see Maclean standing in his prow, hand to mouth, shouting to the galleon. Lennox urged Argyll to draw in still closer to the great ship, closer than was Maclean, despite the gaping mouths of all those rows of cannon.

On the towering aftercastle of the English flagship, a colourful group of men stood, most handsomely dressed in the height of fashion, an extraordinary sight to see at this time of the morning on a war-vessel at sea. One of these, a tall, slender, handsome black-bearded man, dressed in what appeared to be crimson velvet, save for the yellow satin lining of his short cloak, had been conducting an exchange with Sir Lachlan through a voice-trumpet. Now he swung on the newcomers.

'Who a God's sake do *you* say you are – in the Queen's name?' he demanded, in a voice weary as it was haughty. 'If you can speak the Queen's English!'

Argyll and Ludovick exchanged glances. The latter raised hand to mouth, to shout back.

'Sir – I mislike your manners, as I mislike your cannonry! Towards lawful users of these waters, and friends of your Queen. Aye, and towards your betters, sirrah! What do you mean by opening fire on the ships of the King of Scots?'

'Insolent!' the Englishman snapped back, at least the weariness going out of his voice. 'Have a care how you speak, fellow – or I shall be sore tempted to send you and your oar-boat to the bottom of this bay! Your name and business in these waters, coxcomb?'

'Within a score of miles of the Scottish coast, no Scot requires to state his business to an Englishman, sir!'

'Fool! Trifle no more, or . . .'

'Very well. I trifle no more. I am the Lord High Admiral of Scotland, Ludovick, Duke of Lennox, Lieutenant of King James's Northern Realm . . . and in cousinship to your Queen, Elizabeth Tudor!'

There was a choking sound into the voice-trumpet, and then a sudden and profound silence from the tall ship's aftercastle. Heads thereon drew close together.

Mary touched Ludovick's arm, smiling. 'Vicky,' she murmured, 'sometimes I love you even more than usual!'

The Duke pressed home his advantage. 'Come, sir – who are you who crows so loud in other folk's yards? And what is *your* business here?'

'H'mmm.' They could hear the elegant clearing his throat. 'I am Sir Christopher St. Lawrence, commodore of this special squadron of Her Grace of England. Here on Her Grace's business. An especial mission.'

'And does that business and mission include opening fire on your Queen's allies, sir?'

'My apologies for that, my lord Duke. A, h'm, an accident of war! No more. We mistook you for . . . another.'

'So! You shoot first, sir, and make your inquiries after? Is that the English way?'

'I am sorry, my lord . . .'

'Then, Sir Christopher – signal your other ships to halt their hounding of my galleys forthwith! Quickly, man – before blood is shed!'

'Yes, my lord Duke. At once . . .' Sir Christopher St. Lawrence turned to give orders to one of the brilliant young men at his side. As he did so, another man, much more soberly dressed, indeed in old and dented half-armour, came hurrying across the aftercastle to him, having just climbed up from the main deck, urgency in every line of him. With almost equal urgency, Mary Gray grasped Ludovick's wrist.

'Vicky – look!' she whispered. 'See you who that is? Who has just come up? It is Robert Logan! Logan of Restalrig!'

'Eh . . . ? Dear God – you are right! Logan! Fiend seize him . . . !'

Astounded, they stared at each other, minds groping for what this could mean.

Sir Christopher, after listening to Logan, was hailing them again, but in their preoccupation they missed much of what he said.

'We must get to the bottom of this,' Ludovick muttered. Suddenly he came to a decision. Raising his voice again, he cried. 'A plague on this shouting! My throat is raw! Lower a ladder, sir – I am coming aboard you.' He turned his back on the Englishman. The Duke of Lennox could play the haughty autocrat with fair verisimilitude also when occasion demanded.

Argyll, who had not spoken throughout this exchange, nodded to Ludovick. 'Well spoken, my lord,' he said quietly. 'You, I think, make a better Lieutenant of the North than ever I would do!'

'Arrogance ever rouses me,' the other jerked, almost apologetically. 'My lord, can your captain bring this craft sufficiently close in for me to board that ship?'

Expertly the galley was manoeuvred so that its high stern eased in gently to touch the galleon's quarter, and was held there by skilful oar-work. A rope-ladder was dropped to her from the high aftercastle. As Ludovick reached for it, Argyll moved close, declaring that he would come with him.

Climbing up the swaying contrivance, the Duke was aided over the side by eager hands, to be greeted with much respect by St. Lawrence and his gentlemen. Even so, he could not but be aware of his humdrum, not to say unkempt appearance compared with that of these elegants – and was the haughtier in consequence. Logan, he noted, had disappeared.

Sir Christopher St. Lawrence, a man of early middle years, was now all suave good humour and aplomb. He expressed renewed regret for the misadventure, as he termed it, but smilingly indicated that he had not expected to discover the Lord Admiral of Scotland in what he had taken to be a Highland pirate galley. From his inspection of Ludovick's person, the younger man also gained the impression that neither had he expected such a dignitary to be a carelessly-dressed and undistinguished-looking twenty-year-old.

Somewhat curtly the Duke introduced MacCailean Mor, High Chief of Clan Campbell, Earl of Argyll and Justiciar of the West, who, at two months younger still, was perhaps equally unimpressive as to appearance.

St. Lawrence's greetings to the Earl were brief, for he was already looking beyond, behind him. 'And the lady, no doubt, is the beautiful daughter of the Master of Gray?' he said, bowing deeply.

Ludovick turned. He had not known that Mary had followed them up the ladder – although he should not have been surprised. She, at least, was no disappointment to the eye, neither unkempt nor insignificant, despite the simplicity of her dress – indeed looking as lovely, fresh and modestly assured as though specially prepared for the occasion. The murmur amongst St. Lawrence's young men was eloquent tribute.

Ludovick nodded. 'The Lady Mary Gray,' he said, crisply. 'My help-meet and close associate in all things.'

'Ah yes.' There was a second round of bows and protestations of service from the impressionable gallants.

Lennox cut short the civilities. 'Sir Christopher,' he said, 'there is much that requires explanation here – and time may well be short. Why are you and your squadron here, may I ask?'

'That is easily answered, my lord Duke,' the other said, shrugging. 'Although, these being the waters of my Queen's realm of Ireland, I need offer no excuse for sailing them – even to the Admiral of Scotland! But that apart, I am here to intercept and put down a wicked and treasonable invasion of the said realm of Ireland by renegade Catholic subjects of your King. MacDonalds from the Isles. For them we mistook your galleys.'

Ludovick rubbed his chin. 'Then we are on the same errand,

sir. But, that you should know of this attempt is . . . interesting.'

'Our Queen is not uninformed of what goes on even in your islands, my lord!'

'Certainly she expends much gold on the business! But your knowledge, in this case, is very exact, Sir Christopher, is it not? And I saw that you had on board your ship a certain subject of my prince – Robert Logan of Restalrig!'

The other paused for a moment. 'That is true,' he agreed.

They eyed each other searchingly.

'I think that we might discuss this matter more privately, later,' the Duke decided. 'But meantime, sir, since we look for Donald Gorm of Sleat and his MacDonalds to appear at any moment,' he glanced seawards, 'it would be wise to make our plans. Sir Lachlan Maclean of Duart, in the first galley there, commands. Kindly summon him aboard, sir.'

The older man, however little he could have enjoyed this assumption of command, gave orders as required with a fair good grace.

When Maclean arrived, he was in no mood for civilities either. His resentment against the English was strong – but some of it seemed to spill over on to Lennox and Argyll also. However, his main concern meantime was for an end to this idling about in open waters, with the Clan Donald liable to be on them at any time. He demonstrated no joy that St. Lawrence was here seeking Donald Gorm likewise, but he agreed that they co-operated at least to the extent of getting back into Kinbane Bay at once, and hidden.

The English did not seem to like the use of the term hidden, esteeming it as undignified. Their combined forces, St. Lawrence pointed out, with his gun-power and the Scots' speed, should be more than ample to ensure that no MacDonalds ever returned to their barbarous islands. What need was there for hiding?

Ludovick intervened to declare that the objective was not to kill MacDonald but to prevent an invasion of Ireland and a Catholic triumph. If Donald Gorm could be turned away, sent back to Skye without battle, so much the better. To that end they should plan.

St. Lawrence eyed him askance.

In the end it was decided that each fleet should put back to its former position, the Scots hidden in the small bay, the English lying in a corner of the large. From whichever direction the MacDonalds eventually came, this should trap them. If Maclean remained undiscovered, he would hold back until St. Lawrence opened fire.

On an impulse, Ludovick decided to remain on board the galleon. He felt that he might be able to exert some slight moderating influence on the Englishmen should it look like becoming a massacre. Moreover, he wanted an interview with Logan. Mary would stay with him, but Maclean and Argyll would go back to their own craft.

Whether St. Lawrence appreciated the continued presence of his self-invited guests, he entertained them royally. As they headed back behind the promontory of Kinbane Head, into Ballycastle Bay, he took the young people down to his own great cabin immediately below the aftercastle, and breakfasted them as befitted any Lord High Admiral and his lady. No more convincing example of the benefits of adopting a lofty and overbearing attitude could have been demonstrated.

Ludovick and Mary did not have to use any great wiles to gain information from their host. He seemed to know the Master of Gray well, at least by repute, and undoubtedly was the more disposed to talk to the daughter. He admitted frankly enough that it was thanks to the Master that he and his squadron were here. The Master had discovered this Catholic plot to aid the Irish rebels, sent word of it to Queen Elizabeth, and then had sent this Logan to bring them down on the Islesmen. The Master had long been a good friend to the Queen, undoubtedly, and one of the most notable men in Europe. Sir Christopher acknowledged it a privilege to meet his daughter.

For once that daughter was less than adequate to the occasion. Set-faced, she mumbled something almost inaudible, and toyed with her food.

The Duke of Lennox was silent also, and the Englishman looked from one to the other keenly.

'You were not aware that the Master has sent this information, my lord?' he said.

'No, sir,' Ludovick answered briefly – since it would have

been futile to pretend otherwise.

The other fingered his small black beard. 'I wonder why . . . ?'

Mary, recovering herself, spoke quickly. 'No doubt my father sent the word to you after my lord had set out for the Isles. This expedition has taken some time to mount, sir.' It was important that St. Lawrence should not suspect that the project did not have the royal blessing.

'Is that so?'

'Yes,' the Duke put in. 'As you will well perceive, sir, it is necessary to hunt galleys with galleys. His Grace's ordinary ships would not serve to catch galleys, any more than these vessels of yours! So the Isles had to be scoured for such ships. And most had already been collected by the MacDonalds. This took time . . .'

'No doubt. But it is strange that the Master did not inform *us* of your expedition, my lord! Logan at least knew naught of it.'

'M'mmm.'

'Robert Logan was in the Isles himself until but recently,' Mary said. 'He cannot have had time for any close contact with my father. No doubt only messages, letters, passed between them, and this matter was not mentioned.'

As explanation, this did not seem entirely to convince Sir Christopher. But fortunately at this moment shouts from above announced the sighting of sails on the northern horizon. Their host hurriedly left his cabin and guests.

'Oh, Vicky!' Mary said, her voice quivering. 'This is . . . this beyond everything! Treachery upon treachery!'

'It is unbelievable!' Ludovick exclaimed.

'No.' She shook her head. 'Not unbelievable. Not when you think of it. Not for Patrick. Indeed, perhaps I should have thought of it. For here is the fine pinnacle and perfection of betrayal! In the cause of balancing power. He uses Elizabeth's gold to bribe the MacDonalds against Elizabeth; then informs Elizabeth that the MacDonalds move against her, so that she may destroy them!'

'But, dear God – why? Not, surely, merely for the reward . . . ?'

'No – although, no doubt, rewards he will gain. But if thus he can have the MacDonald power destroyed, there is none other to whom Huntly can turn. Yet the Catholics will still believe him their friend. As, of course, will Elizabeth. Patrick gains on all hands, trusted by all. At no cost to himself.'

'Not to himself. The cost is eight or nine thousand Mac-Donalds!'

'Vicky – we must save them! Somehow!'

They hurried aloft.

Donald Gorm was approaching from the north-west, having used the bulk of the long island of Rathlin to mask his descent upon the Irish coast. It could not have been better from St. Lawrence's point of view, for it meant that the invaders would not see into the west side of Ballycastle Bay, and so would have no warning of the English squadron's presence there until the last moment. How soon they discovered Maclean's fleet of galleys would depend very much upon the MacDonald's angle of approach. But strategically the situation could hardly have been improved. The fires on the headlands had now been extinguished – for these, it transpired, had been lit by English parties, to give warning to St. Lawrence. All unsuspicious, therefore. Donald Gorm bore down on his fate.

From the galleon, of course, nothing of the developing situation could be seen; but St. Lawrence had pinnaces out, lying below the very point itself, to signal back information.

Ludovick, adopting his most hectoring and authoritative tone, left the English commander in no doubt that the approaching MacDonalds, although misguided, were nevertheless King James's subjects, and must be treated with no more severity than was necessary to cause them to turn back. Any undue violence and bloodshed would undoubtedly be construed as an attack upon the dignity and privileges of the King of Scots – who of course was Queen Elizabeth's heir. This warning was not enthusiastically received. Ludovick hoped that Maclean, for his part, would be content with the moral defeat of his hereditary foes, rather than seek any blood-bath. His behaviour over the Clanranald business gave some grounds for this, probably.

The waiting, inactive, anxious, was trying. When, however, action did develop, it was not heralded by the anticipated appearance of MacDonald galleys round Kinbane Head, but by the crash of a single cannon. This, after a few moments' pause, was followed by others, but only in scattered, haphazard shooting, not in a concentrated cannonade.

Angrily, St. Lawrence ordered his squadron to move out into open water. 'Curse him! God's wounds – the fool has warned them off!' He swore.

Mary caught Ludovick's eye. Perhaps Lachlan Mor drew the line at allowing Englishmen to massacre fellow-Islesmen, even MacDonalds?

The great English ships, wholly dependent on sails and wind, seemed to take an unconscionable time to beat out of the bay. When they did reach a position where they could gain a wide view, it was to discover an astonishing situation. The sea seemed to be littered with galleys, score upon score of them, oar blades flashing in the new sunlight, swirling, weaving, darting round each other in a milling mass, in negation of any order or formation. Occasionally a cannon would boom out, but this seemed to be more in the nature of a conventional accompaniment to all the urgent movement than any determined attack – an impression reinforced by the fact that no crippled or sinking vessels were in evidence. It was clear, at least, that both fleets were involved – but that was all that was clear in the position. All else was a confusion, a positive vortex of ships, in which it would have required much more expert watchers than any in the English squadron to tell Maclean galleys from MacDonald.

St. Lawrence could scarcely contain his wrath. 'Dolts! Numbskulls! Knaves!' he exclaimed. 'Here's the folly of all follies! Look at them! I can do nothing. Nothing! I cannot fire, lest I hit friend instead of foe. If you can name Maclean friend – which I much misdoubt! Beshrew me – I do not even know which is which!'

'Why so eager to fire your cannon, if the matter may be resolved otherwise?' Ludovick demanded. 'They are not child's playthings, sir! Men's lives are at stake.'

Although St. Lawrence could not fire, he and his squadron drove straight on into the mêlée of ships. It could now be seen that the slower transports of Donald Gorm's fleet had been sent in a tight group northwards again, under escort of the birlinns, as far from danger as possible.

'Make for Sir Lachlan's galley,' Ludovick urged St. Lawrence. 'Yonder, with the ship painted on its sail. Demand a parley. There is naught else to do.'

This indeed seemed to be the case, and even Sir Christopher could think of no other practical course in the circumstances. He set bugles blowing on his flagship and bore down as best he could on Maclean's craft. Sir Lachlan made it easy for him, coming to meet the Englishmen.

Ludovick hailed him. 'Maclean – we must have a parley,' he shouted. 'With Donald Gorm. Where is he? Which is his ship?'

'That with the great banner and the eagle prow. You would parley?'

'Of course. What else is there to do?'

'This is madness, man!' Sir Christopher put in, through his voice-trumpet. 'Play-acting! Mummery! What are you at? You have ruined all, I tell you!'

Maclean ignored him.

'Donald Gorm will talk, I think, Duke of Lennox,' he called. 'He is held. He saw us in the bay, coming from this side. We had to issue out, or be trapped. I have sought to break up this array...'

'Aye – to be sure. You could do no other. Come with me, to Donald Gorm.' Lennox turned to St. Lawrence. 'Sir Christopher – steer for that galley with the great banner. And I'll thank you for less talk of madness and play-acting!'

The Englishman looked daggers but said nothing.

The play-acting jibe was not far from the truth, of course, for there was no actual fighting going on, and even the demonstrations of cannon-fire had died away. It was stalemate, and all knew it.

Donald Gorm MacDonald of Sleat proved that he perceived this as clearly as anyone else, by waiting in his more or less stationary galley for the other two flagships to come up with him. Surrounded by a group of spectacularly colourful chieftains, he stood on his forecastle, silent.

Ludovick was in a fever of anxiety lest wrong words should be spoken at this stage, for the proud MacDonalds would be sore and touchy, and much evil could yet eventuate this day. He was about to hail the other, before they were suitably close, to forestall any arrogant bluster on the part of St. Lawrence, when Mary touched his arm.

'The trumpet,' she murmured. 'Sir Christopher's trumpet.'

'Ah, yes.' He turned and stepped over to reach out for the voice-trumpet which St. Lawrence held in his hand. 'With your permission, sir, this will aid, I think.' Firmly he took the instrument from his host's reluctant fingers.

The device was a great help, lending the shouter confidence and authority, as well as easing his vocal strain. 'This is the Duke of Lennox, Lieutenant of the North and Admiral of Scotland,' he called. 'I would speak with Donald MacDonald of Sleat.'

A voice came back, coldly. 'MacDonald of the Isles is here, and listens.'

'The position must be clear to you all. You cannot now land on this coast to aid the Irish. We can do battle. But whose advantage will it serve? It is time to talk.'

There was a brief pause. Then in sing-song English came the answer. 'Talk, then. Donald of the Isles hears.'

Ludovick bit his lip, as, at his side, Sir Christopher smiled thinly. He surely could look for some co-operation from the Mac-Donalds in this situation? Their spokesman was a tall bearded man in vivid tartans; but each time before speaking he bent to have word with a short squat clean-shaven man beside him, plainly clad in half-armour, leather jerkin and small helmet.

'Are you Donald Gorm?' Lennox demanded.

'No. Donald of the Isles does not shout,' he was informed briefly.

Ludovick flushed, the more so at St. Lawrence's bark of mirthless laughter. A hot answer was rising to his lips when the girl again touched him.

'Be patient, Vicky,' she whispered. 'They have been sore hit. All their hopes dashed. Agree with him. On the shouting. Invite him to this ship. As your guest. He is proud. He will not wish to seem fearful to do so.'

'Tell him that I have forty cannon trained on him!' Sir Christopher cried, from his other side. 'They will make him shout – for mercy!'

Frowning, the Duke raised the voice-trumpet again. 'I dislike shouting also,' he declared strongly. 'I invite Donald of Sleat aboard this ship. That we may discuss this matter like gentlemen. His safety and free return is assured – upon my honour!'

Long seconds passed, and then there came the answer. 'Donald of the Isles accepts your invitation.'

'It is as though the fellow was a prince!' St. Lawrence snorted.

'As he considers himself to be, sir. He would be Lord of the Isles, a prince indeed, but for the stroke of a pen. And the authority of that pen he does not recognise!'

The MacDonald galley nudged in alongside the big ship aft. Two Highlanders leapt aboard, to aid their chief, but the stocky dark man ignored them and mounted alone, with marked agility. Two of his chieftains came after him.

It was strange what an impression of strength, contained force and quiet dignity the newcomer made. It was easy to see why he was known as Donald Gorm, *gorm* meaning blue; for he was so dark as to be almost swarthy, and his shaven square chin was blue indeed. He was not really a small man at all, however short-seeming, being in fact immensely broad and of a compact masculinity, with no fat to his curiously squat person. A man of early middle-age, he stood there on the English ship, silent, assured, self-sufficient, as though a victor awaiting the formal surrender of his foes.

Ludovick bowed slightly. He gestured towards his companions. 'This is Sir Christopher St. Lawrence, commodore of the English ships. And the Lady Mary Gray.'

Sir Christopher turned away, and stared into the middle distance. Mary sketched a curtsy, and smiled.

Donald Gorm inclined his head. 'Roderick MacLeod of Harris, and Angus MacDonald of Dunyveg,' he mentioned, deep-voiced.

The two chiefs made no sort of acknowledgement.

Ludovick swallowed. 'Perhaps Sir Christopher will invite us below to his cabin? Where we may discuss our problems more suitably?' he suggested.

The Englishman frowned blackly. But before he could raise his voice, Donald Gorm spoke.

'No, sir,' he said, with a decisive shake of his head. 'What is to be said may be said here.' His English was good but careful. And final.

'As you will.' Lennox glanced over to where a slight commotion heralded the re-arrival of Lachlan Mor, uninvited. Ludovick was unashamedly glad to see him.

'Sir Lachlan – come!' he exclaimed. 'We seek to resolve this situation. Fighting between us, I say, would be foolish. Is indeed scarcely possible. And would gain nothing, for neither side could win a clear victory...'

'I could crush these galleys with my cannon as I would crush eggs!' Sir Christopher declared scornfully. 'Why this talk of no clear victory?'

'Some of them, no doubt, sir. A few. While they remained within your range. But since they can out-sail you with ease, most would elude your guns. And so long as they remain amongst Sir Lachlan's ships you cannot fire. On the other hand, they cannot attack you either. Nor can they do what they came to do – land to aid the Irish. We can prevent any large landing, and destroy the ships of any who do land. Is that not all true, gentlemen?'

None could deny it. But that did not mean that it could be just accepted and agreed, there and then, nevertheless. Too much of pride and prestige was involved.

Donald Gorm himself said little; he appeared to be a man of exceedingly few words. But his two companions, Angus of Dunyveg and MacLeod of Harris, said much, the former in diabolical English and the latter in Gaelic, both of which Maclean had to translate. Their main points seemed to be that they outnumbered the combined opposition by more than two to one; that they were without doubt the finest fighting-men on the seven seas; that the English cannon might damage a few of their vessels, but that they could twist and turn their galleys in mere moments and so avoid the enemy broadsides; that they would cut off and board the slow English ships one by one, as hound-dogs pick off stags from a herd; and that Maclean knew Clan Donald's mettle too well to dare become involved in any close fighting.

Sir Christopher's angry denials, taunts and challenges, though well-sustained and insulting, never quite reached the stage of breaking off the discussion and ordering the Islesmen off his ship. For his part, Ludovick found himself become a mediator more than anything else, while Sir Lachlan, when he was not translating, contented himself with comparatively mild and modest assertions as to his prowess and powers.

Fairly soon deadlock seemed to have been reached on the diplomatic front, equally with the strategic.

Ludovick was racking his brains to think up some face-saving formula which would allow both sides to step back, with dignity more or less intact, from the positions thus taken up, when Mary Gray, with every appearance of extreme diffidence, made a suggestion.

'My lord Duke – sirs,' she said, hesitantly. 'Forgive me if I speak both foolishly and immodestly, a woman meddling in men's affairs. But it seems to me that here is occasion for a compromise. An honourable compromise – a treaty, indeed. A treaty between Donald and the Confederation of the Isles, on the one hand, and the representatives of the King of Scots and Queen of England on the other. Whereby each acknowledges the other's potency and right, and each agrees that all should return whence they have come, unmolested and with full honours and unassailed authority. Leaving the situation as it was before this morning's light. Such treaty would harm the repute of none. And it would absolve the Clan Donald from its undertaking in this Irish adventure, with . . . with whoever they made the compact!'

Donald Gorm had been eyeing the girl keenly. 'A treaty!' he said slowly. He inclined his dark head. 'There, perhaps, is the first sense spoken this day!'

'I sign no treaty with rebels!' Sir Christopher announced, flatly.

As Angus of Dunyveg, blazing-eyed, began to make hot reply, Ludovick held up his hand.

'These are subjects of the King of Scots, sir – so how can they be rebels to you! As the King's Lieutenant, *I* shall decide who is rebel and who is not! Moreover, there is no need for you to sign anything, Sir Christopher. As senior here, Admiral of Scotland, in alliance with your Queen, I only sign.'

'As well, my lord! For I will not! Here is weakness and non-

243

sense, also, by God's death!'

'And yet, sir, I think were my father here, this is what he would counsel,' Mary put in, quietly.

That produced a sudden silence, as men considered its implications according to their knowledge – as was the intention.

The young woman went on, looking at Donald Gorm now. 'He is not here – but his emissary is, his associate. Logan. Logan of Restalrig. He is here. Ask him.'

The dark man stared. 'Logan! Logan of Restalrig! Here? On this ship...?'

'Yes.'

The other swung on Ludovick, on Sir Christopher. 'Is this true? A prisoner...?'

'It is true. But no prisoner,' St. Lawrence said. 'He led us here. He it was who informed us of your coming...'

'*Diabhol*! Here is treachery, then!' Donald Gorm actually took a step backwards, as though nearer to his own ship. 'We have been betrayed.'

No one spoke.

'This man – Logan. Fetch him here. To me.' the Mac-Donald chief commanded, tight-voiced.

Sir Christopher looked him up and down. 'No!' he said bluntly.

'Sir – I insist!'

'On my ship, MacDonald, only I may insist! Mark it!'

As angry Highland hands slipped down to broadsword hilts, Ludovick intervened. 'Gentlemen – such talk aids nothing! Whatever Logan may have done, and wherefore, alters nothing of the situation. This treaty – is it agreed?'

Donald Gorm searched Lennox's face with those intensely alive dark eyes, and then nodded. 'Very well. Be it so. But a few words will suffice, whatever. That all go whence they came, with full honour. If honour is a word that may be used towards those who deal in treachery!'

Ludovick nodded, ignoring that last sentence. 'Sir Christopher – paper and pens, if you please...'

A single sentence was all the wording necessary for the body of their compact, all perceiving that the fewer words the better. The title however was more difficult, and seemed to be the most important part as far as Donald Gorm was concerned. He declared that the word treaty must be used – obviously the term assuaged his wounded pride somewhat, that he should be making a treaty with the King of Scots and Queen of England. As, of course, Mary had intended that it should. He wished also that the term 'Donald of the Isles' be used; but this Ludovick could not agree to, since it implied that he was indeed Lord of the Isles, a title now incorporated in the Crown of Scotland. A compromise, again suggested by the young woman, of 'Donald, of the Confederation of the Isles' was eventually accepted. Under that heading and the single sentence that followed, Donald and Ludovick signed side by side, with Sir Lachlan adding his name just below.

With a stiff bow to Lennox, an inclination of his head to Maclean and an eye-meeting lingering glance, even the glimmered beginnings of a smile, to Mary Gray, Donald Gorm of Sleat turned about, ignoring Sir Christopher altogether.

In silence they watched him and his companions return to their own ship.

It took some time for that eddying confusion of vessels to disentangle, but at length the watchers saw the Clan Donald armada pull away north-westwards, to join up with its birlinns and transports to the west of Rathlin Island. Maclean's fleet drew off a little way to the east, only Sir Lachlan's own galley remaining close to the galleon.

Ludovick turned to St. Lawrence. 'We now may go our several ways, I think, Sir Christopher. Your duty is done. There will be no invasion of Ireland. The Islesmen are gone.'

'They may turn back.'

'No. They will not do that, I warrant. Donald Gorm will not go back on his word. Besides, he conceives himself to have been betrayed. By those he compacted with. He will return to his own Skye, now.'

'My galleys will shadow him all the way, to see that he goes,' Maclean added grimly.

'Before we leave, however, I would have word with Robert Logan,' Ludovick added.

The Englishman looked doubtful. 'To what purpose my lord?'

'For my own purposes, sir! Must I, the Admiral of Scotland,

explain my purposes to *you*? Logan is a Scots subject – and an outlawed one! Bring him to me.'

Shrugging, St. Lawrence left them.

'What can you do?' Mary asked, low-voiced. 'He will not give up Logan to you.'

'I do not want him. But I can at least confront the fellow. Question him . . .'

'To what end? We know who gives Logan his orders. None of all this is of his conceiving, I am sure.' She glanced at Maclean, who was hailing someone on his own galley. 'Talk with him here, before others, will serve us nothing. It could be dangerous. Be content, Vicky. We have spoked Patrick's wheel, and saved the MacDonalds. Avoided bloodshed. It is enough, is it not?'

It had to be. When at length Sir Christopher returned, it was to announce that Logan was nowhere to be found. At Ludovick's protest, blandly the Englishman suggested that he must have slipped away into one of the Scots galleys. Three, after all, had been alongside his ship.

There was clearly no answer to this. Lennox had to seem to accept it.

Their leave-taking of St. Lawrence was formal, less than cordial. His young men were clearly much disappointed in Mary Gray. As a parting thrust, he requested that his respects be paid to the Master of Gray – and to Logan of Restalrig when they found him.

Back in Maclean's galley, Sir Lachlan considered his two passengers quizzically. 'Whose day was this, think you?' he wondered.

Ludovick rubbed his chin. 'I do not know,' he admitted.

'*I* know,' Mary said quietly. 'It was Scotland's day. Whoever lost or failed or gave way, Scotland gained. No one of the King's subjects has died, I think. The realm's honour is saved, and the Protestant faith suffered no hurt. It might have been much otherwise. King James should rejoice.'

'Should, perhaps – but will he?' Sombrely the Duke turned to gaze away eastwards, towards Scotland.

'It must be our task to make him see it,' she answered. 'We can do it, I believe – with the help of Sir Lachlan Maclean and my lord of Argyll.

Chapter Fifteen

Wonderingly, Mary and Ludovick looked around them at the narrow crowded streets of Stirling town, as they rode behind Sir George Home and a detachment of the Royal Guard. No one was either jeering or cheering, but the citizenry was obviously out in force, and showing a lively interest in their passage. Young Home was being fairly affable, but that might be only sympathy – although, as one of the most insufferable of the King's youthful favourites, sympathy was not much in his line. The Provost of the burgh had met them at the Drip Gate – a highly unusual circumstance. Was all this to confirm their fears or relieve them?

Home had arrived at Methven Castle at midday, with the royal summons – and the travellers had only reached that pleasant sanctuary, from the Isles, the day before. They had assessed this as ominous indeed, for the King was not usually so well served as to information, and they took it to mean that Patrick Gray was behind it, had been watching and waiting for them, and that this demand of their immediate presence at Stirling was his doing rather than James's. Moreover Home had been commanded to bring them both, Mary as well as the Duke, which struck her as alarming. A royal command they could not disobey, but they had ridden the score or so of miles to Stirling in some trepidation. This was not the way that they had planned to make their return to Court – indeed, Mary had intended to stay at Methven and avoid the Court altogether if she could, save for a quiet and unannounced visit to the Gray house in Broadgait, to collect young Johnnie and have a word with the Lady Marie. The inevitable interview with her father, thereafter, could as well be held at Methven as anywhere else, private as it must be.

Outriders of the Guard had hurried ahead, and at the great gatehouse of the fortress on its rock they were met by no less a person than the Earl of Mar himself, Keeper of Stirling Castle. He was barely civil – but then, that was quite normal with Mar, and he and Ludovick had never loved each other. They were to be conducted into the presence of the King forthwith, was all that he told them, and curtly.

He led them to the Lesser Hall of Audience, the second greatest chamber of the castle, whence came the sound of music. Mar told them to wait at the door, and himself went within. In the few moments which they had before he re-appeared, they spoke to each other low-voiced.

'This is no ordinary summons,' Ludovick murmured. 'James himself is in this. It is not all Patrick's doing. I fear he must be very wrath. Our letters cannot have moved him.'

Lennox had written lengthy letters to the King, in advance of his return, sent by swift couriers, one from Duart Castle and one from Inveraray, whence they had sailed on with Argyll on their long road to the south. These had informed James of what had happened – or at least, some of it – and made clear the gain to Scotland's cause and reputation of the confrontation off Ireland. They had prevailed on Sir Lachlan and Argyll to write also, separately, claiming the entire affair as a victory for the King and for the Protestant religion. The Master of Gray's name had not been mentioned in any letter, although his daughter's hand had inevitably featured fairly prominently.

'It is my fault,' the girl said. 'The King will not lightly forgive me for deserting Prince Henry, and for leaving his Court secretly ...'

'No, no – that is nothing,' the Duke shook his head. 'A mere peccadillo compared with what he will hold against me! I have left the North-East without his knowledge. Taken liberties with his name and authority. Conducted a campaign in the Isles without reference to him or the Council. Aye, and annulled Maclean's forfeiture. But – it was necessary, God knows ... !'

Mar threw open the door in front of them. 'Come,' he said.

The music had died away. In silence they followed the Earl into the crowded hall, and up between the long tables towards the raised dais at the further end. Never had either of them felt such culprits, somehow. Scotland's Lord High Admiral certainly was sensible of nothing of the confidence which surely ought to go with that high office that May afternoon.

At the dais-table, King James was dressed with great elaboration and deplorable taste. On his immediate right was a stranger, a courtly-looking individual with peculiar hooded eyes, richly but discreetly clad. On his left sat, surprisingly, the Earl of Argyll, who could have returned to Castle Campbell only the day before. And next to the Earl sat the Master of Gray, at his most dazzling. The Queen was not present.

James, sprawling forward over the table, high hat somewhat askew on his oversized head, watched the couple's approach intently, plucking at his lower lip. Patrick was smiling brilliantly.

The King waited until the newcomers were close, bowing and curtsying at the other side of the table, before he spoke.

'Aye, Vicky,' he said thickly. 'My lord Duke. I rejoice to see you. And you Mistress Mary. Welcome back to my Court, after your much journeyings and labours.'

Bowing again they waited warily.

'We have awaited your comings with interest. Aye, with interest,' the monarch went on, as though reciting a rehearsed piece. 'It has been long since we have seen you. Long.' He nodded portentously.

'Yes, Sire.'

'You have been right active. Both o' you. We havena failed to note what you were at, Vicky.'

'My royal mistress also has not failed to take note, my lord Duke,' the dark stranger at the King's side put in.

'Ooh, aye. Vicky – here's the new English envoy. Sir George Nicolson. New up frae London. We are dining in his honour, see you.'

'I vow it should be in the Duke's honour rather, Your Grace. And . . . this lady's,' the Englishman asserted. He actually rose, and bowed to Mary.

'Aye, to be sure. I'ph'mmm. But bide your time, man! We are coming to that.' James coughed. 'Vicky. Mistress Mary. It is our pleasure, our royal pleasure and desire, to express our thanks. And gratitude. To you both. Aye, both. For your services to the realm. In this business o' the Isles. And the Irish. It was well done. As our Lieutenant. Wi' the help of my lord of Argyll. And yon man Maclean. Aye, it was well done. We heard tell you were wounded, Vicky? In battle . . . ?'

'It was nothing, Sire. No more than a scratched shoulder . . .'

'Hail the Duke of Lennox! And Mary Gray!' Patrick's voice rang out.

Cheers arose from all over the hall.

Ludovick and the girl exchanged glances.

The King tut-tutted, indicating that there were limits beyond which, in the royal presence, acclaim became unseemly. 'Aye, well,' he said, tapping the table. 'Because of the service you have done the realm, we are disposed to overlook, aye, overlook certain . . . certain matters. Irregularities – certain irregularities. You'll both ken what I mean?'

'I thank Your Grace,' Ludovick replied. He took a deep breath. 'But I would point out, with your royal permission, on behalf of the Lady Mary as well as myself, that these irregularities as you name them, were entirely necessary. Otherwise we could not have done what had to be done.'

'Aye, some o' them, no doubt. Vicky – some o' them. But we'll no' pick that bone the now! Come you and sit in – both o' you. I'd hear your tale. My lord o' Argyll here has told me some o' it. And we had your letters. But, waesucks – Elizabeth o' England seems to ken mair than me about it!' And he frowned in the direction of Sir George Nicolson.

Places were made for them at the dais-table, one on either side of Argyll, the Duke next to the King and Mary next to her father.

Patrick kissed her warmly. 'My dear,' he said, 'how good to see you again. And how beautiful you are! To be good, beautiful *and* clever, is given to few of us!'

She found herself scarcely able to answer him, trembling with a strange emotion, torn between revulsion and fascination, shrinking and affection. She muttered something, staring down at the table.

'I vow I must needs be proud of my daughter,' he went on. 'Since it is undoubtedly your guiding hand that is to be seen behind all. This was far beyond our Vicky. I, h'm recognise the Gray touch, my dear!'

'So, to my sorrow, did I!' she got out.

He ignored that. 'Did you enjoy your first visit to the Hebrides? I understand the prospects there to be magnificent, in a barbarous way. Myself, I have never been further west than Dumbarton. The people, I believe, are quite extraordinary. Little better than savages. You were, I think, over-rash to venture amongst them, Mary.'

She glanced to her right. Argyll was involved in the King's converse with Ludovick. On Patrick's other side, his father-in-law, the Earl of Orkney, was fully occupied with and all but fondling a handsome lady whom Mary did not know.

'They are far from savages,' she said, her voice low but tense. 'I would that you *had* travelled in the Isles, and learned to know them. Then, perhaps, you might not have sought to throw thousands to their deaths, for a whim, for one of your wicked plots!'

He blinked. 'Plots? Save us, girl – what's this now? Thousands to their deaths? Have you taken leave of your wits again?'

Wearily she shook her head. 'Spare me, and yourself, the denials, Patrick,' she urged. 'We know each other too well. I have traced your hand in this all the way. None other, indeed, could have conceived it all! Think you that Robert Logan could have thought of it himself? Such double betrayal!'

'*I* am not Logan's keeper!' he said, shrugging. 'If you think to see me behind him in this business, you mistake, I assure you. Even you, Mary, bewitched as you are bewitching, can trace no possible link, I swear! It is all in your head, child.'

'You forget Sir Christopher St. Lawrence, Patrick, I think!'

She heard his quick intake of breath. 'He admires you greatly,' she went on, almost in a whisper now. 'He esteems you one of his Queen's best friends! He sent his respects and grateful thanks. He did not know, of course, that the gold you paid Donald Gorm and Clanranald was Elizabeth's. English!'

She saw his knuckles gleaming white as his fists clenched there on the table, and for a little he did not speak. But when he did, his words were calm, controlled, reasonable.

'It is a great sorrow to me, my dear, that you are forever discovering evil, plotting, treasons, behind all that I do – and more that I do *not* do! It has become something of an obsession with you, I fear. It cannot but poison the well of our mutual fondness, unfortunately – and I am very fond of you, Mary, as you know full well. A pity, too, to spoil this happy occasion.

This welcome back to the Court...'

'Yes, Patrick,' she interrupted. 'Why did you do it? Plan this welcome for us? It is your doing, I know well. The King would never have done it, to be sure. He is none so pleased with us. He has not forgiven either of us, that is clear. You arranged this, convinced the King to do it did you not? Why? When we have spoiled your plot...'

'You have spoiled nothing of mine, girl. Save, with your accusations, the pleasure of this day. Can you not credit me with a father's affection and regard?'

'In some matters, yes. But not this. You did not move the King against his will, and swallow a rebuff to your plans, out of fatherly regard and affection! Even for me, Patrick! I think that you must be afraid. Afraid that we are in a position to hurt your schemes further, perhaps? To talk. Is that it, Patrick? You would keep us quiet, lest we tell King James what we know? Or the Kirk? Or even Queen Elizabeth, through her envoy?'

'A pox, Mary – what next? This is beyond all! You but dream, child. For I tell you that you know nothing, in this. Nothing which could injure me with the King. Or the Kirk. Or Elizabeth. You only guess, conjecture, surmise. And make nonsense! You can show nothing of proof, establish nothing. Think you that any would believe your insubstantial phantasies against the word of the Master of Gray?'

'Yet you did send word to Elizabeth that the MacDonalds were moving to aid Tyrone. That can be proved.'

'To be sure I did. When Logan sent *me* word of it, my duty was clear. Such folly would have greatly damaged the King's good name in Elizabeth's eyes. So I sent her warning. It was necessary. I am thankful that I was in time.'

She gazed at him, speechless now. He was armoured, impregnable, with an answer to everything. Suddenly she was very tired. She shook her head, and the faintest droop might have been discerned in her shoulders.

He smiled, as suddenly, warmly. 'Poor Mary! Dear Mary! As I said, you are good and beautiful and clever. But I fear that you lack just a little in judgement! A small matter, that years will no doubt mend. Experience, my poppet.' He actually patted her arm. 'In time, sweeting, that will come. Meantime, however, it would be less unnatural, would it not, if you sharpened your pearly teeth on other than your sire! And, probably, more successful!' Sighing humorously he leaned back a little in his chair. 'Ah, me – little of reward I get for all my efforts on your behalf over those bairns! The devil of a task I had with our peculiar monarch over that puny princeling of his – especially with the bawling brat turned up in my own nest, as it were! I tell you, there had to be plotting and scheming then, if you like! To soothe the King, to find a new governess for the child, to win back my own wife to my bed! Heigho – you set this Court by the ears then, Mary Gray! As well, I think, that you had me for a father!'

She considered him, for her, almost helplessly. 'Does nothing reach you, Patrick – reach past that clever, mocking head of yours into your heart?' she demanded. 'No prick of conscience, ever? How it can live with your head, in one body . . . !'

When he only smiled for answer, she sighed, and went on, level voiced. 'How is Johnnie? Marie would see to him well, I know.'

'Your Johnnie thrives. He laughes and eats and laughs and sleeps and laughs. A true philosopher, and excellent company. He seems to have much of his grandsire in him! He and I esteem each other highly.'

She bit her lip. 'Where is he? Here, in the Mar Tower still? With the Prince Henry?'

'Ah, no. He is with us in our house in the town. We had to stay in the castle until new arrangements could be made for the ever-wailing prince, since the King would by no means hear of him being taken out. You may be sure that I wasted no time in relieving Marie of that infant's burden, for I mislike being shut into this place, and I find Mar's close company insupportable. Lady Mar is now the child's governess – and she is welcome to him.'

'Poor sad bairn! You would think that he had no mother! Will not the King relent? Allow the Queen to have her son?'

'Not James! He believes that she would but use the child against him. Hand him over to some faction seeking power. As indeed she might for Her vixenish Grace becomes ever more concerned with power, and meddling in affairs of state.'

'She but turns to that, no doubt, lacking her child. Could you not mend this matter, Patrick? Since you now control most other matters of the realm. It should not be beyond your powers? Although perhaps you do not wish it mended – since I think it is your aim to keep King and Queen separated? That you may wield more power, playing one against the other, as you play Catholic and Protestant, Kirk and Council, noble against noble.'

'Ha – more phantasies, girl!'

'Are they? Who was it held that to divide is to govern? Davy Gray says that it has been *your* guiding principle always. And I believe him. You are a notable divider Patrick! You cannot deny it.'

'Davy was ever prejudiced. Full of honest worth, but lacking judgment. A common complaint! You both mistake. My aim is not to divide but to balance. It is not the dividing that governs, it is the holding of the balance. Only so may a weak king and a torn realm be governed – by holding a delicate balance. No light task, I may say. Someone must hold it if Scotland is to survive.'

'Ever it comes to that – the excuse for all! For that, you would do anything ...'

She stopped, as along the table King James beat on the wood with an empty goblet, for silence.

'My lords,' he called out. 'Hear me. I have now listened to more o' this matter. From the Duke. This o' the Islesmen and the Irish. It was a notable ploy – aye, notable. Acting as our Lieutenant, the Duke has achieved much. In conjunction with the ships o' our good sister Elizabeth o' England, the forces o' rebellion have been vanquished. Or, leastways, dispersed. Aye, dispersed. A right happy eventuality. Mind, I'll no' say it wouldna have been better if he had informed us o' what was to do. It would have been more seemly ...'

Patrick Gray cleared his throat with some vigour.

'Aye. Umm.' James glanced along the table at the Master, his great expressive spaniel's eyes rolling. 'That is so. In consequence o' all this, it behoves us to look with increased favour on our good cousin o' Lennox, young as he is. Aye, young. Anything that has been amiss, we can justly blame on his youth, I say – for mind, he's no' yet of full age.' James paused, as though

254

to let that fact sink in. 'So, my lords, it is now our pleasure to show our thanks to the Duke by more than words, just. In token o' his services to this realm, I now release him frae his duties as Lieutenant o' the North. The which will revert to my lord o' Argyll here. Instead, I appoint him to be Governor and Keeper of my royal fortress o' Dumbarton Castle – as was his father before him. Also President o' my Privy Council.'

He paused, and there was some polite applause, while James wiped his ever-wet lips with the sleeve of his doublet. For his part, Ludovick looked doubtfully along at the Master of Gray and Mary. That man smiled and nodded in genial congratulation.

James resumed. 'Further, it is our royal will and pleasure to advance our good cousin Ludovick, Duke o' Lennox, in other fashion likewise. Aye, as is suitable and seemly. That he may more meetly carry out the duties o' Lord President and High Admiral o' this realm. I therefore – he being no' yet o' full age, o' the royal house – do hereby bestow on him in matrimony the hand o' the Lady Jean Campbell, relict o' the umquhile Master o' Eglinton and daughter o' the umquhile Sir Matthew Campbell o' Loudoun, one o' the greatest heiresses in this my realm!' And the King leaned forward to leer along the table at the lady who sat at the other side of his uncle the Earl of Orkney.

The great room seemed positively to surge with the sensation. Seldom indeed could a royal pronouncement have produced such startled effect. Everywhere, despite etiquette, voices were raised in astonished and excited comment and exclamation. The piquancy and drama of the situation required no explaining to even the least informed.

Mary Gray had listened to the King as though in a dream, a nightmare. Scarcely able to grasp the reality of it, she crouched there dazed, a pulse beating in her head.

Ludovick had half-risen from his seat, fists clenched, wild of eye, the picture of angry protest, seeking for words.

James flapped him down, imperiously. 'Sit, man – sit!' he ordered. 'I'm no' done yet. Wheesht, you!' He raised his voice. 'It is my will and command that this marriage shall take place without delay. In the shortest possible time. Aye. In my royal presence and at my charges. And now – Lady Jean!'

'Sire!' Ludovick cried. 'This is not possible! Hear me . . .'

'Quiet, I say! It is more than possible, Vicky – it is my royal command. And here's the lady . . .'

The Master of Gray had risen, and slipped round to aid the Lady Jean from her seat. He now brought her along behind the chairs, to the King. She curtsied low to James, murmuring something – but her glance was on the Duke of Lennox.

Jean Campbell was a tall, well-built young woman, just a little less than strapping, with a proud carriage, strong and striking features, a wide sensual mouth and a firm chin. Six or seven years older than Ludovick, she was obviously nobody's fool – and by no means young for her years. Magnificently gowned, comporting herself with a nice mixture of assurance and modesty, despite the distinctly awkward position into which she was thrust, she looked what she was, a woman of experience, strong character and hot appetite. Beside her Ludovick Stewart seemed almost younger than his score of years.

Desperately the young man looked from her to the King, along to Mary, and back again.

'Houts, man – where's your manners?' James demanded, ponderously playful, poling the Duke in the ribs. 'Have you no civilities to show the lassie?'

Ludovick got to his feet, and bowed briefly, curtly.

'My lord Duke,' the young woman said, smiling faintly. 'Yours to command!'

He stared at her, shaking his head and biting his lip. Then he swung on the King again. 'Sire – your permission to retire, I pray. With . . . with this lady. There is much to say, to discuss. Not meet to do before all these . . .'

'Na, na, Vicky – no' so fast! Be no' so hot, man!' James chuckled now. 'A fast change, hey? One look at the lass and he's for off wi' her, for privy chambering! Na, na – sit you, man. And you, Lady Jean. See – the Master's brought a chair for you. We're no' done yet. Later. Aye, later, you'll get to be alone wi' her. Ooh, aye – plenty time for that! Meantime there's the matter o' my lord o' Argyll, who also deserves well o' us. And the reversal o' forfeiture on Sir Lachlan Maclean to pronounce . . .'

Quietly, Mary Gray rose from her seat, and without seeking

the royal permission or saying a word to anyone, head down, moved swiftly over to a side door behind the dais-table. If the King saw her, he made no comment. A guard at the door opened it for her, and she slipped out.

Hitching up her skirts and almost running, the girl hurried out into the great paved Upper Square of the castle, and down the steps cut in the living rock, past the Chapel-Royal and the Inner Barbican to the cobbled ramp which led down to the great gatehouse. Men-at-arms, palace officials and servitors looked at her in surprise, but she scarcely saw them, saw anything, in her anguish of mind. The guards at the gatehouse knew her well, of course, and let her through. Her feet drumming on the drawbridge timbers, she ran out, and down the open marshalling-ground towards the town, a slender figure of distress.

Up the stairs of the tall narrow Gray lodging in the Broadgait she stumbled. The door was not shut this fine May evening. Within the Lady Marie was aiding a tire-woman to settle young Johnnie in his cot beside that of her own baby daughter. Into the older woman's arms Mary flung herself, panting, sobbing as though her heart would break.

Never before had Marie seen the girl lose control of herself, her normal quiet serenity and innate composure shattered. She held her close, stroking her dark hair, soothing her with gentle crooning words, like one of the children, while at the same time she gestured for the maid-servant to leave them alone.

'Oh, Marie! Marie! I have lost him! Vicky,' she gasped brokenly. 'They have taken him from me. I have lost Vicky, Marie!'

'No, no, my dear. Not lost him. Not Vicky. I am sure not. Hush, my love, my sweeting. Hush you.'

'I have! I have. He is to be married. The King said so. In front of all. To the Mistress of Eglinton. Forthwith. A royal command. I have to leave him. Leave Methven. Oh, Marie . . . !' That ended in a wail.

'My precious Mary!' The other almost rocked her in her arms. 'This is a wicked thing. Shameful. But . . . do not despair, my dear. It may not be quite so ill as you fear . . .'

Mary broke away from her. She darted to the cot, and snatched up her little son, to cover his smiling round face with salt kisses, and then to clutch him to her fiercely, possessively. Over his small head she stared at the other.

'This is Patrick's work!' she cried, almost accusingly.

The Lady Marie shook a sorrowful head, but did not answer.

'It is! I know it. His revenge for us having interfered in his wicked plot. The King would never have thought of it. He has agreed to it because of that folly of the Queen. When he accused Vicky of being her lover. But he would never have thought of this. It is Patrick – the thinking of it and the way it was done, there before all the Court! Where we could do nothing – Vicky could do nothing. It . . . it *stinks* of Patrick! Can you deny it?'

She did not give her friend opportunity to deny or admit it. 'This is Patrick's love for me!' she exclaimed, chokingly. 'He brought us here – for this! He has ever sought to come between Vicky and me. He does not love me – he hates me!'

'Ah, no, Mary – not that! Patrick does love you – that I swear. Whatever else, that is sure. This may be his doing indeed – though I have known naught of it. But even so, he loves you . . .'

Mary was not listening. She paced the floor, hugging and kissing her child. 'Johnnie! Johnnie dear!' she gulped, thickly. 'My bonnie baby, my own darling! What are we to do? Oh, what are we to do? Your father – they have taken your father from us!'

Marie Stewart watched her, her grey eyes sombre, hurt in all her lovely features. This abandon was so unlike Mary Gray as to be alarming in itself, over and above the grim circumstances which produced it. But presently to hurt was added firm decision. She moved over to the younger woman and put an arm around her, propelling her quite strongly to a chair by the smouldering log fire.

'Come, now – sit Mary. Calm yourself, my dear. You must, and you can – for you have the strongest will I know. Stronger even than Patrick's, I do believe! Yes it is. This is not like Mary Gray! You must be yourself. I shall fetch you a posset. As I did last time that you were here. You remember? Then you were anxious, fearful, also – but strong. Fighting. The Mary I know. As you must be again, my sweet. For Johnnie's sake. For

Vicky's sake. Even for *my* sake – for we have a compact, you and I, have we not? That we shall fight and counter, where we may, the evil Patrick does. That we must still do. Only we can do it – his wife and his daughter!'

Her words, and the firm level tone in which they were spoken, affected the younger woman, calming and at the same time challenging her. Gradually she relaxed.

'See – I shall make the posset here beside you,' Marie went on. 'Tell me it all . . .'

Ludovick Stewart shut the door of the ante-room, and turned, leaning his back against it. They were alone, at last. Heavily he gazed at the young woman.

The Lady Jean spoke first. 'Well, my lord Duke – do I so repel you? Am I so ill-favoured, so repugnant, that you must needs treat me like one of the Furies?'

He moistened his lips. 'I am sorry. It is not you. Not you yourself . . .'

'But it is, my lord. Me. Me that it seems you have to marry! Aye – and you that *I* must! Which is a minor matter perhaps – but of some small consequence to me!'

'Then fear no more, ma'am, for I shall not wed you. Nor you me! We shall not quarrel over that!'

She looked him up and down frankly, assessingly. 'I did not esteem you a fool, my lord,' she said. 'Nor am I, I'd have you know. I know that we must wed – as do you. Since it is a royal command. I am a ward of the Crown, and you are under full age. We cannot shut our eyes to it. We have no choice in the matter. For me, I may say, if I *had* my choice, it would be . . . otherwise.'

Ludovick started to stride about the little room. 'Royal command!' he repeated, almost snorting. 'What is a royal command but the mere spoken word of my havering, spineless cousin James Stewart! It is not the voice of God Almighty! What he has said he can unsay. Many's the time I have heard him do so.'

'Perhaps, my lord. You know the King better than do I, no doubt. But he will not unsay this command, I think, given before all the Court and the ambassadors of other princes. How could he, without losing all respect? Moreover, what would the

Master of Gray say?'

'Aye – the Master of Gray! Little need to question whose hand is behind James in this! Curse him!'

'Hush, my lord! That is a dangerous thing to say in Scotland today, is it not? Besides, the Master is something of a friend of mine!'

He paused in his pacing, to stare at her, narrow-eyed. 'Ha! Is that so, indeed?'

She nodded. 'As you are of his, he assures me.'

'Then he is a liar, ma'am – amongst other things!'

She shook her head at him. 'It seems that I am to have a rash husband indeed! And, my lord, since we are fated to be bed-mates, must you be ever calling me ma'am? As though I was your mother! I am older than you, yes – but even so I am no more than twenty-six years. Even though I have a daughter of five.'

'You have a daughter . . . ?'

'Yes. Does that offend you?'

'No. No – but . . .' Ludovick, with an effort, took a grip on himself. 'Lady Jean,' he said, 'listen to me. I do not wish to hurt you, God knows – but while you may accept this marriage, I cannot! It could never be aught but a travesty, a hollow pretence. I am already married, in all but the name. To Mary Gray. I love her. We look on each other as husband and wife. We have a child, a son.'

'All this I know,' she said, quietly now. 'I am sorry also. But . . . it alters nothing. You are not married to Mary Gray. And if you were, the King would have it annulled. Your child by her cannot heir your dukedom. We might have a son who could.'

'Damn the dukedom! It is Mary Gray that I want. And our son Johnnie. Not to provide heir to the dukedom . . .'

'But you can have both, my lord. Why all the pother?' She shrugged strong shoulders at him. 'Think you I care about your mistress? Many husbands have mistresses. I shall not keep you from your Mary Gray.'

He came up to her, frowning. 'You say that? What is there in this marriage to advantage you?' he demanded. 'Why do you seek it, woman?'

'I do not seek it. Indeed, I would have chosen very differently,

260

had it been possible. But I have learned – as should you, my lord – that where circumstances may not be mended they are best accepted with a fair grace. I was not asked if I would wed the Duke of Lennox – I was told that I must. So I make the best of it.'

Despite himself, Ludovick rose to that. 'So you do find some merit in me as husband?'

'Oh, yes. I have seen worse-made men! And clearly you *are* a man, and no painted boy, like so many around the King. That I could scarce have stomached! Then, I shall be a duchess – the only such in this land. That will not be without its advantages, I think. I shall be able to queen it over many proud countesses who now look down their noses at me – including my haughty good-sister the Countess of Eglinton, who hates me. A prospect no woman would despise! I suppose that I might even be the Queen, one day – although that might be a better dream than a reality! All that – and I might think of more. For instance, having a husband who would not be like to watch me with too doting and jealous an eye ... !'

'Sink me – you are frank, at least!'

'Yes, sir – as I hold that you should be also. In our state there is virtue in frankness, is there not? For yourself the marriage will not lack advantage. A wife who will make no great demands upon you. The use of great wealth ...'

'I do not want your money, woman!'

'So you say now, my lord. But perhaps, when it is there to your hand, you may find otherwise. Moreover, I am a Campbell, and to be allied to that clan might serve a man very well – even a duke! Where broadswords are needed.'

'You need not think to buy me with fighting-men, either ...'

'I do not seek to buy you. We are sold already, both of us! I but look for what gain there is for us in it.'

'But ... God's mercy! You may accept all this as sure, settled – but I do not. *I* am no ward of the King. I shall be of age in September. Four months, no more! Thereafter none can force me to anything.'

'Which is no doubt why His Grace hastens the wedding! The more proof that he is determined in this.'

'If I was to bolt. To go away. Where James could not reach

me. Back to the Isles, perhaps. Before any wedding. Until September. Then I could not be forced. James would be angry – but could do nothing . . .'

'Think you that this has not been thought of?' she interrupted. 'They have been preparing this for weeks, see you, awaiting your return. I cannot think that you will be allowed to leave the walls of this Stirling Castle until you are safely wed, my Lord Ludovick!'

'You mean . . . ?' Almost he made for the door, there and then, but restrained himself. 'You think that I am a prisoner, then – to crown all?' he cried.

'If I was the King, you would be.'

'But – this is monstrous! Beyond all bearing. And you?'

'I also, I have little doubt.'

He strode to the door now, and threw it open. In the stone corridor outside no fewer than five guards stood about, armed, alert. They eyed him stolidly.

'Take me to the King,' Ludovick barked, with all the authority he could muster. 'I would have word with him.'

'His Grace has retired for the night, my lord Duke,' one of them answered. 'He gave orders that he was not to be disturbed.'

'This is important. Business of state.'

Nobody spoke, or moved.

'The Master of Gray, then. Bring me here the Master of Gray.'

'He has left the castle, my lord.'

Ludovick bit back a curse.

'If your lordship wishes, I will conduct you to your room,' the young officer went on, stiffly.

'No – I am not staying at the castle.'

'On His Grace's express command, my lord, you are! A room is prepared for you.'

'And for me?' Jean Campbell asked, at the Duke's back.

'Yes, ma'am. Your rooms are . . . together. In the Albany Tower.'

'How . . . thoughtful!' the young woman murmured.

'If you will follow me, my lord Duke . . .'

Patrick Gray strolled into his modest house in the Broadgait, humming tunefully to himself. At sight of the two women sitting by the fire, his face lit up with pleasure.

'So you have the runaway, Marie my dear!' he said. 'I thought that she might possibly be here, come to see young Johnnie and yourself.' He came over, to pat Mary's hunched shoulder. 'The trouble this young woman is to me!' he sighed, but humorously. 'Do you know what she did, Marie? She up and left the royal table without permission! Without so much as a nod at His Grace! Our liege lord, when he discovered, was like a clucking hen . . .'

'Patrick!' his wife interrupted. 'Spare Mary this, for a mercy! She is sore-hearted and in no mood for your witticisms. Nor, indeed, am I!'

'Nor was His Grace, if you will believe me! But let it pass. Mary is sad? I feared she would be. Indeed, it could scarce be otherwise. But it will pass, my dear – it will pass. This marriage of Vicky's was bound to come. The Dukedom of Lennox must have a legitimate heir.'

'Patrick – will you stop it!' his wife exclaimed. 'Have you no heart?'

'Heart, my love? Need *you* ask that . . . ?'

'Where is Vicky?' Mary asked levelly, without intonation.

'He is still at the castle. There is much for him to see to.'

'He sent me no message?'

'Not by me, my dear. Would he know that you were here?'

'He would know where I would come.' She raised her head to eye him directly. 'Is he held? In the castle?'

'Hardly held, lass. He will be stopping there meantime, I should think . . .'

'Yes. I should think so also! You will not let him leave, I warrant! In case you do not see him again until he is of full age! It is only till September. Why will you not be honest with me, Patrick? If, indeed, honesty is something of which you are capable!'

'Mary, my child – you are distrait, downcast. Do not take it so hard. You must have known that Vicky would marry again. He was married before, to Sophia Ruthven, poor creature . . .'

'That you arranged also. That, as well as separate us, you

263

might lay hands on her great wealth. How much will you gain from the Mistress of Eglinton?'

'God save us, girl – what do you take me for?'

'For what I have long known you to be, in my heart – the greatest rogue in this realm! Caring not who you hurt, or how many, so long as you gain your own selfish wicked will!'

The Lady Marie bit her lip, but said nothing.

'You, h'm, exaggerate, my sweeting!'

'Do I? Is it possible? To exaggerate? About the man who got my mother with child – and then left her for Davy Gray to take the blame, care for and marry? The man who betrayed Mary the Queen to her death? The man who brought down Vicky's father, his friend? Who betrayed the Earls of Moray, Arran, Bothwell, Huntly and God only knows how many more? Aye, who would have sold Vicky, on false charges to Queen Elizabeth, had I not halted it! And who now has betrayed the whole Clan Donald? Do I exaggerate, Patrick? Is there indeed anyone who you have *not* betrayed? Or would not . . . ?'

He did not answer her, did not speak. White to the lips, teeth clenched, he swung on his heel and strode for the door, without a glance at either of them, out of the room and out of the house. They heard the click-click of his high-heeled shoes as he ran down the outer stairs to the street, and then silence.

After a few moments staring after him, Mary turned to look at the Lady Marie. At the stricken face she saw there across the hearth from her, she gulped and sprang from her seat.

'Oh, Marie! Marie!' she cried, hurling herself over the intervening space, to sink on her knees beside the older woman and clutch her convulsively. 'What have I done? I am sorry! Sorry! I have hurt you. Oh, fool that I am – I have hurt *you*! Forgive me, Marie! Can you forgive me? You, in all the world, I would not wish to hurt.'

'There is nothing to forgive, my dear – nothing,' the other said, stroking the girl's dark hair. 'It was all true, I have no doubt. But . . . did you have to say it all!'

'No,' Mary whispered. 'No, I did not! It was ill done. But then, I am Patrick's daughter you see! Of the same black blood!' Abruptly she got to her feet. 'I must go, now,' she said.

'Go? What do you mean, Mary? Go – at this time of night?'

'I must go away. From this house. I cannot stay here. This is his house, Patrick's house. I cannot remain in it, after what I have said. Or my son. And what he has done. You must see it, Marie.'

'It is my home too, Mary.'

'Yes. All the more reason why I must go. I come between you and your husband.'

'No. You are wrong. But – where can you go? Back to the castle?'

'No – I cannot go there. Not now. They would not allow me to be with Vicky, I know. And they might take Johnnie from me. As they took Henry from *his* mother!'

'It is too late for you to ride back to Methven tonight . . .'

'Not too late, no. I care not where I ride, by night or day. But I cannot go to Methven either. It is not for me, now . . .'

'Do not be too proud, my dear. It is your home.'

'No. Not now. It is where Vicky must take his wife. My home is with Davy Gray and my mother, at Castle Huntly. There I will go.'

'But, child – you cannot go all that way tonight!'

'Not now, no. Tonight I know where I shall go. Where I went last time that I was here. When I left Johnnie with you. I shall go to Castle Campbell, at Dollar. My lord of Argyll will take me in. Archibald Campbell and I understand each other, I think. That is where I shall go. If you will lend me a horse again, Marie? And a plaid to wrap Johnnie in. Please, Marie. My mind is made up . . .'

And so, a couple of hours later, in the grey half-light of a northern May midnight, Archibald Grumach Campbell was awakened, with the somewhat startling information that a young woman and her baby had come to Castle Campbell, seeking shelter and his charity. She had sought only some corner, and would not have his lordship disturbed – but since she was, it seemed, the Mistress Mary Gray, daughter of the Master, the gatehouse porter reckoned that he should be told.

Pulling on a bed-robe, the young Earl hurried below. He did not have much to say to his untimely guest, but as he conducted her up the winding stone turnpike stair, calling to sleepy servants for food, wine, firing and the like, he held her hand in his.

Chapter Sixteen

The wedding was celebrated in the Chapel-Royal of the castle, by Master David Lindsay, the King's chaplain, before a select but highly interested, not to say intrigued, congregation. If it seemed a very rushed affair, everyone recognised the reasons therefore, many comments being made that they were at least not the usual ones for hurried marriages.

Ludovick made a sullen and unco-operative bridegroom, refusing even to dress at his best. He had not been allowed to leave Stirling Castle in the eight days which had elapsed since his arrival there, and had been forced to perceive that he had no option but to submit, with whatever ill grace. Obviously he would be married even though he had to be brought in chains to the ceremony. The King's decision was law, and there was nothing that a minor could do to invalidate it short of putting himself physically beyond the hands of the authorities.

He had ample time and opportunity, at any rate, to consider the situation, in the fretting confinement of those late May days. At first he had been puzzled to understand James's determination in the matter. Patrick's motives were clear – revenge for interference in his affairs, and to separate Ludovick and Mary; also, almost certainly to gain control of some part of the bride's wealth. But, although vengeance and gain to some extent might also influence the offended monarch, more than that was surely involved. He had had only the one interview with the King in the interim, and that not alone; but he had talked with various others. He had come to the conclusion that James's urgency to have him married was largely on account of the Queen. James actually believed Ludovick to be a menace to him, not only in the Queen's affections, but that, unwed, he was in a position to marry her if James himself was removed, and so to control the child Henry or even make himself the King. So he was to be wed, and not to any great lord's daughter who might conceivably push him towards the throne, but to the heiress of a simple

266

knight, however influential. That the King could be so mistaken in the assessment of the situation would have been laughable had it not been tragic – but no doubt Patrick Gray had carefully nurtured these delusions.

As a consequence, the Queen had been brought to the wedding, and the duchess-to-be was already appointed to be her principal lady-in-waiting, that the lesson be well and truly rubbed in.

The days of waiting had at least somewhat improved the Duke's opinion of his unwanted bride. Inevitably he saw a lot of her, for their apartments were side-by-side and they had to share a single public room. This could have been quite intolerable, for Ludovick at least, with most women; but Jean Campbell was understanding, tactful after a forthright fashion, and cheerful without being aggressively so. Her philosophical treatment of the whole affair was entirely practical, even humorously resigned. Since there seemed to be no way out of their entanglement, he might have had a much worse partner in it.

She at any rate had dressed for the occasion, and was now looking very fine in richly jewelled brocade. Since it was a second marriage for both of them, the dispensing with many of the frills and extras was entirely seemly. It gave the greater opportunity, however, for Master Lindsay to preach a really notable sermon, on the sins, follies, and temptations of those in high places, the dangers of wealth and the pitfalls of pride – more than making up for any brevity in the actual ceremony. As an exhortation to those about to enter upon holy matrimony, it was salutory.

James himself gave the bride away, and the Master of Gray acted groomsman – as was suitable for one who had brought the boy from France to Scotland ten years before. He it was who produced the ring as required, and, when Ludovick himself showed no interest in it, placed it on the lady's finger for him. If the Master did not actually say the responses it was not because the groom did so himself; they were taken as said. Ludovick and Jean were duly pronounced man and wife, in the sight of God and according to rites of the Kirk and the law of Scotland.

The reception thereafter was a brilliant affair such as Patrick delighted to organise, with a wealth of pageantry, masque and allegory – to be paid for, no doubt from the lady's deep purse. James had written a poem for the occasion, mercifully brief.

Ludovick came face to face with the Queen for the first time in many months. She eyed him searchingly and then beckoned him close, conspiratorily.

'I know that this is none of your doing, Vicky,' she declared in a penetrating whisper which neither the King nor the Lady Jean nearby could fail to hear. 'You are leal and true to me, without a doubt. Believe me that I trust you.'

Embarrassed, Ludovick coughed. 'Your Grace – I, ah . . . I am ever your servant, of course, I, h'm, rejoice to see you.'

'I understand, Vicky.' She pressed his arm. 'We shall speak together on another occasion. Not now.'

James looked at them sourly, but said nothing.

Patrick strolled up, and having skilfully involved both King and Queen with the new English envoy on the ever-burning question of Elizabeth's non-payment of James's pension, drew Jean Campbell over to Ludovick's side.

'A word in your pretty ear, Duchess,' he said – the first to accord her her new title. 'And yours, Vicky. You will be glad, I vow, that having both of you been wed before, you can be spared the unseemly business of the public bedding – a mercy indeed! Nevertheless, I hear that there is a move afoot to escort you presently to your bridal chamber. I thought that perhaps I should warn you.'

Ludovick snorted. He could scarcely bear the close proximity of the Master, and had to hold himself from abruptly turning his back on the man. He would have preferred to ignore any remark he made – but this information penetrated his hostility. 'A plague on them!' he exclaimed, hotly. 'Let them but try!'

'I think, nevertheless, we ought not to have a scene,' his bride said, sensibly. 'That would be unsuitable.'

Patrick nodded. 'I thought you might wish to slip away quietly. Not perhaps to the Albany Tower. Away from Stirling altogether. It is too late for Methven tonight, but perhaps . . .'

'We do not go to Methven tonight or any night,' the Duke snapped.

'No?' Patrick raised his brows.

'No. Mary is at Methven.' That was flat.

'Ah. H'mm. Well no, Vicky – she is not, I fear. She is . . . otherwhere.'

'Eh? Where is she? Do not say . . . do not tell me that she is taken also! That you have held Mary as you have held me here?' Blazing-eyed he swung on the other man.

'Tut, man – do not be so plaguey hot! *I* have not held you, anywhere! And Mary certainly is not held. She has, er, gone where she will.'

'Where?'

'I am reliably informed, Vicky, that, curiously enough, she went to Castle Campbell. To our young friend Argyll. The very night you parted. I take it that she established some sort of association with him on your, h'm, travels!'

'I do not like the way you said that,' Ludovick jerked.

'Dear me – do you not? I assumed, since she went to him, that they must have become friends. Forgive me if I mistake!'

'If Argyll took Mary to Castle Campbell, it would be to shelter and protect her. We became friends, yes. In the Isles.'

'Ah, yes. Quite. Only, Argyll did not take her. Mary went there by herself. Late that night. Leaving my house to do so, where she was surely sufficiently sheltered and protected!'

'Ah! Then, Patrick, I commend her choice!'

'Indeed. I wonder at that. But perhaps, as a married man now, you see matters differently! At any rate, there is nothing to prevent you and Jean going to Methven now.'

'But there is. Methven Castle is no longer mine. It is Mary's home. More than that, it is made over altogether, by charter, to our son John Stewart of Methven, in her care. I do not take this lady there!'

Patrick stared. 'You mean . . . ? That you *meant* that nonsense? About putting the barony in the name of the child? You have left yourself without a house!'

'*I* do not do all with intent to deceive!' the younger man retorted. 'I provided for Mary and the child – as was my least duty. Would you have me to other – to your daughter?'

'Then . . . you have nowhere to go now? Nowhere to take your wife, man!'

'Should that concern *me*?' Ludovick smiled, albeit mirthlessly. 'Though to be sure, have I not Dumbarton Castle now? From my generous liege lord. There will be a house there, I've no doubt – and myself the new Governor!'

The Lady Jean intervened. 'Why all this talk of houses to go to? I have houses and lands a-plenty. And if you do not wish to live in Cunningham or Kyle, we can buy a house near to Stirling.'

'Aye. Are you not fortunate in your wife, Vicky? But, to-night? Where will you go?'

'I am content with His Grace's provision,' the Duke said. 'We both are well enough suited. In the Albany Tower. Would you have us spurn the royal hospitality? We shall continue to enjoy it.'

As Patrick, looking from one to the other, was about to speak, the young woman caught his eye.

'We shall do very well there, meantime,' she said, nodding. 'Do not concern yourself further, sir. If you can but aid us out of this hall unnoticed, we shall be in your debt . . .'

And so, presently, in the confusion attendant upon the exit of a troupe of tumblers and acrobats and the setting up of a tableau representing the Marriage at Cana of Galilee, with water being poured in at one end of a barrel and red wine being tapped off at the other, the bridal couple managed to make their discreet departure. They crossed the crowded Upper Square, where servants, men-at-arms and performers were at their own noisy merry-making under the May night sky, to the Albany Tower that had been their prison. Their eyes met as Ludovick opened the door for his Duchess to enter.

Upstairs, at first floor level, was the large public room which they had used in common that past week. Ludovick paused at the door there, but the young woman continued on up the winding turnpike stairway. When she perceived that he did not follow her up, she turned and looked back.

'Which chamber do we use, Ludovick?' she asked. 'Yours or mine?' That was calmly, factually put.

Much less calmly, he cleared his throat. 'Which? Why, both. I assumed that we would be using both. As we did before . . .'

'But we are not as before, Ludovick. We are now man and wife.'

'In name, yes. But...'

'In fact. We are as truly wed as any man and woman in the land. And will remain so. There is little sense in shutting our eyes to it.'

'There is more in marriage, woman, than a few mumbled words in a kirk!'

'True. That is why I ask – which chamber!'

He frowned, tapping a toe on the stone landing. 'Mistress... Jean I prefer to bed alone! If you please.'

She looked down at him thoughtfully. 'What you mean, I think, is that you would prefer to bed with your mistress. With Mary Gray.'

His head jerked up, at that. 'Very well. Put it so, if you will. I would prefer to bed with Mary Gray!'

She nodded. 'That I well believe and understand. And, as I said, I shall not keep you from seeking to do so again. But this day you married me, Jean Campbell. I am your lawful wife, the Duchess of Lennox, and this is our bridal night. Do I have to demand my rights, Ludovick?'

When he did not answer, she went on. 'I am not hot for you – think it not, my lord Duke! I too would prefer to be . . . elsewhere! In a certain small castle in Kyle. But I am in Sterling Castle, not Kyle – just as Mary Gray is not here, but apparently in some other man's house. We have to take life as it is, Ludovick – not as we would wish it. Be we dukes and duchesses, or lesser folk. We are wed, the two of us, and must accept it.'

'You are a great accepter!' he charged her.

'I have been well trained in it! You, it seems, have not. Facts, even hard facts, are best accepted – and can be made thereby the softer, I have found.'

'So you have said before. You are welcome to your convictions – but mine are otherwise!'

'You would deny facts? Deny that we are man and wife . . . ?'

'I deny nothing – save that it is any duty of mine to go to bed with you this night!'

'No? But suppose the boot had been on the other leg, sir? How then? How many women are left in no doubt that it *is* their duty, God ordained, to lie with their husbands, this first night, or any night, of their marriage? Still – let that be. Did you marry me with the intent that we should never bed together?'

Biting his lip, he kicked at one of the stone steps. 'H'mm. I . . . ah . . . no. Not so. But that is . . . well, it is for the future. Not tonight. Tonight it is different. Too soon . . .'

'Is that a man speaking? Or a mouse?' she exclaimed. Then the young woman quickly changed her tone, coming indeed a couple of steps down the stair. 'See, Ludovick – it is better thus. Tonight. We are not children. We know that in matters of this sort there can easily be difficulties, barriers, stumbling-blocks. Put off, delay or shy at it, and it becomes the more difficult, the harder to come together . . .'

'God be good, woman – you make it sound as though we were horses to be broken to bit and bridle! Of a mercy, spare me more of this!'

'Very well,' she said, shrugging. 'Lord – what have I married? My late lord, to whom I was wed at fourteen, was a stallion! Now, I am tied to a gelded palfrey!'

Flushing hotly, Ludovick flung into the room in front of him, and slammed the door shut.

For a considerable time he paced up and down there, scarcely aware of what he did. Young, vigorous and far from undersexed, the woman's strictures hit him hard. What right had she to speak so to him? Right or reason? Excuse? It was beyond all bearing that, just because, for their own unholy purposes, the King and Patrick had forced this match upon him, he should be faced with this ridiculous quandary. The fact that, from one point of view, Jean had the rights of it, made it the more damnable. What was a man to do, in the circumstances? The situation would not get better, as she said. Was he fated to battling with her on this of all subjects . . . ?

Ludovick found a flagon of wine, and drank deeply.

He waited for quite some time longer before leaving the room and going upstairs. He did not slam the door behind him on this occasion; indeed he all but tip-toed up the steps.

Ignoring the part-opened door of the young woman's room, he went into his own chamber – to find Jean Campbell sitting up in his great four-poster bed, a robe around her shoulders. The light from the small window at that hour was not good, and she had a single candle burning nearby. She smiled at him, but said nothing.

He halted uncertainly, perplexed. 'I . . . I do not congratulate you!' he got out, at length.

'No? Is it part of a husband's duty at such a time? I shall survive the lack, I think! You have been long in coming, Ludovick.'

He did not answer that, but moved over to the bed, to stand nearby looking down at her. The robe she had only loosely thrown about her, and it was clear that she wore nothing beneath.

'Why do you do this?' he asked. 'You say that you are not hot for me. Would you have me believe that?'

She shrugged, and one white shoulder slipped out from the robe. 'Believe it or not, as you like. It is both true and untrue, I think. I am not hot for *you*, Ludovick Stewart, in especial. But I am a woman not unappreciative of men – and I have been widowed over long! Moreover, this is my wedding-night. Does that answer serve you, my lord?'

'Aye,' he said, on an exhalation of breath. 'You are frank now, by the Powers! I vow I prefer it to all the talk before. Of what is best for me, the duties of marriage and the like.'

'I thought that you might,' she allowed, low-voiced but smiling again. She beckoned him closer. 'Come!' she said.

He ignored her invitation. 'That does not change matters,' he asserted heavily.

'No? Why do you look at me so, then? Your eyes betray you, my lord Duke! I think that you are a man, after all!'

'A man can have more attributes than the one,' he got out, from lips that were somehow awkward, mumbling, reluctant. 'A man is will, as well as body. Loyal. Able to keep himself . . .'

'Yet you vowed, a few hours ago, before all men, to keep *me*! Must I trade words with you? Bicker and argue? Here and now, at this pass? What ails you, Ludovick? Am I so ill-favoured? Others have not esteemed me so, I tell you! But, Lord – enough of words!'

With a toss of her head she threw off the robe and kicked

back the bed-clothes, to sit there naked before him, in invitation and challenge both.

She was very desirable. A big woman in every way, generously made, she was none the less rousing on that account, although she lacked, for instance, Mary Gray's perfection of proportion and subtler loveliness. There was indeed nothing of subtlety about Jean Campbell's great thrusting breasts, strong arms, rounded belly and massive thighs. But she was all woman nevertheless, urgent, essential, demanding.

Ludovick all but choked at what he saw and sensed, and despite himself took that final pace forward which brought him to the side of the great bed. As he did so, the girl reached out to grasp his arm, to pull him bodily down on top of her.

Once his hands were on her robust and vehement flesh, there was of course no further holding back. In a mounting, ungovernable surge of fierce, dominant desire, he took possession of her with a masterful passion which no other woman had ever roused in him.

Sobbing, Jean abandoned herself.

When the storm was past and they lay spent, relaxed, she was the first to speak.

'I shall not call you mouse again! Or gelding!' she murmured, idly combing a slack hand through his hair. 'Not that I ever truly thought you such. Or even King James could not have forced me into this marriage.'

He grunted. 'It was all lies, then? All your talk.'

'No. Not lies. I meant what I said. That it is best this way. Best for us both. Since it must come to this, better sooner than later.'

'It came to this – because you made it so!' he said, shaking his head free of her hand.

'Ha! Who is now the liar?' she demanded. 'Your eyes, your hands, your body, all your manhood belies your words, Ludovick. You wanted me, whatever you said. Do you think a woman does not know? Aye – and now you keep your eyes shut lest they, and all the rest, do so again! As will be so. You know, and I know. You fight the wrong enemies, husband! Open your eyes, Ludovick Stewart. And unclench your fists. Why waste your fine strength? I can use it ... !'

Chapter Seventeen

Mary Gray, in the act of setting and pressing the oat-sheaf firmly against its neighbours to complete the stook, raised her head to glance ruefully over to where young Johnnie Stewart, on plump but unsteady legs, was doing his tottering best to pull apart the last stook that she had built. The smile died on her lips, however, as her eyes lifted, to narrow against the golden blaze of the declining September sun, westwards towards the frowning red stone castle which towered half a mile away on its rock above the wide levels of the Carse of Gowrie.

'Company, Father, I think,' she called. 'Armour glinting. My lord does not ride at such speed these days . . .'

Davy Gray straightened up from the back-breaking task of gathering the cut swathes of oats into great armfuls, and binding these together with a twisted rope of their own long stalks. He followed her gaze.

'Gilbert, it may be, from Mylnhill? Or William from Bandirran? To demand that my lord's steward does this or that for them! To borrow men or beasts. But neither of them, you may be sure, to set dainty hand to my lord's corn!'

The girl smiled, but said nothing. David Gray's scorn for his younger legitimate half-brothers was best treated as a joke.

She made a delightful, vital and lightsome picture, standing there in the harvest-field, all glowing health and essential femininity, flushed with her exertions, browned by the sun, her bare arms powdered by the oat-dust, flecks of chaff and straw caught in her dark hair. Dressed with utter simplicity in a brief white bodice which clung lovingly to her young rounded excellence of figure, skirt kilted up to the knees, with legs and indeed feet bare, she had never looked more enticing – and never less like a lady of the Court.

David Gray considered her fondly – as he had been doing off and on as he worked, for he found it hard indeed to keep his eyes off her. She loved the satisfying and fundamental work of the harvest-field, as he did, and they were seldom happier than when they were so employed together. The past summer months had been happy ones for the man – and, he thought, after the first weeks, to some extent for the girl also; peaceful, uncomplicated, undemanding. She had slipped back into the old life of Castle Huntly, after the years of absence. as though she had never been away – save that now she had her little Johnnie with her. And Castle Huntly had been the sweeter for her return, the old lord more bearable to live with – for Mary had always been the apple of that irascible tyrant's eye – and her mother Mariota rejoicing to have her back and almost like a girl again, for there were only the fifteen years between their ages.

'Two riders only,' she reported. 'And in a hurry. I hope they do not bring ill-tidings . . .' She stopped, stiffening in her posture. 'Dear God,' she whispered, 'I think . . . I think I know...' She bit her red lip.

Quickly he looked at her, and back to the advancing horsemen. 'Aye,' he nodded, frowning. 'He it is, I think.' Heavily he said it. 'Och, lassie . . . !'

One rider came spurring ahead, his magnificent horse lathered with hard riding – Ludovick Stewart.

He was off his mount and running to her before ever the brute had halted. Stumbling amongst the swathes of cut corn in his tall heavy riding-boots, he flung his arms around her and swept her up bodily off her feet.

'Oh, my dear! My little love! My heart's darling!' he panted, the words tumbling incoherently from lips that sought hers. 'Mary, my own, my precious . . . !'

She clung to him, returning kisses almost as fierce and vehement as his own, trembling in his arms.

Nearby Davy Gray moved slowly over to take the unsteady toddler's hand, and to watch them sombre-eyed.

When eventually Ludovick set her down, the girl's lashes were gleaming wet with tears. She tried to speak, but could not against the spate of his endearments and emotional release. She could only smile and shake her head helplessly.

At last he paused for very breath, but even so Mary could find no words to express the chaos of her feelings. It was David

Gray indeed who spoke, and brought her back to realities.

'My lord Duke,' he said, levelly. 'I am glad to see you well. And honoured, of course, by your presence But is your coming here wise, seemly or proper?'

Ludovick looked at him over Mary's head. 'I think so,' he said. 'I believe so.'

'Yes, Vicky,' the young woman cried, although she still clung to him. 'Why did you come? Oh, why did you come?'

'It was necessary. I had to come, my dear. And . . . 'fore God – I should have come long ago!'

'No! No!' she said. 'You know that is not so. You have had my letters . . .'

'Letters!' he exclaimed. 'Aye, I've had your letters, Mary. Letters that have had me near to weeping! Oh, they were kind, and I cherished them. But what are letters compared with your own self? In especial, when they tell me to keep away from you!'

'The letters spoke truth, nevertheless, Vicky. Oh, you must know it, my dear? You should not have come.'

'I came for good reason. Although I yearned to see you, Mary, I would not have come. Not now. But for my lord of Gray. Your grandfather, I came to see him. But he is not at the castle. They told me that you were here, in the fields . . .'

'What of my lord?' David asked sharply. 'Why should he bring you to Castle Huntly?'

'This morning, sir, at Falkland, I saw an edict of the Privy Council, signed by the King. It ordered the arrest of Patrick, Lord Gray, on pain of treason. On a charge of rebellion. The said arrest to be executed forthwith. By the Sheriff of Forfar!'

'Rebellion . . . !'

'Arrest? Granlord? Oh no, Vicky – no!'

'Yes. Arrest, in the King's name. I thought it right to come in haste. To warn him.'

'But, dear God – Granlord has not rebelled! He has done nothing against the King. What folly is this . . . ?'

'I do not know. I would not have thought my lord to be engaged in anything smacking of treason or revolt. I believed him to have taken no part in affairs of the realm for many years. The warrant but charges rebellion. Anstruther, Clerk to the Council, showed it to me – for I, for my sins, am now Lord President thereof. No details are set forth. I made excuse to James that urgent matters called me to my Priory property at St. Andrews, and came forthwith.'

Mary swung on the older man. 'Granlord has not been doing aught? In plotting or the like? You would know, Father, if he had? It is not true, is it?'

David Gray stroked his pronounced clean-shaven chin. 'Not rebellion. Against the King. Of that I am sure,' he answered slowly. 'But . . . he has been seeing a deal of certain ministers of the Kirk, of late. In Dundee and St. Andrews. Always he was of the Kirk party, of course, though taking no great part in its affairs. But of late he has talked much of the Kirk. I took it to be but an old man's concern for his latter end! But, who knows? He has twice seen Master Andrew Melville at St. Andrews. And Master James, his nephew, was here but two weeks since.'

'But there is nothing of rebellion in that!'

'No. But a clever man might make it seem so, in certain circumstances, to the King, perhaps.' He paused. 'I note that the Sheriff of Forfar is named in this!'

Mary drew a long breath, but said nothing.

Ludovick nodded. 'That is why I came hot-foot!'

'No – he would not do that!' the girl cried. 'Even Patrick would not act so to his own father!'

'He did not hesitate to betray his own daughter!' the Duke said heavily. 'Why should he balk at his father? They do not love each other, Mary. He ousted my lord from the sheriffship, did he not?'

'I cannot believe it, Vicky . . .'

'Whether this is Patrick's doing, or other's, *we* must do more than talk about it,' David jerked. 'You thought, my lord Duke, that there was need of haste?'

'The thing was secret, and had been hurried before two or three members of the Council – all creatures of Patrick's, as it happens. He rules Scotland now, does the Master of the Wardrobe, openly – the more so since Maitland is dead. So that, when he acts secretly, as here, I believe he will act the more swiftly . . .'

'Maitland dead? The Chancellor . . .'

'Had you not heard? He died at Thirlestane two weeks ago. Loudly repenting of his sins, I'm told! And there is to be no new Chancellor. Patrick has convinced James to rule without one. Which means, in truth, to rule through the Master of Gray. James has written a poem declaring this, indeed. An epitaph. He read it out to the Council, choking with laughter. A welter of words, but saying that he was resolved to use no more great figures or chancellors in his affairs, but only such as he might chide or hang.'

'You do not think, then, that Patrick himself covets the Chancellorship?' Mary asked. 'He acted Chancellor before.'

'No, no. He is far too cunning for that. The Chancellor is responsible. He can be called to account. He must bear the burden of his policies. Patrick prefers the power without the responsibility. He moves from behind, not in front...'

'Aye,' David interrupted. 'See you – I think I know where I may find my lord. If I may take your horse, my lord Duke, I shall ride fast. To warn him. You and Mary have matters to discuss, I have no doubt.' He handed the bronzed and chuckling little boy to his mother. 'I shall see you at the castle later – if your lordship has not already gone!'

Ludovick looked after the strong and effective figure of the land-steward as he vaulted into the saddle, supple as any youth, and wheeled the beast round, to spur away westwards.

'He does not like me greatly, does Davy Gray!' he said, shaking his head.

'No, no – he esteems you very well, at heart, Vicky,' the girl asserted. 'It is but your position that troubles him. Always it has been that. That you are a great lord, a duke. He cannot see that our ... our closeness can bring us anything but pain and sorrow.' She controlled the quiver in her voice. 'As seems may indeed be true!'

He shook his head strongly. 'No – it is *not* true! We have had great happiness together, Mary – and will have again. I know it. Swear it. And, look – this young man here is the sign and surety of it! Johnnie is the token of our closeness, Mary – and has not brought us pain and sorrow. Has he?' Ludovick took the child from her. 'Save us – how he has grown! Eh, my fine warrior? You are a son to be proud of, John Stewart of Methven!'

279

The young woman looked from the face of the man to that of the child, so close, and back again. She sighed, wordless.

Signing to the man-at-arms to ride on ahead, Ludovick settled his son firmly on his right arm and shoulder, and taking Mary's elbow in his other hand began to walk her towards the distant castle. They went slowly across the golden rustling stubbles, bare-footed and heavy-booted.

'Vicky,' Mary said, 'If Granlord is taken and warded, how could this serve Patrick?'

'I do not know,' he admitted. 'I thought that you might. You it is that has the sharp wits. That best perceives his schemes. And what is behind them. Could it not be just spleen? Revenge? They have been long at odds.' He spoke stiffly, stiltedly, well aware that his talk would not long postpone what had to be said otherwise.

'Patrick does not act for spleen and spite,' she answered. 'He always has reasons for what he does ...'

'*You* can say that? After how he spited us? *There* was spleen enough, I say!'

'I do not believe that he did it just to spite us, Vicky, nevertheless. He was determined to part us, yes – but not out of mere spleen, I think. Oh, I believed so at the first, and was bitter, bitter. But I have thought much on this, and now ...'

'Mary! Do not tell me that he was worked on *you*! Changed you? Turned you against me? Is that what your letters meant? Keeping me away. Mary – say that it is not true ... !' He had stopped walking, to stare at her.

'Or course it is not true, Vicky! How could you think it? Be so foolish? Dear heart – you are my very life! How could I turn against you ...?'

'Yet you have kept me away, Mary. All these months. Would not have me here now ...?'

'Only because I must, Vicky. Surely you must see it? You are married, now. You have a wife. A duchess. All is changed.'

'A duchess, may be! But a wife? You call this marriage, Mary? Two people forced at the King's command to go through the marriage ceremony! Is that being wed? Does that make us man and wife, in truth?'

'I fear it does, Vicky. Certainly in the eyes of men. Perhaps in God's eyes also – since you took the vows in His house . . .'

'I took no vows! I did not open my lips in yonder Chapel-Royal! I was there only because I was forced to be there. And for no other reason.'

'But you live with her, as man and wife, do you not? You . . . you have bedded with her, Vicky?'

He swallowed. 'Ay, I have. I have, Mary – God forgive me! I tell you . . .'

'I do not think that you need God's forgiveness for bedding with your wedded wife.'

'I do, Mary – I do! I did not mean to. I suppose that I am weak, weak. It was not my wish. At least . . .' He hesitated, frowning blackly. 'How can I make you understand? It is difficult, when two people share the same house, the same rooms . . .'

'I do understand. It is . . . as it must be, had to be. But, surely, you must see that all is changed? For us, Vicky. I cannot . . .' Her voice shook a little. 'I cannot *share* you with your duchess!'

Ludovick rubbed his chin on his small son's curly head, eyeing the young woman sidelong. 'It is only you that I want, Mary. Only and always you. It is you alone in my heart.'

'Your heart, yes – but not in your bed!'

He shook his head. 'Then . . . then I must deny Jean Campbell my bed, also. It will be difficult – but I must do it. If you will but come back to me, Mary . . .'

'No, no! That is not possible. Do you not understand, Vicky? I cannot, I will not, dispossess your lawful wife. It would be most wrong, sinful, shameful. It is not to be thought of.'

He wrinkled his brows in some bewilderment. 'But, Mary!' he protested. 'I do not understand. These years we have been together, you would not marry me, often as I pleaded. You said that the marriage would be broken by the King and Council, and that you were content to be called my mistress. You have been named Lennox's courtesan – and cared nothing. Yet now, mistress in name, you will not be mistress in fact! There is no sense in it . . .'

'No doubt you are right, Vicky, I am foolish, wilful. But that is how I feel. I am sorry . . .'

He gripped her arm tighter than he knew. 'See you – do you not remember that day at Hailes Castle in Lothian, Bothwell's house? Three years ago. The morning after you had forced Patrick to flee Scotland. Have you forgotten what you said to me then? You said that you had made your choice, and that your eyes were open at last. You said that I was to take you away, away to Methven. To be with me, you and me together. You said that you would not marry me – for they would part us if we wed. You said that you would cleave to me always, bear my children – but as mistress, not wife. Aye – and do you remember what else you said? You said I was to help you not to be jealous! Have you forgotten that?'

Silent, she hung her head.

'You said that you would try not to be jealous when I had to marry again. You said I would assuredly have to marry. Some lady of high degree. To produce an heir for the dukedom. You said that she must have her rights. But that you might be weak, and jealous, and I must help you then. But that you would cleave to me always. That was our compact, Mary, was it not?'

She put her hand in his, nodding. 'I said it all, Vicky,' she admitted. 'I remember.'

'But now . . . ? Now that it has come to the test, you say differently?'

Again she nodded.

'Mary – I have never known you like this! To go back on your word . . .'

'I said that I might be weak. I . . . I am weaker than I thought, I fear.'

'No! Always you were the strong one. Stronger in will than anyone I know. Much stronger than I am. For you to act so is not just weakness. It must mean that you have changed. Changed towards me! Have you changed, girl! Do you no longer love me?'

'I love you, yes, Vicky. More, I think, than ever. I believe that I always shall. But . . . I find that I cannot do what I thought to do. To share you. To have only a part of you. To take what your duchess leaves. Oh, I know it is wrong of me, wicked – just sinful pride. But I *am* proud – shamefully proud. I have tried and tried to fight it. But I cannot. Not now, Vicky. Perhaps . . . . perhaps later. Give me time. Please try to understand, to bear with me.'

When it was the man's turn to be silent, she clutched his arm urgently. 'Vicky – feelings are not things which we may command – deep feelings. Even if I was to come back to you, to live with you again, it could not be the same. There would be a barrier between us. No doubt it is different for men. But for me, I could not forget the other woman.'

'Then . . . Patrick has won? He has parted us, possibly for ever!'

'No! Not that. Do not say it, Vicky. In our love he cannot part us. It is only in this of living together. Give me time. It may be that, in time, it will be different . . .'

Unhappily they walked side by side for a while, nearing the tall, arrogant castle. At length Ludovick spoke.

'At least, Mary,' he pleaded, 'go back to Methven. Live there. It is your home, now . . .'

'How can you say that? It *was* our home. But all is changed there also. It is your house, and therefore your wife's . . .'

'No. Nothing is changed at Methven. It is not my house. You'll mind well that I settled it on this child. John Stewart of Methven. His it is. He should be living in it. With you. For in settling it on him, it was to *you* I gave Methven in truth. Until Johnnie is of age, Methven is yours.'

'You are kind, Vicky – generous. But . . .'

'Here is no generosity. It is but what we planned. For Johnnie. Because you have changed, and let pride rule you, will you deny the boy his rights? Here he is but a child born in bastardy. At Methven he is laird of a great estate. If you cannot think for me, Mary, think for Johnnie.'

'All that is but ink and parchment. His lairdship is only in name . . .'

'Not so. It is fact. All is his. All rents and revenues are paid in his name. The moneys wait and grow for him. I have touched nothing of them since . . . since we parted.'

'But . . . your wife? What of the Duchess Jean, Vicky? How can she be dispossessed by her husband's bastard?'

'Jean is not concerned in it. She knows that Methven is Johnnie's, not mine. She has never been there, nor will I ever take her. I have bought another house, in Monteith. There we are living. Methven Castle has stood empty all these sad months.'

'It has? Empty? You have never gone there?'

'*I* have, yes. To look to affairs. That all should be ordered aright for you and Johnnie. But only that. I have never spent a night under its roof. Nor shall, until you are there with me.'

Helplessly she spread her hands. 'There it is, Vicky! Do you not see? Until I am there with you, you say. If I go to Methven, with Johnnie, I could not keep you out, even if I would. And if we are living together in the same house, then . . . oh, you must see what would happen!'

'I see that we might yet find some peace and happiness together.'

The girl sighed, looking up at the castle towering above them, the living rock and then seven storeys of red masonry seeming to grow out of it.

'Let us talk no more of it now, Vicky,' she said, almost pleaded. 'I am sorry . . . but you must give me time . . .'

Before ever they had climbed to the level of the courtyard, they heard the stamping of horses' hooves and the raised voices of many men. Apparently the Lord Gray had returned. Involuntarily they both quickened their pace.

More than this they heard, as they crossed the flagged court within the curtain walling, where the score or so of men-at-arms of my lord's bodyguard were wiping down and unsaddling their sweating horses; out from the doorway of the great central keep of the castle, an angry voice was declaiming loudly, harshly. The young people exchanged glances, and Mary reached over to take the child from Ludovick.

They found Patrick Gray senior stamping up and down the great hall of Castle Huntly in a fury, bellowing like a bull; indeed he was bull-like in ever way, a massive, heavy man, gross of body and florid of feature. Although no more than in his late fifties, he looked much older, the marks of lifelong dissipation strong upon him; but though sagging jowls and great paunch spoke of indulgence and physical degeneration, there was no hint of weakness about the thrusting bullet head, the jutting jawline and the keen, shrewd, pig-like eyes. A more unlikely father for the exquisite and beautiful Master of Gray would have been hard to imagine.

He was shouting now at Davy Gray as he paced his hall,

every now and again emphasising his harangue by smashing down his great ham-like fist on the long central table as he passed it. The lofty stone-vaulted and otherwise empty chamber seemed to shake and quiver to his fury – yet the sole recipient of all this wrath and invective appeared to be by no means overwhelmed by it. The situation was far from unusual, of course, even though on this occasion the older man was more than normally roused. Davy Gray, the land-steward and schoolmaster, had since early youth been whipping-boy and butt for his potent father's lashing tongue – and despite his bastardy and employed position, refused to be daunted by it much more successfully than had any of his legitimate half-brothers. In fact, Lord Gray had long relied upon this early by-blow of his for the efficient running of his great estates and the management of his household. At heart, the arrogant lord knew well that though he was proud, this modest-seeming, self-contained offspring of his was prouder.

At sight of the newcomers, Gray paused only momentarily in both his pacing and his diatribe, to point a finger at them which trembled with ire, not weakness, and forthwith to launch into a vehement denunciation of the King, the Privy Council, the Court, and all connected with it – including, it seemed, the Duke of Lennox – as abject fools, weaklings, and knaves, at the beck and call of that epitome of all ill, iniquity, impiety and infamy, the son and heir whose name he seldom allowed to pass his thick lips. On and on he ranted, growing ever more purple in the face, until sheer lack of breath and evident dizziness forced him to pause and to put out his hand to the table, this time to support and steady himself rather than to pound and beat.

Mary it was who spoke into the quivering silence, gently. 'Granlord,' she said, 'you have cause to be angry, there is no doubt. It is wicked, shameful. But this is but a poor welcome to your house for my lord Duke, surely? Who has hastened here, at cost to himself, to warn you.'

It was only a mild rebuke, but no one else of my lord's household or family would have dared to administer it. Her grandfather glared at her, lips working, but no words coming. After a moment or two he transferred his glare to Ludovick, and that seemed to help.

'Young man . . . !' he got out, with something of a croak. 'Young man . . . !'

'My lord,' the Duke said, 'it is my sorrow to be the bearer of ill tidings. But I would not have you taken unawares.'

'Would you no'? That's kind, aye kind, my lord Duke! But I'm no' that easy taken, see you, awares or otherwise!'

'H'm. Nevertheless, sir, I would urge that you make haste to leave this house. To seek some secure hiding-place where they will not find you.'

'So I have been pressing,' Davy Gray declared. 'I say that he should be off without delay. Up into the hills. He would be safe up in Glen Isla or Glen Prosen. None could come at him there . . .'

'God's death, man – would you have me skulk and slink? Like some Hieland cateran! Me, Gray! On my own lands. And from one o' my own brood, base, unnatural hell-hound though he be! Enough o' such talk!'

'Granlord – you must heed us,' Mary pleaded. 'You are to be arrested. In the King's name. What for, I know not. But they will come here seeking you. Vicky thinks very soon. They must not find you here. For you cannot resist the King's officers . . .'

'Can I no'? Fiend seize me – I'll show them who rules in the Carse o' Gowrie! Think you that accursed scoundrel that Satan spawned on my wife will send me fleeing to the hills? Think you that the minions o' shaughling, idiot Jamie Stewart can lift Gray out o' Castle Huntly? Devil burn them – let them try!'

'But Granlord dear – do you not see . . .'

David Gray's voice, level, almost toneless, but somehow with a quiet vehemence and power that was fully as potent as his father's raging, overbore the girl's. 'My lord,' he said sternly, 'Hear me. Great swelling words will serve you nothing in this pass. You are accused of rebellion. The King and Privy Council have issued a commission against you. Whether on Patrick's prompting or otherwise. If you have not rebelled, little can be done against you. If you are from home, gone to travel your hill country properties, that cannot be held against you. But if you are here, and you resist those who come in the King's name – than that *is* rebellion. Worse – if you seek to hold this castle against the King, it is treason. No cursing will alter that. With your men-at-arms you may hold out against the King's forces for a time. But you cannot remain holed-up here for ever. When you do go forth, the King is still King. And you are in treason and rebellion undoubted.'

That was a long speech for the laconic David Gray, and it was some tribute to the unstressed force behind his words that his puissant sire for once heard him out without scornful interruption. From under heavy bull-like brows he glowered upon this bastard of his, chin outthrust, silent.

Mary, still holding her child in her arms, ran forward to grasp her grandfather's arm, his hand. 'Do listen,' she urged. 'Go while there is yet time. You should not have delayed thus long, Granlord. It is . . .'

Even as she spoke, all their eyes turned towards the windows of the hall which overlooked the courtyard, whence came a renewed noise of horses' hooves and shouting. Ludovick, nearest to one of the windows, was across to it in a few swift strides, to peer out and down.

'Too late!' he announced grimly. 'Here are the King's officers. It is young George Home again. And James Elphinstone. You have waited overlong, my lord!'

'Slay and burn them . . . !'

'No, no!' Mary cried. 'There is still time. You can still escape. By the privy stair. The wicket-gate. Down the cliff path . . .'

'Tut, lassie! Wheesht! Enough o' your womanish havers!' the old lord growled. 'Peace, for God's sake! Think you Gray is the man to scuttle from Gray's castle, like any rat? Before a wheen Court jackdaws! Foul fall them – if they come chapping at Gray's door, Gray they shall see!'

'No, Granlord! Oh, this is folly!'

'Out o' my way, girl!' Roughly her grandfather pushed her aside, and marched for the door with his limping stride.

Biting her lip, Mary turned to Ludovick, and thrust young Johnnie at him. 'Take him, Vicky. I must go after my lord. I must stop him, if I can. From worse . . .'

'I shall come also.'

'No. Not you. They must not see you here, Vicky. Or it will

be known. The King will hear. That you came to warn him . . .'

'I care not.'

'But *I* do. You must stay with Johnnie.'

She turned after Davy, who was following his father down the stairs to the courtyard door.

The emissaries from Falkland had dismounted, leaving perhaps a dozen armed men sitting their horses and looking doubtfully at four times their numbers of Gray's retainers who lounged about the cobbled yard. At sight of Lord Gray standing in the keep entrance, they quickened their pace, a slight sallow man of early middle years, and the over-dressed and somewhat effeminate-seeming George Home of Manderston, the King's favourite.

'My lord of Gray,' the latter said, inclining his fair head just sufficiently to indicate that he did not feel the need to bow. 'I am George Home, Groom of the Bedchamber to His Grace. And this is James Elphinstone of Invernochty. We require you to attend us, in the King's name. To the Castle of Broughty.'

Gray opened his mouth, and shut it again, his whole bulky person seeming to quiver with ill-suppressed rage. At his back Davy Gray stared stolidly.

Elphinstone spoke, less offensively. 'My lord, it is our misfortune to bear a Privy Council commission against you, signed by His Grace. It requires us to bring you before the Sheriff of Forfar, at Broughty Castle, forthwith.'

'Broughty . . . !' the older man burst out. 'My own house o' Broughty! God's eyes – jackanapes! Daws! Prinking ninnies! Dare you come here and name Broughty to *me*, Gray! Prate to me o' the Sheriff o' Forfar – who was Sheriff for twenty years! Burn your bones – is James Stewart gone clean mad, to send the likes o' you to Castle Huntly! If he esteems me so ill, of a sudden, at least he could have sent *men* to me!'

'Beware how you speak, my lord!' young Home cried, taking an involuntary step backwards at the virulence of the old lord's fury. 'We are the King's representatives . . .'

Elphinstone held out a folded paper with a red seal dangling therefrom. 'Here is our commission, sir. Charging you with rebellion. Read it, if you doubt our authority.' He stood well back from Gray, however, who would have had to step forward some paces to take the document.

'Keep your bit paper!' the older man snorted.

At his back, Davy spoke low-voiced. 'My lord – this will not help your case. Abusing these will hurt only yourself.'

'Quiet, you! If puppies and lickspittle upstarts think to require this and require that o' Gray, in the Carse o' Gowrie, in all Angus, by the foul fiend they'll learn differently!'

'Granlord!' Mary exclaimed desperately at his other elbow. 'Why . . . why do you play Patrick's game for him? Oh, should you not rather play your own?'

'Eh . . . ?' That reached him, piercing the armour of his prideful wrath, as she intended that it should. 'Patrick's game . . . ?'

'Yes. This is what he hoped for, no doubt. This charge of rebellion – it can be but a stratagem, a device. To rouse and anger you. But if you play his game, resist these officers from the King, refuse to go with them to Broughty – then he has made his false charge of rebellion come true. Do you not see it? You are rebelling *now* – which is what Patrick wants you to do!'

'A pox! Would you have me truckle to such as these? Painted bed-boys and up-jumped clerks? Go their meek prisoner to my own house o' Broughty . . . ?'

'Go to Broughty – yes. But not a meek prisoner. Go as Lord of Gray, on Gray land, to a Gray house. Go to face Patrick there – if that is where he is. You have your men-at-arms – more than these. Ride with them. So you do not disobey the King's command – but you show who is lord here in the Carse.'

He stared at her for a moment, and then slapped his great thigh and bellowed a hoot of laughter. 'Precious soul of God, girl – you have it! Aye, you have it. Mary, lass – you have a nimble wit for a woman, I swear! So be it. I ride to Broughty. And if these . . . these Court cuckoos choose to ride with me, let them! Aye – you hear that, witlings? I go see the Sheriff o' Forfar in my castle o' Broughty. You may ride with me, or no', as you choose. Davy – have my guard out again, every man o' them. Quickly. We'll go see the Master o' Gray – may he roast in hell eternally!'

Doubtfully David looked from his father to the perplexed envoys and then back to Mary. She nodded.

'And horses for us also,' she added quietly. 'This is a family matter, is it not?'

It was almost dark as they approached Broughty Craig, which thrust into the sea five miles beyond Dundee town, its castle glowing pale and gleaming with lights as it seemed to rise out of the very waters of the widening estuary of Tay. It had been a gloomy crumbling fortress of a place, semi-ruinous and bat-haunted on its little promontory, until a few years before, my lord in a savage gesture of finality had bestowed it upon his son and heir as his inheritance, his single and sole patrimony out of the vast Gray lands, this rickle of stones on a rock in the sea, with not an acre, a tree or a penny-piece else, as ultimate reckoning between them. Patrick had sworn then that he would make his father rue that day, that he would turn the ruin into a palace which would far outshine Castle Huntly, that men's eyes would turn to Broughty from far and near, and that its former proud lord would come seeking admission on his bended knees. He had largely fulfilled that angry vow. Broughty Castle had been restored, extended and remodelled beyond all recognition, externally and internally. Its walls soared high to dizzy battlements, turreted, corbelled and embellished in the French fashion, rough-cast over naked stone kept dazzling with white-wash. Plenishings, furniture, tapestries, pictures, gleaned from all over Europe – even carpets, a thing scarcely known in Scotland – graced its many chambers. Patrick had very quickly prevailed upon the King to deprive his father of the Sheriffship of Forfar and to bestow it upon himself, so that Broughty became the seat of jurisdiction of all Angus, where men must turn for justice and favour. And during James's long absence in Norway and Denmark, when he went to fetch his bride, Patrick as acting Chancellor, with the young Ludovick as Viceroy, had ruled Scotland from here, with the royal banner and those of Lennox and Gray all flying from its topmost tower – to the unutterable fury of his father, who not only had sworn never to set foot in the place again but at great inconvenience had frequently had to make long detours inland in order to avoid even setting eyes on its soaring, flaunting whiteness.

Now, for the first time in five years, the Lord Gray approached Broughty Castle.

It was a strange cavalcade. In front, with his trumpeter and standard-bearer, my lord rode under the great streaming white lion on red of Gray, setting his usual headlong pace. In close-packed ranks behind him came no fewer than seventy men-at-arms, the greatest number that he had mustered for many a day, some of them only doubtful warriors, herd-boys, farm-hands and the like. Following on, having some difficulty in keeping up, after their long ride from Falkland, came the two King's officers and their much smaller band of armed men. And lastly rode David Gray, Mary, and the Duke of Lennox with his two attendants. Ludovick had insisted on accompanying them, declaring that, if on no other account, as President of the Council he was entitled to see this affair to the end.

The castle was practically islanded on its rock, but the drawbridge, was down, and cantering through the huddle of small fishers' and ferrymen's houses, that clustered round the harbour, Lord Gray thundered across the bridge without pause, lashing porters and servitors out of the way with the flat of his drawn sword, his trumpeter at his back keeping a loud and imperious if somewhat unmelodious summons the while. Across the inner court, striking sparks from the flagstones, he clattered, to pull up his massive powerful white stallion to a standing, pawing halt in front of the main arched doorway of the keep.

'Gray, to see the Master!' he cried, above the noise of hooves behind him. 'Fetch him, scum! Have him here, to me. Quickly. Off with you, filth! Ordure! Do you stand gawping at Gray?'

The alarmed and uncertain men who stood in the doorway scuttled off, none hindmost.

'Blow, damn you!' the old man commanded. 'A plague – what do I keep you for? To belch and wheeze? Blow, fool!'

However breathlessly and brokenly, that trumpeter blew and blew, and the white enclosing walls of Broughty echoed and reverberated to the shrill neighing challenge.

Lord Gray sat his restive mount in towering impatience.

No one came to receive the visitors.

Wrathfully Gray stared up and around at the castle's many lit windows, shaking sword and fist, while the exhausted musician's efforts grew weaker and more disconnected.

Still no sign or movement showed about the buildings around them.

'Dear God – he will burst his heart!' Mary groaned to Ludovick. 'He is too old for these mad rages.' She began to push her way through the press of horsemen in that crowded courtyard.

But her grandfather's scant patience was exhausted. Cursing steadily, he flung himself down from his horse, and went storming indoors, sword still unsheathed. Behind him, dismounting in haste, hurried the two courtiers, Mary, Ludovick and David.

'Foolish! Foolish!' Mary declared, almost sobbing. 'He has thrown away his advantage.'

Because of the formation of the rock site, the hall of Broughty was at courtyard level, not on the floor above as was usual. Stamping along the white-walled, sconce-lit corridor therefore, my lord had no stairs to climb to reach its door, which stood slightly ajar, more light streaming therefrom. With a great kick of his heavy riding-boot he flung it back with a crash, and limped within.

The Master of Gray, dressed in the height of fashion in silver satin slashed with maroon, pearl-seeded ruff and lace at wrists, lounged at ease at a small table with two other gentlemen – his sheriff-depute and one of his brothers, James Gray, who like Home was a Groom of the Bedchamber to the King. A decanter of wine, glasses – not the usual goblets – and playing-cards littered the table. At sight of the old lord, these two started to their feet, but when Patrick remained sitting, his brother, looking uncomfortable, sat down again.

'Ha, my lord and presumed progenitor!' the Master greeted, smiling genially. 'It is you, is it? I thought it might be. I heard a bellowing and braying somewhere. I vowed it must be either yourself or a cattle drove! Come in. I rejoice to see you at Broughty, at last. A great joy, long delayed. But . . . dear me – why the ironware? You do not have to *break* your way into my house with swords, I do protest!'

It is to be doubted whether his father actually heard any of this, so astonished was he at the transformation which had overtaken the hall of Broughty Castle. Formerly it had been but a great vaulted barn of a place, ill-lit with tiny windows, damp and gloomy. Now the windows were large and many, such naked stone as was to be seen on the vaulting was washed a warm rosy pink; colourful arras hung to cover the walls, and a notable Flemish tapestry dominated the far end of the chamber. Carpeting, rugs and skins of animals hid the floor flagstones, and instead of the usual massive table to run the length of the room, with benches, many small tables and richly carved chairs, settles and couches dotted the apartment. In two great fireplaces cheerful log fires flamed and crackled, while candles innumerable blazed from branched silver candlesticks and wall-brackets. Never had the lord of Gray seen anything like it.

Patrick waved a friendly hand. 'Ah, Davy! More joy! And Mary!' He actually rose to his feet at the sight of the girl. 'This is a delight indeed. Is it not, Jamie – a family gathering.' Then abruptly his expression changed, as he perceived Ludovick standing behind the others in the doorway. 'So-o-o!' he ended, on a different note. 'My lord Duke also! This is . . . interesting! I wonder . . . ?'

He got no further. Lord Gray recovered his voice, although it quivered a little.

'Silence!' he exclaimed. 'Hold your lying, treacherous tongue! Dastard! Ingrate! Mountebank! Have done wi' your mockery. We'll talk plain, for once, knave!'

'Gladly, sir – gladly. Talk is so much more comfortable than shouting. I must confess that I never could match you at bellowing! But come inside, do. Poor Vicky is having to peep and peer behind you! Sit here, where we may talk in comfort. Wine . . . ?' He resumed his seat.

'No! Any fare of yours would choke me!' The older man stamped into the room nevertheless, the others following him. 'I am here for but one reason – to discover what new wickedness you brew with the King! This, that these popinjays prate of . . .'

'Then, to some extent we are at one, my lord – since the wickedness which these King's envoys speak of is also my concern, as Sheriff of this shire. But – is it not what new wickedness *you* have been brewing, sir? So it seems to the Privy Council, at least. I hope, of course, that these inquiries will prove it all to be a mistake, a mere indiscretion on your part...'

'God damn you, Patrick! I warn you – do not think to ensnare *me* in one of your foul plots!' His father crashed his sword hilt down on one of the small tables, and a porcelain vase thereon jumped, to fall to the floor and smash in fragments. 'I warn you – keep your traitor's hands off me. Or I tell what I know. To the King and Council. To the Kirk. To all. O' many matters that will gar you grue! Of your base betrayals. Mary the Queen. Gowrie the Treasurer, Esmé Stewart, this lad's father – *your* friend, whom the King loved! Of Moray and Arran and a dozen others. Keep your dirty hands off me, I say, or you'll rue it!'

The Master raised his hands and brows, and glanced around him, a man perplexed. 'On my soul,' he said sadly, 'it looks to be as I feared. Your wits are becoming affected, my lord – you dream, imagine, wander in your mind. I thought it must be so. A sad state of affairs, sad – for you are not so devilish old.' He sighed. 'And yet . . . and yet, perhaps it is better so. It would account for so much. Yes – that is it. How this folly of yours may be explained...'

'Fiend seize you! You dare . . . you dare accuse me! To doubt *my* wits! Nincompoop – you!' His father was all but choking, heavy features darkening alarmingly.

'Patrick! Granlord!' Mary cried, starting forward to stand between them. 'Stop! Oh, stop! This is . . . this is shameful! For sweet mercy's sake, do not so misuse each other. Patrick – can you not see what you do . . . ?'

'Bless your heart, Mary – of course I see. Fortunate indeed that I do! I see that our, h'm, noble relative cannot be held to be fully responsible for his words and actions. For the present. No doubt it will pass – a temporary aberration. Unfortunate – but not uncommon as we grow older. Better, at all events, than rebellion and treason against His Grace!'

'Treason?' his father croaked. 'Fool – I leave treasons to you! I have done naught against His Grace, as well you know . . .'

'Oh come, come, my lord! Or . . . is your memory going likewise? All too much evidence has been laid before the Council. Have you forgotten how close you have become with certain ministers of the Kirk?'

'A pox! Is it treason now to worship God? In this Reformed realm?'

'Ha – a point indeed! Some I could name, of the Old Religion, have been asking that for some time! But the charges of rebellion do not rest on your worship, my lord. Nor on colloguing and engaging with such as our good and worthy parish pastors here in the Carse. It is black crows of a different feather who endanger the realm. In Dundee and St. Andrews. Notably the Melvilles, Andrew and James. And . . . others.'

'Melville? Andrew Melville is of the Council himself! Moderator o' the General Assembly. Rector o' the University. God be good – is it rebellion to deal wi' such?'

'Not, h'm, necessarily! Not yet. Though, who knows how soon it might become so? Our fiery prophet of the New Order becomes increasingly indiscreet. Increasingly hostile to His Grace . . .'

'To yourself, you mean – you and your Papist friends! Everywhere you are bringing them creeping back. The Kirk, the true religion, is threatened. It must be stopped, before . . . before . . .' The older man's choleric words died away.

'Yes, my lord?' Patrick's voice was silky. 'Pray proceed.'

His father swallowed, glaring, but said no more.

'Yes. Perhaps you are wise to leave it there, my lord. Masters Andrew and James are gathering round them an obnoxious covey of corbies indeed. Who not only seek but caw loudly about the downfall of the King's realm and the setting up in its stead of a Kirk-state, where ministers shall rule, not King and Council. To this ill company you, unfortunately, are no stranger, my lord.'

'Have I no' always been o' the Kirk party? Never a secret Papist like yourself!'

'You flatter me! I fear that my hold on religion is less certain than yours. I have ever been a sad doubter, where dogma is concerned. A sorry case! But . . . here we are not concerned with faith and creed. We are concerned, my lord, with rebellion, treason and matters of state. For your friends have overstepped the bounds of religion and dogma. In especial one – Master

David Black, of St. Andrews!' That name was shot out.

Lord Gray opened his mouth, and then closed it almost with a click.

'I see that you are sufficiently lucid in your mind to take my point!' Patrick went on. 'Master Black, aided and abetted by others in higher places, who should know better, has gone too far. Even for our forgiving liege lord and a patient Presbyterian Council. He has publicly declared all kings and princes to be bairns of the Devil, with Satan the head of both Court and Council, and called for the overthrow of the throne and the setting up of the supreme rule of the Kirk. Can you deny it?'

'What is it to me what Black preaches from his pulpit?'

'Much, I fear. When such as the Lord Gray, Andrew Melville and others, see a deal of a hitherto inconspicuous preacher who mouths such sentiments, it behoves the Council to take heed. More than that, had this loud-tongued clerk contended himself with public outcry against his own prince, he might have been dismissed with a warning. But he has seen fit to declaim against Queen Elizabeth of England likewise, naming her an atheist. This has been reported to her by her ambassador Nicolson. She takes it ill, and has even sent up her old envoy, Sir Robert Bowes again, to take order with His Grace. Elizabeth demands redress, restitution, threatening much. Do you understand, my lord?'

There was silence in the great room save for the noise of the fire and the heavy breathing of the older man. All eyes were fixed on him.

'I do not,' he got out thickly. 'Burn you – what has this to do with me?'

'Master Black has been summoned before the Council. He has refused to appear, and left St. Andrews. He is to be taken into custody, to answer for his preachings. Our information is that he has crossed Tay to Dundee, in this my sheriffdom. And I have further information, with sworn witnesses to testify, that you my lord spent three hours closeted with him in Dundee town but two days ago!' He paused, and then snapped out. 'Where is David Black?'

The old lord stared back at him, fists clenched, wordless.

'Come – tell me. You must know. We have combed Dundee for him. He is not there. Where is Master Black hiding, sir?'

'Curse you – think you I would tell you? You! If I knew.'

'I think you would, yes. If you have any wits left at all! For I'd remind you that I am Sheriff of Forfar, under express command of the King to find this preacher. To refuse to aid the King and Council in such a matter is flagrant and deliberate treason, sir! As well you know. Whatever you have done or have not done hitherto, if you refuse to tell me now, before these witnesses, then I declare you are guilty of treason.'

'May . . . you . . . burn . . . in . . . hell . . . eternally!' Word by individual word the father spoke the shocking thing to the son, dropping them like evil stones into the pool of silence.

There was a choking sob from the girl.

At her side Ludovick Stewart raised his voice, to break the appalled hush. 'So it is Andrew Melville's turn to be pulled down, Patrick? The same sorry business. Build up, use, and pull down! You no longer need the Kirk?'

'The Kirk, or part of it, is seeking to pull down the King, Vicky.'

'Is it? I have not heard of it. Only that the ministers protest that the Catholics are coming back.'

'Aye – there you have it!' Lord Gray burst out. 'This is naught but another Papist plot, you may be sure. Erroll and Angus are back in the north, from France. None molests them. Huntly's Countess is back at Court, sharing the Queen's naked bed – aye, and gaining more o' the Queen's kisses than does her husband, they tell me! The shameful hizzies! Is there wonder that the Kirk cries out on such lewd abominations!'

'Tcha – spare us such talk, my lord!' Patrick said, frowning. 'In front of our Mary. Aye – and the Duke. The Countess of Huntly is Vicky's sister, after all! Had you forgot? And 'tis all a, h'm, mere matter of hearsay.'

Ludovick looked straight ahead of him, tight-lipped.

'Hearsay, is it? There's folk to swear to it. Aye, and is it to be wondered at, wi' the King himself no better?' Angrily scornful, Gray glanced over at George Home and his companion. 'These gentry will tell us, maybe, if Jamie Stewart's unnatural lusts are but hearsay! Eh, my pretty boys?'

'Enough, sir! In my house, I insist on it!'

'Na, na! I'm no' finished wi' my hearsay yet, man! I've heard

297

tell that but three nights ago Huntly himself landed secretly in Scotland again. From the Continent. At Eyemouth, they say. In the Merse. Huntly's back!'

'Eyemouth!' That was Ludovick, turning to stare from Mary to Patrick. 'Eyemouth is but a mile or two from Fast Castle. Logan's house. Lord . . . !'

'Tush! Vapours and rumours!' The Master dismissed the matter with a wave of his hand. Neverthless those who knew him best detected a hint of discomfort in his normal complete assurance. 'Some of our spiritual guides and shepherds see Catholics behind every stone! Smell a Popish plot in every Court breeze . . .'

'Do *you* deny that Erroll and Angus are back, whether Huntly is or no?' his father interrupted. 'And lesser Papists with them?'

'I do not. They have given assurances of their repentance. Seen the error of their ways. Expressed themselves contrite and willing to receive all instruction in the Reformed faith. To support Presbyterian chaplains in their houses. His Grace has been gracious. Wisely, I think. He has shown mercy. For these are our fellow subjects. Are they not, my lord Duke? You were concerned for this, I mind. And they have already suffered much for their adherence to the unpopular faith. They are, of course, now confined to their northern estates, warded in their own castles. And with my lord of Argyll strong in Aberdeen, as Lieutenant of the North, they can do no harm. For princes to show mercy and forbearance, with strength, is commendable, is it not . . . ?'

'Hypocrite! Dissembler!' Lord Gray shouted. 'You prate of mercy and forbearance, knowing what you know! What you yourself devised! When it is all a covetous, grasping plot for money! Aye, Patrick – I know what you are at. You and the King. The treasury is empty. Elizabeth isna sending gold, any more. You are spending silver like water. And so you are desperate for money. You sought money from the Kirk – and when it wouldna give God's ordained tithe into your clutching hands, you turned to the Catholics. They are *buying* their way back. Huntly, Erroll, Angus and the rest. Pouring gold into your coffers that they may once again harry the land and flaunt their idolatrous worship . . .'

'Have done, sir!' Patrick actually rose from his seat. 'Who

now can doubt that you are crazed? Deranged? Only a madman would conceive such charges. If your Kirk friends have told you this, taking advantage of your senility . . .'

'God's Passion, you . . . you . . . !' His father gulped for breath, for air, as well as for words.

'On my soul – that I should have sprung from such a doited fool!'

'Patrick!' Mary's voice rose almost shrilly. 'No! Stop! For the love of God – stop! You will kill him. He is your father. You are blood of his blood!'

'Aye – it is enough, Patrick.' That was David Gray, speaking for the first time in this encounter, levelly, but strongly, authoritatively. 'Have you not enough on your conscience? Be done with this evil play-acting – for that is all it is . . .'

'Sakes, Davy – do you name high treason and the commands of the Privy Council play-acting? *You* should know better. This peculiar sire of ours has been dabbling in pitch. As well indeed that he is proving himself to be clouded in mind. That I may attribute his folly, to the King and Council, as mere dotage . . .'

David moved forward slowly, deliberately. 'I said enough, Patrick!' he repeated. There was something infinitely menacing about the stocky plain man's advance upon his elegant half-brother, as about his few quiet words. 'Do you require that I should teach you your lesson again? After all these years. Before these?'

At the sheer fist-clenched and jaw-outthrust threat of the other's approach, the Master backed a pace, his fine eyes widening. He forced a laugh. 'Ha – use your head, Davy! As I do. Can you not see it, man?' His words came much more quickly than usual, almost breathlessly. 'Aye – and my lord's head, likewise! We must use the fact that he has lost *his* head, to save it! That his wits are gone . . .'

The clatter of Lord Gray's sword falling to the floor as its owner brought up both hands in strange jerking fashion to his thick throat, drew all eyes. The older man was staggering, mouth agape, eyes protruding, heavy features the colour of mahogany. Thick lips tried to form words but failed. Great choking gasps shook him. Then his leg-booted knees buckled beneath him, and the heavy gross figure fell with a crash like a stricken tree.

In the confusion that followed it was Mary who took swift command, running to kneel beside her prostrate grandfather, loosening his doublet and neck-cloth, wiping his foaming mouth, demanding space and air. The old lord was unconscious quite, twitching and stertorously breathing.

His three sons, after a little, picked him up as the girl cried that he must be got to bed and a leech summoned to bleed him. Staggering under the awkward weight of him, with Ludovick's help, they were making for the door and the main turnpike stairway to the sleeping accommodation of the upper chambers, when Patrick directed them otherwise, pointing to a smaller door at the side of the great hall fireplace, declaring that this was better, easier. Here, behind the arras, a narrow straight stair led within the thickness of the walling, down not up. It was the usual laird's private access to his wine-cellar, which could thus be kept locked away from thirsty servitors. Down this constricted dark flight of stone steps, stumbling and with difficulty they bore their groaning, snoring burden, Mary and George Home bearing candles before and behind.

In the cellar at the foot, Patrick directed them out through a door into a dark vaulted passage, and gestured towards another stairway at its end. This again led down. Mary alone had breath to protest – but she was once more told briefly that this was best, that all was in order. Broughty Castle's foundations no doubt followed the uneven surface of the thrusting rock on which it was built; nevertheless, here they must be nearly underground.

Down this second flight they lurched, to another damp-smelling corridor where the candles revealed a row of four heavy doors ranged side by side. Nothing more typical of a castle's dungeons could have been imagined. Patrick, turning a great key in the lock, opened the second of these, and signed the others in.

Mary at least was surprised. A lamp already burned in here. The place was no more than a small vaulted cell, otherwise lit only by a tiny barred slit window high in the arch of the vault at the far end. But despite this, there was comfort here, a small fireplace whereon logs smouldered, a bed and other furnishings, rugs on the stone floor, even two or three books on a desk.

They laid the unconscious man on the bed, and Mary and David busied themselves in getting off his harness and outer clothing.

When they had done all that they could for the sufferer, and must await the physician whom Ludovick had gone to fetch from Dundee, the girl found that only Patrick and David remained in the chamber. She looked from one to the other.

'You planned this, Patrick, did you not?' she said quietly. 'All arranged for. Nothing overlooked.' And she gestured around her.

Her father shook a faintly smiling head. 'Now, now, Mary – even you will not credit me, I think, with arranging my lord's bodily condition, his health and sickness!'

'I would not swear to that!' she told him. 'You knew well that he had over-much blood. When last you spoke with him, years ago in this same house, you made him ill with your baiting. You have not forgot that, I swear! Tonight, with your wicked talk of dotage and senility, you as good as drove him to this. Why?'

'A marvel! *You* answer that, my dear, since you are so clever!'

'I think that I can, Patrick. You swore to humble Granlord over this Broughty – swore it before Davy and me, that day. You have done much to bring it about – but you could not get my lord to come here, to force him to acknowledge your triumph. Now, with this charge of rebellion, you have got him here at last. But that does not content you. You must make him eat the very dust at your feet – your own father! You itched to see him locked up here, in the very deepest dungeons of the castle he flung at you! Did you not? You prepared this cellar for him – but you could not be sure that you could win him here without using force. And he has more than seventy armed men fretting in your courtyard. So you devised to get him here otherwise – and succeeded! By working upon his anger and rageful choler. Deliberately. Time and again I pleaded with you to stop . . .'

'Nonsense, girl!'

'Is it nonsense? You cannot deny that, knowing how it must infuriate so proud a man, you continued to taunt him with being witless, wandering in his mind . . . ?'

'For his own sake. Can you not see? That he might escape the full consequences of this charge of rebellion and treason.'

'Which you arranged likewise, did you not?' She waved her hand. 'And this chamber, this cell! Down in the rock itself. It is a pit, a prison. You made this ready for him – not one of the rooms which you would give to a guest, where there is light and air. For the Lord of Gray, whose castle this was . . .'

'Are you as blind as he is, child? Do you not see that, as Sheriff of Forfar I must obey the King's edict? In name at least. To ward him and charge him. I must seem to do my duty. Imprison him. Then go plead his failure of wits before King and Council. If I install him in any honourable room in this house, who will take my warding seriously? Will he? My lord? Will he abide quietly in any proper chamber? I tell you, it had to be down here. But I have made it comfortable for him. More so than most of the rooms of his own house. Than ever was *my* room at Castle Huntly. I have sought to think of all things . . .'

'Aye, Patrick – you have thought of all things!' David repeated heavily. 'God forgive you, if He can!'

'You too! God grant me patience, you mean!' The Master swung about, and thrust out of that cell.

Later, with the blood-letter at his unchancy trade, and the Lord Gray still unconscious, Ludovick Stewart came to the girl in the vaulted passage outside the sick-room.

'Mary,' he said, 'the hour is late. Come away now. You are weary, pale as a ghost. There is no more that you can do here. Come away. With me.'

She shook her head. 'I must stay here.'

'Why? What good can you do? You will not budge Patrick in his course. You should know that, by now!'

'Granlord needs me, Vicky . . .'

'I need you likewise. More than he does.'

'That I cannot believe, Vicky. Want. Desire, perhaps. But not need. Any more. Granlord *needs* me. I must stay with him here, meantime.'

'*I* cannot stay in this house, Mary. Patrick does not want me, and makes it plain. Nor do I wish to bide under his roof. Besides, I must get back to Court, to Falkland . . .'

'Yes. And to your wife.'

He frowned. 'I did not say that. But James will look for me.'

At the stiffness in his tone and bearing, Mary bit her lip. Her hand reached out to his arm. 'You are hurt, Vicky. I am sorry. Oh, I would not wish to hurt you, my dear. But . . . I cannot help myself. It must be this way. At least, meantime. Try to understand.'

'I do not understand you,' he told her flatly.

'Then . . . then, Vicky, at least forbear and forgive. For love of me.'

He paused, and then swallowed. 'I can try,' he said. 'For love of you, Mary, I can attempt anything. But, you? How of your love of me?'

'My love of you is sure. Certain. For always. For my life and beyond my life. That you have, my beloved.'

'And yet – this!'

'This, yes – to my sorrow. Now go, Vicky, Go – before my heart is broken quite.'

Hard he stared at her, almost glared. 'I shall come back,' he said, tight-lipped. 'I must. I cannot leave it so. I must come, hoping. Believing. That one day you will change. See it all differently. Need me as I need you . . .'

'No more, my heart – for sweet pity's sake! For I cannot bear it.'

He took a step forward, as though to take her in his arms, and then thought better of it. Set-faced, sighing, he bowed swiftly, jerkily, and turned blindly away.

Even so, it was the young woman who spoke the last word, hesitantly, faltering. 'Vicky,' she got out, from constricted throat. 'Is she . . . is she kind? Warm with you? A . . . an able lover . . . ?'

He did not so much as glance back, dared not, but made for the narrow mural stairway almost at a run.

Chapter Eighteen

In all his affairs, save only one, the world wagged well for
Patrick Gray. And, it must be admitted, for Scotland likewise –
in consequence or as a mere coincidence. With no new Chancellor appointed, and Maitland's lieutenants quietly got rid of,
the Master of Gray now guided the King in all matters, and
through him ruled the land. He did so well, efficiently and tact-
fully, without seeming to push himself forward – so that James
himself, it is probable, scarcely realised how firm was the hand
that controlled his own, how hollow a façade was the personal
government by divine right of which he was so vocally proud.
Patrick claimed no other Court position than that of Master of
the Wardrobe still – which of course gave him the readiest
access to the monarch's person at all times. He also had his seat
on the Privy Council. These were sufficient for his purposes.
And, for Scotland, the ship of state sailed a comparatively steady
course, however strong and warring the underlying currents.

The religious dichotomy which had bedevilled the land for
half a century was brought once more to a state of precarious
balance, by effective however peculiar means. The Kirk, while
still apparently paramount, had its vaunting power and political
pretensions curbed. The law was invoked against certain of the
activities and pronouncements of ministers; dissension was
created amongst the ranks even of the elect by the introduction
of bishoprics of the King's appointment. Andrew Melville was
got rid of by a judicious linking with Masters Black, Davidson
and others, some of whom were, it was whispered, in fact *agents
provocateur* in the King's pay. He found his closest associates
arrested on charges of treason, and was manoeuvred into a
position where every word that he spoke was weighed and tested.
Like a wounded and baited lion eventually he could stand no
more, and lashed out against earthly tyrants who set themselves
up against the supremacy of Christ, quoting passages of the
Basilikon Doron, King James's own book, as yet unfinished,

written for the future instruction in kingship of Prince Henry. How Melville obtained knowledge of these passages was a mystery, for they could only have been supplied by someone very close to the King; but they served their purpose. The royal wrath was unleashed in a flood. Melville fled the land.

In matters of administration the realm was being served more effectively than almost ever before. No Lord Treasurer was appointed in place of Patrick's old enemy, the Master of Glamis, one of the first to be disposed of. Nor was there appointed a new Secretary of State, a post formerly held by Maitland's nephew. Instead eight new men were brought in, without specific title, to handle, under the Privy Council all the business of the realm. All were able, reliable, and of comparatively humble origin, the most prominent being James Elphinstone, a son of the Lord Elphinstone – and all were associates of the Master of Gray. They became known as The Octavians – and Scotland had never before known their like. They made an interesting contrast to Robert Logan of Restalrig, who now returned swaggering to Court banishment annulled.

Another swaggerer to return at almost the same time as Logan, and from the same direction, was George Gordon, Earl of Huntly, forgiven by a gracious and forbearing monarch. Melville's sentence of excommunication upon him was solemnly revoked by the Kirk – for was he not daily receiving instruction from a patient Presbyterian catechist? His grim murder of the popular Earl of Moray now conveniently laid at the door of the late Maitland, Huntly strutted and postured as effectively as ever – and with good cause, for James had ever a weakness for him. He was reappointed Joint Lieutenant of the North, with Argyll. His wife being the Queen's closest companion, he had his feet well planted in both Court camps.

That there were indeed two distinct camps at Court was now undeniable, even by James himself. The Queen was as open and frank in her political manoeuvrings as she was in her contempt of her husband and hatred of Mar, her son's governor. Moreover she was showing much interest in Catholicism and was said to be closeted frequently with Jesuits – these, some suggested, being supplied by the Master of Gray. However unkind this might be, Patrick did in fact make a point of remaining on good terms with the difficult and unpredictable Anne – to James's relief, who evidently felt that he could leave this awkward personal problem, like so many others, in the Master's capable hands. Despite the fact that she was allegedly pregnant again, seldom indeed now were the monarch and his consort seen together. Despite the usual questions and rumours anent the paternity of this putative embryo, James made no accusations, against Ludovick or others. Anne, indeed, although she still carried on an occasional arch exchange with the Duke, now appeared to be more interested in the company of young women than young men – which suited her spouse.

One hitherto unfailing source of trouble faded most fortunately from the Scottish scene – Francis Hepburn Stewart, Earl of Bothwell. After Glenlivet and the collapse of the Catholic cause in the north, this fire-eater, excommunicated, fled to Orkney, there apparently to take up the trade of pirate. He was less successful in this profession than might have been expected, however, and soon found his way to the Continent, where quite suddenly, at Naples, he died in somewhat mysterious circumstances. It is safe to say that few mourned him.

The Master's more private affairs fell out in almost equally satisfactory pattern. His father, never fully recovered from his providential stroke at Broughty, remained in his cell at the castle for months on end, a changed man – scarcely a man at all indeed. In the end Patrick packed him off back to Castle Huntly, the suddenly feeble and querulous old man being not worth fighting. Mary had taken up her residence at Broughty, unasked, to look after him – another good reason for getting all charges against his father dismissed and sending him home.

With Mary herself the situation was somewhat improved, in that she was making little or no trouble, refraining from meddling in his affairs, however damnably reproachful and unforthcoming she might be when they met. By arranging that the King sent Ludovick away on prolonged embassages, one to the Court of Elizabeth and one to that of France, this source of friction and disharmony was removed – for the meantime at least.

All this was satisfactory. But there was one fly in the ointment. Financially, matters were far from well. This was nothing new in Scotland, of course, where money had always been the scarcest of commodities. But in the circumstances it greatly hampered Patrick Gray, tying his hands at every turn, hitting him both in matters of state and person. The cream was just not there to be skimmed. Good government was more expensive than the almost non-government of the previous era. It is always more difficult to get contributions out of people in time of peace and comparative prosperity. The Kirk and the nobility saw no need to dip hands in pockets – and the ordinary folk had never had to.

Patrick and his Octavians were busy on schemes of taxation, after the English model – especially directed at the burghs, the craft-guilds and the mass of the people, who were prospering as never before. But this was a long-term prospect, and immediate funds were urgently necessary. The raising of a permanent and sizeable body of royal troops solely at the disposal of the Crown, was a first priority – but there were numerous other clamant demands for public works which no private purse was going to defray. Long years of misrule and misapplication of moneys had left the Exchequer not only empty but in serious debt; eighty thousand pounds was owed to the late Earl of Gowrie's heirs alone, moneys advanced by him at a time of the Crown's grievous need, and unrepaid.

All Patrick's not inconsiderable wits, these days, seemed to be bent on this intractable problem. If only Queen Elizabeth would die, and in dying make it clear that her heir was indeed her distant cousin of Scotland, the entire matter would be solved – for the English Treasury bulged indecently. Yet she had not even paid James his agreed pension for years. The King of France, having turned Catholic, was disinclined to aid his impoverished partner in the now somewhat blown-upon Auld Alliance – though this was the ostensible reason for Ludovick's mission to Paris. King Christian of Denmark, on approach, proved to be in even greater financial embarrassment than was his brother-in-law. Patrick toyed with the idea of making a personal visit to London. But his successes with the Virgin Queen in the past had been largely attributable to a delicate blending of sex, wit, and blackmail; it was doubtful whether the ageing lady, with no gift for growing old gracefully, would still respond to such treatment.

It was with a certain trepidation then, even for Patrick Gray, that he turned his speculative eye still further afield. There was one unfailing and acknowledged source of great wealth in the world, hitherto quite untapped. Admittedly it would take a very bold, quick-witted and agile man to tap it – but was there not just such a man in Scotland?

After considerable cogitation and some little research, on an afternoon of October 1598, in the modest quarters of the Master of the Wardrobe in the Palace of Holyroodhouse, Patrick sent for James Elphinstone of Invernochty.

Elphinstone came in haste. Third son of the impoverished third Lord Elphinstone and of a Catholic Drummond mother, he was a peculiar man, abler than he looked, and younger. He had a diffident, almost retiring manner, unusual in his class, and a deprecating smile. But he had a good brain and a trained mind, having been bred to the law. Indeed he had been made a judge, a Senator of Justice at the age of thirty; the reason for his reaching such eminence so early was as mysterious as for his sudden deprivation of the office a year or two later. Now he served the Master of Gray as the senior of the Octavians.

'James, you look weary,' Patrick greeted him pleasantly. 'You are working too hard. That is foolish. The realm's cause requires diligence, yes – but hardly such desperate devotion. A glass of wine? You need it by the colour of you.'

'There is much to do, Patrick. Pleas. Petitions, Causes. Tax schedules...'

'No doubt. But you must find others to aid you with these. You are too valuable a servant of His Grace to so squander your talents.'

The other looked swiftly, almost uneasily, at the speaker, and made no comment.

'Too much toil is not only wearisome, James – it is to be deplored, avoided at all costs. Do you not agree? For it defeats its own end. The keen mind – and God knows there are few enough of them! – can become blunted, lose its cutting edge, by the dull grind of unremitting labour. Myself, I always seek to play rather more than I work – for the work's sake. I believe it to be a sound principle.'

Elphinstone sipped his wine, and waited warily.

'It occurs to me,' Patrick went on conversationally, 'that successful as has been our experiment in, h'm, fourfold responsibility, the time may be near when a change might be made, with profit. It seems to me that while His Grace's affairs may well proceed satisfactorily without a Chancellor, or even a Lord Treasurer, yet in matters of administering the state, some single man should bear the principal authority. Bear the authority, I say, rather than do the work. You will note, also, that I speak of administering, not of policy. Does your experience not lead you to agree?'

The other blinked rapidly. 'It might well be so,' he temporised.

'It is possible that the office of Secretary of State ought to be revived. And filled. You, James, might make an excellent Secretary of State, I think – if you could be prevailed upon not to work so devilishly hard!'

His visitor's sallow face flushed, and he swallowed.

'It might possibly be arranged,' the Master observed, and then paused. 'You are a good Catholic, are you not, James?'

Pleasantly, almost casually, as this was said, the colour drained away from Elphinstone's features. Tensely he sat forward, gripping his wine-glass. 'Not . . . not so!' he got out. 'I am not active in religious matters. I leave that to others. I have not, perhaps, leant strongly towards the Kirk. But . . .'

'Tush, man – we can talk plainly, here in the Wardrobe! Your lady-mother is of a strong Catholic family, the Drummonds of Inchaffray. Your cousin Drummond is Bishop of Vaison, is he not? Close to the Vatican. You receive Jesuits in your lodgings, on occasion. As, of course, do I – though perhaps for different purposes!'

The older man looked down. 'If I have been indiscreet, I will rectify it. I assure you, Patrick, that you . . . that His Grace need have no doubts as to my behaviour and loyalty. The Protestant cause is entirely safe as far as I am concerned . . .'

'M'mm. I am glad to hear that, James. That is as it should be, in this godly Reformed realm. It would be quite insufferable, would it not, if the monarch's principal Secretary of State should be known to be an enemy of the Kirk?'

'I am not, Patrick. Never have I lifted a finger against the Kirk. I swear it . . .'

'Quite. No doubt.' The Master lounged, toying with his glass. 'Nevertheless, you know, there could be advantages in the situation also, James. *Your* situation. So prominent a Catholic family, the Drummonds. Even His Holiness himself, I dare say, will know of your name, fame, and, er, inner faith!'

'His Holiness . . . ?' the other faltered.

'Exactly. His Infallible Highness the Supreme Eminence. The Holy Father. The Pontiff and Vicar of Christ . . . or Satan's Principal Disciple and the Keeper of the Whore of Rome. Depending upon the point of view!'

'It is possible that the Pope may know of my name, my family. But that is all. I swear it. He cannot esteem me as more than, than . . .'

'A good Catholic at heart, as I said. And that is all that is required, I think. Sufficient for our purposes, James.'

Bewildered Elphinstone gazed at him. 'I do not understand,' he said. 'What is required of the Pope? What purposes?'

'The most common requirement of all, James – man's universal need. Gold. The filthy mammon of unrighteousness – of which, if you ask me, the Holy Father has accumulated an embarrassing superfluity! He should be grateful for the opportunity of disposing of some small proportion of the wicked burden of it all! To us. To, h'm, further the cause of the one Church, Holy, Catholic and Apostolic, in this far northern realm of Scotland. Is that not so?'

'You mean . . . ? You mean that you will ask the *Pope* for money?'

'Tut, man – not I. I am but the Master of the King's Wardrobe. It is not new clothing that we need in Scotland! Besides, I have – whisper it – sought money from His Holiness before! With but indifferent success. No – the request must come from a loftier source. The highest, indeed. And if it is endorsed, amplified, buttressed and given some detail and explanation by His Grace's new Secretary of State, so much the more impressed will be His Holiness as to the possibilities, the lively possibilities, of the re-establishment of the good and true faith in this sadly lapsed Scotland. With consequent suitable and substantial contributions from the Vatican vaults to aid along this happy development.'

'God, Patrick – you think to gain the gold we need from the Pope!' That was a whisper.

'Why not? All know that the walls of the Vatican are in sore danger of falling with the weight of gold, jewels and the like within! For centuries wealth has been pouring in from all Christendom. Notably, of late, from the Spanish Indies, with the Dons making sure of heaven. Absurd that this small corner of Christendom should fail in good and godly government for lack of a moiety of the Pope's gold! If His Holiness is sufficiently impressed by the probability of success in Scotland, he will loosen his purse-strings, I vow. For Scotland today could mean England tomorrow. Elizabeth cannot live for ever. And a King of Scots soon to become also King of England ...'

'But King James is no Catholic. Why should the Pope credit such a possibility?'

'*You* will convince him, my dear James. As will ... others! By many notable signs and portents. And one of the most notable will be that His Grace is appointing the good Catholic James Elphinstone – h'm, we might say *Sir* James Elphinstone, possibly – to be his Secretary of State! Think you that this would not be a convincing sign, in itself?'

There was silence in that small panelled room for a space. At length Elphinstone spoke. 'I do not understand,' he said. 'How can His Grace be brought to this?'

'Leave you His Grace to me, James.' The Master smiled. 'Indeed, I think you may safely leave all to me – save your signature on the letter to His Holiness! Is it agreed?'

The other let out a long breath. 'I ... I can but bow before your superior knowledge and experience, Patrick,' he said. 'But ... I confess that I am surprised. For this Papal gold you are prepared to turn Scotland Catholic again?'

'A pox, man – what's this? Do I mis-hear? Or have I mistook my man? I had not thought you stupid.' Patrick stretched, and lifted easily to his feet. 'A stupid Secretary of State would not do, at all, I'd remind you! Who said anything about turning Scotland Catholic ...?'

The ante-chamber was warm, too warm, and there was an aura of women about it which amounted almost to an odour, a little too strong even for Patrick Gray, admirer of the sex as he was. Two young women sat therein, amongst a surplus of furnishings, one working at a frame, the other sitting at a virginal. He exchanged pleasantries with them even as his finely chiselled nose wrinkled a little.

The inner door opened, and the satisfying, almost challenging figure of the Duchess of Lennox emerged on a further waft of heat, her high colour heightened by the temperature.

'Her Grace will see you, Master of Gray,' she announced formally – but raised her brows at him as she said it, making a tiny grimace. Instead of waiting at the inner door, she came over to escort him thither.

As he strolled beside her, the man raised a hand to run his fingertips lightly up and down the inside of the Duchess's bare arm. ''Tis a wicked waste, I vow, Jean – you, in this assembly!' he murmured in her ear.

'Who put me here, Patrick?' she asked, in return.

'Did I do you an ill turn, then?'

'I have made no complaint, have I? As yet.'

'Nevertheless, I must do what I may to console. To compensate, Jean.'

'Further?'

'Further.' He nodded, glancing down appreciatively at her magnificent and frankly displayed bosom.

She smiled, and threw open the inner door. 'The Master of Gray seeking audience, Your Grace,' she called.

The Queen's private boudoir was like a hot-house, despite the October sunshine. Anne sat over at the window-seat, clad in the flimsiest of bed-robes, her pale, distinctly foxy features red at the cheek-bones, her quick glance busy. Beside her sat another young woman, taller, fairer, but strangely colourless. She rose, as Patrick was shown in, as though to move away – but the Queen held out a hand to keep her close.

The visitor bowed low. 'Highness,' he said, 'I am, as always, dazzled by your presence. And rejoiced at my good fortune in being admitted to it.'

'Flatterer, as ever, Patrick!'

'But, no, Madam. There are times when flattery is impossible. As now.' He inclined his head briefly to the other woman. 'Lady Huntly – your devoted servant.'

'And what is it in my poor power to do for the influential Master of Gray, Patrick?' the Queen asked, a little breathlessly. 'Since I cannot conceive of this visit as being purposeless.'

'If I could but answer that, Your Grace, as my heart dictates! But since it is not permissible . . . ' He paused and sighed – but at the same time glanced over towards Huntly's wife, Ludovick's sister, who was looking at him with her peculiar lack-lustre eyes. 'I must needs fall back on matters of mutual concern, in the realm's affairs – while still basking in the sun of your royal presence. But, h'm, somewhat close affairs, Highness – for your private ear alone.' And again he looked towards the other woman.

The Lady Henrietta Stewart, Countess of Huntly, was only two years older than her brother, but made him an unlikely sister. Brought up in France, and hardly knowing Ludovick, she had been sent for by the King ten years before to be married to George Gordon at the age of fifteen, an odd marriage which had produced little of co-habitation, for most of these years the wife had spent at Court while the husband was in more or less active rebellion elsewhere, or else in exile. Yet the lady appeared to be anything but the strong-willed woman determined to lead her own life – such as was Ludovick's wife; on the contrary, the most distinct impression that she gave was of negativity.

'I have no secrets from Hetty,' Anne declared sharply, and again her hand reached out to the other.

Patrick inclined his head, and shrugged slightly at the same time. 'As you will, Highness. As well that it is the Lady Hetty, and none other, however, in this instance.'

'What do you mean, sir?'

'Merely that her ladyship's discretion is well known – and here discretion is essential. Moreover, she is of course also known to be of the Old Religion – which is relevant to the matter.'

The two women exchanged quick glances.

'What matter?' the Queen jerked. 'What is this, Patrick?'

'Nothing to distress you, Highness – be assured,' the Master told her, soothingly. 'No sudden crisis. I have been meaning to speak with you on the subject for some time. And this seems an apt opportunity...'

'Come to the point, sir! What do you want?' That was sharp. 'You seek my aid, do you not?'

'It would be my joy to be even more indebted to Your Grace than I am now,' the other answered smoothly. 'But in this instance, the boot is rather on the other leg! The matter in case refers to, shall we say, two interests which I know to be very close to Your Grace's warm heart. Have I your royal permission to sit down?'

Eyeing him closely, the Queen nodded, unspeaking.

'In the past, Madam, knowing your interest in religious and, h'm, moral questions – comparative theology I believe, the savants call it,' Patrick went on genially, 'it has been my privilege and pleasure to find for your information learned men with whom you could discuss these profound but no doubt enthralling issues...'

'Say Jesuit priests, man, and be done with it!' Anne interrupted tersely.

'Very well, Highness – Jesuit priests. I do not know what stage you have reached in your investigations into these matters – but if you feel that the time has come for carrying them a stage further, the opportunity seems now to present itself. Also, there is the matter of your son, Prince, er, Frederick Henry.'

The Queen sat forward abruptly at mention of that name – and for the first time Patrick wondered whether there might not be something in the current rumours that she was pregnant again. Slenderly, almost boyishly built, she had scarcely shown signs of the previous infant's presence until close indeed to her time of delivery, so that up till the last moment most of the Court had assessed it all as but one more of her innumerable and much advertised false alarms.

'What of Frederick?' she demanded urgently.

'Just that he is now five years of age, and his instruction in matters religious, as in other things, ought properly to be considered. Does Your Grace not agree?'

'God be good – do not play with me, Patrick Gray!' the Queen exclaimed. 'Do not presume to mock me, I warn you! Nor to cozen me. I am not such a fool as is my husband! You know well how dear is my wish that my poor child should receive true and honest instruction. Not pedantic vapourings such as his father writes for him in that stupid book. Nor the heretical ravings of the Kirk's zealots ... !'

'H'rr'mm.' Patrick glanced around him expressively, warningly. 'As well, Madam, that your ladies are beyond doubt trustworthy!' he told her. 'Nevertheless, if I may be so bold ...'

'Would you seek to muzzle me, your Queen, in my own bower?'

'Ah, no. Far from it. Only remind Your Grace that there are more effective ways of obtaining one's ends than stating them loudly enough for enemies to hear!'

'What do you mean? Come to the issue, Master of Gray. Where does all this talk lead us?'

'It leads us, Highness, to the Vatican.'

The indrawn breaths of both women were ample testimony to the impression that he had made.

He went on. 'In strictest secrecy, I have reason to know that an approach is to be made to the Pope. On a matter of state. A special courier will be entrusted with this most delicate mission. This courier, however, could carry more letters than one! I have long known and sympathised with Your Grace's distress at being unnaturally kept apart from the young prince. Here, I submit, is an opportunity for you to alter this sad situation. The state, the realm, requires the Pope's aid in a matter of policy. If Your Grace was to write to His Holiness urging that he insist to the King that the young prince be brought up, if not in the Catholic faith, at least in full knowledge thereof, with a grounding in the elements of the true religion – then I think that King James and the Council might be hard put to it to refuse. Or to deny due and natural access to the prince's lady-mother.'

The Queen was clasping and unclasping her thin hands, eyes glistening. 'You think this? You believe this? Is it possible ... ?'

'More than possible – almost certain. If you ask this of the Pope, he cannot refuse you, since it must coincide with his own wishes and policy. It must be his anxious desire that the Prince of Scotland, who will one day be King of England also, should be on the way at least to being a good Catholic. Is it not so?'

315

'Glory be to God – I had never thought of that! Hetty – do you hear?' The Queen turned, with hands out, to her pale-eyed friend. 'My son. Do you understand?'

'It could be a notable endeavour, Your Grace,' the Countess said more cautiously, in her flat voice. Patrick eyed her thoughtfully.

'I shall write the letter. Now. At once,' the Queen declared. 'You will guide me, Patrick in what I should say?'

'Gladly, Highness.' He stroked his chin. 'It would be as well I judge, if you were to encourage His Holiness, at the same time, with some intimations that the Catholic interests in Scotland are by no means in eclipse. If you were to mention that the Catholic earls are all returned from exile and in good favour again. That many of the faithful are in high office, including James Elphinstone, who is much in the King's confidence. That your Jesuit friends come and go unmolested . . .'

'Yes, yes. And the Master of Gray himself, who is the key to all, is favourable to the true religion!'

'Ah no, Madam – to state that would be injudicious, I fear. To my sorrow. In the past, I have had the misfortune to seem to be at odds with the holy Clement, on occasion. My dealings with Queen Elizabeth have no doubt been misrepresented to him. I am told that he once asked why I was not excommunicated! In the circumstances your plea would carry more chance of success without my name being mentioned.'

The Countess of Huntly emitted a curious brief snigger, and then was as silent as before. Undoubtedly she blamed her marriage, and possibly other things, on the Master of Gray.

Patrick nodded towards her, while still addressing the Queen. 'It might be as well, Your Grace, if the Countess also addressed a letter to the Holy Father. As the wife of Scotland's premier Catholic nobleman. She might inform His Holiness, for instance, that the King is considering the bestowal of a notable mark of his favour on my Lord of Huntly, an increase in his already lofty stature. And therefore of her own!' He paused significantly. 'With other reports of royal, h'm, tendencies, it might well impress the Vatican.'

The Lady Henrietta opened her mouth, but seemed to decide against speech.

'Is this so, Patrick?' Anne demanded. 'I have long besought James to honour Hetty. But he would not.'

'It may come about this way. Your Grace, and you, Lady Hetty, may rest assured that I will do what I can in the matter.'

'Excellent! Then – the letter . . .'

'I will pen a few words to aid you, and have it sent to Your Grace forthwith. Meantime, I think that I need not stress that none must know of this. Any of it. Even your other ladies.'

'Have no fear, sir . . .'

Although Patrick Gray dined with the King that night, in the company of Nicolson the English ambassador, Mar and Huntly, he made little mention of affairs of state and none of any gesture towards the Vatican. It was the following afternoon that he ran James to earth in the royal stables, where he was rapturously admiring a magnificent pure white Barbary mare, running his hands over the creature's shining flanks and cooing and drooling with delight.

'Look at her, Patrick!' the King commanded. 'Is she no' bonny? Two years, no more. The finest bit horseflesh I've seen this many a day.'

'No doubt, Your Grace, a handsome animal. Have I not seen her somewhere, before . . . ?'

'Aye. She was Huntly's. Geordie brought her back frae France wi' him. You'll have seen him riding her.'

'But she is now in your royal stables, Sire?'

'Aye. Is she no' a notable gift, Patrick? Geordie Gordon gave her to me in a present. Was that no' right kindly o' him?'

'My lord is very good.' Patrick sighed. 'He is fortunate in being able to afford such gestures.'

'Ummm,' the King said.

As James continued to fondle the mare, and point out her excellence Patrick said not a word. At length his liege lord turned on him. 'Man – what ails you?' he demanded. 'You're byordinar glum! Soughing and puffing . . . !'

'Your pardon, Sire. Think nothing of it. I have had some ill news from England, that is all.'

'Eh? Frae England? What's ill there, Patrick?'

The Master raised his eyebrows towards George Home who,

as so frequently these days, was in close attendance on the King. James flapped a hand at the young man, as though shooing away a hen.

'Off wi' you, Doddie,' he ordered. 'We hae matters to discuss.' Then, to Patrick. 'What's amiss, man?'

'It is the Queen's health, Sire. Reports on Her Grace of England's state are not encouraging, I fear.'

James leered. 'Is that a fact? Guidsakes man, 'tween me and you, is that cause for a long face? The auld Jaud's had her day. Ower long a day! They could do fine wi' a new bottom sat on the throne o' England, I say!'

'Quite, Sire. Undoubtedly. It is what we have worked for, all these years. If it was only Her Grace's bodily health that was failing, I could contain my distress! But her mind also, they tell me, is growing enfeebled. And since she has not yet named you finally and certainly as her heir, there is danger in this.'

'Hech, me! D'you say so!' Anxiously the King licked thick lips. 'But she'd no' go by me now, man? Who else is there?'

'It is not so much the danger of her naming another, Sire. But if Elizabeth's mind goes, altogether, before naming you – there is the danger.'

'But, Patrick – who else could they choose? Yon Arabella Stewart's a right glaikit crittur – and no' near it in the blood as am I. Vicky Lennox is nigh as near it as she is. Waesucks – it's no' that? You're no' telling me that there's any thinking on Vicky as King o' England, in place o' me!'

'No, no, Sire – that at least I think you need not fear! The trouble is otherwhere. The only other claimants who have any possibility even of being considered, are the Infanta Isabella of Spain and Edward Seymour, Lord Beauchamp, great-grandson of Henry the Eighth's sister Mary. These two, separately, scarce menace Your Grace's position. But combined, it could be otherwise.'

'Combined, man? How could that be? The Infanta is married to the Archduke Albert. Beauchamp couldna marry her, Forbye, he's a Protestant and she's a Catholic.'

'Not that, Sire – not marriage. My dread is that their *support* might be combined. The Infanta's claim is supported by the English Catholics – and there are not a few of them. But neither

Queen nor Council nor yet the mass of the people would have her. Beauchamp is a different matter. The late Queen Mary Tudor considered his aunt, Jane Grey, near enough to the crown to have her executed. But he is a man of straw and unpopular...'

'What, then?'

'My tidings, Sire, that distress me, are these. There is a move afoot, they say, that the English Catholics should transfer their support from the Infanta, whom they recognise as having no hope, to Beauchamp, under a secret agreement that he should turn Catholic. That is the danger that lengthens my face, Your Grace!'

'Christ God, man – no! It's no' true! They couldna do that to me – James o' Scotland!' In his agitation, the King grasped Patrick's arm and shook it vehemently. 'No' for a crooked carle like yon Beauchamp. It's shamefu' even to think on it!'

'Shameful, yes, Sire – but possible. The Infanta's and Beauchamp's support combined could be no light matter. And if sustained by the Pope and the Catholic powers . . . with many who mislike the Scots, in England...'

'Fiend seize me, Patrick – what's to be done, then? What's to be done?'

The other took a pace or two away, over the stable cobblestones, and back. 'I have been thinking on this, Your Grace. Seeking to find a way out. It seems to me that the solution of the matter lies with the Vatican. The Pope. As supreme leader of the Catholic world, he could change all. If he was to tell the English Catholics *not* to lend their support to Beauchamp, then there is no longer a problem.'

'Aye – but how is that to be done?'

'If His Holiness was to be convinced that Your Grace would be a better King of England, from the Catholic point of view, than would Beauchamp...'

'But, man, he kens fine I'm no Catholic. I've ay been the Protestant monarch.'

'Even Protestant monarchs can turn, Highness – as witness Henry of Navarre, now of France! And Beauchamp is also a Protestant – so far! Not, of course, that I am suggesting that Your Grace should turn secret Catholic – God forbid! But if it could be made clear to the Pope that, unlike Elizabeth, you would be kindly disposed towards Catholics. That you would work with them, and with the Pope himself. That you are the least prejudiced of princes ...'

'Ooh, aye – but how to convince the Pope o' this? Eh?'

'If you were to send a letter to His Holiness. By special courier. Secret, of course – since it would never do for it to be known that the King of Scots was in communication with the Tyrant of Rome! A letter which would leave the Pope satisfied in his mind that you were very favourably disposed towards his people ...'

'Och, Patrick man – yon Pope's no fool! D'you think he'd no' ken? If I was to write to him of a sudden, yon way. Fine he'd ken I was wanting something. He'd soon sniff it out what we were at.'

'Therefore, Highness, you must indeed seem to want something from him. Something other than your true requirement. And something, if possible, that further confirms your goodwill. Your acknowledgement of the Papal authority in its own sphere. But yet that does not commit you to anything dangerous. For instance – you might write to him hoping that he might be graciously pleased to create a Scottish Cardinal.'

'Eh ... ?' James blinked at him, mouth open.

'A Cardinal, Sire. A Prince of the Church. It is long since there has been such appointment, of a Scot. But a Scottish Cardinal could be most useful, in dealing with the other Catholic powers – and most of Europe is still Catholic. So Your Grace might well make such a suggestion. And the Pope would esteem it as grace, I am sure!'

'On my soul ... !'

'It would cost you nothing, commit you to nothing. Yet the impression on His Holiness would be great, I swear. Especially if it was supported by one or two other indications of Your Grace's open mind in such matters.'

'But ... but ...' Helplessly the King scratched his head. 'Who, Patrick? Where are we to find a man to name? We havena any ...'

'I think I know just the man, Sire. One Drummond, Bishop of Vaison. A prominent cleric, much in favour at the Vatican. By birth a member of the Inchaffray family – and indeed uncle to our good James Elphinstone. The Lord Elphinstone married a Drummond of Inchaffray.'

'You tell me that! Och, my goodness me! But . . . it's a notion, Patrick – it's a notion. Elphinstone, you say? Well, now. Yon's a canny chiel, James Elphinstone. Right eident and diligent. His uncle? But . . . wouldna this Drummond, this Bishop, wonder why for I should be naming him, Patrick? Would it no' smell right strange? Since I've never heard tell o' the man? Would he no' maybe go to the Pope and say there was a twist to it, some way . . . ?'

'I have the answer for that, Your Grace. You must seem to honour James Elphinstone. Make him Secretary for State. It is necessary that this position be revived. The work demands it – work that Elphinstone is already doing. There should be one senior of the eight men who serve you so well – if only to sign the papers. He is the only one of noble birth, and the hardest worker. Make him Secretary of State. Perhaps knight him. Then, Sire, it will seem to the Bishop, and to the Pope, that it is but *he* who presses his uncle's name with you. All will be credible, natural.'

'Guidsakes, man – you think o' everything!'

'I but seek to serve Your Grace to the best of my limited ability. Unlike my lord of Huntly, I cannot present you with costly gifts. Only the products of my poor wits.' He paused. 'As to the same lord, it occurs to me that you could show your appreciation, Sire, of this kindly token of affection, as well as of probable future benefits to come – for the Gordon is passing wealthy – by bestowing upon him some token of your own, some suitable token. In the state of the Treasury, it must cost you nothing. But Your Grace is the fountain of honour. And honours cost you but the price of a piece of parchment and some sealing-wax!'

'Hey – what's this, now? I'd like fine to honour Geordie Gordon some way – but how can I? He's an earl already, and Lieutenant o' the North again. I couldna raise him to be duke, for he's no' o' the blood royal . . .'

'No, that is not possible. But the English whom, pray God, you will soon be ruling, have found a new title, midway between. That of marquis. Higher than earl but less than duke

– taken from the French. You might create Huntly Scotland's first marquis. At no expense to yourself.'

'M'mmm. Uh-huh. I could, aye. Marquis, eh? Think you Geordie would like that?'

'I am sure that he would. He likes strange titles, and revels in calling himself Cock o' the North and Gudeman o' the Bog! He would be suitably grateful, I feel sure. But, what is more important, I think that the Pope in Rome would be the more impressed. With your magnanimity towards the Catholics. In having bestowed this signal honour on your foremost Catholic subject.'

'Aye – that's so. There's something to that, maybe. Marquis o' Huntly! Cardinal Drummond! Aye – and no' costing me a penny-piece! Man – where did you get your wits, eh? No' frae that auld donnert father o' yours!'

'Perhaps it was from the Ruthvens, Majesty. My mother was Barbara Ruthven of Gowrie.' He looked suddenly, directly, levelly, at his monarch. 'Gowrie – to whom the Treasury owes so much money!'

'Ech? Hech, hech! Och, man Patrick. H'rr'mmm.' Hastily coughing and looking away, the King changed the subject. 'Where's . . . where's this place? Vaison, did you say? Where the man Drummond's Bishop?'

'I have not a notion, Sire. Somewhere in France, belike. But we shall find out. Shall I pen some small points to aid you in your letter to the Pope?'

'Do that, Patrick – do that. Aye.'

'Then, with your royal permission, I shall to my desk, Sire . . .'

Reasonably satisfied, Patrick Gray bowed out of the stable.

Chapter Nineteen

King James thrust his chair back violently from the head of the long table, so that it scraped harshly on the Council-chamber floorboards, and started up, to stamp the great room with his shambling, unsteady gait, ramming down his ridiculously high hat more securely on his head. Everywhere, turning eyes to the ceiling or to each other, the entire Privy Council had to rise likewise and so stand in their places while their sovereign paraded. This sort of thing was becoming almost routine at Council meetings, unfortunately.

'Ignorant fools! Presumptuous dolts! Numbskulls!' The King had difficulty in getting the words round his oversized tongue, and, as always when he was excited and upset, his voice went into squeaks. 'They'll pass this folly and that! The Estates o' the Realm will have this done and that done! Ooh, aye. But they'll no' pass my stints and taxations. They'll no' put their hands in their pouches. It is resolved to do this, and resolved to do the next thing – but, waesucks, never a cheep o' where the siller's to come frae! I tell you, my lords, it's no' to be borne! They refuse my right clamant demands. They delay and hold over the right fair and necessary taxes and imposts that Patrick . . . that the Master o' Gray has devised. They say the realm must be strong and I must build up an army. But who's to pay for it? Do they think I'm *made* o' siller?'

Happening to be passing the bulky person of the Earl Marischal, James poked him strongly in the back. 'You, my lord – do you think the like?' he cried. 'How much have you given to my royal Treasury o' late? Eh?'

A little startled by this unexpected attack, the Keith chief gulped. 'I . . . I sent five hundred crowns no more than three months back, Sire . . .'

'Five hundred! What's five hundred crowns frae half The Mearns? And you, my lord o' Cassillis? What has Carrick sent? Tell me that. What o' the broad lands o' Carrick?'

'I am gathering what I can, Your Grace. But at this season it's no' easy. After the harvest, may be . . .'

'Harvest! Houts, man – I canna wait till harvest! This is June. I may need ten thousand men any day – and you say wait till after harvest! A hundred hands are clawing out at me for siller – and you say wait for harvest! You are as bad as the Estates yesterday, my lord!'

A Convention of the Estates, the Scottish parliament, had held one of its infrequent meetings the previous day, the 26th of June 1600. Presented with an excellent and comprehensive scheme of taxation, broadly-based, fairly-designed, it had temporised, hedged and voted for delay – whilst enthusiastically adopting the Octavians' projects of good government and public works. The King himself had presented the demands, and had been mortified by the rebuff.

He stormed on, waving his hands. 'It's no' right. It's no' right, I say. That the King o' Scots should be thus vexed and constrained. For lack o' money to rule and govern his realm. And to support his just and lawful claims to another realm – England! My lord o' Atholl – what o' you? When last did *you* put your hand in your pocket, for your king?'

Emboldened perhaps by the fact that he was himself a Stewart, a far-out cousin of the monarch, Atholl spoke out. 'Sire – my duty is to protect you, to support you at need with armed men – not with pounds and shillings. I am an earl of Scotland – not a merchant!'

The murmur of acclaim that greeted his assertion was faint but eloquent – and significant. James gobbled in anger. 'My lord . . . my lord . . . !' he got out thickly, and then turned help-lessly to look for aid from Patrick Gray.

That man, standing near the foot of the table, close to Sir James Elphinstone the Secretary of State, did not fail him. 'Your Grace,' he said, mildly, easily, 'perhaps my lord of Atholl, in his remote mountain fastness, has not perceived that times have changed? That the sword no longer rules in Scotland. That a tail of blustering men-at-arms is no longer the standard authority in this realm. It is four years, five, since Your Grace last called upon any of your lords for fighting men. All of you . . .' He amended that. 'All of us, my lords, have had these years of peace, to tend our lands and mend our affairs. Do we owe nothing to His Grace for these years when he has made no call upon our duty? When he has maintained the King's peace with but little aid from us? Is the continuing good government of the realm no concern of ours? Are swords all we are good for, my lords?'

There was silence in that Council-chamber of Edinburgh Castle. Many men frowned darkly, but none spoke.

'Aye. Well said, Master o' Gray', James commended thickly. In the lowered tension, he shuffled back to his great chair at the head of the table, and sat down. Thankfully all followed suit. 'The Master speaks truth,' he went on, banging on the table for quiet. 'He does right well to reprove you, my lords. For it's little enough the most o' you have contributed, this while back, out o' the great lands you hold o' me, the King. Mind you that! You hold your lands o' *me*. At my pleasure. You'd scarce think it, whiles. Wi' the most o' you. But no' o' the Master himsel'. Na, na. I tell you, this past year and more, the realm couldna have been managed lacking the Master putting his hand in his pouch. His own pouch, mind. God kens where he got it, but . . .'

'God . . . and the Pope!' a voice said quietly, from half-way down the table.

There was a stir, with exclamations, muttered charges and counter-charges.

The King was slapping the table again. 'My lord! My lord o' Gowrie!' he cried. 'Watch your tongue, I say! It ill becomes you – aye ill. To make sic-like observes. And against your cousin! You, but who yesterday raised voice against me in the Estates.'

'Not against you, Sire. Never that. Against your advisers, only. Upon a demand for more moneys that your subjects have to give – your poorer subjects. And for a purpose which all true men must conceive to be dishonourable.'

Clearly, firmly, and unflurried, the youthful voice answered the King. The speaker was a man of only twenty-one years, good-looking, fine-featured, well-made – John Ruthven, third Earl of Gowrie and sixth Lord Ruthven. Son of the late Lord Treasurer Gowrie, who had been executed fourteen years before for alleged treason after a murky Court intrigue, he and his family had long been under official royal displeasure – for had it not been to Ruthven Castle that the young King James had been kidnapped and held prisoner for nearly a year, in the lawless 1580s. After his father's execution, the young Earl, with his brother, at the age of fifteen, had been sent abroad, and had spent six years at the University of Padua – to such good effect that he was now in fact Rector of that great seat of learning. He had been back in Scotland only since April, and was already making his presence felt. The day previously he had been the only great lord actually to raise his voice against the King's demand to the Estates for one hundred thousand crowns as an immediate levy on the burghs and lesser barons and lairds.

James was all but speechless. 'Dis . . . dishonourable!' he croaked. 'You! You, to say the like! You, son o' a beheaded miscreant! Grandson o' yon black devil who knifed Davie Rizzio in my own mother's presence! You . . . !'

Only Gowrie's clenched fists betrayed how he disciplined himself. 'Sire, my father's and my grandsire's actions are not my affair. And were dearly paid for. My father's in money as well as blood – for did Your Grace not accept a loan of eighty thousand pounds no less, from his hands? As Treasurer. Which moneys have not yet been repaid . . .'

Again there was near uproar in the Council.

It was not the excited clamorous voices which prevailed, but the young Earl's calm and measured statements. 'What I hold to be dishonourable,' he managed to resume, 'is the policy of raising an army to invade England. This costly threat to enforce Your Grace's claims to the throne of Queen Elizabeth . . .'

'Have done, I say!' James interrupted him furiously. 'Do you dare so decry your prince's legitimate endeavours? We a' ken why you're so kindly concerned for Elizabeth! We ken that you spent two months at her Court on your way home – aye, often close-chambered wi' the Queen hersel', we've heard! No' for nothing, my lord – no' for nothing, I'll be bound! Meddling in matters that are no concern o' yours. To your prince's prejudice – aye, prejudice.'

'Not so, Sire . . .'

'Silence! You will remain silent, sir! This, I'd remind you, is *my* Privy Council – no' yours! Learn you how to behave! My lords,' James declared agitatedly, great eyes rolling as he looked round at all of them, 'the situation o' my royal succession to England is serious. Most serious. Elizabeth is auld and crabbit, and daily grows less clear-like in her mind. She refuses most contumaciously to name me heir. I have ay been her true heir, a' these years. You ken it, she kens it – a' true men ken it. But she'll no' say it, the auld . . . the auld . . . !' He swallowed, but even so, a deal of the royal saliva was lost.

'I had' done a' that man can to bring her to the bit, my lords,' he went on. 'Cecil, her Secretary, and Willoughby, likewise. But to no avail. The stupid auld woman has it in her head that if she once names her heir, she is as good as a corpse! Heard you ever the like? Hersel' a sick and failing husk, and England lacking the sure knowledge o' who'll be on her throne to-morrow! It's wicked, my lords – wicked! And as a conse-quence, the land is fu' o' plots and schemes. To put this on the throne, and that! God kens a' the claimants there are now sprung up – wi' no' least title o' right to them! There's even a party, they tell me, for Vicky Stewart here, Duke o' Lennox . . .'

Ludovick, sitting at the King's right hand, as nominal Presi-dent of the Council, had sat silent throughout – as indeed was quite customary when he attended at all. Now he spoke, briefly but strongly.

'Your Grace knows very well, as do all others, that I have no interest in the throne of England, or any other throne. Indeed, if all England, and your royal self, offered it to me in gift, I would refuse it without a second thought. I seek nothing of kings and rule and courts.'

'Aye. I'ph'mm. Just so.' James looked sidelong at him. 'But that's no' the point, Vicky. The point is that on account o' Elizabeth's right stubborn silence as to the succession, there's folk scrabbling for her throne like hound-dogs for a bone! That throne is mine by right, in blood, in reason, and in the policies o' our two states. And, as God's my witness, I shall have it! These two kingdoms shall be united under my reign – to the glory o' Almighty God and the peace and prosperity o' both peoples!'

There was even some applause for this resounding affirma-tion of faith, led by the Master of Gray.

Encouraged, the King went on, leaning over the table. 'You a'

327

ken, my lords, how we'll benefit – *you'll* benefit. It's to your most notable gain. No more wars. Peace on the Border, for a' time to come. A share in England's wealth, my lords. Appointments at my English Court. Offices o' profit and honour. Broad English lands in my gift. Trade for your burghs and merchants. Aye . . .' That goodly catalogue, ending in a long royal sigh of contemplation, had not only James Stewart licking his lips.

'It's near, my friends – near!' the King went on eagerly, if wetly. 'It could be the morn's morn. Ours! But . . we maun be prepared to *take* what's ours, if others seek to steal it frae us. If Elizabeth doesna name me heir, before her death, there'll be plenty seeking to get sat on her throne the moment she's awa'! Seeking, wi' armed force. They're no' a' like Vicky Lennox, here! There'll be war, my lords. I must have a Scots army standing ready on the Border, a stronger host than any the others can raise, to march south the instant moment the word o' Elizabeth's death is brought. No less will serve to win me what is mine. And for that, my lords, I must have siller. Much siller.'

Now, he had most of the Council with him, or at least interested. White-faced, set, Lord Gowrie stared straight ahead of him. Ludovick looked down at his finger-nails, expressionless. Certain others frowned or murmured. But by and large the general air of hostility was abated.

'I must have that hundred thousand crowns I asked the Estates for, and more,' James told them, nodding portentously. 'And at once. If no' frae them, frae you, my lords! You'll get it back, mind – ooh aye, you'll get it back. Wi' interest. Once I'm in yon London. You can do it fine and easy, if you set your minds to it – you ken that. Some, mind, ha' been right generous already. My lord Marquis, in especial . . .'

Huntly, who had seemed to be asleep, opened his eyes, nodded casually in the direction of his monarch, a crooked grin on his big red face, and shut his eyes again.

'Aye. And the Constable, my lord of Erroll, has done right nobly likewise.'

There was some throat-clearing at the especial mention of these two Catholics. James nodded again.

'Others, o' maybe a different conviction, havena yet seen fit to do the like,' he added.

Ludovick almost opened his mouth to observe that his Protestant wife's deep coffers, at least, had been most thoroughly and consistently raided – but thought better of it.

'So there it is, my lords,' the King declared. 'If you would have your prince King o' England – wi' a' that will mean to you – then waesucks, you'll just ha' to find me the siller! And forthwith. I must raise and equip an army, without delay. How many ha' we got there now, Patrick? And in what-like state?'

'Sir James, I think, can best tell us such details, Sire.'

The diffident but efficient Secretary of State kept his eyes down-bent on his papers, even though he did not require to consult them. 'You have four thousand and three hundred men enrolled, Your Majesty. Some three thousand trained and equipped. But horses only for eleven hundred. More horses are coming from the Low Countries, and arms from France. But ... these are not yet paid for, Sire.'

'Aye. And I need at least ten thousand, my lords!'

Into the murmur of talk which arose, Patrick Gray raised his melodious voice again. 'Your Grace – may I point out our especial need? I hear noble lords saying that they will supply men, rather than money, as formerly. But this will not serve. Bands of men-at-arms, my friends, are not sufficient for His Grace's purpose, however many. This host must be disciplined sternly. To stand and wait. Possibly for months, even years. It must obey no orders but the King's. If it has indeed to march into England, it must do so under strict control – for it must not assail or offend the English people, the King's new subjects. You know your men-at-arms, my lords – we all know them, all too well! They will not serve, in this.'

None could controvert him.

'Moreover, it is not only the soldiers,' he went on. 'There are many in England who will support the highest bidder! Unprincipled gentry, no doubt – such as none here would countenance!' He smiled round them all, genially. 'Such disbursements and subventions, to carefully chosen persons in the English Court circle, although costly, will afford most handsome interest. But, alas, His Grace's coffers are empty, scraped clean as a bone. As is my own humble purse.' He nodded with entire goodwill in the direction of his cousin Gowrie. 'God – or even the Pope, my lord – are but unchancy contributors, I fear, and the widow's cruse would appear to have run out!'

There was a laugh at that, for young Gowrie was known to be of a notably religious turn of mind, almost a Puritan indeed, and the Biblical reference apt. The statement also was literally true, although the speaker hoped that only he and Elphinstone knew how true. The Pope's largesse, which had so largely kept the protestant ship of state afloat this past year and more, had now dried up. His munificence had amounted to more even than the hundred thousand crowns demanded of the Estates. But in the continued absence of any sign of Scotland turning Catholic or King James making any public pronouncement towards that end, His Holiness was now limiting his benevolence to promises – even if princely promises. Two million crowns, no less, would be despatched from Rome the moment that James published liberty of conscience for all subjects of the two kingdoms, and moved his forces over the Border for London. Patrick Gray, of a night, was apt to dream longingly of that two million.

'Aye, my lords – that's the way o' it,' James took him up. 'I've been Elijah ower long. I charge you a' to reckon up forthwith what moneys you can raise out o' the lands you hold o' me, and inform the Secretary here. Aye, and dinna be grudging, my friends – if you'd have me remember you kindly in London-town! Then awa' wi' you and gather together the siller. Is it understood?'

If the depth of silence was the measure of the assent, then there was no misapprehension in the Privy Council

The curiously unsteady yet for once determined royal glance made a slow circuit of all the faces at that table, until it came to that of the Earl of Gowrie, and there halted. For seconds on end these two eyed each other, as all men watched – and it was the monarch's regard which dropped first.

'Aye,' James jerked. 'Mind it! I say, mind it.' He got to his teetering feet. 'This Council stands adjourned. God preserve you my lords!'

As the others rose, he was already making for the door.

Patrick Gray was there first, nevertheless, to open the door wide, having signed Elphinstone back. 'Magnificent, Sire,' he murmured as the King lurched by. 'I am lost in admiration! Only – Your Grace omitted to mention the Duchess of Lennox's contributions, as I suggested. It would have been wise, I think.'

'Guidsakes – I clean forgot! It was yon Gowrie – yon ill limmer, Gowrie! A curse on him! To owe the likes o' him a' that siller! Eighty thousand Scots pounds! In this pass. It's scarce to be borne, Patrick – scarce to be borne!'

'As Your Highness says – scarce to be borne,' the Master repeated evenly, and bowed to the royal back as the Guard outside escorted the sovereign hence.

Ludovick Stewart stroked the dark curly head of the six-year-old son at his side – and quickly the boy broke away and darted across to the edge of the tiny terrace garden carved so cunningly out of the cliff below towering Castle Huntly, keeping his small square shoulders stiffly turned away from the visitor.

'See you that!' the man complained. 'He scarce knows me – his own father. Is that right? Is that proper, Mary?'

The young woman bit her lip. 'It is near two years since he has seen you, Vicky. Do not blame him . . .'

'I do not blame Johnnie,' the Duke answered her. 'It is you that I blame. It is not his fault that he and I are all but strangers, Mary – it is yours. You who keep us apart. Will you not, for his sake if not for mine, come back to me? Back to Methven, at least. His heritage. Where we can be together at times, if no more than that. It has stood empty, waiting, all these long years. It is all that I live for, I swear.'

Troubled deeply, she eyed him. He had never seen her look so lovely, in her simple country gown, with the basket of cut flowers on her arm. Now twenty-five, Mary Gray was in the fullest bloom of fair womanhood, of an exquisite beauty of feature and figure to tear at the man's heart, patrician grace and carriage in every line of her however humble her attire and modest her demeanour.

'Not . . . not in front of Johnnie, my dear,' she murmured, low-voiced. 'I beg of you – not now.' She moved a little away over the short turf of the narrow terrace in the warm July sunshine. 'You have ridden far today, Vicky?'

Shortly, abruptly, he answered her. 'Only from Falkland. The

331

Court is there again. Since four days. I crossed the ferry at Erroll. No great distance, as you know.' He glanced down at himself, frowning. 'It seems to be my fate ever and only to come to you thus, covered in dust, booted and spurred, smelling of horses...'

'Do you think I care for that – so long as I see you?' she asked, reaching out to touch his arm lightly.

'You can say that – when still you keep me from you!'

'To be sure – for I did not cease to love you, my dear, when we were forced to part. You should not visit me here – that is certain. But when you do, can I help it if my heart all but bursts at the sight of you?'

'Mary...!'

Quickly she went on, before he could make too much of that. 'It is twenty long months since last you came to Castle Huntly, Vicky. That black day when... when...'

He nodded. 'I have been far since then. In London. And Paris. Burgundy. The Low Countries. Sent on embassages, now here, now there. Sent, I do believe, to get me out of the King's sight, out of Patrick Gray's sight – even out of *your* sight!'

'No!'

'But, yes. Who knows, perhaps out of Jean Campbell's sight, also!'

'Your wife...!'

'I prefer to call her my duchess!'

Mary drew a deep breath. She turned, to call the boy over to her, to hand him the basket of flowers. 'Johnnie – take these up to Granlord's room. Tell him that I shall come to see him very soon. Talk with him, Johnnie. Tell him of the martin's nest you have found in the cliff, here...'

'How is he? The old lord?' Ludovick asked, as the boy ran off.

'A broken, done old man,' she answered, sighing. 'But the empty shell of what he was. He seldom stirs from his chamber, high up at the battlements. Staring and staring out over the Carse all day. Lips moving but not speaking. He will see only Davy and myself. And Johnnie. And even us he does not seem to know, at times. Oh, Vicky – how terrible a blow Patrick struck him, that day!'

'Aye. When Patrick strikes . . . ! God only knows – perhaps I should never have come, that day. To warn him. Perhaps it would have been better, kinder, to have let the matter take its course. He would have resisted the arrest – Lord Gray. There would have been fighting. And that would indeed have been treason. But he would have gone down like a man.'

'No. You did what was right. And generous. This would have happened anyway – this of Granlord. The bad blood has been working its ill between them for long. All my life. Indeed, it may be that my life was the cause of it all – my birth that raised the wicked barrier between them. Sometimes of a night I lie and think of that, Vicky . . .'

'That is folly, lass. Those two would have clashed on any and every issue. And sooner or later Patrick would have struck. As he always strikes – unexpectedly, like a scorpion, a snake, a viper! As, I fear he will strike again . . . !'

Tight-lipped she turned to him, eyes asking, but wordless.

He nodded grimly. 'Aye, it is Patrick that brings me here again – since I must needs have an excuse to come to you,' he told her bitterly. 'Patrick, and the King. I fear now greatly for another man – Gowrie. I fear for him, Mary.'

'The Earl of Gowrie? John Ruthven? The Lady Beatrix's brother?'

'Yes. And your cousin. The Lady Gray, Patrick's mother, was sister to Gowrie's father, was she not?'

'I scarce know him, nevertheless, Vicky. Always he has been away. Abroad. I had heard that he was back, that is all.'

'He is back. And putting himself in Patrick's way, the King's way. Honest and fearless, but not knowing what he does, what he hazards. I have tried to warn him – but he will not heed me.'

'You think . . . you think that Patrick means him an injury?'

'I know it. Is not anyone who opposes Patrick in danger? Gowrie opposes his policies openly. He condemns the English succession policy. He openly refuses to contribute to the King's levy. He cares not what he says, so long as he believes it right – noble behaviour but dangerous, fatal. *You* know it. We have seen so often what happens to those who run counter to Patrick. Gowrie is in deadly danger. I am sure of it. I see all the signs. I have sought to tell him. Twice I have spoken to him.

But to no avail. There is so little to point to, for Patrick is never obvious. And Gowrie does not know him. He was only a child when he left Scotland, six or seven years ago. He does not know that he is dealing with the Devil himself!'

Patrick's daughter gulped, but said nothing.

'Gowrie, I think, conceives me as but a fool, or worse. He sees me as close to the throne, a tool of the King's party, warning him off. To keep him quiet. Also, he does not love me, on account of his sister, Sophia. My first wife – if you could name her that. God knows, I had no responsibility for her death! But the family think the less of me, in consequence. I spoke to the other sister, the Lady Beatrix, your friend. But to no better avail. I urged that she tell him to leave Scotland. To go back to Padua. He is a scholar, Rector of the University there. But she herself does not know the danger, as you and I know it. And her brother is noways close to her, almost a stranger to her, seeing her also as of the King's company, a lady-in-waiting to the Queen. So . . . I come here, Mary.'

'But what can I do, Vicky?'

'You, and Davy Gray. I thought that Gowrie might listen to you, perhaps. Patrick's daughter and brother. You might persuade him. You are clearly not of the King's company . . .'

'Davy is away. Visiting Granlord's properties in The Mearns.'

'You are the more important in this. Gowrie is at his townhouse in Perth. He left Falkland yesterday. If you would ride there, with me, to speak with him. It is not two hours riding. He might listen to you, Mary – for all men listen to you! You are related to him. You can speak of Patrick as no other can . . .'

'You are asking me to . . . to witness against my father? To this stranger?' That said low-voiced.

'I suppose that I am, yes. That he may possibly be one less stain on your father's name and conscience! As I fear he will be, otherwise.'

She said nothing.

'Mary – if, by speaking to Gowrie, you can save an evil deed being done, should you not do it? How would you feel, my dear, if you withheld, and later Gowrie was brought low by some wicked intrigue? *I* am no friend of his – but that is what I ask myself. That is why I am here.'

'Very well.' She raised her head, decision taken. 'I shall ride with you, Vicky. First, I must see to Granlord. Then, in an hour, I shall be ready . . .'

Accompanied by two of Ludovick's grooms, presently they rode through the July afternoon the fifteen miles along the fertile cattle-dotted Carse of Gowrie to Saint John's town of Perth. So long it was since the girl had ridden at this man's side, that at first she could only delight in it, despite the object of their journey. To begin with she was almost gay – and Mary Gray, like her sire, could be sparkling gaiety itself. But as they neared Perth, following the narrowing Tay by Seggieden and Kinfauns a silence descended upon them.

'Mary,' the Duke said, after a long interval. 'How long is this to go on? How long will you keep me away from you? Hold me off? Is there to be no end to it? When we love each other. When our son sees his father only as a stranger? It has been three years now – three endless years.'

'I am sorry, Vicky,' she answered him, almost in a whisper.

'You said the same two years ago! You said to wait. I have waited, Mary – God knows how I have waited! How much longer must I wait?'

'I do not know. I only know, my heart, that I cannot share you. Not with any prospect of joy or peace between us. I am sorry. I know that it is my grievous fault – wicked pride, no doubt. But I know myself sufficiently well to be sure that if I made myself come to you, shared your bed again, there would be always that other between us! The true trust and dear unity would be gone, my love – broken. And that I could not bear. We would be less happy than we are now. Believe me, it is so.'

'Then, shrive me – what is there to wait for? Do *you* wait for a miracle? For Jean to die, maybe? Do you wish her dead . . . ?'

'Ah, no! Do not say that. It is not true. I am a wicked proud woman, Vicky – but not so vile as that. I swear it! No – I ask you to wait for something in myself. Some change . . .'

'I would seek a divorcement – since it was no true marriage. But the King and the Kirk would never hear of it.'

'No. For it was true enough marriage to produce a child,

Vicky. You have a daughter, I hear. Is she . . . is she fair? A joy to you?'

'No. I scarce know her. I am unfortunate with my offspring, am I not? Her mother keeps her close. I seldom see the child . . .'

'Vicky – is that fair to the bairn?'

'I know not. I would not have the child to suffer – although she has been a sickly creature from the first. But Jean hides her away. We can hardly be said to live together, you understand. Have not done so for many months. She goes her way – and goes it boldly, as I know – and I go mine. Though, to be sure, mine is a more lonely way than is hers! We see each other about the Court – that is all.'

'Oh, Vicky – what a tangle it is!'

'No such great tangle, Mary. Nothing that we could not cut through this very night – had you the will for it!'

She lowered her head, and they rode on unspeaking.

Crossing the bridge of Tay into Perth town, they were quickly at Gowrie House, which indeed faced the river, its gardens running down to the water's edge. It was a great rambling establishment, turreted and gabled, forming three sides of a courtyard, with one wing flanking the street of Speygate. With the tall Kirk of St. John, it dominated the town – as indeed had done its family for long. The young Earl had been but a week or two back in Scotland when he was appointed provost of the town and chief magistrate.

The visitors were first received by the Earl's brother, Alexander, Master of Gowrie, a cheerful, smiling youth of nineteen, who had been playing tennis with a page. Obviously much taken with Mary Gray, and suitably impressed by the eminence of the Duke, he led them by many corridors and stairways to a moderate-sized room off a great gallery on the second floor, evidently a library. Here his elder brother was surrounded by books and parchments strewn on tables and floor, and was dusting and arranging them. Although he envinced no great joy at the interruption of his task, he greeted his guests courteously, requesting the Master to have wine and refreshments set before them, and explaining that the house had been long standing unoccupied and that he was concerned to discover what of value might be in his father's library.

Ludovick was little of the diplomat, and came quickly to the point. 'This, my lord, is the Lady Mary Gray, mother of my son – who would be my wife if I had been able to have my way. She is natural daughter to the Master of Gray – and therefore your own cousin in some degree. I have brought her here because I believe that what she can tell you is of the highest importance to your lordship.'

Gowrie looked at Mary keenly, thoughtfully, and inclined his head. 'I am honoured by your interest,' he said quietly. 'I have not failed to hear of the lady. But how do my poor affairs so greatly concern her, my lord Duke? Or indeed, yourself!'

'Myself, I have already spoken to you. To but little effect, I think. The Lady Mary may be more successful. I pray so.'

'My lord,' the young woman said earnestly. 'My position is difficult, unhappy. When you have heard me, you will absolve me, I hope, from any charge of meddling, of undue interest in your concerns. I am a woman of no position or importance – but I have this one qualification, that I know my father, the Master of Gray, very well. Sometimes to my sorrow!'

'Whether this is a cause for congratulation or for sympathy, madam, is for you to say. For myself, I have had few dealings with the Master, cousins though we be – nor have ambitions for more!'

'Anyone who takes any hand in the affairs of this realm, has to deal with the Master. Whether he knows it, or not, my lord! If you run counter to the King's present policy – as I am told that you do – you run counter to the Master of Gray. And that can be dangerous!'

'Is it so? All must agree with His Grace's every notion, then – or risk my cousin's righteous displeasure! Is that the way of it? A dire matter!'

At the young Earl's tone of voice, Mary shook her head. 'I am sorry,' she said. 'Be patient with me. Small disagreements, minor dissensions, would not matter. But you, my lord, I understand to oppose the King on a great issue – the issue nearest to his heart. The English succession. The matter above all others which over the years my father has worked for. You are against the finding of this money, as the Duke tells me, for the raising and providing of an army, to hold in support of His Grace's claim. You may well be right – indeed, although my poor woman's opinion is of no value to any, I would think also that this is not how the succession should be assured. But this is scarce the point...'

'You will forgive me asking it,' Gowrie interposed stiffly. 'But what *is* the point? If the rights and wrongs of the matter are not!'

'It is hard, sore, for me to say it, my lord – but that because of this course, you are in real danger, I fear.'

'Danger, madam? Of what? And from whom?'

'From the Master of Gray. Of what, I cannot say. My father is not one to make his moves apparent, to be guessed at. But this I do know all too surely, that those who oppose him in major matters are always in danger. Most real danger. It has been proved too often to be in doubt, my lord.'

'A most convenient reputation for the Master to cherish!' the other commented coldly. 'None must oppose him – or they suffer terrible but undisclosed dangers! A valuable celebrity, fostered and published by his household and friends!'

'Do not be a fool, Gowrie!' Ludovick burst out. 'We are not here on the Master's account, but on yours. We fear – we more than fear, we are certain – that some move will be made against you. What we know not – but I have observed all the signs . . .'

'You would have me jump at signs and shadows, my lord Duke? I note your warning, and shall be on my guard. But I cannot esteem such shadowy fears to have any justification. I do naught that any other member of the Council has not a right to do – to oppose the expenditure of moneys on a policy which was before the Estates. It is no more than my duty, if I conceive the policy wrong. As I do. Are all who voted against it in the Estates likewise in danger of the puissant Master's ire?'

' 'Fore God, man – can you not see this as it is? Not as you would wish it to be? It is not some mere taking of sides in a debate on the state's policy. It is a direct attack on the King's most cherished project, his lifelong ambition. And today the Master of Gray is behind all the King's projects, and moreover believes this succession to be the greatest good that Scotland can achieve. At the Estates, it was your voice raised that turned the tide against the King's tax. And in the Council you could not but see how hot was the King against you for it. Since then you have stated that you will give nothing towards the levy which is being demanded of all great land-holders. No others have seen fit to say as much. Others may hedge and delay and seek to win out of it. But you, of all men, ought not to have cried your refusal to the heavens.'

'Why me, of all men, I pray?'

'Because, my lord, the Crown owes you for eighty thousand pounds! That is why. And no debtor on this round earth could love the man to whom he owed such a sum!'

There was silence for a few moments. For the first time, Gowrie seemed in any way affected or concerned. The Master and a servitor came in with food and drink, and no more could be said until the latter at least was gone. The Earl dismissed his brother also.

'I have not demanded any immediate repayment of these moneys,' he told them, presently. 'Knowing, indeed, that I would not get them. Am I now expected to throw good money after bad?'

Ludovick shrugged. 'I care not if you never give James another silver piece. But to oppose him openly, and to lead others to do the same, is folly.'

'Such is to break no law. What can they do against me?'

'My lord – you do not know my father or you would not ask that!' Mary Gray declared. 'If you stand in the way of anything to which he has set his hand, he will find a way of pulling you down. Many have discovered that, to their cost . . .'

'*My* father did!' Ludovick interrupted harshly. 'His close friend. I now know that he brought him low, to his ruin and death. His own father, the Lord Gray, he has recently dragged down likewise, without shame or compassion, for his own ends. And *your* father, my lord – what of him? The first Gowrie – Greysteil. He was beheaded on a charge of treason, was he not? After making a secret confession, under promise of pardon, and so brought to his doom. Whose hand was behind that, think you?'

'That was on account of the Ruthven Raid. Patrick Gray, they told me, worked for his pardon. That was Arran's work, was it not?' The Earl stared.

'Arran scarce moved a hand, in statecraft, without Patrick behind him. He was Chancellor only in name. The business bears all the marks of the Master's hand.'

'I'll not believe that. His own mother's brother!'

'Who gained the administering of your great Ruthven estates while you were under age, my lord? Who had your sister Sophia married to me – bairns, both of us? And why?'

The other plucked his chin, looking from one to the other of his visitors.

Mary was wringing her hands. 'My lord,' she said, 'this of your father, I do not know. I was too young. It may not be so. But . . . there have been others, I fear, in plenty. Patrick . . . Patrick is a strange man. He has great qualities – but he can be the Devil incarnate! He is, many will say, the most able and clever servant that any King of Scots has known. The realm has never been better ruled, most will admit. But he has no least scruple, where his path is crossed. I urge you. I pray you – do not fail to heed us. Do not dismiss your warning . . .'

'In God's name – what would you have me to do?'

It was the Duke who answered, 'Go back to Padua,' he told him tersely. 'Before it is too late.'

'Shrive me! Padua! Do you jest? Leave Scotland . . . ?'

'Aye, my lord. Just that. Leave Scotland – while there is yet time.'

'This is nonsense! Unthinkable! I shall return to Padua in due course. Next year, it may be. For my affairs there are still to settle. I am still Rector of that University. But not now. I am but three months home! Think you I will go running, like some whipped cur? From the Master of Gray. I – Gowrie!'

'It is not only from him – from the one man. It may be from the whole power of this realm. Which he may use against you. Do you not understand? It is for your own safety and weal . . .'

'Is it, my lord Duke? Of a truth? Is it not perhaps for Patrick Gray's weal, rather, that you come? Perhaps a device to get me out of his way, at no cost? Are you sent to scare me off . . . !'

Ludovick jumped to his feet. 'Have a care, sir, what you say!' he exclaimed. 'Lennox is no lackey of the Master of Gray, or any man, I'd have you know! You will not speak to me so . . .'

'Nor will *you* frighten me with bogles!' Gowrie also rose. 'I will not be threatened . . .'

'Vicky! My lords!' Mary cried, 'Not this – I beseech you! Be patient – there is so much at stake. Hot words will serve nothing . . .'

'No words will serve with my lord of Gowrie, I think!' the Duke asserted. 'I, for one, will waste no more on him.'

'For that, at least, I am grateful, sir!'

'Come, Mary . . .'

'Is our journeying to be quite fruitless, then?' the young woman asked, helplessly. 'Will you not be warned, my lord? Perceive your danger . . . ?'

'I perceive, of a truth, that Patrick Gray would have me out of his path! That, at least, is clear,' Gowrie said, moving after Ludovick towards the door.

'You will take heed, then? Take precautions . . . ?'

The Earl did not answer. They went down the stairs singly, the Duke hastening in front, Gowrie next, and Mary lagging in the rear. At the outer door, where the grooms waited with the horse in the stone-flagged courtyard, the girl turned again to the stiff younger man.

'You will do something?' she urged. 'Be guarded well? Ready to fly if need be . . . ?'

'I shall pleasure myself by keeping away from Court, at any rate,' he told her, distantly. 'I have lands in Atholl which I have not seen for long. There I may visit. But I fly for no man . . .'

With that they had to be content, and took their departure with only bare civilities.

As they clattered over the cobblestones of Perth, Ludovick alternately raged against the stiff-necked folly and blind self-sufficiency of the man they had set out to succour, and apologised for having brought the young woman on this thankless errand. Loudly employed thus, he did not at first hear when Mary presently called urgently to him – and by the time that she had succeeded in attracting his attention and directing his gaze where she indicated, it was too late.

'Amongst that throng of drovers and Highlandmen,' she called. 'Around the alehouse. It was Logan! Logan of Restalrig.

I swear it was he! Looking at us. He turned and hurried off. When he saw I perceived him. Down that vennel. It was Logan, Vicky!'

'Restalrig! Here, in Perth? That bird of ill omen! You are sure?'

'I would not mistake that face. It has cost us too dear, in the past.'

'Patrick has had his outlawry annulled. He hangs about the skirts of the Court. I have never seen them together, but . . .'

'Should we go back? Tell the Earl? Warn him?'

Ludovick snorted. 'Warn that one! Tell him what? Think you he would thank us for the information that one of Patrick's bravoes is in his town? Besides, it may have nothing to do with Gowrie.'

Preoccupied and with no hint of gaiety left to them, they crossed the bridge over Tay and turned their beasts eastwards for the Carse.

Chapter Twenty

The Duke of Lennox drew rein, and the steam from his panting, sweating mount rose to join the mists which, on this still August morning, had not yet had time to disperse, caught in all the shaws and glades of the great marshy forest of Stratheden. He cocked his ear – but could hear only his horse's snorting breathing and the hollow thud of hooves on sodden ground as his falconer came cantering up behind him.

'I thought that I heard the horn,' he called back. 'Did you hear aught, Pate?'

'No, lord. No' a cheep.'

'It is early to have killed. But we are on the wrong track, that is clear. The brute must have circled round to the north. Do many follow us . . . ?'

Thin and high, from some distance off, a hunting-horn sounded.

'North, as I jaloused. By west, some way. It has made for higher ground, then – swung away from the river. A pox on it – the King was right!'

'Aye, His Grace is right canny when it comes to the stags, lord. He seems to ken the way a hunted beast will think, will turn.'

They could hear other riders who had followed the Duke's mistaken lead approaching now. Ludovick pulled his spume-flecked black's head round to the right, and spurred on, to pick his way amongst the alder, birch scrub and hollies, northwards.

There did not sound to be many behind him. Most must have followed the King when, about two miles back, the stag and baying hounds had taken the south flank of a wooded hillock, and James had pulled off to the north. He shone at this, did their peculiar monarch; in the forest, with deer to chase, he was a different man, with a sheer instinct for the business that was more than any mere experience and field-craft. His heart was in it – to the woe of most of his Court.

It would not be much after nine now – and they had been in the saddle for almost three hours. Small wonder that the numbers riding were small, despite royal disapproval – and most of these resentful. A man had to be an enthusiast indeed to be up day after day at five of the clock, wet or fine – and no women, however ambitious or spirited, would face it. Ludovick himself, in his present restive and fretful state of mind, made no complaint. He too was fond of the hunt, the vigorous action of which gave scant opportunity for gnawing thoughts, broodings and repinings, the long days in the saddle which left a man too tired to care overmuch for his lonely nights, to pine for the presence which meant all to him.

Riding north now, in answer to the horn's summons, to what must be an early kill, with the headlong pace of the chase slackened, Ludovick could not keep the sore and aching thoughts at bay – more especially as it was not so very far from here that once, on just such a morning and occasion as this, he had contrived a meeting between Mary Gray and the King, which had led to the return from his first exile of the Master of Gray, and so to a co-operation between them, the Duke and the land-steward's reputed daughter, that culminated in their loving taking one of the other. The contemplation was bitter-sweet indeed.

The intermittent winding of the horn guided him in time to the more hilly ground that lifted towards the foothills of the Ochils between Strathmiglo and Balvaird, where the trees grew smaller and stunted and gave place to whins and thorn. Here, on an open grassy terrace, about six miles from Falkland and the palace, the stag had been cornered, almost prematurely, in a re-entrant of outcropping rock, and brought down, a big beast with a magnificent head but too much weight to its forequarters. A score or so of horses were being held by grooms and falconers, deer-hounds were pacing about with lithe grace, and men were grouped here and there.

But although Ludovick rode straight to the spot beside the rocks where the chief huntsman was kneeling, busy at the bleeding and gralloching of the quarry, James was not there; which was strange, for desperately as he hated and feared the sight and presence of blood and naked steel, the King never appeared to find any displeasure in this messy business of the gralloch – and indeed was apt to offer pawky advice to the operator, with proprietorial interest in the slain, and sometimes even to lend a hand himself. On this occasion, however, the royal victor was not crowing about his prowess, as usual, but standing some distance away, talking to a single individual. Another little group, including the Earl of Mar, George Home, and John Ramsay, the present favourite page, stood nearby, presumably beyond hearing, watching. And the remainder of the hunt stood further off, all eyeing the King, not the ceremony of the gralloch.

Ludovick was not so enamoured of his cousin's company and presence as to hasten to his side. But a movement of the King's ungainly form suddenly revealed to the Duke the slender figure of the man he spoke with. It was Alexander Ruthven, Master of Gowrie – whom Ludovick had not set eyes upon since that day at Perth a full month before. Frowning, he moved over.

Johnny Mar told him that the Master, with a cousin, Andrew Ruthven, had come up behind them as the stag turned at bay. They had certainly not started out on the hunt with the rest. He had requested to speak with the King apart. Some request for office or position, no doubt – one more pretty boy, the Earl suggested, with a scornful glance at Home and young Ramsay.

'He came seeking the King, then?' Ludovick asked. 'It was not the King that sent for him?'

'Would he be like to send for the fellow in the heat of a hunt?'

Presently James, who seemed much interested in his conversation, perceived the Duke's presence and beckoned him forward.

'Hech, hech, Vicky – you missed it! Aye, missed it! You were smart enough, back yonder. You should ha' held to me, man.' The sovereign chuckled his triumph. 'But, see – here's Sauny Ruthven, Gowrie's brother. He's come tell me that my lord his brother has something for me, at Perth. Aye – maist interesting.' And he shot a quick glance at the handsome young Ruthven.

'Indeed, Sire,' Ludovick said flatly.

'Aye. It's . . . it's right kindly intentioned. He would have me ride there, forthwith. To Perth.'

'*You*, Sire? Ride to Perth? Now? At Gowrie's behest?'

'Aye. You see, it's this way, Vicky. Gowrie has yon ill loon the Master o' Oliphant, some place in Perth. Him that's at the horn. You ken I've been to take order wi' him for long, and couldna lay hands on him. Now he's done this new vile and proud oppression in Angus, and he'll have to pay for it. Guidsakes, yes. He's lying in Perth . . .'

'Even so, Sire, I see no reason why you, the King, should go in person to apprehend him. To call off this hunt and ride a dozen miles just to act sheriff! Send a party. Send Gowrie authority to arrest Oliphant himself – although he needs it not, for he is provost of the burgh.'

'Na, na, Vicky – I maun' go mysel'. He's an unco proud and agile rogue, this. He's old enough to be Gowrie's father, and would befool him, to be sure. It'll need the King himsel' to put the King's justice on yon one.

Mystified, the Duke shrugged. 'As you will, Sire – but I cannot see the need of it.' He looked doubtfully at young Ruthven. 'Has my lord of Gowrie not sufficient stout fellows in Perth town to apprehend old Lord Oliphant's son?'

The young man coughed. 'I fear not, my lord Duke. It's a kittle matter . . .'

'Aye, just that,' the King said brusquely, finally. 'Kittle, aye. We'll ride. But no' a' this throng. Vicky – do you and Johnny Mar select a number decently to company me. And pack the lave back to Falkland. Bring you my Lords Lindores and Inchaffray. And Sir Thomas Erskine and Jamie Erskine. Ummm. And Geordie Home and Johnny Ramsay, there. Aye, and the physician-man, Herries. Och, aye – wi' yoursel's, that's aplenty. See you to it. Come you, Master Sauny . . .'

So presently a reduced and somewhat bewildered company of sportsmen thus nominated, with the Duke at their head, were pounding after their liege lord on the twelve-mile ride to Perth, while the others were left, ruefully or gratefully as it might be, to escort the single trophy of an abortive day's hunting back to wondering Falkland town.

James had waited for none, and superbly mounted on the splendid white Barb which had been Huntly's gift, was already well in advance, young Ruthven being hard put to it to keep up with him.

346

They went, by the little valley of the Binn Burn, down into the steep winding defile of Glen Farg, forded the river thereof down near the mouth of the glen, and thereafter went thundering at a fine pace across the level haughlands of the great River Earn, mile upon mile, scattering cattle and raising squattering wildfowl from the scores of pools and ditches. It was not until Bridge of Earn itself was reached that Ludovick caught up with the King, who was now somewhat held back by the Master's tired horse. It was always a mystery how James, who looked so ill on a horse, like a sack of meal in the saddle, in fact rode so well and tirelessly. His great-grandfather, James the Fourth of sad memory, had been the same.

He seemed to be in excellent spirits, despite this extra-ordinary interruption of his beloved hunting. 'No' far now, Vicky,' he called out. 'But three miles beyont this brig, ower the side o' yon Moncrieffe Hill. We'll soon ken the rights o' the business, now!'

'There are doubts, Sire? Of the rights of it? Anent the Master of Oliphant?'

James rolled his great eyes, from Ludovick back towards Ruthven, who was beginning to fall behind. He pulled his white over closer to the Duke's side.

'It's no' Oliphant, Vicky – no' Oliphant, at all! Yon was but a device, see you. Necessary, you understand, to keep the matter close. And it is a right close matter.' The King had dropped his voice, so that the other had great difficulty in hearing him. Yet he sounded notably pleased with himself, almost gleeful. 'Right close. Weighty. Aye, o' great consequence.'

Ludovick looked at him keenly, wordless.

'I can tell *you*, Vicky – but no' a word to the others, mind. It's no' a matter to be shouted abroad, this! Guid kens it's no'! There's gold in this, Vicky – yellow gold! Gowrie and his brother ha' gotten their hands on a mannie wi' a pot o' gold!'

'What!'

'Gold, I tell you! A byordinar strange discover. Last night, it was. Sauny Ruthven, here, came on this mannie. Out in the fields some place, beyond Perth, he says. A right mysterious carle, muffled to the nose in a cloak. Ruthven had never seen the like. When he challenged him, the crittur was fair dismayed, and began to run. But Sauny's young and quick. Forby, the stranger was sair weighted down. Sauny got a hold o' him, and off wi' his cloak. And, man, under it he had this pot o' gold. A great wide pot, full o' gold pieces! Have you ever heard the like?'

Lennox's almost open-mouthed astonishment was answer enough.

'Aye, then. A most notable employ, you'll agree, Vicky? Sauny was right exercised. So he haled the carle to Gowrie House, wi' his pot, and has him secure in a bit privy chamber there. Then, at cock-crow, he's up and on the road to gie me the tidings. What think you o' that Vicky Stewart?' All this in a confidential if gabbled undertone, with much glancing over padded shoulders and around.

'But . . . but . . . !' Ludovick had seldom had more difficulty in finding words. 'You don't tell me . . . Your Grace isn't riding to Perth on such a, a bairn's gullery? A fable!'

'Ah, but we maun discover the matter aright, Vicky. Sauny has the man lockit up for us to see. To question. And his gold wi' him. Foreign gold it is, too – all Spanish coin, Sauny says. It will be a Jesuit priest, belike – a Jesuit, wi' moneys to raise a rebellion.'

'Sire – Jesuit plotters, I'll swear, don't travel the country carrying pots of gold pieces under their oxters! This is the sheerest invention . . .'

'How d'you ken what they do, Vicky? What do *you* know o' Jesuit priests? They peddle Spanish gold – we a' ken that. They maun carry it some way. Why no' in a pot?'

'But . . . Sire, this is madness! Never have I heard so unlikely a tale! And if it were true, why bring the King all this long road to Perth, to see the prisoner? Surely the man could have been brought to you?'

'Och, well – there might ha' been a rescue, see you. The carle was for taking the gold some place, mind. His friends in the business will be right put out. They'd likely try a rescue. The gold's safer at Gowrie House.'

'If any gold there is!'

'You . . . you misdoubt the business, Vicky'

'I do, Sire. As I say, I cannot think of it all as other than a fable. A madness. But for what purpose . . . ?'

They rode on in silence for a little, and it was noteworthy how the King slackened his pace. The Master of Gowrie was almost up with them again when James spoke to his companion in a hoarse whisper.

'Madness, heh? Are you thinking, maybe, that Sauny Ruthven's gone clean mad? Is that it, Vicky?'

At the sudden change of tune, Ludovick blinked, shaking his head. 'No. No – that was not my thought. He seems sufficiently sane. The madness, if such there is, would seem to be elsewhere!'

'Ummm.'

They were now topping the shoulder of Moncrieffe Hill, with the fair valley of the silver Tay spreading before them, and the grey roofs and walls of the town of Perth huddled directly below. Young Ruthven, who had drawn level, on the other side of the King, sought permission to ride ahead the remaining mile or so, in order to warn his brother of his liege lord's approach, that he might welcome him suitably. James agreed, and the youth spurred on.

The rest of the party had now reached them, and were speculating on the possibility of resistance to arrest on the part of the Master of Oliphant, and likelihood of sword-play – for all were practically unarmed, clad in green hunting costume, and bearing only dirks and hunting-knives; indeed the page, John Ramsay, was the only member of the company equipped with a whinger, or short sword. James made no attempt to reassure them, or to admit that Oliphant's capture was not the real object of the journey. His only expressed concern was with the dinner that he was likely to get at Gowrie House.

The royal party was through the gates of Perth and into the narrow streets before the Earl of Gowrie and his brother, with two or three hastily gathered representatives of the town, came hurrying to greet the King. It was a somewhat stiff and formal encounter, for unlike the Master, the Earl was no dissembler and showed his feelings all too clearly. James indeed was the more affable of the pair, affecting a heavy jocularity. Neither made any reference to the object of the visit, in front of the company. Gowrie, after a single brief bow and exchange of cold glances with Lennox, ignored the Duke's presence.

Gowrie House was as empty-seeming and bare as at Ludovick's previous call, and gave no impression of being prepared for a royal occasion. The Earl explained that he was but two days back from his Atholl property, and that his mother and main household was at Dirleton Castle, his Lothian seat, where he intended to join her in a day or two. He hoped that the King would bear with him if he had to wait a little while for a modest dinner, himself having already dined early. There was a grouse or two in the larder, and he would have a hen killed . . .

This seemed to Ludovick almost as extraordinary a situation as that indicated by the story of the pot of gold. It looked, indeed, as though the Earl had not expected the King's visit, and was in fact upset and embarrassed by it. Could it be that his brother had not told him of his ride to Falkland? Or even, perhaps, of the mysterious captive in the privy chamber?

As strange as all this was the fact that, despite all the urgency and speed of their coming here, neither James nor young Ruthven now showed any hurry to go and inspect the prisoner or his treasure. James sat in the pleasant if somewhat overgrown garden, sipping wine and holding forth on the history of the former Black Friars Monastry on which this house was founded, to any who would listen to him, while hungry huntsmen, who had not eaten for nearly seven hours, waited with less patience. Ludovick, low-voiced, asked once when the King was going to investigate the matter they knew of but was waved away with a royal frown, and told to bide in patience like the rest of them.

This supposed reference to the delayed meal raised a growl of feeling, particularly from the Earl of Mar who was a great trencherman.

Admittedly the Gowrie House kitchens seemed to be singularly unequal to their task, that day, for although it was just after twelve-thirty when the visitors arrived, it was after two o'clock before Gowrie himself came to announce that some humble provender now awaited them in the dining-hall. In the interim there had been not a few comments on the well-known Puritan habits and frugality of his young lordship, one of the wealthiest men in the kingdom – criticisms which were by no means stilled by the eventual sight of the provision made for them within.

The Master was presumably giving a hand in the kitchen, for he had not shown himself since their arrival.

The King was served at a small table by himself, the Earl waiting upon him personally – and if he did not fare sumptuously, he at least did better than did his supporters; Master Herries, the royal physician, who had been bred for the Kirk, remarking that a miracle of the loaves and fishes was sore required in Saint John's godly town of Perth.

At least it did not take long to demolish the meal. Even James, who was a dawdler with his food, had finished and was back to sipping wine, when young Ruthven appeared at last, and approached the royal table, to say something in the King's ear.

The monarch rose, as of course did all others. He began to accompany the youth towards the door, but when Ludovick and others started to follow, he waved them back peremptorily, declaring that Master Sauny had something private to show him, above. They should all go out into the garden and await him there. He passed through the hall doorway, making for the main stair.

There was a sniggering murmur from sundry of the company. The Master was a personable youth, and the King's peculiar tastes were only too well-known. Ludovick glanced at Gowrie himself, who seemed to be unconcerned and only glad that the problem of feeding his many visitors was disposed of.

In the garden there was considerable debate about the real object of this peculiar visit – since it seemed apparent that the apprehension of the Master of Oliphant was, to say the least of it, scarcely preying on the mind of the monarch. On the other hand, it did not seem likely that any mere assignation with young Ruthven would have brought James all the way to Perth, especially with such a tail of followers – when all could have been achieved a deal more effectively at Falkland. Ludovick said nothing.

Some of the guests were wandering about the garden, seeking to supplement their dinner by eating cherries off the trees, when Thomas Cranstoun, Gowrie's equerry, came to announce to the Earl that he was told that the King was away. Had left the house by the little Black Turnpike, as he called it, a narrow winding turret stair that led down from the corner turret that overlooked both street and garden, at second floor level.

Gowrie, staring, interrupted him 'Away? What do you mean, man – away?'

'They say, my lord, that His Grace came down the Black Turnpike, went to the stables, mounted his horse and rode away. He is even now riding across the South Inch.'

There was not a little commotion at the news. Men started up, and led by Gowrie, hurried round to the stables, calling for horses to follow the King. Doubtfully indeed Ludovick followed on. It was highly unlikely that James had done any such thing. His disbelief was confirmed, when he reached the stable-yard and saw the King's white horse still standing beside his own black.

He turned, to point this out to Gowrie, who was questioning the gate porter, this man asserting that nobody had in fact issued through this main gate, and that the back-gate was locked and he had the key here in his lodge. Gowrie, at Ludovick's announcement, frowned.

'Stay here, my lords,' he called. 'I will go up and discover the verity of all this.' He hurried off.

Mar and some of the others were already mounting, but the Duke declared that he was quite sure that the King had not gone, that it was all some stupid mistake started by a servant. Nevertheless, he was uneasy. The entire affair was so strange and indeed nonsensical that there was obviously more behind it than met the eye. He did not wish to break the royal confidence by enlarging upon the ridiculous story of the pot of gold.

Gowrie had just come hurrying back, saying that he could see no sign of the King or of his brother in the long gallery or elsewhere upstairs, and that it looked as though they must indeed have ridden forth, when there was a dramatic development. There was the sound of a window being thrown open directly above them, and then the King's voice sounded, high-pitched, excited, and even more indistinct than usual.

'Treason! Treason!' it cried. 'Help! Vicky! Johnny Mar! Help! I am murdered!'

At least, that is approximately what most thought had been cried, for there was no certainty about it. Not unnaturally, for as they all stared upwards at the small window of the round turret, it was to see the King's agitated and indeed contorted face there-at, with a hand at his throat, his mouth – whether his own hand or another's was impossible to tell at this angle. James was hat-less and his thin hair awry.

Immediately, of course, there was pandemonium, as men shouted, cursed, threw themselves down from horses, and rushed for the house door. Ludovick ,who had not been mounted, led the way. He ran indoors and leapt up the main stairway. At the second-floor landing, above the hall, he came to the door of the same long gallery off which had opened the library where he and Mary had had their interview with the Earl a month before – and from the far end of which the turret chamber must open. The door was locked.

Mar and the others came panting up as the Duke beat upon the door's panels.

Ludovick was desperately looking round for something to use to force or break down the heavy door. A small ladder lying on the landing, for access to a loft trap-door, was all that he could see. Grabbing it, he and others began to better it against the timbers. But without avail. The ladder's wood was less solid than that of the door and broke away.

'Hammers! Axes!' Mar shouted. 'God's death – find axes! Where's Gowrie?'

'It's a plot! A trap! Gowrie will be in it.'

'The other stair,' Ludovick cried, as he continued with his battery. 'The Black Turnpike! The turret stair. Try that . . .'

Lord Lindores and some others ran off downstairs again, to seek Gowrie, axes and the small back stairway.

Some were still down in the courtyard, including Gowrie him-self, who seemed to be completely bewildered by the sudden crisis and clamour. Sir Thomas Erskine, a cousin of Mar's, after shouting encouragement to the King above – whose face had now disappeared from the turret window, but whose shouts could still be heard suddenly swung on the young Earl.

'Traitor!' he cried. 'Traitor! This is your work!'

His brother, James Erskine, a Gentleman of the Bedchamber, leapt forward to grab Gowrie at one side, Sir Thomas at the other. The Earl did not resist them at first, only crying out

353

that he knew nothing of it all, what had happened and what it meant.

The gate-porter and other of Gowrie's servants could not stand by and see their lord mishandled. They flung themselves upon the Erskines and freed Gowrie. That young man, seeing Lindores and others come running upon him, from the house, backed alarmedly out into the street, panting. Then, in a sudden access of courage or fury, he ran back, snatching out the gate-porter's sword from its scabbard and crying that he would take charge in his own house or die in the doing of it. His equerry, Cranstoun, now also drew sword, and men fell back before their flickering blades as these two raced for the turret stair nearby.

Meanwhile, at the head of the main stair, Ludovick was still battling fruitlessly with the locked door. Somebody brought a heavy poker from the hall fireplace, and this, when inserted between door and jamb, using the broken ladder as fulcrum, looked as though it might effect an entrance. He thought that he could hear shouting from within as well as from without, which led him to believe that the King's murder was, at least, as yet incomplete.

Mar had arrived with a mattock from the garden, and somebody else with a great lump of stone with which to assail the lock. All the door's attackers, however, got much in each other's way, and Ludovick's curses were not all for the stoutness of the timbers and lock. In the event, while still the door withstood their efforts, shake as it did, they heard a great outcry from within, the sound of many upraised voices. Clearly an entrance had been gained elsewhere.

A few moments later the hinges of the door began to give, before the lock, and furious blows soon had it swinging open drunkenly from the top. Staggering, the batterers struggled through into the long gallery.

At the far end, where the turret room opened, men were milling about. King James was one, dress in disorder, wild-eyed, blood on his sleeve. He was clutching the arm of John Ramsay his page, and of all things appeared to be trying to catch a hooded hawk which was fluttering about trailing its chain. Ramsay had had the bird, the King's favourite goshawk, on his wrist all day. The same Ramsay, the only member of the King's party who had been equipped with a sword, now bore this naked in his hand – and no two glances were needed to see that it was bloodstained. One other drawn sword was in evidence. It was no longer the Earl who carried it, however, but Sir Thomas Erskine. And this sword was bloodied also. Lindores and others, who had followed Gowrie and Erskine up the small back stairway, were in agitated movement around the monarch. One man knelt on the floor – Herries the physician.

Ludovick ran forward to the King's side. 'You are safe, Sire? Unhurt?' he panted.

James was far too excited to answer, or even to hear. But it was evident that the blood spattered upon his person was not his own, and that however distressed he was not seriously injured. He was gabbling incoherently, now stroking Ramsay's arm, now making ineffectual grabs at the blinded, bewildered hawk, and now pointing back into the turret chamber.

Ludovick was about to hurry therein when he all but fell over the kneeling Herries – and was brought up short by what he saw when he glanced down. The physician was examining a body on the floor, twisted and crumpled – that of John Ruthven, third Earl of Gowrie. As the Duke stared, he had a vivid mind-picture of another body that he had once gazed down at, some years before, in similar conditions, state and posture, and another earl likewise – that of James Stewart, Earl of Moray, the Queen's friend. The Earl of Gowrie was not so handsome as the bonny Earl of Moray – but he was equally dead.

Feeling sick, Ludovick mumbled, 'Who . . . who did this?'

At his side, Lindores answered him. 'Ramsay. Johnnie Ramsay. We came up the wee stair. The King named him traitor. Gowrie. Said had he come to do what his brother hadna been able to do? Gowrie had his sword, but when the King cried on him he dropped his point. Ramsay ran him through. Aye, through the heart. A shrewd stroke, by God!'

'God!' Ludovick echoed. He stared from the body to the gabbling monarch, to the young, brilliantly smiling Ramsay with the reeking weapon, and back to the corpse on the floor. 'And the other?' he faltered, all but whispered from dry lips. 'His brother? The Master?'

Lindores jerked an eloquent head towards the turret room,

from the window of which James had called for help. The Duke strode therein.

The little room was bare, empty – but the floor-boards were shockingly splashed and befouled with gouts of blood. At one side, a lesser door stood open, also blood-smeared. From this the narrow turnpike stair descended. And lying asprawl on the steps, head downwards, arms outflung, was the body of Alexander Ruthven, the Master, hideously butchered.

As Ludovick gazed, a groan escaped his lips. At his elbow Lindores, who had followed him in, spoke.

'We came on him as we came up. He wasna dead then – though sair stricken. Tam Erskine finished him off wi' the man Cranstoun's whinger. He was struggling wi' the King, Ramsay says – this Sandy Ruthven. Another man too. Ramsay was right quick to find this bit stair. He was the first here. Aye, and ready wi' his blade, seize me!'

'Aye. Ready with his blade!' the Duke repeated slowly, grimly, and turned back towards the gallery, heavy at heart.

Somebody had caught the ridiculous goshawk and it was now secured again at Ramsay's bloody wrist. Everyone was talking loudly, the King loudest of all, in a jumbled, breathless stream, recounting the dire nature of the attack upon him, declaring the wicked and vile treachery of the Ruthvens, and making much both of his own courageous resistance and the valour and vigour of his deliverers, Ramsay and Sir Thomas Erskine. It was noticeable that it was on these two that he showered his encomiums, the two who held dripping swords in their hands, touching and fondling them – James Stewart, who had never been able to abide the sight of either blood or naked steel. Noticeable too, to the Duke at least, that Erskine received almost as much praise as young Ramsay, despite the fact that he had done little more than the rest of them in rescue, other than apparently wantonly stabbing at both Ruthven brothers' bodies after they had been laid low by the martial page.

Ludovick did not join in the flood of excited exclamation, congratulation and question. His mind was busy in a number of directions, somewhat numbed as it was by the sudden and ghastly tragedy. He looked at the flushed and grinning Ramsay, a slender youth of no more than eighteen, and it came to him that he had not seen him in the garden with the others, after the meal. With that hawk on his wrist, he would have been apt to catch the eye.

Perhaps, even in his elevated state, the King noticed his cousin's silence, for he suddenly turned to him – and the glance he gave him was strange indeed, sly almost, with triumph and something that might have been fear commingled.

'Vicky – are you no' blithe to see me? Safe delivered? Frae this most vile attack. And conspiracy – aye, conspiracy. Did the Almighty no' confound my enemies quite, and deliver them into my hand? Should we no' a' give thanks? Wasna Johnny Ramsay here raised up as a tower o' strength against the wicked? Aye, strength and fury.'

'He was certainly sufficiently furious, with his sword! Your Grace's safety is cause for rejoicing, yes. But was it necessary that they should be slain? That both the Ruthvens should die?'

'You ask that! O' traitors? Treacherous miscreants! Yon Sauny had hands on me, man – violent hands. On me, the King!'

'He attacked you, Sire?'

'Aye. Wi' most murderous intent.'

'But he was not armed, Sire. He wore no weapons.'

'Eh? Eh? Hech, man – what o' that? He put his hands on me, to my throat. He could ha' throttled me, could he no'?'

'But why should he seek to do any such thing? What would it serve young Ruthven to throttle the King? Alone with you in this small room? Do you believe, Sire, that he brought you here to strangle you?'

'How should I ken, Vicky? But he laid hands on his King.'

'So Ramsay found you so, and slew him out of hand? Unarmed as he was?'

'Aye. But . . . but there was another man. Another man in it. And he was armed, Vicky. A right savage and terrible man. Standing there!' James pointed vaguely into the turret room.

'So you were *not* alone with the Master?'

'No. There was this other. When we came in here. I dinna ken who he was. Armed. Wi' mail beneath his coat. Eh, Johnny?'

'That is so, Sire. A stranger. Wearing mail,' the page answered promptly.

'So Ramsay slew the unarmed man, and left the armed one!

357

What then, Sire? Where is this stranger now?'

'Houts – how should I ken that? He went off. In the stramash. I didna see where. I was right put about . . .'

'If he went off, he could only have gone down the turnpike stair here – since the gallery door was still locked. From the inside. Others came up that stair, but moments later. Did they see this man? Sir Thomas? Herries? Did you see him?'

Nobody could claim to have seen the mysterious stranger. But Erskine declared that he could have left the stair at the first floor landing and gone to hide elsewhere in the house.

'Aye – search the house!' James cried. 'Let no murderous plotters escape!' As some ran off to do his bidding, he turned on Ludovick. 'I mislike this, Vicky Stewart – aye, I mislike it! You sound more concerned for Sauny Ruthven than for your sovereign lord! When I'm new escaped frae the jaws o' death, here's you putting me to the question like a common felon! I'll no' have it!'

'Your pardon, Sire. I but seek to learn the full extent of the matter. For Your Grace's further safety and, h'm, repute.'

'You choose an ill time, then! Aye, and you werena so timeous, back there! In coming to my rescue, Vicky Stewart! I could ha' been throttled quite, for a' *your* haste!'

'H'rr'mm.' The Earl of Mar, who had been equally held up by the locked door, intervened. 'We couldna get in, Sire. The door was steikit. But there's no profit in this. We've more to do than talk, I say. The main matter is that this, this carrion's dead!' And he spurned the fallen Gowrie with his boot-toe. 'But there may be more to it than this. A further attempt against Your Grace. These two would not be the only ones. We'd be safer out o' this town o' Perth, I'm thinking.'

'Aye, you're right. That's more wise-like talk than the Duke's, my lord! But first, my friends – let us give thanks to God for His most notable mercy and deliverance. On your knees, sirs, as becomes guid Christian gentlemen.' And leaning on Erskine's arm, the monarch got down on his knock-knees beside the crumpled body of his slain host. All, however reluctant and embarrassed, must needs get down with him, Ramsay the slayer, hawk on wrist, with the rest.

At this precise moment the bells of St. John's Kirk began to ring, to be followed almost immediately by other bells. 'See you – the very bells canna contain themsel's, my lords!' James declared, uplifted. 'Shall we let them outdo us in thanks to our Maker?' And composing his voice to its most pious, the King addressed the most high protector of kings and support of princes, thanking Him for a truly miraculous deliverance and victory. He acknowledged that he had most evidently been preserved from so desperate a peril in order to perfect some great work to God's glory. Developing this theme enthusiastically, he went into a sort of court of enquiry, there on his knees, as to what this work might be, coming to the eventual conclusion that it must be the bringing of both the peoples that the Almighty had entrusted to his care, the Scots and the English, to a proper understanding of how they should be governed in unity, in church as in state.

How much more detailed the revelation afforded by this curious act of worship would have grown, only James and possibly his Maker knew. But the thick and unctuous voice was now having to compete with more than the clangour of bells; another sound arose, which grew louder and more strident rapidly, and set all men glancing uneasily towards the windows At length, carried away by his devotions and visions as he was, the King became aware of it, and faltered to a stop. It was the sound of many voices, upraised, the voice of a crowd and undoubtedly an angry crowd.

Hardly had the royal words ceased than men were scrambling to their feet and hurrying to the windows at the end of the gallery and in the turret, which overlooked the street of the Speygate. A mass of townsfolk were approaching, filling the narrow thoroughfare, and being added to every moment by others flooding out from each wynd and vennel, townsfolk in an ugly mood, most evidently.

'The bells werena just for thanksgiving, then!' Mar commented grimly.

'They've heard!' Herries exclaimed. 'Somebody has told them. That the Earl is dead.'

'He was provost here. The Ruthvens – they have a great following in this town...'

'The gate!' Ludovick interrupted sharply. He ran to the

turret window, pushing aside others there, to lean out and look down. The courtyard gate still stood open to the street. Neither the porter nor any of the Gowrie servants were to be seen. Two or three townsmen stood out there, gazing in, but nobody appeared to have entered as yet.

One or two of the royal party's grooms were standing about the yard. 'That gate! Shut and bar it!' the Duke cried to these. 'Haste you. Do not stand gaping there! Get it shut – if you value your skins!'

He was only just in time. The startled grooms had barely got the massive double doors closed and were sliding the heavy greased oaken beams out of their deep sockets to bar them, before the crowd was surging and seething at the other side, yelling and banging on the timbers. In the forefront of the throng were the gate-porter himself and two others in the Ruthven colours.

There was no doubt as to the hostility of the mob, nor of the reason for it. To the accompaniment of much fist-shaking and brandishing of weapons, the shouts of 'Murderers! Assassins!' and the like arose. Some stones came up, and broken glass tinkled to the floor.

Ludovick held up his hand for silence, trying to speak to the crowd. But they would not listen to him, although he shouted that he was the Duke of Lennox, Admiral of the Realm, and that the King himself was within. At length he desisted. The gate remained secure, and the high courtyard wall would keep out intruders so long as they did not bring ladders to scale it.

Turning back, he discovered the King to be a changed man, his exaltation gone and replaced by a trembling, mumbling fear. 'Tullibardine!' he kept repeating. 'Where's Tullibardine?'

'Your Grace must needs speak to them,' Ludovick urged 'They will perhaps heed you, the King. If you show yourself, it may quieten them. Gowrie was popular, good to his people. They have heard that he is foully murdered . . .'

'Na, na – I'll no' can speak to them, Vicky. No' to yon yowling limmers! I canna do it. If Tullibardine would but come, wi' his Murrays . . .'

'The Lord Murray? What of him? Why should he be here, Sire?'

The King darted a glance at him, nibbling his nails. 'His house is no' that far away, is it no'? He has plenty o' men, to come to my aid.'

'He cannot know that you need help. His house is miles away. You must speak to these folk, Sire. Quietly. Firmly. Tell them that there has been attack upon your person. But that you trust the burghers of Perth. Say that all is now in order. Command that they retire to their homes. They will not heed me, but you they may obey.'

With the greatest of reluctance James was led to the turret window. At sight of him, however, the yells and jeers redoubled, and he shrank back at once, and nothing would bring him forward again.

'Murderer!' someone screamed. 'You murdered the faither! Now you murder the sons!'

'Come down, son o' Seigneur Davie!' another mocked. 'You've slain an honester man nor yoursel'!'

'Aye – gie us our provost. Or the King's green coat shall pay for it!'

James retreated to the farther side of the gallery in an agony of apprehension. Mar went to the window and leaning out shook his fist at the mob.

'Fools that we were, to ride unarmed!' he stormed. 'Wi' two-three hagbuts we'd send these curs scuttling to their kennels!'

But they had no firearms, and only two swords to the entire party. A search of Gowrie House might discover one or two more – but clearly they were not going to be in a position to withstand an attack by the townsfolk. It would be only a question of time, with the crowd in this temper, until they found their way over the courtyard wall.

'The back gate?' Ludovick suggested. 'The gate His Grace was said to have left by.'

A visit of inspection was made to this rear exit, only to find that a smaller crowd was congregated behind this high wall also. But Ludovick learned from the terrified Cranstoun, the Gowrie equerry, held close by some of the King's people, that there was a third way out of the establishment – the river gate, a seldom used postern at the bottom of the garden which opened on to the river bank. A boat or two lay there, for catching the Tay salmon.

Investigation revealed nobody in sight outside this gate, save a couple of small boys playing by the waterside. But the boats were small and would not take the entire royal party save in relays – and without their horses. The King, in consequence, although anxious to be anywhere but in Gowrie House, would not hear of making a bolt for it and having to entrust himself to his own two feet across the river. He was, in fact, now rapidly nearing the stage where it would be impossible to do anything with him.

It was at this impasse that an alteration in the quality of the noise and shouting from the streets revealed a new development. From the house windows the cause of this could not at first be ascertained but soon it became evident that the crowd was now becoming agitated on another score – its own safety. Which could only mean that it was being assailed somewhere by another and possibly more powerful faction. Presently the clattering of shod hooves on cobblestones proclaimed that the newcomers were mounted. The packed throng in the Speygate began to surge and eddy and thin out.

Then a large troop of men-at-arms, their armour glinting in the watery late afternoon sunshine, came into view from the south, the other direction from the river, forcing their way with the flats of their swords. A banner at their head fluttered blue with the three white stars of Murray.

'It's Tullibardine!' Mar cried. 'God save him – I have never loved John Murray but I'll shake him by the hand this day!'

'Aye,' the King muttered. 'Aye. He's no' before his time, the man!'

Ludovick turned to consider his cousin pensively.

Soon John Murray, Lord Tullibardine, was sitting his horse beneath the turret window, in the midst of his tight steel-clad company, but with the Perth crowd still in evidence all round and beginning to raise their voices again. Clearly he was not happy about his position and not wishful unduly to provoke the townsfolk – who, after all, outnumbered his troop twenty to one. To his invitation that the King should come down and be escorted to safety through the streets by the Murrays, James would by no means agree. He would not even allow the great gate to be opened to allow either Sir John in or himself out. Instead, it was arranged that he should now slip quietly out by the river gate, to be rowed across Tay, and there to be met by half of the Murray company whilst the rest maintained their present position in front of the main gates as a blind.

So, at last, the King of Scots left Gowrie House, furtively, in fear and in scowling silence. He was in ill temper with all, even with Lord Tullibardine his rescuer – and as for the Duke of Lennox he did not so much as address a word to him all the weary ride back to Falkland. Not that that young man was in any cheerful or conversational mood himself, having a sufficiency of dark thoughts of his own to occupy his mind.

In one of the King's few remarks, however, that now wet and gloomy evening, Ludovick did take a keen and silent interest. They were nearing Falkland, Lennox riding close behind James, when the latter beckoned one of the escorting Murrays, Sir Mungo, to his side, and spoke low-voiced, urgently. Ludovick could not hear just what was said, although he did distinguish the word Dirleton. Neither did Murray hear, however, and the monarch had to raise his voice.

'I said, I have a task for you, Mungo,' he declared, and this time the Duke missed nothing. 'Take fresh horses frae my stables at Falkland, and ride you, wi' some o' your lads, this night. For Dirleton. In Lothian. The auld bitch, Gowrie's mother, and her two other sons, are biding at their castle o' Dirleton. I want them, Mungo. They're just laddies – but the ill blood's in them. Young vipers frae the same nest! Arrest them a' – the Countess, too. In the King's name. Before they get word o' this, and flee. You understand, Mungo? We'll make an end o' the Ruthvens. It's an ill night for riding – but you'll be none the poorer for it, man, I promise you!'

'Yes. Sire. Dirleton. Near to North Berwick. I know the house. But it is a far cry – twenty-five miles to Stirling, thirty-five more to Edinburgh. Then twenty beyond. Perhaps better by early morning light . . .'

'No – tonight, man. Tonight, I said. Ride to the Queensferry. Rouse the ferrymen. In my name. That will save near thirty miles.'

'Very well, Your Grace...'

Ludovick hurried straight to his quarters in the Palace of Falkland, demanding his page, Peter Hay – which young man had to be ravished from the company of some of the Queen's ladies.

'Peter – you have some fondness for the Lady Beatrix Ruthven, I understand?' the Duke said, without preamble. 'Aye – then you have opportunity to serve her, poor lassie. The Earl and the Master, her brothers, are dead. Foully slain. Ask me not how – not now. You must ride forthwith. Secretly and fast. For Dirleton Castle, in Lothian. To her mother and the two young boys, her remaining brothers. They are in gravest danger. Tell the Countess to flee with them. To England, or where she will. But at once. Before morning. They are to be arrested. You understand? Sir Mungo Murray is on his way to take them. In the King's name. If he does, God help them! You must reach them first. Ride to Dysart – that is quickest. Ten miles only. Get a boat there, fishermen, or others. To put you across Forth. Here is money. If you have trouble, demand it in the name of the Lord Admiral. But... as secret as you may, or we both may suffer for it! Have the boat to put you in at the little landing behind Fidra Isle. Thence it is but a mile or so inland to Dirleton Castle. Ride at once, Peter – and you should be there much before Murray. He goes by the Queensferry. And Beatrix Ruthven will have cause to thank you...'

Chapter Twenty-one

With but surly assent, Sir David Murray obeyed Ludovick's peremptory command and ordered the half-troop of the Royal Guard to turn in, with their burden, towards Castle Huntly, from the Dundee road.

'The man's as good as dead, my lord Duke,' he said. 'You'll no' save him. And it was the King's command to bring him to Falkland forthwith.'

'He must have the chance, I say. To live. I take responsibility for this, sir. Besides, what use to the King is a dead man?' That last was purely rhetorical. The Duke knew as well as did Murray that Harry Younger was indeed of more use to the King dead than alive – for so at least he could not talk. That is why he now lay unconscious, bleeding from many stab wounds, tied like a gralloched stag on his own lathered horse that was led behind one of the guard.

The deed had been done perhaps three miles back, nearer Dundee. Younger, a far-out cousin of the Ruthvens, had been summoned to Falkland. But the very next day, the King, impatient, had sent this half-troop under Murray to fetch him from Dundee. Ludovick, seizing the chance and excuse to pay even a brief visit to Castle Huntly, and also hoping that he might be able to question the man before the King did, had volunteered to accompany the party – to no one's enthusiasm. They had met Younger himself, near Invergowrie, riding alone from Dundee to obey the royal summons. Murray had immediately treated him as a dangerous malefactor, insisting that he be bound there and then with ropes. Although Ludovick had declared vigorously that this was not necessary, Younger had taken fright, as well he might, and spurred off, apparently making a dash for the fastnesses of the Sidlaw Hills. Murray had engaged the Duke in altercation while the troopers raced after the fleeing quarry. When Ludovick had eventually caught up with them, in a corn-field, it was to find Younger lying below a stook, little better than a corpse. That it had been all arranged so was not difficult to perceive.

The Duke's presence gained them entry to Castle Huntly without delay, and Davy Gray came hurrying to meet them as they rode into the courtyard. One glance at the bleeding body on the horse and he took charge in his curt and efficient way, having the victim carried carefully into a chamber of one of the flanking towers, sending a groom hotfoot to Longforgan for the physician, and shouting for Mariota his wife to come and aid him and for Mary Gray to provide refreshment for the Duke and Sir David.

Ludovick's meeting with Mary therefore, the first since their abortive ride to Perth together, was again not as he would have wished it. He took her aside, as soon as he decently could do so, and left Murray to consume his regalement in his own company.

'Oh, Vicky!' she burst out, whenever they were alone. 'Here is evil! That poor man – he cannot live. He is almost gone, now. What wickedness is this? How come you to be in it? Here, in the Carse?'

Briefly he told her, stroking her dark hair and holding her to him.

'So it is more of this of Gowrie!' she whispered. 'That shameful savage work! That terrible sin is not done with, yet!'

He shook his head. 'Far from it, I fear, Mary. Gowrie's and his brother's deaths were only a beginning. There will be much ill done yet, before the cup is full, I believe.'

'But why, Vicky? Oh, why? What does it all mean. Has the King run mad indeed? I know so little of it. Only what you told me in your letter. And the common talk. How does all this murder help the King?'

'It is that bloodshed breeds bloodshed. Mouths must be closed. Some men bought to keep them quiet. Others quieted thus! Having set his hand to evil, James must needs continue in it, lest men learn the truth. This man died, I think, because the mysterious armed stranger whom the King says was in yon turret at Gowrie House with the Master, has to be found. To colour the King's story. I do not believe that any such man existed – therefore a dead man, a relative of the Ruthvens, is

366

better witness than one who could still talk! Especially if he can be said to have fled, in guilt, when being taken before the King!'

'Dear God – so this man had done nothing? Was wholly innocent?'

'So I believe. As innocent as was Cranstoun, the equerry, who was executed. As were Craigengelt, Gowrie's steward, and the gate-porter. All arrested, tortured and hanged. Even Gowrie's old tutor, broken with the boot, to have him confess to a plot against the King, of which he could know nothing even if it had ever existed – which I do not for a moment credit. And there will be more – never doubt it!'

'But, Vicky – *why*? Why do you say there will be more?'

'Because the King's name and fame is at stake – and James perceives it. That is why he ordered bonfires to be lit on half the hills of Scotland, in celebration of his great deliverance! Why he ordered every church in the kingdom to hold services of thanksgiving, and the fifth day of August to be in all time coming a day of public rejoicing in the realm. Most of the Kirk has refused to obey, since all honest men cannot but doubt the King's story. So he is in fear and fury. And when kings are so, no man is safe. Any minister refusing to hold the thanksgiving service is now forbidden, under pain of death to preach in any pulpit – or even to come within ten miles of Edinburgh! Summonses of treason are issued against the two children, Gowrie's remaining brothers. Also their mother. Thank God that they escaped in time, to England! The very name of Ruthven is proscribed, forbidden to be used, written or spoken. Even the turret chamber in Gowrie House is pulled down and demolished. All to cover up James's guilt.'

'You are so certain, Vicky? That there is no truth in the King's story?'

'As certain as that I stand before you, Mary. I dare not say it to any but you – or my own head would roll, close to the throne as I am. It was a plot, yes – but *against* the Ruthvens, not by them. A plot in which a few carefully chosen men were concerted. With the King. Men who have been well rewarded indeed – and whose mouths are successfully stopped! One of them is in this house this moment. It was partly for that reason that I came with this company today.'

'You mean Sir David Murray?'

'Aye. The Murrays were in it. They ever envied the Ruthvens. Why else has this one been given the great Gowrie lands and lordship of Scone? For, of course, all the Ruthven estates and moneys are forfeit and confiscate. Why has Sir Mungo Murray been given Ruthven Castle – so long as he names it by another name? Tullibardine himself gets the Perth lands, Gowrie House and the Sheriffship of Perthshire. All this, that they do not talk. Explain how it was that they rode into Perth that afternoon a month ago, three hundred strong, in time to rescue their King – when they should not have known that he was not still hunting at Falkland? The Murrays were in it – although they were a little late! James was asking where Tullibardine was an hour before they appeared!'

'So false? All these?'

'Aye – and more than these. Sir Thomas Erskine, a kinsman of Mar's gets Dirleton Castle, the plum of it all. Aye, he is a great man now, the Lord Erskine of Dirleton no less! Which is strange, for he seemed to play a secondary part to young Ramsay – who is now, of course, Sir John Ramsay, with a handsome pension for life! I have not yet discovered why Erskine was the most favoured – when he only stabbed fallen, dying men! Perhaps Herries, the physician, could tell me – save that he also is now knighted, and laird of the fat barony of Cousland! Others too will remain silent for similar reasons.'

The girl shook her head. Then, staring out of the narrow, iron-grilled window, she spoke from tight lips. 'Vicky – in all these names there is one that you have not pronounced. Patrick's! Does it mean . . . is it that, for once, after all, Patrick is not one of them? It was against Patrick that we warned the Earl of Gowrie – not the King. Were we wrong? In all this, what of my father? What of Patrick Gray?'

'Well may you ask, Mary – what of Patrick Gray! Despite the fact that his hand is behind the King's in almost every matter of state, most men would say that Patrick is not concerned in this evil. At no point, that I have heard, does his name come into it. He was not there, nor at the hunt – for he seldom hunts. Indeed he had left Falkland for Broughty the day previous. I have not heard that he has gained anything of the Ruthven riches. And yet ... and yet ...'

'And yet what, Vicky? You believe otherwise?'

'Aye, Mary – I do. Leastways, it is not so much belief as instinct. Somewhere behind it all, I sense Patrick's hand. It is not just that we feared it ...'

'Might it not be? We feared it, yes – and so we must discover it – ? But – it may not be so, Vicky. After all, it is not like Patrick's work, all this. So bungled, so evidently false, so lacking in the subtlety with which he always acts.'

'I wonder. May not this be, rather, the greatest subtlety of all? That it may seem all to be the King's own doing. That Patrick himself must seem most assuredly to have no hand in it. That, this time, there be no whispers, no questions, no fingers pointing at *him* ...'

'But is that not *too* clever, Vicky? Are we not in danger of making him into a demi-devil, a nightmare? Seeing him in every shadow ...?

'Perhaps. There is that danger, yes. Often I tell myself so. But certain aspects of this matter, not in its carrying out but in its results, do point to Patrick, say to me that he *ought* to be concerned in it. Not only that nothing of great import touching the King happens without him knowing, if not arranging it. He has not sought at any point to halt this wicked course – as surely he would have done had it lacked his approval. But there is more than that. Queen Elizabeth, out of it all, has turned towards James. She has sent him the kindest letter, in her own hand, that she has written for long years. She declares her joy at his escape from death, assassination, and her horror of the attempt. And though she ends by warning him against anticipating her own funeral and intriguing with her courtiers regarding the succession, she does imply succession and signs herself His Grace's loving sister and cousin. This is esteemed to be a great step towards the English throne – goal of Patrick's policy. Elizabeth, ever since she ordered our Queen Mary's death, has been haunted by a terror of the violent death of princes. It is her great weakness, I think that Patrick played on it.'

'It could be, heaven knows! But also it could have happened otherwise.'

'It could – although we were looking for him to arrange something against Gowrie. That eighty thousand pounds of debt can now be forgotten, and much Ruthven silver added instead to the empty Treasury. There is that, also. But there is something else – something strange, which has the smell of Patrick to it. You remember how you spied Robert Logan at Perth, yon day? I told you how he was back at Court, his horning annulled. Now he is at the horn again, and fled abroad, a ruined man, all his goods and lands being forfeit to the Crown. For being art and part in the conspiracy of Gowrie!'

The young woman stared. 'But .. but . . . ? If there *was* no conspiracy? What can this mean? How can this point to Patrick, Vicky? Logan was ever Patrick's man. Does this, if it is true, not point against Patrick having plotted the business?'

'You think so, Mary? Remember Patrick's power in the land. He could have halted this new outlawry against Logan, had he wished – just as he had the old outlawry annulled. He has not done so. Why?'

'Perhaps Logan *was* intriguing with Lord Gowrie? On his own part, not Patrick's. For he was always a rogue...'

'Consider this, my dear. Just days before this new horning was proclaimed, and he disappeared to France or wherever he is, Logan signed deeds of sale of his estates. All except Fast Castle. And to friends of Patrick's. Elphinstone the Secretary got Restalrig, for eighteen thousand merks. And George Home the Berwickshire properties for forty-five thousand. Which moneys have not yet been paid. Nor ever will be, I reckon – since Logan and all his possessions are now outwith the law! You see what this means, Mary?'

She wrinkled her brows. 'Can it be . . . ? Can it mean that Patrick has deserted his henchman? Has thrown Logan to the wolves?'

'Aye – but more than that. It means that Patrick was privy to what was to take place regarding Gowrie – for he must have had Logan's part and implication arranged beforehand. And the sales of the lands drawn up. For all was done within a day or so of Gowrie's death. Patrick *must* have known.'

'Oh, Vicky! Can it be so?' She drew a long, quivering breath. 'It can, of course. How well we know that it can! How familiar the pattern.' Wearily she asked it. 'What was Logan's part? What was he supposed to have done, in the plot?'

'He was to have had a boat ready to carry the King captive, in Gowrie's power, to Fast Castle. To be held there, while Gowrie and his friends ruled the land in his name. The Ruthven Raid of 1582 again! Only, this time, a fable, a chimera without foundation, backed by forged letters. So one more is added to the list of those whom Patrick has betrayed – his own creature and tool! And I shall be surprised indeed if the revenues of Logan's lands – and that includes much of the town of Leith – despite the names of those who seem to have bought them, do not find their way into Patrick's pocket!'

Mary almost groaned. 'This, at least, sounds like my father!' she said.

The Duke nodded. 'Logan is scant loss. But, Mary – I said I feared that the evil was by no means finished yet, the cup not full.' He took her hand in his. 'I believe that there is much yet to come. Innocent folk still to suffer. It may be that I can do some little to halt it. With your help, my dear. As we have done before. I want you to help me. You, who are better able than any other. You cannot do so here, at Castle Huntly. Come back to Court, my heart – and work with me.'

Almost in panic, it seemed, for that usually so serene and assured young woman, Mary Gray looked at him. 'No, Vicky – ah, no! Not that. Do not ask me . . .'

'You are afraid? It is not like you, Mary, to be timorous, frightened.'

'I am afraid,' she nodded.

'Of what? Of whom? Not of me?'

'No – not of you. Of myself.'

Sombrely he gazed at her, for a moment. 'I think that you are wrong, Mary – all wrong. But . . . even so, be afraid for someone else, I say. Be afraid for Beatrix Ruthven, for one. She is your friend, is she not?'

'The Lady Beatrix! She . . . is she in danger also?'

'Need you ask? She is Gowrie's sister, still unmarried, and the last Ruthven left in Scotland. Only the Queen's protection has saved her hitherto. For the Queen declares openly that she disbelieves this of a conspiracy. She refuses to dismiss her lady-in-waiting. But . . . I fear for Beatrix. The King rages at her whenever he sees her. Declares that she poisons the Queen's mind against him. She is a simple creature, and requires a wiser head to advise her. Wiser than the Queen, or that sister of mine, Hetty. And I do not trust my . . . the Duchess. You could help her, Mary.'

She said nothing.

'And you could watch Patrick. As you have done before. As only you can do. You . . . you have hidden away here, Mary, for long enough.

She looked down at the stone-flagged floor. 'You think that?' she said, almost below her breath. 'Think that I hide myself here?'

'Yes, I do.' That was blunt, almost harsh.

Mary gulped. 'But . . . I cannot live with you. That is not possible. And the Queen would not have me back, even though I wished to go . . .'

'You can go back to lodging with Patrick. I saw the Lady Marie, his wife, before I came here. She said that I was to bring you back with me. She said that I was to tell you that she loved and needed you, sorely. That wherever they lodged, room awaited you. And Johnnie. She said that I was not to come back without you.'

'Marie said that? Sweet Marie! Dear Marie! But – Patrick . . . ?'

'He *is* your father.'

'But . . .'

Davy Gray came seeking them, grim-faced. 'Your prisoner is dead, my lord Duke,' he said. 'It was too late for aught we could do. Here was dastard's work, I think.'

Ludovick nodded. 'Well may you say so. God rest his soul. And God forgive the men who decided that his life was worth less than a black lie! Have you told Murray?'

'Aye. And he seemed no' ill-pleased, the man.'

'No doubt. Since he is little better than a hired assassin! A knightly cut-throat! Although he that hired him has the greater charge to answer.' He shrugged. 'At least I may spare myself the displeasure of his further company. He may carry his trophy back to his master at Falkland lacking my aid. I will go tell him so – and we shall breathe the sweeter air for his absence! Mary will give you the bones of the matter, sir.' And the Duke strode off to get rid of the unwelcome guest.

When he came back, presently, it was Davy who addressed him, heavily.

'I hear, my lord Duke, that you are to have your way! Or something of it. That Mary is going back to that den of iniquity, the King's Court. It is against my wish and counsel. But she is her own woman – not mine. Nor, my lord, any other man's! I'd mind you of that!'

'I do not need reminding, sir.' Ludovick could not keep the surging elation out of his voice. He turned to the girl. 'Mary – you have decided? I thank God!'

'Vicky – be not too thankful! I warn you – I have not changed my mind. I come only because my conscience will not allow me to stay here. That I may serve perhaps to counter a little of Patrick's wickedness, once more. That, if possible, I may aid the Lady Beatrix. I do not return as your mistress, Vicky. You understand? I shall not permit that you see overmuch of me ... or I of you! However great the temptation. And it will be a notable temptation, God knows – for I love you fully as hotly as you love me, my dear. But on this condition I come, and this alone – that even though tongues wag, as indeed they will, we remain ... we remain ...' Her voice broke.

He inclined his head. 'As you will, Mary.'

'You have a wife. And at Court. I will cheat no woman. Slight none – nor be slighted. Is ... is it a compact, Vicky?'

'It is a compact, my dear. At least I shall see your loveliness, hear your voice, share the same air you breathe. And hope – always hope.'

'That, at least, it is not in me to deny you, Vicky,' she said.

Chapter Twenty-two

The Parliament Hall in Edinburgh was crowded to suffocation point. But the smell of humanity and not over-clean clothing was sweet nevertheless, compared with that other stench. Ludovick, all but nauseated by both what his eyes and his nose told him, was astonished that the King seemed not at all affected, in either sense, and indeed leaned forward in his chair of state, avidly drinking in the scene and all that was said, apparently oblivious of the stink. It might have been noticed that, earlier, the Master of Gray, making an appearance at the door, had taken one glance at the packed assembly, wrinkled his fine nose in disgust, and straightway left the hall.

Not only King James was sitting forward now. There was a stir of urgent interest throughout the entire great chamber, as the Lord Advocate, Sir Thomas Hamilton, the gross, coarse but shrewd Tam o' the Cowgate as his monarch delighted to name him, called what all understood would be the key figure of this strange trial, to the witness stand.

'I call Andrew Henderson, lately chamberlain to the accused,' he rumbled. 'Andrew Henderson to the stand, to testify, I say.'

Then came a murmur of disappointment from all around. Here was anti-climax indeed. An utterly unknown name, a mere nonentity, a house-steward! Rumour had been busy with all sorts of impressive identities for this so important witness, found after long searching, the mysterious stranger on whose testimony it was believed the King's case would be established. Even Ludovick himself was surprised. He had never so much as heard the name of Andrew Henderson.

Nor was the man, whom the guards now ushered in, any more impressive than his name and style. A small, tubby, ruddy-featured individual, with sparse, receding hair and anxious, indeed hunted expression, he came in, bowing obsequiously to all whom he could see, all but prostrating himself before the burly figure of the Lord Advocate – but curiously, quite overlooking the King, the only hatted person present, in his chair at the side of the court – until, that is, Hamilton roared out his omission, pointing an imperious finger, when the little man doubled himself up in his agitation, to the titters of the crowd. He was thereafter hustled to the witness-stand.

After administering the oath to the trembling man, Hamilton declaimed, 'You are Andrew Henderson, until the fifth day o' August last chamberlain and house-steward to the accused John, Earl o' Gowrie, at Gowrie House in Saint John's Town of Perth?'

'Aye, sir. Aye, my lord. That is so. Aye.'

'You recognise and identify the panel? Aye – both o' them?'

'Eh . . . ? What's that? I . . . I dinna take you, my lord?'

'Recognise, I said. Identify. Your master. The accused. And his brother. Look, man – and tell the court.' And again the Lord Advocate threw out a pointing hand to accompany his bellowed command. This time he pointed to another corner of the cleared central well of the hall, flanking the witness-stand, so that Henderson had to turn to peer – and turning, all but choked in strangled horror, the blood draining from his ruddy face. It appeared indeed that he could have slid to the floor had not the guards grabbed and supported him.

At the bar of the court, two figures sat – or, at least, were propped up – the grey face of one seeming to grin toothily in hollow-eyed mirth, the other to sleep, the decomposing bodies of the brothers John and Alexander Ruthven, former Earl and Master of Gowrie, dead for fourteen weeks.

Henderson, being for the moment in no state to make coherent answers, his recognition was taken for granted, and Sir Thomas declared in sonorous tones that this Andrew Henderson, apprehended at Gowrie House on the 5th of August last and confined in the Tolbooth of Edinburgh since, on charge of treason as having been art and part in the murderous and desperate attempt on the life of their beloved sovereign Lord James, by the grace of God, King, Protector of Christ's Holy and True Kirk, the said Andrew Henderson had of his own free will and decision sent a letter from the said Tolbooth to Master Patrick Galloway, Minister of the Gospel, declaring that he it was who was the armed and mail-clad man present with Alexander, Master of Gowrie in the turret-chamber of Gowrie House, on the occasion of the wicked and treasonable attack upon the King's Majesty. In consequence of which letter, a deposition had been taken from the said Andrew Henderson, and thereafter His Grace had been graciously pleased to waive and revoke the aforesaid summons for treason against him in order that he might give proper and lawful evidence, according to the laws of this realm, at this the trial of the said John and Alexander, formerly Earl and Master of Gowrie.

Ludovick could scarcely believe his ears. Was anyone expected to believe this masquerade and mummery? Was this the best that they could do? Was this frightened little man the savage and terrible armed stranger who had allegedly played so strange a part in that turret-chamber? Henderson, the house-steward! Who had escaped so mysteriously down the Black Turnpike? And if Henderson, what of Harry Younger? That unhappy individual seemed to have died entirely in vain.

The Lord Advocate having given the witness time to recover from his shock, now began his examination. But Henderson was clearly not of the stuff of heroes, and was much too overcome by the grisly presence of his late master's corpse to make a satisfactory witness. He mumbled and mowed, mis-heard and mistook, and ever his eyes were drawn round to the horror at the bar of the court. Eventually, in disgust, Sir Thomas had to content himself with perfunctorily asking the witness to confirm its truth, and accepting any sort of reaction, gabbled incoherences, nods, blank stares or complete silence, as confirmation.

The story he pieced together was little more convincing than was the witness. Henderson deponed that on the early morning of the 5th of August last he had ridden to Falkland from Perth with the Master of Gowrie, to seek interview with the King. The Master had informed His Grace that he had captured a suspected Jesuit priest with a hoard of gold pieces, and desired His Grace to come to Gowrie House to put the prisoner to the question. When the King agreed to do this, he, Henderson, had ridden on ahead with all speed, to inform the Earl that His Grace was on his way.

There was a stir of interest throughout the hall. This was the first public reference to the curious wayfarer with the pot of gold. Ludovick looked across the court, to find the King's eyes fixed upon himself. James had never told the rest of the courtiers this tale; as far as others knew, it was some hope of catching the elusive outlawed Master of Oliphant that had decoyed the King to Perth. This item of testimony, then, presumably had been put in to keep him, Lennox, quiet. Ludovick was puzzled. Also, he was sure that he had not seen the man Henderson at Falkland, or at the hunt – or indeed ever before in his life. And if the Earl of Gowrie was thus informed of the King's coming, why had he made no provision to entertain the royal party?

Sir Thomas Hamilton continued with his reading of the deposition. The Master of Gowrie, soon after his arrival with the King, had ordered Henderson to arm himself and wear a pyne-doublet, or vest of chain-mail, under his coat, and had then taken him to the turret-chamber and there locked him in. Later, after dinner, he had come back, bringing His Grace, and again locking the doors behind him. His Grace had mistaken him, Henderson, for the Jesuit priest, but the Master had delayed no longer with play-acting. Laying hands on the King's person, he had cried out that he was now in his power, that this man was armed and ready to use his weapons, and that the King must do as he was told. Henderson here had inserted a telling touch of dialogue. 'Sir, you must be my prisoner,' the Master had declared. 'Remember on my father's death!'

King James thumped his staff on the floor at this quotation, apparently much moved. The Lord Advocate bowed towards him, as though in receipt of applause. The Lord President Seton and his fellow Lords of Session on the Bench, nodded in shocked concern.

The witness, seemingly enheartened by the impression his composition was making, gained a better possession of his faculties and even went so far as to interject that he had not known that it was His Majesty that he was to be armed against, that he had indeed understood that he was to apprehend some Highlandman.

'Ha! So you've found your tongue, my mannie!' Tam o' the Cowgate commented. 'You'll maybe answer my questions now, more like an honest Christian! Will you tell the court what

377

was the Master of Gowrie's intention in laying hands upon his liege lord's sacred person?'

'It was to capture and carry off His Majesty, sir. Aye, carry off. To hale him awa' to the Laird o' Restalrig's house. To Fast Castle, on the Border. The same as his father did, mind, lang syne, when he held the King's Grace at Ruthven Castle. That was . . .'

'Silence, man! Have a care of your words. You have used a name that is forbidden and proscribed by law!' Sir Thomas turned to the King, and then to the Bench. 'Your Grace – my lords – I crave your indulgence for this witness. This once. He was carried away by the thought of the odious attack on Your Grace.'

Graciously the King waved a hand, and the judges inclined sage heads.

'So the King's Grace was to be captured and taken to Fast Castle? There to be held by the prisoners at the bar and that outlawed rogue Robert Logan, formerly of Restalrig? How was this to be achieved, man?'

'Eh . . . ? In a boat, my lord.' Henderson was flustered again. 'He . . . His Majesty was to be bound fast. And carried down the Black Turnpike. To the side gate. There two men were waiting wi' horses . . .'

'Two men? What men?'

Henderson hesitated, and glanced at the King. 'Hugh Moncrieff, sir. And Patrick Eviot. They had the horses at the side gate,' he said, in a rush.

'Hugh Moncrieff and Patrick Eviot. Aye – we'll no' forget their names! But you didna take to horse, with His Grace a prisoner? Why?'

'The King, sir. He got to the bit window. And shouted. The Master pulled him back. Then the laddie . . . the young gentleman Ramsay. He came up the turnpike. Into the turret yon way. He had a whinger in his hand. He ran the Master through.'

'That door was open, then? The turnpike door wasna locked?'

'Eh . . . ? I . . . ah . . . I dinna ken. No. No, it couldna have been . . .'

From across the court the monarch's own thick voice spoke. 'Locked frae the *outside*, man – the outside! Johnnie Ramsay turned the key and came in.'

'H'rr'mmm.' The Lord Advocate, with a darted glance towards the Bench, bowed hurriedly to the King, and resumed, 'And you, man? What did you do then?'

'Me, my lord? I wanted no part in it. No. no. God kens I was innocent o' any o' it! As John Ramsay sworded the Master, me, I ran out the way he had come in. Doon the turnpike and awa', afore any should take me. Out the gate and into the town.'

'Aye – a right heroic course! That is a' you have to say relative to the matter? In which case ...'

'I never kenned there was to be aught against the King in it, sir. I thought ...'

'Quite, quite. But the court isna interested in your thoughts, my man. You may stand down.' Sir Thomas seemed suddenly, perhaps understandably, anxious to be done with the witness. 'Take him hence,' he directed the guards.

As Ludovick watched the stumbling, unhappy Henderson bowing himself out, he marvelled that in fourteen weeks, and with half of the realm to choose from, James had not been able to produce a more eloquent witness and at least more convincing liar. After all, almost anyone would have served equally well, and many better, to represent the unknown and terrible stranger in the turret.

Even though it was only to bear corroboratory evidence, as Hamilton now declared, the next witness was indeed more eloquent. Master Patrick Galloway was called, and strode through the hall in his black gown, to mount the witness stand as though it was his own pulpit. He scarcely allowed the Lord Advocate to enunciate his identification questions before he lurched forth into full and resounding flood.

Yes, he was Patrick Galloway, as all men knew, shepherd of Christ's erring sheep, and chaplain to His Grace. Yes, he it was who had been God's chosen messenger and humble emissary in this matter, in that it was to himself that the wretched Andrew Henderson, tool of the traitors before them, had decided to confide his part in the foul and shameful conspiracy against the King's Majesty, writing to him the letter which proved him to be the armed accomplice of the vile plotters now arraigned at the bar to receive the court's verdict on their wickedness – God Himself having already pronounced and carried out *His* verdict on their sinful bodies, and no doubt now dealing justly and terribly with their thrice-damned souls.

Master Galloway proved himself to be a bolder as well as more fluent witness than the other, by pointing a long and jabbing finger directly at the two Ruthven corpses, and plunging into a thunderous condemnation of their enormities, concentrating more especially on the elder brother, who admittedly had been somewhat neglected hitherto, declaring that not only was he a would-be regicide and traitor, but an incarnate devil in the coat of an angel, a studier of magic and a conjuror with devils, many of whom he had at his command – a revelation which had James rubbing his hands and the company agog. Thereafter, completely ignoring the Lord Advocate's attempts to get a word in, he proceeded to curse the accused, jointly and severally, in detail and in general, their name, their forebears, their kin and memory, comprehensively, scorchingly, breathlessly, hand raised high. Lack of breath, indeed, alone seemed to bring the denunciation to a close. And without a glance at Hamilton, the judges or even the King, he stepped down unbidden from the stand and stalked out, head high, beard bristling.

As the crowded hall seethed and surged in emotive reaction, Sir Thomas, who himself would not have been where he was had he not been something of a showman, perceived that to call other and lesser corroboratory evidence now would but lower the temperature and create anti-climax, wound up briefly and succinctly by resting his case upon their lordships' sure judgement and demanding the maximum penalty within the court's power to impose.

The Lord President raised his hand to still the clamour, and with scarcely a glance at his fellow judges, proceeded in a broad and matter-of-fact voice to read a previously written judgement. The court, after full consideration of the evidence, found the said John and Alexander, sometime Earl and Master of Gowrie, guilty of highest treason. It passed sentence of forfeiture to the Crown upon all that they had possessed whatsoever, and declared their posterity infamous. The court further ordained that their bodies be taken forthwith to the Cross of Edinburgh and there hanged upon the common gibbet. Thereafter the said bodies were to be drawn and quartered at the said Cross, and the heads befixed upon the top of the Tolbooth, and their several members taken to the towns of Perth, Dundee and Stirling there to be affixed in the most patent places. God save the King.

James rose and nodded all around, grinning. Then patting his high feathered hat more firmly on his head, he commenced his teetering walk to the door. After a few paces, however, he paused, and looked across the well of the hall.

'Vicky,' he said loudly. 'I'm for the Cross. Come you wi' me, man.'

Stiff-lipped, Ludovick answered him. 'Sire – I pray you to excuse me. I fear that I have a delicate stomach!'

'Aye, Vicky Stewart – I'm thinking you have. Waesucks – sometimes ower delicate, I do declare! For a leal support o' the Crown. Come you, I said. Can you no' see they're a' waiting on us?'

Despite the short notice, the Master of Gray had worked wonders, and not even Nicolson, the English ambassador, always critical, could report that the evening was not a notable success, either the banquet or the masque and ball which followed. It seemed incredible that all should have been organised and arranged in two days – but there was no question that this was so, for the Queen's unexpected delivery of a second son had been a matter of weeks earlier than anticipated – some said brought on by shock at her husband's gleeful and graphic announcement to her of the disposal of the bodies of the Gowrie brothers; although this was probably a mere malicious canard set afoot by the same people who said that Her Grace had been over-fond of Alexander, the young Master. Be that as it may, the birth of the new Prince Charles had taken place the self-same night as that in which the unfortunate Ruthvens were dismembered and their heads spiked up atop the Tolbooth, not far from Holyroodhouse, to the cheers of the crowd – and old wives gloomily foretold that the young prince would be bound to suffer some derangement in consequence, some preoccupation with beheadings and dismemberments possibly.

Undoubtedly only Patrick Gray could have carried out the King's command to have this great entertainment two nights thereafter. It was a double celebration, to mark the birth of a second son, and to commemorate the King's miraculous escape from the Gowries. The Queen, of course, could not take part, but this was perhaps as well, for the royal partners were scarcely on speaking terms – this time over Anne's sustained refusal to dismiss the Lady Beatrix Ruthven, who lived more or less a prisoner in the Queen's apartments, afraid to venture out, Anne still declaring to all who dare listen that she believed nothing of her husband's story of the conspiracy, trial or no trial. However, James, after the banquet, had paraded the thronged Great Hall of Holyroodhouse with the new and bawling infant in his arms. Moreover he had at his side for most of the evening the seven-year-old Prince Henry, Duke of Rothesay, a weakly and frightened child, ridiculously over-dressed in velvet and sham jewels. The Scottish succession appeared to be assured; undoubtedly the English one was advanced thereby.

The entertainment, if scarcely up to Patrick's highest standards, was commended on all hands, the motif and theme being the royal fondness of the pursuits of the forest. Almost half of the vast hall was transformed into a forest glade, the trees and bushes – since it was mid-November – being evergreens and fir, hung with fairy lanterns. In and out amongst the greenery nymphs and satyrs flitted, roguishly enticing adventurous guests to sample their varied charms, embraces and delights. In the centre was a clearing in which arose a turfed mound, perhaps six feet in height, mounted by rustic steps, on the summit of which was an ingenious fountain, contrived in the form of a great bowl in which stood four naked figures, two male and two female, holding up pipes from which spouted red wine, pumped up by hidden, busy workers beneath the mound. From this happy source all might drink who would – and the surplus overflow splashed down into the bowl over the feet of the living statuary, and back into circulation.

Against this background were staged throughout the evening the usual tableaux, spectacles, charades, dances, feats of skill and mimicry, of a catholicity and cheerful variety, from flauntingly pagan to highly moral, to suit all tastes. A bearded Kirk divine, for instance, preaching furiously to a congregation of sketchily clad nymphs and goat-men, himself fully dressed in Geneva black gown and white bands in front but wholly unclothed behind, preceded an appearance of Sylvanus, the Wild Man of the Woods, uttering congratulatory verse to the royal parent and the new prince in stanzas both subtle and broad. And following on this came a mermaid with a ten-foot tail blowing Satan in front of her with puffs of wind, so that the crown-topped ship behind might come safe into Leith haven – a commentary on King James's single venture into heroics and the dangers of his journey to fetch his bride from Denmark.

Watching this last, and well back in a corner of the huge apartment, three people stood somewhat apart – the Duke of Lennox, the Lady Marie Stewart, Mistress of Gray, and Mary Gray. It was the first Court entertainment which Mary had attended for years, and despite her state of mind and all the circumstances, she could not but respond to it all in a pleasurable excitement. This was reflected in her sparkling eyes and vivid, alive loveliness; dressed in one of the Lady Marie's gowns, she was, as ever, drawing almost as many eyes as was the display. In consequence, Ludovick stood by in a fever of mingled pride, love and frustration. He saw so little of her, even now – for he could scarcely haunt the Master of Gray's quarters, where she lodged; and since she held no official position at Court and eschewed the giddy round, opportunities for meeting were not frequent, consistently as he sought to contrive them. Tonight, even, she would not have come, had she not been assured that the Duchess of Lennox, being in attendance on the Queen, would not be present.

'I wonder whether James ever senses the malice behind Patrick's masquerades and confections?' the Lady Marie murmured. She was drawing her own meed of attention, both as a maturely handsome woman of quiet but assured beauty, and also as wife of the powerful Master of Gray. 'How he ever seems to flatter – but always there is the sting, the mockery, their veiled contempt. As here. The mermaid playfully banishing the King's dread enemy, Satan, with such ease. The allusion that his fears were of naught, his terrors groundless. And yet, James seems to approve of it all. Look how he chuckles and simpers!'

'James, I swear, sees more than we credit, nevertheless,' Ludovick said. 'He has a shrewdness of his own that even Patrick would be wise to heed. A fool and a buffoon, he is, in some ways; but in others he is clever enough. Knowing. And a monster, God knows!'

'Softly!' Marie warned.

'Who is the mermaid?' Mary asked.

'The daughter of my new Lord Balmerino. Lately Sir James Elphinstone, the Secretary of State.'

'She is well-made. And fair.'

'Not as you are, Mary. She is not fit to hold a candle to your sun. Indeed, I cannot think of any other who is!'

She touched his arm lightly. 'You are prejudiced, Vicky! But leal. And ... lacking something in tact!'

Marie smiled. 'I say he is honest. Which is more than are most men. Moreover, I agree with his judgement.'

Ludovick was not listening. He had stiffened, his rather square and far from handsome features set. Weaving his way through the chattering, colourful throng, smiling, tossing a word here and there, but most evidently making for this retired corner, came Patrick Gray at his most brilliant.

Mary touched the Duke's arm again, but this time with a different pressure. The two men were now apt to avoid each other, even when in the same room.

'On my soul, what need is here for spectacle and lesser delights, when you two are present to be admired!' Patrick greeted the ladies. 'I might have spared myself a deal of trouble. Vicky – you choose excellent company, I'll say that for you.'

The younger man bowed, curtly, stiffly, and said nothing.

'Your spectacles and delights are very successful, nevertheless, Patrick,' his wife said. 'All appreciate and applaud. Even ... His Grace.'

He considered her. 'You think, perhaps, that His Grace might have reason to do otherwise, my dear?'

'I think that you should not mock him so obviously.'

'Obvious! Sink me – here is damnation indeed! To be obvious – that is anathema. I must be failing, I fear. You slay me, my heart, if you name my small efforts obvious. My aim, as you

384

should know, is to make my point by what I leave unsaid, rather than by what I say.'

'Aye!' That was Ludovick, brief but eloquent.

'I am glad that my lord Duke agrees with me in this small issue.'

'You can tie us up in words, Patrick, always – or, at least, Vicky and myself. With Mary it is otherwise! But heed me in this. It is dangerous, I think, even for you, so to mock and disparage the King.'

'Who says that I mock and disparage His Grace – save only you, sweeting?'

'It would be strange if you did not – since you do all others!' Ludovick said. 'To their sore cost.'

'Folly, Vicky, mocks and disparages itself. Digs its own pit...'

'Patrick,' Mary intervened. 'Have you spoken to the King about the Lady Beatrix? To urge that she be spared further hurt and hounding? You said that you would...'

'His Grace is very obdurate about that unfortunate family, my dear. He will hear no good of any of them. An interesting subject for philosophical inquiry. I fear that the daggers of my uncle Greysteil and his father, when they let the life out of David Rizzio in Queen Mary's presence, let something equally unpleasant into the unborn James. After all, the Italian was probably his father – since Henry Darnley was scarce capable of begetting offspring. And so the debt is worked off. The sins of the fathers...'

'But Beatrix can do the King no harm. An innocent girl.'

'That is not the point, Mary. She is Gowrie's sister, Greysteil's daughter, the old lord's grand-daughter. James sees her only through a veil of blood.'

'Nevertheless, you could save her if you would, Patrick. You *must* save her.'

Her father stroked his scimitar of moustache thoughtfully. 'I said that I would do what I can. I can make no promises...'

'What would they be worth, if you did?' Ludovick demanded. 'Since I have no doubt but that you were behind the fall of her brothers! However carefully you hid your hand. To talk of the sins of the fathers is surely sheerest hypocrisy.'

'Have a care what you say, Vicky!' That was very softly

385

spoken. 'I will stand only so much – even from such as you. Do not try me too hard.'

'Do you assert that you, who move the King in all affairs, knew nothing of this great matter? In which so many were engaged – the Murrays, the Erskines, Ramsay and the rest?'

'None of these are associates of mine. You exaggerate, as do others my influence with the King. Do you not realise that there is a great part of his affairs in which I have neither influence nor interest? Thank the good God! Has it not occurred to you that this was a business which *would* keep from me? Since the Ruthvens were kinsmen of mine.'

'Robert Logan was also a kinsman of yours!'

'What do you mean by that?'

'I mean that Logan is, or was, your jackal. You have used him in your unsavoury plots ever since I can remember. Since he was so deep engaged in this conspiracy – so the high court of Parliament declares – could you still know naught of it? A singularly uninformed Patrick Gray!'

'On my soul, you would try the patience of a saint in heaven! Think you that Logan lived only to do my bidding? He was a rogue with a hand in a hundred ploys. I neither knew nor desired to know a tithe of them.'

'Leave Logan, then. But there is one side of it all which I think you will find it hard to claim ignorance of. Queen Elizabeth was much put about. As she was meant to be, no doubt. She wrote a long letter to James very shortly after the murder of the Ruthvens; speaking in detail of much that had happened. James showed me the letter, with much relish. Therefore, she had been most fully informed. And swiftly. James himself did not write to her. He sent Captain Preston, of the Guard in due course, to acquaint her. But she knew it all before Preston left Falkland. Do not tell me that Her Grace of England has other correspondents at this Court more prompt than the Master of Gray!'

All three of them waited while Patrick looked away, craving forgiveness, to consider the progress of the current display, pointing out that unfortunately he had duties as Master of Ceremonies which must in some measure preoccupy him. When he turned back to them, he was smiling, wholly himself again. Mary, at least, noted the fact as significant.

'Now – let me see. What was it? Ah, yes – Queen Elizabeth. Her Virgin Grace, Vicky, has a quick-witted and thorough ambassador to this Court, with ample means to gain information for his mistress and to transmit it swiftly to her. Elizabeth is well served. There he stands, the nimble Master Nicolson, talking with my lord of Mar. I warrant that by daybreak tomorrow a swift courier will be on his way to London bearing word of what is done here tonight; whether His Grace was pleased or displeased; which royal favourite is receiving preference; the weight of the new prince and his likelihood of survival. And much else. Aye, much – including, I have no doubt, tidings anent the Duke of Lennox.'

It was Mary who took him up, quickly. 'What do you mean – the Duke of Lennox?'

'Why, my dear, merely that His Grace proposes once again to show his entire confidence and trust in his ducal cousin, by sending him to Elizabeth's Court at London as his envoy residentiary and ambassador in attendance.'

'Ah, no!'

'What? Ambassador? Resident? Me?' Ludovick jerked. 'I'll not go!'

'No? Against a royal command? Come, come, Vicky – you know better than that. You know that if your liege lord is determined on it, you cannot refuse and yet remain in Scotland. And consider the virtues of it, man – Gloriana's brilliant Court, instead of this dull company which you claim to like so little . . . !'

'This is *your* work, Patrick! You are seeking to have me banished the realm . . .'

'Tut, man – do not talk nonsense! His Grace requires an especial envoy, close to himself, with authority to deal with the various factions in England, that all may unite to call for his succession on the Queen's death. The faction of the Earl of Northumberland, Raleigh, and the Lord Cobham, in particular – in opposition to the Secretary Cecil and Howard. These must be brought to favour strongly our monarch's translation to the English throne – as Cecil and Howard do. And who more suitable to convince them than the Duke of Lennox?'

'Patrick, must this be?' his wife asked, almost pleaded. 'Would not another serve equally well?'

387

'Even the suggestion is unjust to Vicky, my dear! Besides, consider the chance it offers him to spy out the land! All England is the prize. When King Jamie does move south, think of the glittering prospect for his cousin and close supporter, the Duke! Of this land flowing with milk and honey. Here is a most happy opportunity to prepare the way for his own translation, to consider what offices, lands and houses he will have. Elizabeth cannot last long now. 'Fore God – most men would give their right hand for this so timely survey!'

'I desire nothing from England. You know that well,' Ludovick declared. 'My only hope for the English succession is that, once James goes to London, he will leave me here free to live my own life. That is all I ask of him.'

'Wait, my friend. Wait until you have considered well what England has to offer! Now – you will excuse me? I must go act midwife to the infant Moses – Charles, born amidst the Queen's bulrushes – lest Pharaoh's daughter makes a botch of it!'

'Patrick,' Mary said, as he made to move away. 'If I have spoken little, it is not that I am unconcerned. You have now the power and authority which you have always desired. Do not, I pray you, now play God's right hand as well as the King's! Lest you be struck down in your presumption. It seems that there is a danger of it.'

He paused, to eye her closely, sombrely, for a long moment. Then, without a word he turned and left them.

The girl emitted a long tremulous sigh. 'Vicky, Vicky – what have we done?' she whispered. 'Were we fools indeed to match ourselves against the Master of Gray?'

Neither of her companions answered her.

Chapter Twenty-three

Mary was right indeed. Patrick Gray had now the power which he had always sought, almost unlimited power, as Scotland moved into the fateful and eventful seventeeth century. And seldom can a man have been more suited to wield power, more competent to use it, more modest in its sway. Since power over men must by its very nature be a living force, and never a mere dominance and control, weighty and inert, which holds the seeds of its own destruction, its successful handling demands the finest, surest touch. The balance of political power is as vital in its own essential quality as in any outward expression and application. The forces which go to produce it, frequently diametrically opposed to each other, must be kept counterpoised as though on a knife's edge, if the delicate balance is to be maintained.

At such balancing Patrick Gray was the past-master. Power was his life, his goal, almost his religion – power itself, not as with most ambitious men, what power could bring him. He was not concerned with gaining wealth as such, or position, or adulation, or fear. He saw himself as born, and able, to wield power, pure power, and to wield it surely, economically, justly. Utterly without scruple as to how the power was obtained, the power itself was sacrosanct, not to be abused. Behind the extraordinary, shambling, uncouth figure of King James, the realm had never known so scrupulous a ruler.

His policy, of course, was aimed at the achievement of still greater power. Scotland was to be well-managed, prosperous and justly governed, not only because such was implicit in the correct use of power and aided the maintenance thereof, but in order that this should be seen and understood south of the Border, so that nothing should prejudice or hamper the overwhelming call to vastly enhanced power in London. King James was but indifferent material with which to work, not the most attractive monarch for the English to desire – but the Master of

Gray set himself to see to it that he *was* perceived as the infinitely desirable successor to the failing Elizabeth by all who mattered in England. To this end all was aimed. It happened that the policy demanded, meantime, effective good government in Scotland.

The interim was longer than any expected. Elizabeth, although nearing seventy, never robust and now a sick woman, had the spirit of a lioness, and clung to life tenaciously. Nor would she so much as countenance the possibility of her demise by naming her successor. Patrick, who knew her so well, had long recognised that she would never so oblige them – even though James himself kept trying to cajole such admission from her, to the end. Patrick's policy was concerned with others – those who surrounded the Queen, and those in opposition to them. He went to work on the susceptibilities, ambitions and the judgement of all in the major factions in England, patiently, systematically, but subtly, brilliantly, by building up his picture of a wise and liberal monarch ruling a contented and prosperous realm, who was the only possible choice as successor to their famous Queen; he offered future privilege, position and reward for present support; and he even reversed the accustomed flow by sending money south, to carefully selected key figures who would use it to best advantage – being something of an expert on the matter of subsidies. This despite the continuing grievous shortage of money in Scotland. A host of Scottish envoys, representatives, informers and spies descended upon England, sounding, probing, subborning, intriguing, under the cloak of the ultra-respectable and patently honest Duke of Lennox, whose lack of both guile and concern about the issue was obvious to all. And all the time, discreetly back from the Borderline, troops waited, in every town and burgh – not so large an army as Patrick would have liked to see, but sufficient to form a swift and ruthless striking-force to spearhead the move on London should more subtle methods fail.

The provision of the necessary funds for all this continued to be one of Patrick's greatest headaches, in a land where money always had been the scarcest of commodities; his success in the matter was probably one of his greatest triumphs, in consequence. The Pope's contribution, although now reduced, was still valuable. At one time it seemed as though His Holiness was going to dry up altogether, in disappointment of any sure evidence of Scotland's return to the true faith. Patrick had to sacrifice Elphinstone on the altar of expediency as scapegoat. The Vatican, in an effort to step up the pressure, published the King's letter suggesting the elevation of Bishop Drummond to the cardinalship, complete with James's incontestable signature – and Elphinstone, as Secretary, had to be made to confess that he had composed this letter and inserted it amongst other documents for signature, so that it was signed inadvertently by the King. However, skilful diplomacy turned even this mishap to good effect, secret assurances being sent to the Pope of James's increasing tendences towards Catholicism to the extent that he was suggesting that he might send his son and heir, Prince Henry, in a year or two's time, to be educated either in Rome or at the Court of Philip of Spain. Mollified and encouraged, the Vatican, noting that Queen Anne was now as good as a Catholic, resumed its subsidies – and Patrick Gray prayed for the speedy translation to a higher kingdom of Elizabeth Tudor.

It was one of his innermost personal satisfactions and proof that his machinations went undetected by the said Elizabeth and her Treasurer, at least, that to retain the good offices and services of Patrick Gray at this same juncture, an award of four hundred crowns a year was sent north, in order to 'aid in the suitable education of Andrew, son and heir of the Master of Gray' – a sum that continued to be paid indeed until the death of the Queen.

The Gowrie business had proved entirely successful, both in its direct and indirect results. Even despite the large grants of Ruthven lands to those who had aided in the matter, there was still a large surplus of the forfeited properties to come to the royal treasury – as well as the cancellation of the deplorable £80,000 debt. Moreover, the King's late colleagues in conspiracy, the Murrays, Erskines and the rest, could now be persuaded effectively to contribute quite large sums, on account of their new holdings and in anticipation of further benefits in England. Even better, the nobility at large, having seen what had happened to Gowrie who had been most outspoken in refusing to contribute to the nation's needs, now hastily chose the wiser and patriotic course, and dipped reluctant hands deep into pockets, their own and even more so, their vassals'.

One other small side issue of the Gowrie affair, which might have proved unfortunate, was happily disposed of by Gray wits – in this case partly by Mary Gray's wits. The King was still hot against the Lady Beatrix Ruthven's continued presence at Court, in the Queen's entourage, and the royal spouses were indeed more fiercely at odds on this subject than on any other. But it was obviously only a question of time until the unfortunate young woman paid the penalty of being sister to the Gowrie brothers, since she could not remain a captive in the Queen's apartments indefinitely. Mary was much worried on her friend's account.

One afternoon she ran Patrick to earth in the new bowling-green being constructed at Holyroodhouse, after considerable searching; for although her father should have been the busiest man in the kingdom, and bogged down in paper-work and affairs, in fact he appeared to be one of the most idle of men, with little of consequence to do much of the time – so adept was he at ensuring that others contributed the necessary labour to put his schemes, ideas and decisions into effective action. No man, he held, with the burden of major decision on him, ought to impare his faculties by dull toil and labour.

'You are the fairest sight these eyes have lighted on this day,' he greeted her, smiling. 'But since you seek me out thus, I fear the worst! What sin have I committed, my dear? What have I done now?'

She shook her head. 'It is not what you have done, Patrick. It is what you have *not* done. I asked you, besought you, to aid the Lady Beatrix. You have not done so.'

'Are you so sure? How do you know, Mary, what I have done? Beatrix does not suffer any hurt. She remains in the Queen's household. No steps have been taken against her. Why are you so sure that I have done nothing to aid her?'

'Because, if you had set your hand to the matter, it would have been to better effect. The Master of Gray does not deal in half-measures! The Lady Beatrix is no better than a prisoner, in fear for her life. The King smokes against her, declaring her to be the last of a viper's brood! Only the Queen's protection saves her. But how long can that last? The Court moves to Falkland soon. It is close quarters at Falkland – little space for any. When the Lady Beatrix leaves the Queen's apartments here at Holy-roodhouse, will she ever see Falkland? Does the King not but wait for that?'

'I fear that you misjudge His Grace, my dear – you who used to play his friend, to speak for him when others decried. Was not this fair ear the repository for many a slobbering confidence?'

'I have learned King James's true nature, to my cost. He is a tyrant, a murderer!'

'A pox, girl – watch what you say! Even I could not save you if word of that sort of talk was carried to his ears.'

'To be sure. It was for less than that that he murdered Lady Beatrix's brothers!'

'Have a care, Mary, 'fore God! It is not like you to be so witless. You cannot, must not, accuse the King of the death of the Gowrie brothers. They sealed their own fate when they conspired against James...'

'Patrick – need you lie to me? Here, where none can overhear us. You know, as do I, that it was not the Ruthvens who con-spired. But the King... and his advisers!'

'Idle tales, Mary. The slanders of false and malicious tongues.'

'No. The truth. Which can be established as the truth. Proven.'

It was as though a mask had been drawn over her father's handsome features, so still did they become. He leaned forward a little. 'What do you say?' he asked slowly. 'Proven? What do you mean?'

'I mean, Patrick, that the Lady Beatrix can establish that the conspiracy was on the part of the King – not of her brothers. She has the proof of it.'

'Impossible!'

'No – proof. And possessing this, she has the wherewithal to bargain for her life, has she not? The price of her silence. That is why I have come to you, Patrick. To bargain for my friend!'

He waited, silent.

'Days before that wicked deed was done, Master Herries the physician, who is now Sir Hugh, of Cousland, was with Beatrix. They are friendly. She railed at him, because of his bound gouty foot, declaring that he was but a feeble physician who could not heal himself. He told her then that she would be singing a different tune very shortly. That certain folk close to her would be sore needing the services of the King's feeble physician, and not like to receive them. That a day of reckoning was at hand, and her proud house would be brought low. He had been drinking . . .'

Beneath his breath Patrick Gray said something indistinct but very vehement.

'So you see, Patrick, Herries knew beforehand that the Gowries were to fall. What happened at Gowrie House was no chance.'

'Here is no proof. No certain warranty. The babbling of a drunken fool . . . !' Although that was equally vehement, the Master sounded just a little less assured than usual.

'I think that others would see it differently. Since few believe all the King's story – even after the trial.'

'Who has she told? Other than you?'

'None. As yet. I said to tell none until I had spoken with you. Conceiving that she would be in a better situation to bargain. You see, Patrick – I have much faith in your ability to reckon up the true values of any situation! Where your advantage lies. No merchant, no huckster, I swear, has a clearer understanding as to when to come to terms . . .'

'Bargain! Terms! Can you not see, child? That this is a matter of the direst danger? For Beatrix Ruthven. I concede nothing as to its worth, its truth. But spread abroad, this story could do much damage. That I grant you. Therefore the wretched girl is in the greatest peril. If the King hears of this – *when* he hears of it – she will fall to be silenced. Forthwith. That is certain, inevitable.'

'Exactly. So I came to you. The King may act swiftly. But not before Beatrix can speak. Tell the Queen. And the others of the Queen's ladies. Then, what advantage in silencing her? I come to gain her life by her silence. Not . . . not her silence by her life!'

He stared at her, through her, for long, scarcely seeing her. Then he paced away from her, over the green turf. When he came back he was his assured self again.

'Very well,' he said, nodding. 'We can be agreed on this, I think. For her own sake, for the sake of the realm, Beatrix Ruthven must be silenced. And silenced for all time. She must not change her mind, after a while. She must never be in a position to give evidence in this matter. Or to call on Herries to give evidence. That is the heart of the matter. And there is only one way to seal her lips effectively – short of her death. She must wed Herries.'

Mary drew a quick breath, started to speak, but changed her mind.

'As his wife, she cannot bear testimony against him – even if she would. By good fortune, he is unmarried. It is none so ill a match for her, now that he is knighted and given Cousland . . .'

'He is old enough to be her father!'

'What of it? That is nothing. Many of the best marriages are such. And you say that they are friendly.'

Mary looked down, swallowing. 'Better, I suppose, to marry Herries than to die. But . . . is there no other course?'

'Not that will keep her quiet. As she must be.'

'Will he agree?'

'Give me but two minutes with Hugh Herries, and he will be running to offer his hand!' the Master declared grimly. 'This must be arranged swiftly, quietly. The King must hear naught of it, at this stage. Go back to Beatrix, Mary, and tell her. And no word, otherwise, to a living soul.'

'But the King . . . ?'

'Leave the King to me.'

And so the thing was done, the crisis was past. The Lady Beatrix became the Lady Herries, and with a suddenly chastened and sobered husband retired from Court to live on the former Ruthven estate of Cousland in Lothian. King James even gave them a wedding-gift – but quietly they were also given the word that he never desired to set eyes on either of them again. The Queen, curiously, mortally offended, said the same – but at least one stumbling-block between the royal partners was removed.

Mary Gray lay awake many a night wondering whether she had done rightly.

So the months passed. The tidings from England were good. Queen Elizabeth was failing steadily, in mind it seemed as well as in body. She had sent her favourite, Essex, to the block on a charge of treason, and was now grieving crazedly for him, often sitting alone in a dark room mourning and lamenting. Her judgement, which had so long been her own and England's pride, was impaired; she was rewarding close servants by allowing them to tax articles in general use, even salt and starch – to the indignation of Parliament and the people. She would sit about on the floor and refuse to move. At the opening of Parliament her robes of velvet and ermine proved too heavy for her, and staggering, she had only been saved from falling by the peer who stood nearest her in his arms.

Her cousin twice removed and would-be successor, rubbed his hands. It would not be long now.

The Duke of Lennox came back to Scotland unannounced and unbidden – and was warmly greeted by neither his wife nor his liege lord. Only Mary Gray rejoiced to see him – but even she still failed to give him the welcome on which his heart was set. Ludovick Stewart was a man at odds with the world.

At least he had had the wit to bring with him a letter from Lord Henry Howard, with which to soften the royal wrath. Lord Henry, brother to the Duke of Norfolk, was a fox, and closest associate of Sir Robert Cecil, the Secretary of State, who was ruling England in the Queen's name. While the peculiar Cecil was circumspect to the point of primness in his communications, Howard was allowed to be otherwise. James was so pleased with this letter that he read it aloud at a banquet to the assembled Court – to the vast embarrassment of Nicolson the English ambassador; and just in case any of his hearers had missed the significance of it, he read the part which he liked especially a second time. It went:

'You are the apple of the Eternal eye, most inestimable King James, whom neither death nor life nor angels nor principalities nor powers, shall separate from the affection and vows the subjects of this fair realm, next to the sovereign possessor, have vowed to you; the redoubtable monarch of whose matchless mind I think, as God's lieutenant upon earth, with the same reverence and awe which I owe to God himself when I am on my knees.'

While, shocked, some muttered about blasphemy, none could

deny that when Cecil's right-hand man wrote in such terms, the signs were propitious to say the least of it. Although Ludovick himself was revolted by the contents of the letter he had brought, the same nevertheless served to make King James applaud the bearer instead of berating him and sending him back to England forthwith. He kept quiet. Keeping quiet, and waiting, it seemed, was to be his role in life – and his cross and burden.

So the months went by.

Chapter Twenty-four

The reeling horseman on the foundered and indeed dying mount clattered alone up to the gatehouse of the Palace of Holyroodhouse, and all but fell from the saddle. The guard had heard those uneven hoof beats on the cobblestones of the Abbey Strand in the silence of the night, and were waiting expectant.

'The King! The King's Majesty! Word for the King's Majesty.' The man's voice was as uneven as had been the sound of his approach, and, added to his English accent, made his words barely intelligible. But there was no doubting the urgency of his demand, or who he desired to see, as he slid, panting, from the horse and staggered up to the gate.

'His Grace is abed lang syne, sir,' the officer of the guard announced. 'Here's no time o' night to see the King! Who are you from, man?'

'Eh . . . ? Who . . . ? Abed?' Stupidly the newcomer peered at the speaker through the interlocking iron bars of the great gate, swaying drunkenly. In the light of the flickering torches he made a sad sight. His once-fine clothing was so befouled by rain, mud, sweat and horse's saliva as to be an offence to eye and nose both, and his unshaven features, although obviously comparatively youthful, were grey lined with fatigue, like those of an old man, and caked with the dried blood of a grazed cheekbone. 'Carey,' the apparition managed to enunciate. 'Carey – for the King's Majesty. I . . . I . . .'

His thick words were interrupted by a crash. Behind him the legs of his steaming, trembling mount had suddenly buckled and splayed, and the brute toppled to the cobbles in sprawling collapse as its heart gave out.

The young man scarcely turned to look. 'The fourth,' he muttered. 'Fourth. No – fifth. Fourth or fifth – God knows!'

They had the gates open for him now, and were just in time to save him from following his horse to the wet ground. The officer, supporting him on his arm, led him into the palace forecourt.

They were turning into the warmth and light of the guard-room, where a blazing fire kept the chill of the wet March night at bay, when the visitor resisted and held back, with un-expected strength and vehemence considering his state.

'The King,' he exclaimed again. 'I demand the King. His Majesty's presence. Take me.'

'His Grace is asleep, man. I darena wake him up at this hour . . .'

'Fool! You dare not *fail* to wake him, I say! I am Carey. Sir Robert Carey. From Richmond. From the Court of England. I must see the King.'

'Will it no' keep till the morn . . . ?'

'No. Now, I say, Forthwith.'

The guard-commander shrugged, and still holding Carey's arm, moved on. He ordered two of his men to hurry ahead, one to waken the duty page and one to inform the Master of Gray.

Up the winding stone stairs of the most northerly of the drum towers he conducted the stumbling Englishman. At the first-floor landing, a sleepy-eyed grumbling youth was dragging on some clothing in the pages' room. The officer demanded a goblet of wine for the stranger before the page went upstairs to arouse the King.

'Tell His Grace that it is Sir Robert Carey. From England. On matters exceeding urgent.'

'Son to the Lord Hunsdon. Cousin to Queen Elizabeth.'

The page returned sooner than might have been expected. 'His Grace will see Sir Robert Carey,' he announced. 'Follow me.'

Up a second turnpike stair they went, to the next landing, where two armed guards stood on duty. They crossed an ante-room, and the page knocked on the door beyond. As they waited, swift footsteps brought the Master of Gray to their side, fully dressed and quite his usual elegant self, despite the hour. He greeted Sir Robert briefly, brows raised in unspoken question, and dismissed the guard-commander, just as the King's voice bade them enter.

James was sitting up in his great canopied four-poster bed, a comic picture, clutching a bed-robe round his nakedness, with a tall velvet hat, hastily donned and askew, replacing a discarded nightcap, presumably in pursuit of dignity. As always when upset or concerned, his heavy-lidded eyes were rolling alarmingly, and he was plucking at his lips. The page had lit three candles from the dying fire. The room was hot and stuffy.

'Hech, hech – what's this? What's this?' he demanded. 'It's no'...? Man, it's no'...?'

'Sir Robert Carey, with tidings for Your Grace,' Patrick said.

Carey, evidently revived by the wine, ran forward to the royal bed and threw himself down on his knees beside it, reaching out to grasp the apprehensive monarch's hand. 'Sire!' he cried. 'Twice, thrice King! Humbly I greet you! Hail to the King! King James, of England, Scotland, France and Ireland! God save the King!'

'Guidsakes!' James said, jaw sagging. 'Och, well now. Mercy on us.'

Swiftly Patrick was at the kneeling Englishman's side. 'This is certain, sir? Sure?' he demanded.

'Certain.'

'You have a writing? A proof?'

Carey put his hand into the bosom of his stained and soaking doublet, and drew out a glittering ring. Silently he handed it to the King.

James gobbled. 'I ken this!' he cried. 'Aye, fine I do. I sent this to her ... to Elizabeth. One time. It was my mother's ring – Mary the Queen's ring.'

Patrick knew it also, since he it was who had handed it to Elizabeth Tudor, years before. He dropped on one knee, beside Carey, and took the monarch's hand, that still clutched the great ring, to carry it to his lips.

'Your most royal Majesty's humble, devoted and right joyful servant!' he murmured.

'Aye,' James said, on a long bubbling sigh. 'Aye, well. So ...so she's awa'? At last! God be praised for a' His mercies!'

'Amen!' Rising to his feet, Patrick smiled slightly. 'May Her Grace rest in peace perpetual.'

'Ooh, aye. To be sure. Indeed aye. Our beloved sister and cousin.'

Carey remained kneeling. 'My sister, the Lady Scrope. A lady of the bedchamber. She drew the ring from Her Majesty's finger, Sire. As her last breath faded. She threw it to me. Out of the bechamber window. I was waiting beneath. All the night. It was a compact, between us. That I might bring it to you. The tidings. I have ridden night and day . . .'

'When, man? When was this?'

'The night of Wednesday, Your Majesty. No – it was Thursday morning. Three of the clock.'

'Thursday? And this is but Saturday night!' Patrick exclaimed. 'Four hundred miles! In three days and two nights?'

'I killed four horses. Or five. I have not stopped. Save once. When I fell. And must have slept awhile where I lay. Near to Alnwick, in Northumberland, I think.'

'Expeditious,' the King commented sagely. 'Maist expeditious. Aye, and proper.'

'I . . . my sister and I esteemed that Your Majesty should know. Be informed. At the earliest moment. I sought the honour. To be Your Majesty's first subject to greet you. First English subject, Sire.'

'A worthy ambition, man Carey. I'ph'mmm. Meritorious. You'll no' suffer for it – we'll see to that!'

'I thank you, Sire.'

'Sir Robert – the succession?' the Master of Gray said. 'The Queen's death is established. That is, h'm, very well. But – was aught said of the succession For, if not, it behoves us to act fast.'

'Waesucks, aye!' James's voice quavered again. 'What o' that, man? Was it decided?'

'Yes, Sire – your royal succession is assured. The Queen decreed it. In the end. Before she sank away. Earlier in the night. I was there present, myself. In the bedchamber. With other cousins. When she was evidently sinking, they questioned her. The Secretary, the Archbishop, the Lord Admiral. To name her successor. She said – and it was the last words she spoke, Sire, "My seat has been the seat of kings, and none but a king must succeed me".'

'Aye. Maist fitting and due,' Majesty nodded.

'Is that all?' Patrick demanded. 'No more specific word? Naught of the Lord Beauchamp?'

'She had said before that she would have no rascal's son in her seat. When he was named.'

'But, for her successor, she spoke no actual name?'

'After she had said this of only a king in her seat, they put names to her. The King of Spain. She showed no sign. The King of France. She did not move. Then they said the King of Scots. Her Grace started. She heaved herself up on her bed and held her hands jointly over her. Above her head. In the manner of a crown. Then she fell back. From then, Sire, to her last breath, she neither spoke nor moved. Three hours and more. While I waited below, booted and spurred.'

James nodded, beaming now. 'Explicit,' he said. 'Full explicit. The auld woman had some glisks and glimmerings o' sense to her, after all! Aye – though she was a fell time about showing it. So – a's by with. England's mine. England's mine, Patrick – d'you hear? I'm rich, man – rich.'

Patrick bowed, unspeaking. He turned to Carey, who at last had risen from his knees. 'What of Cecil? And the Council? What of a proclamation?'

'I heard Cecil say to the Archbishop, sir, that the succession of King James would be put to the Council so soon as it could be assembled, in the morning. And the proclamation issued thereafter. That same Thursday morning.'

'So I've been King o' England for two days, no less - and didna ken it! Guidsakes – you wouldna think it possible! It's a right notable thought. I could indite a poem on it – aye, a poem. An opopee. An ode. I'll do that, Patrick – get me papers and pens. Here's occasion for notable rhyming.'

Carey stared, as Patrick bowed and murmured. 'Excellent, Your Grace. But . . . at this hour?'

'To be sure. What has the hour to do wi' the divine creation? The ardent excogitation? Paper, man. And have the bells to ring. The Kirk bells. A' the bells. To be rung until I command that they cease. Aye, and bonfires . . .'

'Sire – might I suggest a small delay? Until the English Council's word arrives. Sir Robert's tidings are joyful and welcome. But they are those only of a private subject, however excellent.

It would be seemly would it not, to await the proper messengers of your Privy Council in England? And to inform your Scots Council before the public rejoicings.'

The King's face fell, and he darted a glance that was almost venomous at the speaker. He shrugged. 'Aye. Maybe,' he conceded shortly.

'Do you wish Her Grace to be informed, Sire?'

'Anne? Na, na – no hurry for that. She'll but haver and bicker on it. Soon enough for her, the morn.'

'Very well. I shall call a meeting of the Council for tomorrow?'

'Aye, do that. And see to Sir Robert here. Now – paper and pens, man . . .'

Chapter Twenty-five

The ranked cannon on Berwick's massive ramparts thundered out as never they had thundered before, it is safe to say, in all the Border fortress's long and turbulent history. Never had the cannoneers been so reckless of powder, and never before had those serried ranks of north-pointing English muzzles belched blank-shot. The echoes rolled back and forth across the winding Tweed and all the green plain of the Merse, tossed hither and thither by the distant encircling hills. To their accompaniment the great company approached the ancient grey-walled, red-roofed town by the glittering sea, which had for so long been the most bitterly grudged bone of contention between the two hostile nations.

It was as good as an army which flooded down from the Lamberton ridge to the north – although a very different army from the steel-clad host which had for so many months kept its silent vigil along the Border, and now was at last dispersing unrequired. This company, although fully a thousand strong, represented the very flower of Scotland. Not since King James the Fourth had led his resounding chivalry to disaster and extinction at Flodden Field exactly ninety years before, had so much brilliance, colour and circumstance come to the Border. Some would go on, across Tweed, and some would turn back, men and women both.

King James the Sixth and First was apparelled for the occasion. Seldom indeed can a man have sat a horse for a long journey happed in such sheer yardage of velvet, cloth-of-gold and satin-ribbon, not to mention the ostrich-plumes, gold chains and sundry decorations. If he did not outshine all his entourage, it was not for want of ornament. His Queen, some way behind, amongst her ladies, was much less adorned – and still in evil humour because her children had been left behind in Edinburgh in the care of the Earl of Mar.

The King rode between Sir Charles Percy, brother of the Earl of Northumberland, and Thomas Somerset, son of Lord

Worcester, the English envoys who had brought north the official news of Queen Elizabeth's death, and the call to her throne from the Privy Council, three days after Sir Robert Carey's spectacular dash. Carey himself, promised a peerage and a pension, rode just behind with the Master of Gray and sundry English notables. The Duke of Lennox, who should have been close at his cousin's and monarch's side, was nowhere near – not even with the Queen's party where rode his Duchess, but far in the rear with Mary Gray, the Lady Marie and her children.

It looked as though even the weather of Scotland was glad to be getting rid of her peculiar sovereign, for the sun shone, the clouds sailed high and the air was balmy indeed for early northern April. This was as well, for the lesiurely progress southwards of this enormous cavalcade would have been a sorry business in bad weather. It was only the second day of the long journey, of course, which so far had been something in the nature of a triumphant procession, with cheering folk in every burgh and village, lairds hastening to provide stirrup-cups and lords greater hospitality; it remained to be seen whether the welcome of the southern kingdom, climatic and otherwise, would be as heartfelt as this northern farewell.

At least there was no doubt about Berwick's greetings and reception. The town had not had time to prepare the masques and spectacles seemly for the occasion – for James had wasted no time in shaking the dust of Scotland off his feet, this being but the 6th of April, he having set out only five days after the official news had arrived at Edinburgh; but, apart from the cannonade, Berwick's entire population showed its appreciation of its new situation, its release from the centuries-old condition of being almost a perpetually besieged city, by packing the narrow streets so tightly that it was almost impossible for the royal party to win through them. At the Scots Gate, the Governor and Marshal of Berwick, flanked by the Wardens of the Marches from both sides of the Border, awaited the monarch of them both – and who thereupon, with droll humour, dismissed them from their ancient offices, as no more necessary in his united domains. The Mayor then handed over the keys of the town – and what was still more welcome, a purse of gold – and commenced to read a lengthy peroration which the King presently interrupted, referring to the worthy as Provost and declaring that what he wanted to do was to inspect the cannon which had made such 'extraordinary exellent displosions'. Up on the ramparts which walled in the town, he started up the cannonade once more, himself gleefully discharging some of the pieces and commanding that there was to be no let up of the noise until all their powder was exhausted. Then, tiring of this, he set off through the crowded streets, to shouts of 'God save King James', his vast following making their difficult way through as best they might, down to the lower part of the town, near the river and harbour, called Ravensdowne, where at the Governor's House immense hospitality was prepared.

It was late in the afternoon before all was ready for the great moment, and the royal cavalcade somehow managed to reassemble, to convoy the royal traveller down to the bridge to cross Tweed into his new realm of England. The river here at its mouth is quarter of a mile in width, and the long, narrow and spidery bridge of timber, patched and mended from shatterings innumerable by storm, flood and war, represented a tenuous link indeed between the two kingdoms. The sight of it, hitherto hidden by the tall enclosing walls of the town, brought suddenly home to many just how significant was the occasion – brought indeed a lump into many a throat.

Many, the greater proportion of the company, were turning back here and there was a great taking of leave and saying of farewells. A large concourse was to be seen awaiting the monarch's arrival at The Spittall, on the other side of Tweed. A couple of hundred or so would accompany James all the way to London. Others would cross the river to but set foot on English soil and say their farewells there. Of this last group Mary Gray was to be one.

While this marshalling and leave-taking was going on, still to the intermittent booming of a few remaining cannon, a single horseman came cantering across the long bridge from the far side, his hoofbeats drumming hollowly on the timbers. It proved to be a young man dressed in the height of fashion, who jumped off his beast and sank on his knees before King James, holding out a large key in his hand.

'Your most gracious Majesty, serene exemplar of learning, humanity and piety, the heart's desire of all true Englishmen,' he cried in fluting tones. 'I am John Peyton, son to the Lieutenant of the Tower of London, the most humble of all your servants. Here is the key to that said dread Tower, Majesty, England's citadel, which I have ridden post to present to you ere you set foot on England's devoted soil.'

The Scots around the King coughed and looked embarrassed at such unseemly and magniloquent language; but James himself appeared to find nothing amiss with it. Smirking and nodding, he took the key, patting the young man's head, and on impulse told him to stay on his knees. He turned to Ludovick, at his side, demanding his sword, and taking it, had some trouble, with the large key in his hand, in bringing it down on the young man's shoulder.

'Arise, good Sir John . . . John . . . Eh, what's the laddie's name?' he asked, in a stage whisper, peering round.

'Peyton, Sire – Peyton,' Somerset said hurriedly. It was the Englishmen's turn to look embarrassed.

'Aye, well – arise Sir John Peyton. Vicky – here, take this key, man. It's ower heavy . . .'

That was but the first of three hundred knightings on the way to London.

'Come, Sir Percy. Come Somerset, man,' the King commanded, beckoning for his horse. 'Aye, and you too, Vicky. Escort me across this unchancy brig. It's gey long and it's gey rickmatick, by the looks o' it. You'd better go first, Vicky. Aye, you too, Percy. See it's safe for me. I dinna like the looks o' it . . . !'

'It is quite safe, Sire, I assure you,' Sir Charles Percy told him. 'I have crossed it many times. Heavy cannon cross it . . .'

'Aye, maybe. But go you ahead, just the same. It's a right shauchly brig, this. You should ha' done better for me, man!'

Ludovick looked back unhappily to where Mary stood; he had intended to cross the bridge at her side, with parting now so near. She waved him on, indicating that she would see him at the other side.

It was no doubt inevitable, indeed possibly essential, that the long bridge should sway somewhat in the middle, constructed of wood as it was and with a dog's leg bend two-thirds of the way across to counter the swift current of the tidal river. But long before they were that far, James was complaining loudly, bitterly, exclaiming at every shake and shiver. Presently indeed he commanded a halt, and hastily got down from his horse, pushing the beast away from him in case its weight should add to his own danger. He would have turned back there and then, on foot as he was – but it was pointed out to him that they were more than half-way across now, with less distance to go forward than back, and that the bridge behind them was crowded with folk. Insisting that Ludovick led the two horses and kept well in front, the King, clutching Sir Charles's arm on one side and the parapet-rail of the bridge on the other, placed the remainder of the way almost on tiptoe, staring horrified at the jabbly wavelets beneath him, thick lips moving in mumbled prayer.

Thus James Stewart entered into his long desired inheritance. He made the last few yards to English soil at a sort of shambling run, and reaching *terra firma*, sank down on his velvet-clad knees dramatically and kissed the ground – to the alarm and confusion of the great gathering here awaiting him, who did not know whether to come forward, remain standing, or kneel likewise. The Earl of Northumberland and the Bishop of Durham, leaders of the welcome party, after a hasty whispered consultation, moved forward and got down on their own knees beside the monarch, who, with eyes tight shut and lips busy, was colloguing with his Maker and apostrophising the Devil in the same urgent breath. The throng stared, enthralled.

When he opened his eyes and found others kneeling beside him, James tut-tutted in displeasure, but used their shoulders to aid himself to rise. Then perceiving that one was in holy orders, he forestalled the address of welcome by launching into a stern and voluble denunciation of a people and nation who expected their prince to take his life in his hands and come to them across a death-trap like that.

'It's no' right or proper, I tell you!' he declared, wagging a finger at the unfortunate Bishop. 'I . . . we are much displeasured. Yon's a disgrace! We might ha' been submerged in the cruel waters – aye, submerged. It wabbles, sir – it quakes. It'll no' do, I say. It is our command – aye, our first royal command on this our English ground – that you'll build a new brig. Aye, a guid stout brig o' stone, see you. That'll no' wabble. Forthwith. See you to it. Our Treasury in London will pay for it.'

'It shall be done, Majesty. Most certainly. A start shall be made at once. And now, Sire, here is my Lord of Northumberland. He humble craves permission to present an address of welcome ...'

Ludovick, standing by with the horses, like any groom, found Mary at his side. He thrust the reins into the hands of the nearest bystander, and taking the girl's arm, led her through the press some little way, to where, at the waterside, they might speak alone.

'Did ever you see such a to-do about nothing!' he demanded of her. 'Such a pother and commotion to make, in front of his new subjects! What they will think of him ...'

She smiled. 'At least they will not *say* what they think, it seems – as some might, in Scotland! The English are most flowery speakers. I think King James more like to drown in a flood of flattering words than the waters of Tweed!'

'Aye – but he revels in their flummery. The more fawning and fulsome, the better! But ... Mary, we are fools to waste time and thought on James Stewart, here and now. When we are so soon to separate. What are his follies and troubles to ours, who love each other and yet must be ever apart? You are sure? Determined? Even now. You will not change your mind? Come south with me? At least, with Patrick and Marie. To London. Even for a little time. You might like it well.'

'No, Vicky. Here I turn back. Here is where I belong. I have been to London, you remember. With Patrick, when he went to see Queen Elizabeth on the matter of the King's pension. I liked it well enough – but I could not bide there. I pined for our own hills, for the great skies and the caller air ...'

'As did I. As I shall. But ... I will return, Mary. And quickly. Nothing shall hold me. Once I have seen James installed on his new throne, I shall be back, hot-foot – that I swear by all that is true and holy. James may forbid it, threaten me with the Tower if he likes! But I will win back to you. To you. And swiftly. Back to Scotland.'

She gripped his arm. 'Do that, Vicky,' she said simply. 'I

shall be waiting.'

'You . . . you will welcome me back?'

'Oh, my dear – can you ask that? I shall barely live until I see you again.' Her voice was unsteady.

'Mary – you can say that now? At this pass! After all the years wherein you have held me from you?'

'From my body only, Vicky – never from my heart. You know that.'

'I know only that I am the most unhappy of men, Mary. To have tasted of heaven, and then to be cast out – while told still that my heaven is there, waiting, yet with me locked and barred from it! For the sake of . . . what?'

'For the sake, I fear, of *me*, Vicky. Myself. What I am. Oh, I am sorry. I am foolish, I know well – stubborn and proud also. And my folly was never more clear to myself than at this moment!'

'You mean . . . ?'

'I mean that I am seeing myself for what I am. And knowing not whether to weep or to laugh. I now know myself to be but a very frail and feeble woman, Vicky . . .'

'That you could never be!'

'My dear – you will discover! Soon, I pray.'

'Soon, aye. Before summer is in, I shall be back to you. I will come with the swallows. Swift, like the swallows. Would I had their wings. To Castle Huntly, in the Carse . . .'

'No, Vicky. Do not come to Castle Huntly.'

'No?' His face fell.

'No. Come to Methven. Back to our own fair Methven, in Strathearn. Johnnie's Methven. I . . . I shall await you there.'

'Mary! Mary!' Uncaring who watched them, the Duke grasped her, pulled her to him. 'My dear! My heart! You mean it? Is it true? You are going back to Methven . . .?'

'Yes, Vicky. Johnnie shall go back to his inheritance. At last. And I with him. To await his father. And my love. There, beneath the blue Highland hills, we shall count the days . . .'

'But . . . thank God! Thank God, I say! But, why, Mary? I mean, what has changed you? At long last?'

She pointed, above the heads of the crowd, to where the Queen's mounted company was now debouching from the bridge. 'Yonder is my reason. So simple, so shallow. That makes a mock of all my fine talking and lofty airs, Vicky! Your Duchess. Leaving Scotland. There is all your answer.'

'Because Jean goes? To London. You will come back to me?'

'Yes. Simple, is it not? Now you know the deeps of a woman's nature! This woman – who has for so long prated of high-sounding precepts and principles. Because your wife will be four hundred miles away, I will return to your side, Vicky! Your Scots wife! I had a word with the Duchess. She spoke me very fair, I cannot deny. She will stay with the Queen. The move to London pleases her well. She will be a great lady there, indeed. She will not come back – any more than, I think, will the King. But *you* will – and I shall be waiting for you.'

He drew a long breath. 'Heaven be praised! I ask no better of life than this! Jean is no wife to me, Mary. She never has been. You are all the wife I have, or desire.'

'Not wife, only mistress, my dear. I have discovered myself to be less proud, less high-souled, than I believed. Your mistress I am content to be – so long as your Duchess is not wife to you. And stays four hundred miles away! It is no noble confession – but at least I see myself, at last, for what I am.'

'You are my heart's blood, my delight, my life, my all!' he said, deep-voiced.

'Then . . . I am content.'

Silent now, merely holding each other fast, they stood, at peace, until querulous royal shouts for Vicky the Duke reached them, and they made their reluctant way back through the throng.

James had had enough of speeches of welcome, and was for pressing on. Final leave-takings were in progress, and already the Queen's entourage was moving off.

'Vicky – where ha' you been?' the King demanded. 'You shouldna jouk off that way. You should be at my side, man. It's yon lassie again, I'll be bound! Mistress Mary. Aye. Well, you'll be quit o' her now – for she's no' coming with us. Na, na. There's some we'll manage fine without, in London!'

'She had no thought of coming, Sire. She goes back. With my lord of Argyll.'

'D'you say so, Vicky? Mysel', I reckoned she'd be going back

411

wi' her begetter, Patrick Gray!'

There was a sudden indrawing of breaths and silence from all near enough to hear. Men stared from the King to each other.

James licked his lips, eyes rolling, and whinnied a peculiar excited laugh. He looked round to where Patrick stood behind him. 'Aye, Master o' Gray,' he said. 'I'm thinking this is where we part company!'

Blank-faced, the blood draining from his handsome features, Patrick stood, lips parted, as though stunned. For moments he, the most eloquent man in two kingdoms, found no words. None other spoke.

'I . . . I do not understand, Your Grace,' he stammered out, at length.

'No? Do you no', Patrick? Yet it's simple, man – simple. *I* go on to this London – and you turn back. You understand now, my mannie?'

Patrick's fine nostrils flared, his eys narrowed. 'Your Grace means that you wish me to return to Edinburgh. Meantime. To complete some business of the state there, before coming to London?'

'No – my Grace doesna mean any such thing. We left a' things well arranged in Edinburgh, you'll mind. Ooh, aye – Edinburgh will manage fine.'

'Then, Sire, I repeat – I do not understand you.'

'It's no' like you, Patrick, to be so dull in the uptak! Most times you're quick enough – aye, ower quick, by far! What's come ower you, man?'

'I think, Sire, that I must ask that of your royal self!'

'Oho! Testy, eh? Vaunty! Paughty! To me, the King! Aweel, Patrick – I needs must discover you the matter, since you'll have it so. And now's as good a time as any. You are a rogue, Master o' Gray – and I've aye kenned you were a rogue! But I needed a rogue, see you. A great rogue, to berogue the lesser rogues around me! And I had them in plenty. Ooh, aye – it's a great place for rogues, is Scotland! But I intend to leave them there, Patrick man – no' to take them with me! The English are honester folk – eh, my lord Bishop? My lord o' Northumberland? And if they have a rogue or two in London-town – waesucks I'll find me one o' their own breed to berogue them! I'll no' need the likes o' you in London, Patrick, Master o' Gray! Now you understand me?'

So quiet were all those about King James, that the shuffling of his feet and the tinkling of ornaments on his person sounded clearly.

Patrick Gray said nothing. He looked his monarch in the eye until the royal gaze faltered and fell. Then he bowed low, but with a thin smile and the elaborate flourish of sheerest mockery. Thereafter he turned his back on the King.

'My horse!' he called out. 'And quickly. I mislike the stink of this place!'

'Master o' Gray!' James cried, his voice quavering with anger. 'I've no' finished wi' you, yet. Wait you. You're . . . you're deprived o' your offices, man. You understand! You are no longer my Sheriff o' Forfar. And there's no wardrobe to master now, in Scotland! D'you hear . . . ?'

But Patrick Gray was not waiting. Without another glance round, he strode over to his horse, and mounted, the beast's head turned towards the bridge and Scotland. 'Where is my wife?' he asked of the silent watchers. 'Where is Marie?'

'Here, Patrick, my dear. Here . . .'

King James plucked at his lower lip, watching. Then his frown faded, and he actually chuckled. '*Alea jacta est*!' he said, and dug the Bishop of Durham in the ribs with his elbow. 'Or, more properly *Jacta est alea?* Aye. Is that no' apt, man? Apt. Hech, aye – Caesar crosses the Rubicon, and I cross Tweed! *Aut Caesar aut nullus*!' He looked round to discover how many recognised his learning and wit. Disappointed in what he saw, he sniffed. 'Come, Vicky – to horse,' he commanded.

Ludovick, aiding his cousin to mount, looked over to where Mary Gray stood watching. Their eyes met, and as though of a single volition turned to consider the receding elegant figure of the Master, already upon the bridge. When their glances returned, and held for a long moment, it was as though a spate of unspoken eloquence flowed between them, sombre and joyous both. Then the Duke mounted, raised his hand high, and spurred after the King.

It took some considerable time thereafter, because of the delay imposed by the constriction of the narrow bridge, for Mary

413

and the Earl of Argyll to come up with Patrick Gray – by which time he had won free of Berwick town on the long road northwards. He was riding at a fast trot, the Lady Marie at his side, his children with the servants and all their baggage falling behind, apart from any other group or company.

Without a word spoken, Archibald Campbell drew back a little, as they neared the Grays, so that Mary might overtake them alone. The girl thanked him with her glance, and cantered ahead.

Patrick was staring fixedly in front of him as Mary rode up at the other side from his wife. He made no sign or greeting as she came up. The two women exchanged looks, but did not speak.

So the trio rode on in silence.

It was fully a mile further on before Patrick spoke, abruptly. 'Who was the greater fool?' he demanded.

Neither of the women presumed to answer him.

'That is what cuts deep,' he went on tight-voiced, as though to himself. 'Not the insult. Not the loss of place and position. Not the ingratitude, even – although he would not now be riding to London had it not been for what I have done. It is the knowledge that I have been fooled by a fool! How could it be?'

Slowly Mary replied. 'Perhaps, Patrick, only a fool *could* have fooled you? Perhaps it required that.'

He turned in his saddle to consider her and what she said. Then he actually laughed, a short bark of a laugh. 'Aye,' he said, 'it may be so.'

It was the girl who spoke next, as abruptly, briefly. 'And now?' she asked.

'Now, yes. What, you may well ask, Mary. This, at least – I am done with statecraft.'

'I thank God!' his wife said, deep-voiced, at his other side.

'You may say that my task is done,' he went on, still as though to himself. 'For years I have worked for this day. To make a unity of these two realms. To end the shadow of war and hatred between them. It is done – whether I go to London or not. That work is finished. I should rejoice, perhaps – like you, Marie? For, heigho – am I not a free man? At last!'

'I have prayed for this day, Patrick, for long years,' Marie said unsteadily.

'Have you, my dear? Is that how you love me?' He did not say that harshly, however.

'Yes, it is. God bless James Stewart, I say! We can now start to live again. Live as man and wife should, in trust and sanity ...'

'In a stone tower on a bleak rock in the Tay! Can you think to roost in Broughty Castle, Marie my love?'

'You know that I can. I can live anywhere with you – so long as it is *you*, Patrick. And not ... the Master of Gray!'

'Was he so ill a husband?'

'He was, I sometimes think, the Devil himself!'

Into the silence that followed, Mary spoke again. 'Why Broughty, Patrick? Why not Castle Huntly? Where you belong. My lord is but a shadow. A shadow that is fading fast. It is too late to alter that. But you will be the Lord Gray before long. *That* task is just beginning. Lord of great lands and many folk. Is it always to be Davy Gray's burden? Davy – who is so excellent a steward. And a father. But ... no lord of Gray!'

'Dear Davy!' Marie said.

'Aye – there you have it!' Patrick nodded, smiling wryly. 'Dear Davy! Davy dear! Dare I take my wife back to Castle Huntly – who loves Davy Gray?'

'I love Davy Gray, yes – always have done and always will. But not as I love my husband!' Marie said simply. 'You may safely take me to Castle Huntly, Patrick. It is my hope that you will.'

'It is my hope also,' Mary agreed. 'For I go to Methven. With Johnnie. There to await Vicky. It is Methven for me.'

'Oh, Mary dear – I am glad, glad!'

'So that is the way of it, lassie, in the end? You have it all plotted and planned and arranged! The daughter of the Master of Gray!'

'That is the way of it, Patrick. In the end.'

Slowly he said it. 'Tell me then, girl,' he wondered, looking at her sidelong, 'Who spoke back yonder at the bridge-end of Berwick? James Stewart? Or Mary Gray?'

'Say that a higher voice than King James spoke there, Patrick – for it was time.'

'God saving King James?'

'Rather, I think, God saving Patrick Gray!'

FOOTNOTE

The history-books tell us that Patrick, Master of Gray, the handsomest man in Europe, the Machiavelli of Scotland, retired from public life after the Union of the Crowns in 1603 – save to sue the Crown in the Scottish courts for the sum of £19,993 for certain services rendered, and to win it; some historians have wondered why. That he succeeded his father as 6th Lord Gray in 1608, and died three years later in comparative obscurity. Let the history-books have the last word, then, as is only right and proper.

In 1612, Sir John Stewart of Methven, illegitimate son, by mother unnamed, to the Duke of Lennox, was, at the age of nineteen, appointed Constable and Keeper of Dunbarton Castle.